PENGUIN BOOKS

Also by Gavriel Savit

Anna and the Swallow Man

the way back

Gavriel Savit

PENGUIN BOOKS

PENGUIN BOOKS

UK | USA | Canada | Ireland | Australia
India | New Zealand | South Africa

Penguin Books is part of the Penguin Random House group of companies
whose addresses can be found at global.penguinrandomhouse.com.

www.penguin.co.uk
www.puffin.co.uk
www.ladybird.co.uk

First published in the USA by Alfred A. Knopf,
a division of Penguin Random House LLC,
and in Great Britain by Penguin Books 2020
This edition published 2021

001

Printed and bound in Great Britain by Clays Ltd, Elcograf S.p.A.

The authorized representative in the EEA is Penguin Random House Ireland,
Morrison Chambers, 32 Nassau Street, Dublin D02 YH68

A CIP catalogue record for this book is available from the British Library

ISBN: 978–0–241–44251–7

All correspondence to:
Penguin Books
Penguin Random House Children's
One Embassy Gardens, 8 Viaduct Gardens, London SW11 7BW

For all of my ancestors and all of my descendants,
Whether they be living today
Or not

the way back

CHAPTER ONE

Two from Tupik

On a bright summer day in the year eighteen hundred and twelve (by the gentile reckoning), a girl left her mother's house—the little house where she had been born—and went to the brambles on the far side of the forest to gather the small summer strawberries that grow in the shade.

These were the best kind of berries, tiny and soft, and the girl crouched in the bushes, staining her lips and fingertips red: one for her mouth, one for her apron, and so on and on.

At first the girl was sure that she must be imagining things. She was far from the village here, far from the road, and she alone knew of the berry bush.

Surely no one else would come to this place.

But she was not imagining things.

The column burst out into the clearing like a ball from a musket: men in orderly rows, stepping in time, their buttons and bayonets shining in the sun, and more and more and more men—the young lady had never seen so very many. Now horses came as well, and taller men in splendid uniforms astride them. Mules and wagons and great bronze cannons thundered past the girl in the brambles, and feet and hooves and studded wheels churned the grass into a muddy slaw.

The girl was not foolish; she kept hidden and did not draw attention to herself. But when one particular man reached the clearing, she could not help but rise up to get a better look.

Even in the heat of the summer sun, he wore his long, pale blue coat. The gray stallion beneath him moved dexterously at his urging, as if it were a part of him, and as he loped out into the clearing, it quickly became clear that the entirety of the column—all the men and horses and cannons and shot, all of it—was simply an extension of his body.

This, of course, was the great war emperor Napoleon Bonaparte.

He had come to take the Russian Empire.

He had come to take the world.

An officer on a dappled charger came cantering up to his elbow, and the emperor turned his head. It was in this moment that he caught sight of the girl in the bushes.

His eyes bore into hers, and she locked her lips tight, unwilling to let even the lightest breath pass between them.

The officer was speaking.

The emperor did not look away.

And then he turned back toward the horizon, answered his officer, and spurred on his horse.

And that was that.

The girl made her way home. The sun sank behind the advancing troops.

The year wore on. Battles were fought. Men were killed. The leaves changed color and fell. Napoleon retreated and, in due course, was overthrown.

Soon thereafter, the girl was led beneath a wedding canopy, where she traded the name of her father for the name of her husband, and from that day on, she lived in his house, cleaned his mess, boiled his chicken soup, and waited for him to return home at night.

But something odd happened: one day, the girl looked into the mirror and found that the face staring back at her was no longer her own. She had loosened, wrinkled, worried herself into something that no longer resembled her at all. Only her lips remained the same—locked in a light, tight frown.

That evening, her husband did not come home.

It was not long before she knew that he would not be returning at all.

The frown deepened.

Before the week was out, the lady who had been a girl took her son, Zalman, and moved far away from the village of her birth to a place where no one knew, and where no one would whisper: all the way to a tiny, out-of-the-way shtetl called Tupik.

She took a small room in the attic of the baker's house and apprenticed her boy in the bakery on the ground floor.

The baker died. The bakery passed to the lady's son, Zalman.

She remained in the attic.

And as if in a chrysalis of silence, the lady in the attic turned into an old woman. Before long, as she was eldest, the women of Tupik began to call upon her to attend the births of children, and for more than a generation, every boy and girl born into the shtetl of Tupik was caught by the old woman's hands.

But only two of them made any lasting impression on her.

The first was a scrawny boy, born before his time into a blustery, rain-soaked evening. When his tiny eyes blinked open, bright and clear and icy blue, they focused perfectly into hers.

She had seen that expression before: once, as a girl, long ago, crouched in the brambles, fingers stained, fear in her heart, sweetness on her lips.

Eight days later, breaking with her custom, the old woman went to the synagogue to hear what name the boy would be given.

It was Yehuda Leib.

And that evening, the child of her son, Zalman, was born— a girl named Bluma—and as the baby emerged, pink and squalling, the old woman found herself filled with a sense of unutterable gladness.

But when she looked down at her granddaughter's face, another feeling stole into her heart: a sort of guilt, of pity and compassion.

There, as if reflected in a little mottled mirror, was her very own mouth, locked in a light, tight frown.

Yehuda Leib's mother, Shulamis, woke before dawn, dragging her clacking bones up from the warm bed hours before it was reasonable. It was unpleasant, but if she wanted a chance of collecting enough odd jobs to afford a bit of food for the evening, she would have to start early.

Her back ached.

Tupik was leaning forward in anticipation this morning, silent and still in the gloaming. The gray clapboard houses huddled over the muddy streets as if to steal the rising steam of the passing people's breath, and at the outskirts of town, the tall pines seemed to bend inward over the roofs as if to better see what might transpire.

Perhaps it was the growing cold, perhaps the thick gray slab of cloud covering over the sky, but whatever the cause, everything felt weighted down—coiled.

Waiting.

In the corner of the little front room, Shulamis's son, Yehuda Leib, pretended to sleep in a twisting of sheets.

She glanced down at the pan by the cooling embers of the fire.

Half a potato. This was all the food left in the house. Even the saltcellar was empty.

With a sigh, stomach moaning, Shulamis rose from the hearth, took Yehuda Leib's warm red scarf from the chair by the door, and tucked it into the crook of his arm. She'd made the scarf with her own two hands, stitch by stitch, the thread passing between her ruddy, cold-stiffened fingers night after night until finally it was done.

Truth be told, there was as much worry as wool in it.

"You'll be good today?" she said.

"Yes," said Yehuda Leib flatly, his eyelids clamped shut, as if he still might manage to convince her that he was sleeping.

"You won't make any trouble?"

"It's never me who makes the trouble, Mama."

Shulamis frowned, as if she just might believe this. "Of course not." And then, crossing to the door, "There's a little potato left in the pan," and, halfway through the door, "Don't forget your scarf."

It was only moments later, the sound of Shulamis's squelching feet fading down the muddy road, that the front door yawned open again to admit a bright-eyed boy into the morning.

A boy with no red scarf.

It was itchy. And it choked him.

Yehuda Leib couldn't stand being constrained.

The sun was rising.

Few mothers in Tupik could see Yehuda Leib coming down the street without feeling the urge to protect their children from the ill influence that seemed to mass around the boy like a crowd of flies. And this was not entirely unjust. Yehuda Leib's name was rarely heard in the synagogue or marketplace without an attendant sigh—*always brawling, climbing, running*—and if a quick glance over the shoulder showed that neither the boy nor his mother was near, the sigh was very likely to be followed up with the remark that *of course, everyone knows what his father was like.*

But if everyone knew that Yehuda Leib had a tendency to do what he wanted—often with some lightly destructive results—there were few, perhaps none, in Tupik who really understood the extent of his capabilities.

Little escaped the notice of his keen blue eyes.

This morning, for example, he was careful not to waste time lounging in bed once his mother made her way out into the world. Judging by the particular glimmer of the light, he could tell who was likely to be awake, who was on his way to morning prayer at the synagogue, who was making her way to the marketplace. Not only could he therefore say which kitchens and larders were likely to go unattended, but he could also guess which routes he might safely take to get into them without being seen—and, consequently, blamed once he'd acquired what he'd gone for.

Not that he was prone to lifting enough to be noticed—on either the taking or the receiving end, for his mother would never approve of his appropriations—but all the same his face and reputation were familiar enough in town that he knew it was best to avoid notice if he could.

Was it honest? No. But the more he was able to thicken their stores of milk and flour and salt, the easier his mother could sleep the next night.

And besides—as everyone knows—a boy cannot grow on half a potato a day. Not even an ordinary boy.

And Yehuda Leib was not ordinary.

This morning, Yehuda Leib managed a decent haul in the brief window of time safe for grazing, and by the time he climbed out of a certain second-floor window and turned his feet toward the synagogue, the pockets of his worn black coat were well laden with the scraps and leavings of a handful of houses: a hunk of cheese, a crust of bread, a half-eaten apple. Even his mittens were full: salt to replenish the dwindling supply in his mother's cellar.

Perhaps he was a nuisance, perhaps a petty thief, but for all the mischief he made, no one in Tupik saw things as clearly as Yehuda Leib.

It was Yehuda Leib's aim each day to position himself on the steps of the study hall opposite the synagogue's front doors well before the morning service concluded. Once the worshippers began to mill about the threshold, the day's schmoozing would start in earnest, and if he slung the brim of his cap low over his bright, keen eyes, huddling into the corner where the railing met the wall, their chat would flow freely: who had what errands to run, who was traveling, who sick in bed. This talk was indispensable to Yehuda Leib if he was to avoid attracting the wrong kind of attention throughout the day, and if he was in his place on time, the talkers rarely took any notice of him.

This was why, today, it was so strange that they did.

Things started out normally enough, the droning hum of prayer within the synagogue dwindling and coming to an end. The

doors were thrown open, and the most industrious of the worshippers squelched off to get their morning's work under way, leaving
the schmoozers to gather around Yankl, a lanky old schlepper who
had gotten in late from Zubinsk the night before.

Zubinsk was the closest thing to a real place anywhere in the
vicinity of Tupik. Nestled at the edge of the wide forest in which
Tupik was located, it could be reached in the better part of a day's
travel, barring any complications on the road.

But as everyone knew, complications had a way of cropping up:
wagon axles broke, donkeys sprained their ankles, men lost their way.

The grandmothers of Tupik had troves of tales hours deep
about the malevolent demons of the forest: how they hid in the
darkness between the overhanging boughs and dropped down
upon your head when you stopped for a drink of water; how they
tempted men off the path with the flicker of false fire and the
aroma of roasting meat; how, if you were foolish enough to stop for
a nap, they would sneak in through your ears and steal everything
away—your thoughts, your memories, your very substance—until
there was nothing left behind but the papery husk of you.

One could never be careful enough.

Men like Yankl, then, who made their living transporting goods
between Tupik and Zubinsk, had a way of collecting charms and
protections about them. Once, Yehuda Leib had heard Yankl cataloging his arsenal: the hunk of iron at the bottom of his heavy pack,
the faded bracelet of thin red thread around his wrist, the amulets
carefully inked onto small squares of parchment, rolled tight, and
stashed in all the pockets of his clothing.

It was, in fact, about a new talisman that Yankl spoke as he
came out of the synagogue door this morning: an old, hard slice of
bread with a small bite taken out of one corner.

Someone asked how on earth he thought a piece of bread would keep away the demons, and at the sound of this word, Yankl spat superstitiously over his shoulder.

"This is no ordinary slice of bread," he said, raising a finger instructively. "This is bread from which the holy Rebbe of Zubinsk has eaten."

This pronouncement was met with a chorus of appreciation. If the stories of the demons were numberless and dark, the stories of the Rebbe were just as numerous and just as bright—his wisdom, his wonders: they said he could see straight into you and pluck out the sorrow like a rotting apple.

A voice spoke from the knot of gossips. "And how are the wedding preparations going, Yankl?"

"The whole town is in an uproar," said the schlepper. "It's as if they've declared a new holiday!"

Two days hence, just before the beginning of Chanukah, the holy Rebbe of Zubinsk was to marry off his final granddaughter, the youngest of five. It was going to be a massive celebration, and for weeks the rumors had been building: so many wagons full of fine food had arrived, and twice as many musicians; the bride's dress had been made specially for her in Kiev; the groom's family was bringing a famous wedding jester all the way from Vilna.

And best of all: the invitation was entirely open. Everyone was welcome, without exception.

Needless to say, this was a tempting prospect, no less to those interested in the holy Rebbe than to those interested in the promise of a good party, and it was in the midst of describing the torrent of arriving visitors that Yankl stopped short.

"Oh!" he said. "And you'll never guess who I saw at the tavern: Avimelekh. *Avimelekh!* Can you believe it? I wouldn't have thought—"

But what Yankl wouldn't have thought went unsaid; at precisely this moment, the rabbi spoke up.

"Yankl," he said, his soft voice cutting through the chatter like
a knife.

All heads turned to where the rabbi stood in the door.

"What?" said Yankl.

The rabbi gave his head a sharp little shake as if to say, *Don't,*
and then gestured to the place where Yehuda Leib was sitting.

Now the eyes of the crowd turned toward him.

Yehuda Leib's cheeks began to burn.

They were all looking at him.

Why were they looking at him?

"What?" said Yehuda Leib, and when no answer came, he repeated himself: "*What?*"

It was in this moment that Moshe Dovid Frumkin, the stern
and pious town butcher, came forward and, mercifully, broke the
silence.

"Yankl," he said. "Yankl, did you get my new hat?"

"Ah!" said Yankl. "Yes!" Yankl stepped back inside, produced his
hefty pack, and set to untying the large, round box secured to its
bulk. This turned out to contain the hat in question: a rich fur
crown of a shtreimel, glossy and fine, for special occasions.

Now the knot of schmoozers split, some gathering in close to
admire the shtreimel, some splintering into their own conversations or drifting off into the day.

But Yehuda Leib was frozen where he sat. His heart was
pounding. He did not care to be stared at—he who was so often
blamed for broken or missing things, who was no sooner seen than
suspected.

Why had they all stared at him?

What did they all know that he didn't?

The morning was not shaping up well.

And this is why—even more than was normally the case—Yehuda Leib found himself growing angrier and angrier at Issur Frumkin.

Issur was the son of Moshe Dovid the butcher and he was the only other boy in Tupik of Yehuda Leib's age. This inevitably invited comparison, and not to Yehuda Leib's advantage: Yehuda Leib was scrappy and small; Issur was tall and broad. Yehuda Leib was dirty, poor, always in trouble; Issur was none of these things. Because his father was prosperous, Issur's hours were rarely occupied with work, and he was free to sit in the study hall reading holy texts; Yehuda Leib had to occupy his hours finding food to eat.

But what made Yehuda Leib jealous was neither the comfort nor the esteem belonging to Issur Frumkin. It was something altogether simpler:

Issur had a father and he didn't.

And, to make matters worse, Issur had two very different faces. The first, which he always wore in his father's presence, was deferential, humble—the picture of Reb Frumkin's expectation. The second, which he had a habit of turning on Yehuda Leib when others—particularly parents—were not around, was bratty, sneering, and superior.

And there he was now, standing in the synagogue door, doting cloyingly on his father, trying on his new hat. It was far too big on him, of course, and it slipped around and made him look even more foolish than he did in the first place.

But still, Issur's father smiled and laid his hand on the boy's shoulder as if there were nothing his son could do wrong.

No one ever touched Yehuda Leib like that.

Now Issur was asking to keep the hat with him at the study hall, and his father answered with the fond admonition that it was new and expensive, and he must be very careful.

The little fire in Yehuda Leib's chest was picking up heat.

By the time Yehuda Leib looked back up, nearly everyone was gone—Moshe Dovid off to his butchery, the rabbi off to his breakfast. But Issur was crossing the road toward Yehuda Leib now, his feet kneading through the well-turned mud.

It was not kind—and it was probably not wise, either—but Yehuda Leib was in no mood to give Issur Frumkin a free pass. Rooting in his pocket for something to eat, he shifted his body into the doorframe to block Issur's way.

"Hey," said Issur, mounting the front stairs. "Move."

Yehuda Leib did not react, keeping his eyes low beneath the brim of his cap, chewing assiduously on a hard rind of cheese.

"Hey! Yehuda Leib!" said Issur. "I know you can hear me. Move, you idiot."

At this, Yehuda Leib sighed and scooted himself over, but rather than clearing the doorframe, he moved farther in, taking up as much space as he possibly could.

"Oh," said Issur. "Think you're funny?"

Now Yehuda Leib looked up and smiled through a mouthful of cheese.

"You're disgusting," said Issur. "Get out of my way."

Again, Yehuda Leib did not budge.

"Some of us have important things to do," said Issur. "Why don't you stand up and move, you little *bastard*?"

It is entirely possible that Issur was not aware that, coming from him of all people—on this morning of all mornings—that word would scorch Yehuda Leib's guts with its injustice. It is, in fact, likely that Issur Frumkin had no idea what he was getting himself into.

But none of this made the slightest bit of difference to Yehuda Leib.

Calmly, he stood. Tossing aside the stripped rind of cheese, he stepped out of the doorframe, and as he passed Issur by, he swatted at the brim of Moshe Dovid's fine new hat, sending it flying up and out into the street, where he trod on it hard, crushing it deep into the mud.

Issur stood quivering on the study-hall stairs above.

Yehuda Leib turned and smiled.

"There," he said. "How's that?"

And this is how the fight began.

The house of Reb Zalman the baker was on the forest side of Tupik. Coming in from Zubinsk, you had to pass through the little cemetery on the hillside to reach it, and if you didn't take care to lose sight of the clutch of leaning headstones before turning to the baker's door, you might have had the uncanny feeling that you carried some residue of the graveyard inside with you.

For this reason as well as others, the baker made sure to leave a cup and basin for hand washing by the door.

The ground floor of Zalman's house was occupied primarily with the necessities of his business: large sacks of flour, wide wooden workbenches, a vast clay oven stoked to blistering temperatures each morning before the sun even had a chance to rise and compete. Baskets of rolls, rugelach, and, on Fridays, shining brown loaves of thick, braided challah crowded close in around the door. If you wished to speak with Zalman, you would invariably find him here, attempting, it seemed, to cover each of his sober black garments thoroughly with flour before his day was done.

It was mainly on the narrower second level that the women of Zalman's house led their lives. His wife, Feygush, insisted on maintaining a second kitchen there, away from public view, which required quite a bit of schlepping—water and other necessities—up the rough wooden stairs.

This schlepping almost always fell to Zalman's daughter, Bluma.

Bluma was widely considered a good girl—pretty, kind, generally receptive to the needs of others. Her only fault was a slight overfondness for the fleeting territory between sleep and waking, where the eyelids are heavy, the blankets are warm, and the entirety of the world seems to be confined behind a thick sheet of glass. Rarely did she rise until midmorning, when she might creep downstairs to steal a wink and a smile from her father—and often a sweet bun besides.

It was because of this abundance of time spent in bed that Bluma was the member of the family far most familiar with the activities of her grandmother, who lived on the third floor.

Third floor, though, was charitable. In truth, it was a cramped attic, almost perfectly triangular, in which Bluma's grandmother lived with her crabby, toothless gray cat. *Attic* even was a bit too kind: there was barely enough space among the rafters to accommodate the bed, the table, the chair, the old woman, and the cat all at once. And what little floor space there was hung directly above Bluma's bed.

Bluma knew the sound that the ceiling made when the old

woman first shifted in bed in the morning. She knew the sound of the cat jumping from the pillow to the windowsill. She knew the sound of tiny old feet shifting onto the floorboards, of the chair being pulled from beneath the table.

And on this particular morning, the floorboards above her were dead silent.

"Papa?" said Bluma.

Zalman looked up from his kneading and smiled. "Good morning, darling," he said.

"Has Bubbe come down?"

Zalman shook his head and began to knead again. "I think she's still upstairs."

Bluma shook her head. "I haven't heard her all morning."

Bluma's bubbe was nothing if not reliable. Reliably, she stumped down from her attic in the morning to retrieve a bit of bread and water, and reliably, she creaked back up without having spoken a word to anyone.

This had been the way for nearly as long as Bluma could remember.

"Hope she's feeling all right," said Zalman, his voice jumping with the exertion of his work. "Here," he said. "Take her a bit of milk and some rugelach. She'll like that."

Bluma's bubbe, as a rule, did not care for people. She took what little food she ate on her own schedule and often in her own room. Once a week, on Fridays, she would come down to make a pot of chicken soup, and when they all sat down to eat it, she would quietly wish her son and her granddaughter a good Sabbath.

She never spoke to Bluma's mother.

Bluma arrived outside her grandmother's bedroom door and tapped lightly with her knuckle, twice.

"Bubbe?"

For a period of time, Bluma had spent her days reading on the little landing just outside her bubbe's bedroom door. She'd hardly meant to make a habit of it, but while she'd lain there one morning, her grandmother had pulled open the door. Bluma had expected to be shooed away, but her bubbe had simply stared down at her. After a moment, she'd left the door hanging open and gone about her business.

They had lived quietly in parallel, then—Bluma reading on the landing with her pillow, and her bubbe within, occupying herself with needlework or tidying. Often she would sit in front of the oblong mirror on her wall and make a silent accounting of the dissatisfactions she found in her face.

And then one day the door had swung open in the morning and almost immediately slammed shut again. When Bluma had gone to use the bathroom, her pillow had been moved back down onto her bed, and that had been that.

All the same, Bluma held the quiet certainty that she had shared something with her grandmother that no one else in the house had ever seen.

And this was correct.

Again: one knuckle, two taps.

"Bubbe?"

There was no answer.

The bedroom door was hung to swing inward, and with every creaking moment that Bluma spent pushing it, she still thought she might find her grandmother there, just behind the opening door.

But she didn't.

Her bubbe was gone.

The sky was heavy, and Yehuda Leib longed for the rain to come and relieve the pressure.

His mouth ached.

Issur had only gotten one good hit in—despite his superior size, he was really worth almost nothing in a fight—but as luck would have it, his fist had caught Yehuda Leib square on the lip, and it was beginning to swell.

Yehuda Leib was too wise to stick around once they'd been hauled apart—it didn't matter who was at fault when one of the combatants was Issur "God's Gift to Tupik" Frumkin and the other was a grubby, fatherless thief, and so he'd made himself scarce among the rooftops.

Up here, there was no one to glare—no one to wish he simply wasn't.

The time passed slowly. Feet and hooves trod the mud below. Fires were kindled, burned, went out. The dim gray sky began to darken.

The hour came and went for afternoon prayers.

It really was a shame. He had promised his mother that he would stay out of trouble.

But he'd had very little choice in the matter. There were a lot of things you could say about Yehuda Leib, but he *wasn't* a bastard. That much he knew.

He remembered his father, though his mother thought this was impossible.

The memory was warm, almost hot, and it smelled of wax and wood and sweat and wool.

It was a very good memory.

He had been a small boy, and his father had held him with one arm. It had been Yom Kippur, he thought, the holiest day of the year, because all around him he remembered clean white garments. His father's garment had been white, and over it he had worn his striped prayer shawl. Yehuda Leib remembered looking up at the raucous, colorful ceiling of the synagogue, painted with vines and figs, eagles, lions, and unicorns, red and blue and tawny and white, and then his father had pulled his attention down to the front of the room, and someone had blown the ram's horn, and there had been a great riot of supplication from the congregation, and he'd looked up, and there had been tears in his father's eyes, and he'd reached out and taken the edges of his father's beard softly in his fat little fists, and his father had smiled, and the tears had fallen onto his cheeks.

That was all he remembered.

Sometimes he thought the memory felt holy because of the synagogue, and sometimes he thought maybe it was the other way around.

He would have given anything to see his father's face again. He would've given the right eye out of his own head.

But it was impossible. Whenever he asked about him, his mother told Yehuda Leib that his father had died, and then she became very sad for a day or two.

After a while, Yehuda Leib learned to stop asking.

But he never learned to stop wondering.

"Rabbi!"

Instinctively, Yehuda Leib lay flat against the slope of the roof below.

He knew that voice. That was Moshe Dovid Frumkin. The last person Yehuda Leib wanted to see was Issur's father, the butcher, a man who wore blood as comfortably as others wore clothes.

"Rabbi," called Reb Frumkin again, and now Yehuda Leib heard the soft, round voice of the rabbi reaching out in response.

"Moshe Dovid," he said. "What can I do for you?"

Moshe Dovid Frumkin let out an aggrieved sigh, and Yehuda Leib wriggled around to see the two men talking in the street below.

"I trust you heard?" said Frumkin.

"About the fight?"

Moshe Dovid scoffed. "The attack, more like. Issur tells me that wild beast of a boy jumped on him out of nowhere. My fine new hat is ruined, my son's nose broken. . . ."

Yehuda Leib's guts squirmed at the injustice of Issur's story, but at the same time, he was pleased he'd managed to break Issur's nose.

"I'm sorry to hear that, Moshe Dovid," said the rabbi.

"You're always sorry," Frumkin said.

"Yes," said the rabbi. "I suppose I am."

The butcher stepped closer. "But the situation isn't getting any better, Rabbi. Something needs to be done."

The rabbi nodded. "And what do you suggest?"

"Well," said Moshe Dovid. "I caught up with that schlepper Yankl, and I asked him about Avimelekh."

Avimelekh. There was that name again. Yehuda Leib had almost forgotten it in all the excitement.

"He says," continued Frumkin, "that Avimelekh has racked up some heavy gambling debts. He's set on coming to Tupik today or tomorrow—before the Rebbe's wedding. Says he can get a good amount of money finding conscripts for the Tsar's army. Now, would it be such a terrible thing if we just let him have the boy?"

The rabbi tugged at his beard and nodded again slowly. "Yes," he said. "Yes, I think it would be."

Moshe Dovid sighed again, so loudly it was almost a word. "You can't keep protecting him like this."

"I don't see why not," said the rabbi.

"Because," said Frumkin, "it's just a matter of time. It's in his blood."

"What is?"

"You know what, Rabbi. And it's going to come out. Let Avimelekh take him off our hands."

"I think," said the rabbi, with a sigh of his own, "that it would be best for you to look to your own house, Moshe Dovid. The way I heard it told, it was *your* little wild beast who did the attacking. Good evening."

Yehuda Leib grinned.

At least someone was on his side.

But something was still bothering him.

Let Avimelekh take him off our hands.

It was growing dark. He should be getting home.

CHAPTER TWO

Crossing Over

Shulamis was bent over the fire when Yehuda Leib pushed through the front door, and she turned at the sound of his voice.

"Mama?"

Shulamis stood, consternation gathered around her shoulders like a heavy shawl.

"I heard what happened this morning."

She opened her mouth to scold, but there was a question burning in Yehuda Leib, and he blurted it out before she could begin.

"Mama," he said. "Who's Avimelekh?"

Shulamis stiffened.

Yehuda Leib did not know what he'd expected, but this was not it. Despite the popping of the fire and the rolling boil of the potato water, it felt as if all the sounds in their little house had fled in fear of the word he'd just pronounced.

"Where did you hear that name?"

Yehuda Leib swallowed hard. "From Yankl the schlepper. He said Avimelekh was in Zubinsk and then everyone—"

"In Zubinsk?"

"Yes," said Yehuda Leib. "And then Moshe Dovid Frumkin said—"

"Moshe Dovid?" said Shulamis. "Does he know?"

"Yes," said Yehuda Leib. "I overheard him saying that Avimelekh was coming here to Tupik because—"

"This isn't funny, Yehuda Leib," said Shulamis. "Who put you up to this?" She had begun to crack her knuckles, which was never a good sign.

"What?" said Yehuda Leib. "No one. Moshe Dovid said that this Avimelekh was going to be here today or tomorrow, because—"

"*Today or tomorrow?*"

"Mama," said Yehuda Leib with a lurch in his chest. "You're scaring me."

Shulamis stepped forward as if to take hold of her son, but whether to comfort or to warn never became clear.

At just this moment, there was a knocking at the door.

Shulamis froze.

After a long, still moment, the knocking came again.

"Yehuda Leib," whispered Shulamis. "Get under your bed, and no matter what happens, you don't make a sound, understand?"

Yehuda Leib's keen eyes were wide. "Yes, Mama," he said, and in a flash he was hidden.

Slowly, Shulamis smoothed herself. She took a deep breath, and, just as the knocking began again, she opened the door.

"Oh," said Shulamis, letting her breath go. "Oh, Rabbi."

"I apologize," said the rabbi's round voice, "for disturbing you."

"No, no," said Shulamis. "Not at all. Would you like to come in?"

"No," said the rabbi. "No, thank you. I just thought you ought to be told: Avimelekh is in Zubinsk, and he could be here as soon as this evening."

"Yes," said Shulamis. "I heard."

"He's in debt again, Shulamis. And he thinks he can get himself clear by selling boys into the Tsar's army."

Shulamis sighed deeply. "Ah."

"Yes."

Now there was a silence—long, empty, immovable.

"Shulamis, I'm so sorry," said the rabbi softly.

"Thank you," said Yehuda Leib's mother, and then, again, softly, "Thank you."

"Of course," said the rabbi. "Keep safe."

"I'll try," said Shulamis. "Good night."

"Good night."

Gently, the door closed.

Yehuda Leib crawled out from under the bed.

His mother's face was as still as a death mask.

"Yehuda Leib," she said.

"Mama?" said Yehuda Leib.

"You have to go away."

"What?" Yehuda Leib felt his throat catch. His jaw was impossibly tight; his chin began to quiver. "Why?"

Shulamis shook her head so softly it was almost impossible to see. "Because he's coming."

"I can fight?"

Shulamis laughed like nothing was funny. "Not against him, you can't."

"Yes I can!" All of a sudden, Yehuda Leib found himself yelling.

His eyes were filled with tears. He felt helpless and frightened, as if he were little again. "Won't you even try to stop him?"

Shulamis turned away and wiped at her eyes. "If I thought it would change anything, I'd let him tear me limb from limb. But it won't." Slowly, she began to walk about the room, taking things from shelves and cupboards: a threadbare knapsack, a spare cap, a bowl, a cup, an extra shirt, a few potatoes. "If you can make it to Zubinsk, you should be able to lose him. Just get yourself as far away as you can."

Yehuda Leib swallowed. "Okay."

Carefully, Shulamis hung the knapsack on her son's shoulders and set to fastening his coat.

"Mama?" said Yehuda Leib.

Shulamis did not look up from her work. "Yes?"

"Who is he? Avimelekh?"

Shulamis sighed. "He's a very bad man. He hurts people, even when he doesn't mean to—and he means to more often than not."

Her voice was trembling; Yehuda Leib swallowed hard.

"If you want to stay the good young man you are—if you want to stay my son, Yehuda Leib—you keep yourself away from him."

He nodded. "I will."

Shulamis's right cheek bunched up as she struggled to keep the tension from her voice. "Don't you make any trouble."

Yehuda Leib shook his head. "I won't."

Shulamis pulled the front door open and stood back.

"Will you be all right?" said Yehuda Leib to his mother, and she sighed long and low before saying, "I will."

They both knew she was lying.

Outside, for the first time that year, fat white flakes of snow were beginning to fall.

Yehuda Leib took a deep breath, stepped out through the open door, and pulled it shut behind him.

Shulamis stood at the window, watching him walk away until she could see him no longer.

Only then did her eyes fall on the chair beside the door.

Tonight—of all nights—she had let him forget his warm red scarf.

It was not until he reached the cemetery on the hillside that Yehuda Leib began to consider what it would mean to flee into the forest at night. He was not wholly confident of the truth of the stories people told: of evil things among those trees, of accidents and mishaps, of long, snatching fingers and sharp, shearing teeth. He was, however, rapidly becoming sure that if he was going to find out, he would prefer to do so in the light of day.

Through the veil of falling snow, the low-hanging trees and leaning headstones met to create the impression of a mouthful of jagged teeth.

No. He would be far safer on this side of the cemetery tonight. He would hide himself somewhere in town, and when the morning came, he would make his way to Zubinsk.

Slowly, the town lay down to sleep; slowly, the eyes of Tupik began to shut.

Presently, things became still, only Yehuda Leib and the snow creeping on through the darkness.

And then, into the hush on the far side of midnight, a door swung open; Yehuda Leib saw light cutting through the snow and the dim.

Bluma. She had always been kind to him.

"You look cold."

Yehuda Leib nodded. "I am."

Bluma shook her head softly, as if this were a very stupid response. "Then why don't you go home?"

"Believe me," said Yehuda Leib, tramping across the snowy road to the door. "I'd love to."

Bluma sighed.

"What are you doing up so late?" said Yehuda Leib.

"Waiting," said Bluma.

Bluma's bubbe had not come home. Her father had gone walking the streets to look for her two separate times, but no one had seen her, and eventually, with no other good option, he'd gone to sleep—or at least to toss and turn in bed.

So Bluma did the only thing she could think to do:

She sat and waited.

"For?"

Bluma didn't seem to like this question, and she tossed her head and changed the subject. "I heard you started a fight with Issur Frumkin today."

Yehuda Leib sighed. "I didn't start it. I never start it."

Bluma rolled her eyes. "Of course not."

Now there was a short, empty silence.

"But did he at least deserve it?"

"Certainly."

Bluma chuckled.

"You didn't say what you were waiting for."

"No," said Bluma. "I didn't. But you didn't say where you were going."

"Well, you didn't ask."

"Where are you going, Yehuda Leib?"

"I don't know," said Yehuda Leib. "Away."

Bluma was standing just inside the door, the candle behind her throwing a warm flicker into the street; Yehuda Leib was standing just outside, the snowflakes on his coat melting away like dewy ghosts.

"Anyway, I can't stay here anymore."

Bluma's eyebrows fell. "Does your mother know about this?"

Yehuda Leib nodded. "It was my mother who sent me away."

Bluma's chin began to twitch, and for an agonizing moment, Yehuda Leib thought she might start to cry.

But instead, an idea seemed to march into her mind, her lips locking into a light, tight frown.

"What?" said Yehuda Leib.

"One second," said Bluma, and she ducked inside, returning quickly to thrust a large braided challah at him. "Here," she said. "Take this."

"What?" said Yehuda Leib.

"Take it," said Bluma. "And eat it sooner rather than later. It's already a few days old, and they go stale quickly."

It broke Bluma's heart to see Yehuda Leib's beautiful blue eyes widen; it was as if no one but his mother had ever given him food before, which was an unutterably sad thought.

"Thank you," said Yehuda Leib, and then, four or five more times, "Thank you," as he stuffed the challah into his little knapsack.

When he finally looked up again, he caught Bluma peering out into the darkness, searching.

"Well," said Yehuda Leib, "good night."

"Good night," said Bluma. "Stay safe."

Yehuda Leib shrugged as if to say, *What can I do?*

"I hope you get what you're waiting for," he said.

Bluma sighed. "Me too."

And, unfortunately, she would.

She came trudging out of the woods haltingly, snowdrifts on her stooped shoulders. She jostled the door as she crossed over the threshold, and in the front room where she'd fallen asleep, Bluma's mother moaned and rolled over.

Bluma's bubbe saw this, and, disappointed she hadn't managed to wake her daughter-in-law, she made a loud, rude noise with her tongue and tramped over to the staircase.

Up, as always.

Up, past her granddaughter, dozing, still dressed atop the bedclothes.

Endlessly, endlessly up.

She was tired—exhausted, really. As tired as she would ever get.

All she wanted to do was lie down and rest.

Arriving heavily at the top of the stairs, she found that someone had been in her room, and she made the rude noise again, this time to the universe at large.

With a weary shimmy, she shook what snow remained about her onto the floor, stumped over to the window, wheezed, coughed, and blew out the two dwindling candles that had been left burning on the sill.

Slowly, she turned back to prepare for bed in the gloom she felt entitled to.

And at this very moment, on the far side of the river crossing, a small bell began to ring.

If you arrived in Tupik at the end of a long day's journey and wished to continue on the next day, the only place for you to go would be back the way you came. Just beyond the far shore of the muddy river, the ground became first unpleasantly moist, and then impassably swampy, and to make matters worse, a series of precipitous drops and rocky rapids in the river downstream made it impractical to pilot a boat, a barge, or any other vessel out on the water.

Tupik was a dead end.

It might, then, be a surprise to learn that an old stonework ferry shack still crouched low on Tupik's riverbank. According to the town's founding charter, as long as the Jews of Tupik provided, at their own expense, a ferryman to work the crossing, they would be allowed to continue to live and trade in the little town by the river. Of course, the nobleman who had granted the charter had been dead for hundreds of years, and his descendants had long since lost track of the bargain, but to the denizens of Tupik—like the rest of their people—it was no small thing to abandon an ancient agreement.

In those days, the ferryman was a fellow named Mottke, a devoted souse who was rumored never once to have bathed.

The entirety of Mottke's responsibility consisted of sitting close to the ferry, waiting to hear the ringing of a small bell that could be pulled from the landing platform across the river. Of course, the bell never rang. But in the event that it did, Mottke's job was simple: he was to climb aboard the little ferry barge that sat tethered on the Tupik side of the river, take hold of the chain attached to the far platform, pull himself across the current, and return with whoever had rung the bell.

But, of course, the bell never rang. There was no road passing anywhere near Tupik on the far side of the river, and it was almost impossible to conceive of someone slogging through the miles and miles of nearby swampland in order to end up there accidentally.

This is why it was so very strange that, just as Yehuda Leib began to think about finding a place to steal a few hours' sleep, his ear was drawn down to the banks of the river by the unmistakable sound of a tinkling bell.

"Mottke."

The ferryman was snoring softly, his breath curling away in little ringlets of mist.

"Mottke!" This time Yehuda Leib jostled the man, and he started awake.

"Hrrrrghm?"

This was not a word. Yehuda Leib had never before heard Mottke make a sound that could be unconditionally classified as a word.

Stillness had descended over Tupik, as if it had stopped breathing in the night. The snow had broken off, the cloud had cleared, and the air was dense beneath the star-riddled sky.

And it was into this heavy hush that the soft tinkling of the bell fell.

Dingadingading. Dingadingading. Dingadingading.

Mottke's eyes were wide. "Beh," he said. "Beh."

Yehuda Leib nodded.

Mottke leapt to his feet, dashing and sliding across the slick icy rocks on his way to the ferry. Down on the water, Yehuda Leib could hear him shatter a thin layer of ice; he could hear the clanking of the heavy chain, and the river beginning to buffet the edge of the ferry as it edged out into the current. The stars were bright overhead, and in the cold light the ferryman could be seen lunging forward and pulling back, lunging forward and pulling back, as he drew himself across the water.

Only when Mottke had finally reached the far shore did Yehuda Leib's eyes fall on the dark stranger waiting on the opposite platform.

Without hurry, the stranger stepped onto Mottke's ferry. There was a murmur of exchanged words, their sense lost in the susurrus of the flowing water. Before long, Mottke was pulling again.

Now the figure on the ferry was moving toward him.

Gradually, it occurred to Yehuda Leib to be afraid.

Yehuda Leib heard the ferry barge bump against the Tupik landing platform. The chain rattled as Mottke returned it to its place. Some further indistinct murmuring of voices.

And then footsteps in the snow.

Slowly, the dark stranger climbed up the riverbank. His coat was black—blacker than the night, blacker than the darkness hidden inside your eyes. On his head he wore a hat, tipped forward, also black, with a brim so wide that it hid nearly all of his face.

The gait of the dark stranger was heavy, weary, and slow, and when he reached the top of the riverbank, he stopped not six feet from where Yehuda Leib stood.

The low fire in Mottke's shack flickered and flared, sending spasms of warm light out into the cold blue dim. Yehuda Leib stared, trying to make out the face of the stranger beneath the brim of his hat.

"Yehuda Leib," said the dark stranger, his lips curling into a grin. "It is a pleasure to see you."

"A-Avimelekh?"

Yehuda Leib's heart was beating very quickly.

"No," said the stranger.

"How do you know my name?"

"I am a Messenger. I have been to many places and spoken with many people."

"And who told you my name?"

The Dark Messenger shook his head. "I do not repeat what is spoken to me."

Yehuda Leib's eyes narrowed. "Are you sure you're not Avimelekh?"

The Messenger nodded. "Yes. And it would be better to save your breath than to ask me a question twice. I have never told a lie."

Yehuda Leib tried to swallow, but he couldn't quite manage it.

"I wonder, Yehuda Leib," said the stranger, "if you wouldn't accompany me into town. My list of errands is long—so very, very long—and it is rare that I have any company on my way."

Yehuda Leib's gut squirmed as if it were trying to escape. The stranger did not look like a man accustomed to refusal.

"All right," said Yehuda Leib, and the dark stranger smiled.

Yehuda Leib began to walk up the sloping market road, and the stranger fell in beside him.

"Where do you go?" said Yehuda Leib.

"I have an errand in Tupik," said the stranger. "But thereafter I go to Zubinsk. A wedding is to be given in that place to which all have been invited, without exception."

"The Rebbe's granddaughter," said Yehuda Leib.

"Yes," said the stranger. "I have been at my errands long now—

perhaps longer than may be borne. I feel I deserve a reprieve, and the joy and celebration of a wedding seems just the thing. But the far better question, Yehuda Leib, is this: Where will *you* go once you have left Tupik?"

Yehuda Leib sighed. "If it were up to me, I would stay in Tupik forever."

The stranger shook his head. "No man lives forever."

"For all the days of my life, then."

"And why in Tupik?"

This was a question to which Yehuda Leib had been trying to find the answer all night.

"Because it's my home. Because I can feel it."

"What do you mean?"

He wasn't quite sure himself. "Tupik. I feel it—the way people's bodies move in the street, the streets themselves, the buildings, the mud, the water in the river—here, just where the back of my neck meets my head. Do you know what I mean?"

The Dark Messenger turned toward the boy and regarded him for a long moment.

Slowly, he grew a grin.

"You have keen eyes," said the stranger, and he began to walk again. "Have you ever met a sheepdog, Yehuda Leib?"

Yehuda Leib shook his head. "No."

"I have a deep affection for such animals. They herd, corral, protect their sheep, and they do it all in a very simple manner: they hunt them."

"What?"

"They hunt the sheep. They chase them, stalk them, stare them down. But they hunt without killing."

Yehuda Leib's eyebrows fell. "Is it still hunting if they don't kill?"

The dark stranger smiled. "Oh my, yes."

"Hmm," said Yehuda Leib.

"What I mean, Yehuda Leib," said the stranger, "is that you might do well to consider the Tsar's army."

This idea shocked Yehuda Leib. "What?"

"Oh, it is a risky business, war," said the stranger. "A risky business, to be sure. One stands to lose more than just his life. But unless I miss my guess, I think you might find the work well suited to your talents."

Yehuda Leib's lips were pressed together tightly. "No," he said. "No."

"You seem," said the stranger, "terribly certain."

"Wouldn't the army . . ." Yehuda Leib swallowed as he looked for the word. "Change me?"

The stranger nodded. "It would. As will all things."

"I don't want to be changed."

"That," said the Dark Messenger, "is unavoidable, I am afraid. If you wish to live."

Now the dark stranger brought his feet to rest, and with surprise Yehuda Leib looked up to find that he was standing again in front of the house of Reb Zalman the baker.

The stranger gave a heavy sigh. "Thank you for accompanying me, Yehuda Leib," he said. "I know my way from here."

"All right," said Yehuda Leib.

"But there is one thing more," said the stranger. "You must do me a service: the ferryman would not accept my payment."

"No, no," said Yehuda Leib. "He's paid by the community."

"So he told me," said the Messenger.

Yehuda Leib had trouble imagining Mottke telling anything to anyone with much success.

"But it is a point of honor with me," the stranger said. "I can leave no debt behind."

Yehuda Leib shook his head. "You have no debt. The crossing is free for all travelers."

"Yes," said the stranger. "But still the ferryman is paid. I must provide his payment."

"Really," said Yehuda Leib. "There's no need."

"I am afraid," said the stranger, "that I must insist," and he held out his hand.

In his long, narrow palm, there were two worn coins.

"Take them," he said.

Slowly, Yehuda Leib stretched out his fingers.

Perhaps he would just hold them and then give them back. Perhaps just for a time. Carefully, Yehuda Leib took first one coin and then the other from the stranger's hand.

"Good," said the stranger.

The coins were odd: two of the same denomination, cold and heavy, battered, gray. On one face they bore the figure of an open eye, and on the obverse the same eye firmly shut.

"Until we meet again, Yehuda Leib," said the stranger.

And by the time Yehuda Leib looked up, he was gone.

The front door of Bluma's house bumped, jostled, and swung open.

The wind was stirring.

Someone stepped across the threshold.

A sudden gust of wind swept through the street and slammed the door shut behind the stranger. Feygush, slumped asleep across the front room, stirred, moaned, and rolled over.

Again, she did not wake.

But she was not the only one in the house.

On the second floor, Bluma's eyelids flew open at the sound of the slamming door.

Bubbe, she thought.

Bubbe is home.

The house gave a groan as a pair of feet shifted from the floorboards to the staircase, and from her vantage point near the wall, Bluma was overjoyed to see the figure of a hunched old woman begin to rise heavily from the first floor.

It was not long, though, before her joy melted away.

The old woman was not her bubbe.

Bluma froze, her breath arrested in her throat.

Who was it?

Slowly, a dark stranger climbed the stairs. Her dress was black—blacker than the night, blacker than the darkness hidden inside your eyes—and over her head she wore a blanket, pulled forward, also black, forming a hood so deep and dark that it hid nearly all of her face.

Only her mouth could be seen.

The gait of the dark stranger was heavy, weary, and slow, and when she reached the top step, she stopped not six feet from where Bluma lay.

With a sigh, the dark stranger looked up the last flight of stairs toward Bluma's bubbe's bedroom. She reached a knobbly hand into the folds of her black blanket and produced an object—some sort of tool that gave a glint in the cold moonlight.

Bluma could not see what it was.

With effort, the old woman began to climb the final flight of stairs.

Who was this?

What was happening?

What did she have in her hand?

Above, Bluma heard her bubbe's bedroom door yawn open and swing shut. Quickly and quietly, she laid her bare feet down on the rough wooden floorboards and crept up after the dark stranger.

She could hear voices.

"Dvorah Leah, daughter of Hindeh." The stranger's voice was husky and rough.

"Oh, for God's sake," said Bluma's bubbe.

"What?"

Outside, the wind sauntered by with a low yowl.

"I tramp around all day making myself ready for you, I go, I sit in the woods, I shiver, I collect snow on my shoulders like it's gold, I think, I say, *Anytime now*, and all the while you're nowhere to be found. Now, finally, I come home, I put in the trouble to get myself ready for bed, and just like that, here you are."

"I did not appoint the time of our meeting, Dvorah Leah."

"Oh, get out of here. No one's called me Dvorah Leah in forty years."

"It is your name."

"I don't care. Take it if you want it."

"I am afraid not, Dvorah Leah."

"Hey," said Bluma's bubbe. "Hey, did you do something to my cat?"

"I know nothing of your cat."

"Sure you don't."

"I do not lie," said the stranger.

"What, I'm supposed to believe that?"

The stranger sighed. "It is entirely immaterial to me what you believe, Dvorah Leah. I am here to do you a service."

"Bah," said Dvorah Leah. "Some service."

"You would be sorry if I were not able to perform it for you," said the stranger. "Believe me."

"I thought what I believed was immaterial."

Floorboards creaked as weight was shifted from foot to foot. "Take my counsel: You begin only once and end only once. There is no reward or exception for the irreverent."

Bluma's brows began to fold. *End?* What did she mean, *end?*

Dvorah Leah laughed. "You think I should be reverent? What have I ever been given that I should be reverent?"

"Life, Dvorah Leah," said the stranger, and the word fell like a heavy load dropped at the end of a long workday. "Life."

"You don't know what you're talking about," said Dvorah Leah. "Do you have any real knowledge of what you're talking about?"

There was no response. Beyond the window, the wind flexed its muscles.

"No," said Dvorah Leah. "I didn't think so. I'll tell you what: why don't you go away and live a lifetime's worth of pain, of fear and want and intimidation and abandonment and betrayal and disappointment, and then you can come back here and tell me how I ought to be reverent. How *dare* you."

For a long moment, the house was silent.

Presently, the Dark Messenger spoke. "It is not given to me to form judgments."

"No," said Dvorah Leah. "Of course not. You're, what, just the messenger?"

"I prune the tree so that it may grow."

"Oh, go piss into the wind. What, did you come up with that while you were killing an actual gardener?"

Suddenly Bluma's heart began to race.

Killing?

"I do not kill," said the stranger. "I retrieve what otherwise might be lost."

"Ah," said Dvorah Leah. "So you're like a dog, then—like a filthy dog."

Slowly, the voice of the stranger began to shift like a gathering storm.

"It is your prerogative, Dvorah Leah, to squander your final moments if that is what you wish to do. But it is unwise to tempt the wrath of such a one as I."

Now Dvorah Leah laughed long and loud, but the laughter was false—pushed and angry.

"At what do you laugh, Dvorah Leah?" asked the rising storm of the stranger.

"At you, whatever you are. You'd like to think you're just a gardener, just a messenger, just a retriever of lost things, but when it comes right down to it, you get crabby when you're taunted, just like anyone else."

The stranger made no response.

"No matter what I do, I'm not going out that door on my own two feet, am I?"

"No, Dvorah Leah. You are not."

Bluma's heart was beating so hard that she was afraid it would be heard.

"All right, then," said Dvorah Leah. "Here's exactly what I think of you."

Bluma heard her grandmother take a hobbling step forward and fill her lungs with air.

And then it happened.

Shuffling feet.

Falling furniture.

Her bubbe was angry, but she was prevented from speaking.

There was something metallic, and as it came into contact with a bedpost or table corner, it rang out reverberantly, like a bell.

Thrashing. Anger.

A bump and rumple of bedclothes.

A choke and a gurgle.

Metal scraping against something rigid—crockery, perhaps, or bone.

Outside, the wind had begun to fly by with greater and greater force, quicker and quicker, as if something were trying to flee, which it was.

Suddenly, terrible, still silence.

Silence.

Tears blossomed in Bluma's eyes.

And then, from inside the bedroom, footsteps began to approach the door.

Bluma flew down the steps, quickly, quietly, as swiftly as possible without making a sound. Feet pressed into the floorboards above her, and she dropped to the floor and slid herself into the small gap beneath her bed.

Too late she remembered that she had been atop the bed before. And if the stranger thought to look . . .

Too late.

The stranger's feet reached the bottom of the stairs. She came to a halt and let out a long, low sigh.

Bluma stopped up her breath and sealed it in, wrapping her fingers tight against her lips. She must not make a sound.

Her heart was thundering in her chest.

She must not make a sound.

"*Unpleasant*," said the stranger to herself. "That is the word. Unpleasant. And unfair."

The stranger's shoes pressed into the floor, one foot first and then the other, and with a surge of fear, Bluma realized that she was moving closer. Her feet were visible now, walking wearily along the side of Bluma's little bed, moving their way up toward her pillow.

The feet stopped.

Bluma started to panic, her vision beginning to whiten at its edges. The dark woman's feet were not six inches from her face, and if she didn't breathe soon—well, she didn't know what would happen.

Above, there was a sound of plashing and plinking, as if . . .

Yes.

The stranger had begun to wash up.

Bluma herself had fetched that water in.

And, all of a sudden, the water stilled.

Something was moving nearby.

The dark stranger had heard it.

Bluma's thirst for breath had grown so intense that she had to gnaw at the inside of her cheek to distract herself with pain. And now the Dark Messenger stood above her, listening hard for any sound of life.

"Who's there?" said the stranger in a hoarse whisper.

Silence.

A creaking floorboard.

Outside, a half-hearted shift in the wind.

Bluma was dying for breath.

And then, all at once, a screech, a yowl, a streak of gray fur—Bubbe's ancient toothless cat leapt out of the darkness, and, out of surprise as much as necessity, Bluma's bottled-up breath broke through her lips, and she gasped sharply. The stranger cursed and stumbled backward at the cat's ambush, and, just as Bluma remembered to stifle the sound of her panting breath, the instrument that the stranger had been cleaning in the water bounced to the floor with a clang.

In time to come, she would look back and ask herself: Had there been some intention in it? Had Bluma meant, on some level, to start what she had started?

But the plain fact of the matter is this: Bluma reached out and laid her hand over the fallen metal instrument because it was clattering against the floorboards and she was convinced—for good reason—that it would draw attention to her.

But now her arm was protruding from beneath the bed.

Now she was out in the open.

Bluma held absolutely still.

Gradually, the dark stranger above found equilibrium between her two feet. Again, she cursed softly to herself.

"Cats," she said. "I hate cats."

Flinging the water from her fingertips, the dark stranger turned and made her way to the head of the stairs.

Wearily, she began to descend.

The front door bumped, jostled, swung outward, and then shut.

She was gone.

It was over.

Slowly, Bluma pulled the stranger's instrument into her tiny hiding place beneath the bed.

And she was surprised. She had assumed it to be a knife or a dagger of some kind—a weapon—but it wasn't.

The Dark Messenger's forgotten instrument was a spoon.

And the spoon was strange—preternaturally cool, or even cold. What little moisture had been left on its surface in the washing was beginning now, bit by bit, to transform into tiny pine needles of crystalline frost.

That was strange. It was cold outside, to be sure, but thanks to her father's oven, of all the houses in Tupik, theirs was by far the warmest. In fact, it was because of the warmth of the upper floors that Bluma's bubbe had continued living in the attic even once her hip had started to bother her.

And, with a start, Bluma realized that she could no longer say that her bubbe continued living in the attic. She could no longer say that her bubbe continued living at all.

Bluma curled up as small as she could, threw the spoon against the wall, and began to sob.

It was only once she looked up again that she discovered the second peculiarity of the Dark Messenger's instrument.

When it was not cultivating frost, the round face of the spoon seemed entirely unremarkable: small dings and scratches marred it, and behind these, a person could easily recognize herself reflected. But the reflection was odd: slow, delayed, as if it had traveled a long distance through something thick and viscous.

This is why, when she looked up, the girl that Bluma saw reflected back to her was curled up as she had been a moment ago, crying.

Bluma dried her tears and shuffled forward, staring intently at her sobbing double.

After a moment, the Bluma in the spoon looked up and noticed her. Soon she dried her own tears and inched closer, just as Bluma had done a moment ago.

And this is how it came to pass that there, beneath her bed, Bluma descended into the sleep of the grieving under the watchful gaze of her own unblinking eyes.

CHAPTER THREE

Ripples

Bluma was wakened by the gentle hand of her father on her shoulder.

She rolled over, bleary on the rigid floorboards, and there he was, kneeling above her, red-eyed, tender, and completely clean of flour.

"Bluma," he said, a quiver in his voice.

Bluma couldn't stand the thought of him speaking it out, and she lunged at her father, wrapping him in a tight embrace, her face buried safe between his beard and his shoulder.

Softly, his big hands fell onto her.

Softly, he began to shudder with tears.

Soon things started to move very rapidly. There were, said Bluma's mother, necessities to think of.

First, the members of the Holy Society were sent for, and they assembled in the front room of the bakery, one by one, somber, respectful, their eyes cast downward. Once their quorum was gathered, they tramped en masse up to the third floor and carried Bluma's bubbe down on her straw mattress.

She did not look like Bluma had imagined.

It was unmistakably her: her face, her body, even her unruly hair. There had been no violence done to her, no cuts or scrapes or bruises or holes made, but all the same there was something missing.

She was a person who had departed.

It was incomprehensible.

The straw pallet was laid down in the front room, and there, in the presence of the Holy Society, Bluma's father mumbled a rote blessing and tore his shirt and jacket in a ritual of mourning. This having been done, the somber company lifted Bluma's bubbe again and carried her out of the house to the small funeral hut near the cemetery, where she would be washed and guarded until her burial.

As the door swung shut behind them, Zalman sank to the floor.

There he remained, leaning back against the stacked sacks of flour, all morning.

For a short time, Bluma and her mother remained with him. Before long, though, Feygush began again to murmur of necessities, and, rising to turn back to the ordering of the home, she beckoned for Bluma to follow.

Feygush climbed to her bedroom and gently tucked away the little looking glass that Bluma was sometimes permitted to use. With effort, she lifted her small, heavy mirror and turned it around to face the wall.

It was in the midst of this task that she spoke to Bluma.

"Blumaleh," she said. "Go upstairs and turn your bubbe's mirror around. Just like this."

This was a horrifying prospect.

Bluma stood, staring blankly, until Feygush noticed her.

"Did you hear me, Bluma?"

Bluma had so much to say that it jammed up her throat: How could she possibly go up there? How could she enter that room?

How could she violate her bubbe's privacy? How could she move things that her bubbe had set in place? How, how, how?

Feygush sighed. "Today is not the day for this. Do as I say."

And so Bluma's feet carried her up to the third floor.

And what she saw was horrific.

Some well-meaning member of the Holy Society had tidied the room. Every possession was laid out in perfect parallel, every piece of linen folded, every edge straightened.

They had taken Bluma's bubbe out of the house and cleared up after.

Bluma wanted desperately to get out, to get away from this violent tidiness, and so she moved swiftly to the mirror. Her reflection startled her—it seemed too quick, somehow, too prompt—and as she turned the glass to face the wall, she began to feel some stirring of memory.

Her reflection.

What had happened last night?

Bluma hurried back down to the second floor to find her mother struggling to move the water barrel toward the top of the stairs.

"Good," she said. "Come help me."

Feygush and Bluma collected all the water in the house, and once it had been arrayed by the door—bottles, buckets, barrels—they began to pour it out, little by little, into the street.

Up until this moment, Feygush had acted with almost defiant practicality, but as they stood in the chill air watching the wasted water run downhill to the river, Bluma heard her mother's breathing catch and shudder, and she looked up to find her wiping her eye.

In the nearby cemetery, the sound of shovels could clearly be heard digging open her bubbe's grave.

As much to block out this sound as for any other reason, Bluma spoke.

"Why?" she said. "Why do we pour out the water?"

Feygush sniffed and cleared her throat.

"They say," said Feygush, "that when the Angel of Death is finished claiming the dead, he washes his knife in the water of the house."

His knife? That didn't seem right.

And suddenly all the events of the previous night came flooding through the dam of grief and fatigue that had held them back.

She had seen the Angel of Death.

And her instrument was not a knife.

It was a spoon.

The news made its way swiftly through Tupik.

As soon as the members of the Holy Society returned, one by one, to their homes, Bubbe's name passed from lip to lip, spreading like a virulent cold.

Dvorah Leah, they said.

Who?

Dvorah Leah. You know, the old woman—Zalman the baker's mother.

Ahhhhh.

Tongues tsked and heads wagged. She had not been a popular woman—she had been very deliberate about that—but just the same she had delivered many of their children, and when death touched even the furthest outpost of their little community, it was a tragedy for them all.

Hands that otherwise might've gone idle that morning grasped onto the hafts of shovels. The digging sped by. Between them all, the grave was ready by lunch.

In accordance with tradition, she was to be buried as soon as possible.

Shortly after noon, when news of the grave's preparation reached the riverbank, people began to tramp uphill. Friends knocked on their neighbors' windows. Tasks were laid aside. Two feet became four, and then eight, twelve, twenty, slogging through the snow and muck toward the cemetery together, and slowly their number increased until the town ran uphill like an impossible river.

The young were nervous. The old were reflective.

Tupik was going to bury its dead.

Yehuda Leib woke woozy and confused, and immediately he was on his guard.

There were voices.

It was a moment before he realized he was in the dusty, dim synagogue attic. Morning prayers were under way in the sanctuary below.

A cacophony of half-chanted melody floated up through the floor, and as Yehuda Leib rose, stretched, began to creep from rafter to rafter, he imagined himself intercepting the rising column of each individual prayer.

Before long, the worshipful murmuration below fell off into light chat, and then into silence. The sanctuary door creaked open and swung shut behind the last straggling worshipper like a final *amen*.

Yehuda Leib was left alone.

The attic was vast. Four or five of Yehuda Leib's houses could easily have fit inside.

The stillness was terrible.

He wanted to go now, wanted to be on his way, but he was in the very center of town, and the man Avimelekh might already have arrived.

Across the muddy snow of the road sat the study house. Issur Frumkin would be there for certain. If he so much as cracked the sliding panel beneath the wide synagogue eaves in order to leave, he could be seen.

He needed a distraction.

And then, as if by some dark miracle, all the people of Tupik began to march past him up the hill.

What was happening?

Where were they going?

No matter. This was the chance he had been waiting for.

As the flow of people began to dwindle, Yehuda Leib slid the entry panel back.

He took a deep breath. Silence held the road below.

Carefully, he climbed down into the snow.

It was time to go.

But there was one last thing he had to do first.

People kept looking at Bluma with pity.

All she wanted was for no one to look at her at all.

Just leave me alone.

The funeral had seemed simultaneously endless and perfunctory. There had been blessings, and the rabbi had said something about an old woman who sounded nothing like Bluma's bubbe, and then they'd done what they'd all come to do: put her bubbe into the earth and, one by one, seal it up above her.

Bluma's father took up the shovel late, but unlike Bluma, Feygush, and the others, he did not stop with a single symbolic clod. In fact, he did not stop at all. People shuffled around him to drop their handfuls of earth into the grave—still, he kept shoveling. Bluma could see the veins bulging in his neck as he shoveled, and shoveled, and shoveled.

And shoveled.

He had worked up quite a sweat by the time the grave was full, and on their short walk home, steam rose from him like silent prayer into the cold, gray afternoon.

People began to arrive at their door, bringing food, smiling sadly. Candles filled the house. Before long, the front room was packed with milling visitors—munching, chatting, looking at Bluma with pity.

Just leave me alone.

Soon she retired to the empty second level. She could not outrun the chatter of the guests on the first floor, but here, at least, it was muted, as if heard through a thick layer of earth.

There had been many distractions, of course, but whenever Bluma's brain had come to rest that day, this was the place to which it had returned.

The spoon.

She could not see it, but she knew it was there, wedged against the wall beneath her bed, just where she had thrown it.

She thought she remembered odd things—frost, cold metal on her skin, a strange, lugubrious reflection—but her mind was not at all calm, and by now she had begun to wonder if she hadn't been imagining things.

Had the old lady climbing the stairs just been her bubbe?

What had she really heard through the bedroom door?

Had she only been dreaming?

Perhaps it was just an ordinary spoon.

Downstairs, the front door ushered in a new crop of guests, and Bluma heard hushed greetings ripple through her front room.

Quietly, she lowered herself to her hands and knees and peeked below the bed.

There it was.

It had frozen against the wall.

Careful not to allow herself to slide all the way beneath, Bluma reached deep under the bed and grasped the frigid spoon, tugging hard, once, twice, before it came up in her hand.

She had not been imagining things.

In fact, the spoon was odder than she remembered, for while her reflection was indeed delayed in the spoon's surface, the setting it depicted was not delayed at all: instead of persisting in showing the dim surroundings beneath the bed, the reflection in the spoon now showed the larger second floor exactly as it was—except that Bluma had not yet arrived.

Shortly, though, in the spoon's reflection, she came padding up the stairs—weary, dour, sad.

No wonder people were looking at her with such pity.

Bluma wanted to see herself better, and, bunching up the hem of her skirt, she began to polish the frost from the spoon.

With a sharp gasp, she dropped it to the floor. Instinctively, she stuck her thumb into her mouth.

Her thumb. She had cut the pad of her thumb.

Was the spoon . . . sharp?

It was. The rim of its basin had been honed to a razor's edge, which both confused and disquieted her. All she could imagine was a big mouthful of soup and a long gash along the inside of either cheek.

Who on earth would want a sharp spoon?

But as she bent to retrieve it, something else—something stranger—caught her eye.

The spoon had landed facing up. A small droplet of her blood was creeping down the inverted slope, and in the glossy red trail it left behind, a slice of someone's face was reflected.

And it was not hers.

Bluma lifted the spoon, waiting for her reflection to arrive, and the blood ran and spread, covering more and more of the basin.

Gradually, the face in the blood began to clarify.

It was her bubbe. Bluma was sure of it.

And as if on cue, Bluma's own face came swimming into focus, perfectly framing Dvorah Leah's: two different faces, united by a common reflection. Or, rather, one death divided between two people.

"Bluma!"

Feygush's voice came echoing up the stairs, and her footsteps followed close behind.

Almost without thinking—almost—Bluma stuck the spoon into the pocket of her apron and wheeled about to face her mother.

"Perla Kraindl's here. She wants to say hello. Will you come down?"

Feygush's face was drawn and weary.

Bluma looked at her with pity.

The old woman was dead and buried.

Shulamis had not known her well, but all the same she lingered at the back of the crowd by the graveside until Zalman packed the very last shovelful of earth atop her casket.

It gave her a chance to cry.

The sun was low and the sky beginning to darken as Shulamis started the short trudge back to her little house. It would be dark, and it would be cold, and it would be empty.

But as soon as Shulamis reached the front of her house, she knew. A little sob broke from her throat, and she found that she was smiling.

Yehuda Leib's familiar footprints led first into, and then back out from, her front door.

And the warm red scarf was nowhere to be seen.

Yehuda Leib straightened his scarf and hoisted his pack high.

Now was as good a time as any.

The shadows between the trees glowered down at him like the darkness between teeth; a breeze stirred the pine needles as if to whisper, *You are too frightened.*

And perhaps he was.

Tupik was far behind him now, over the hill and downriver nearly half an hour's walk, but he could still smell the toasted aroma of its fires.

He still might find his way back.

As much to buy time as to warm them, Yehuda Leib stuck his chill, stiff fingers into his coat pockets. He had mittens, of course, but he didn't like to wear them. He couldn't stand being constrained.

But at the bottom of his coat pocket, Yehuda's fingers met something cold and hard.

Two somethings, in fact.

The coins were thick and heavy in his hand, and when he opened his fingers to look down at them, he felt a little jolt of shock. They had come out of his pocket well spaced, and for a moment he could've sworn that they were living eyes, looking straight back up at him.

Or one living eye, at least. The coin on the right was flipped to display its closed lid, as if frozen in a perpetual wink.

Somehow, this bothered Yehuda Leib.

"No," he said to himself, flipping the coin on the right. "Eyes open."

A low, stalking breeze rifled the tree branches.

The sun was sinking with every passing minute. If he didn't go now, he would lose what little light he had left.

Pocketing the coins, Yehuda Leib took a deep breath and began to climb.

The forest between Tupik and Zubinsk was mostly evergreen, and the snow clumped together atop the boughs and needles, forming a barrier against the low sun.

Gradually, Yehuda Leib was wrapped up in creeping darkness; quietly, almost furtively, the snow began to swallow up his tracks.

Everyone in Tupik had heard stories of the demons among the forest trees, and Yehuda Leib did his best not to think of them now. As long as he could find the path to Zubinsk before he lost the light entirely, he thought, he would be all right.

But nightfall is a terrible trick in the forest: just when you think the darkness is complete, it finds a way to grow thicker.

The ground was completely covered in snow, and the path might've been nothing more than a gap between the trees.

Had he missed it?

Like a nearing drum, Yehuda Leib began to hear the beating of his heart growing heavy in his chest.

He had to find the path.

But now he was unsure where he had been facing just a moment ago. From which direction had he come?

The long fingers of the darkness had begun to work their way into his mind.

And then, all of a sudden, the jangle of a bridle. Hoofbeats in the snow.

A horse meant a person.

A person meant a path.

Without thinking, Yehuda Leib charged forward.

It was only once he could see the equine silhouette looming up between the trees ahead that he remembered the threat of Avimelekh.

"Who's there?"

Warm lantern light shone out like a rupture in the darkness.

"Hello?"

Yehuda Leib's heart fell. The face that swam into view in the flickering light of the lantern was not Avimelekh's, but possibly it was worse.

"I know you're out there," Issur Frumkin called into the trees.

Swallowing his pride, Yehuda Leib stepped forward into the light.

"Oh," said Frumkin. "*You.*"

What Yehuda Leib had taken for a horse in the dim was

nothing more than the Frumkins' stocky little donkey. Issur was seated behind her in a battered two-wheel cart, reins in hand.

"What are you doing out here?" said Yehuda Leib.

"I'm going to Zubinsk. For the wedding."

"Your father agreed?" This was surprising to Yehuda Leib.

Issur scoffed. "I don't need my father's permission."

Yehuda Leib cocked his head to the side. "But you do need his donkey."

Issur grimaced as if this notion were so stupid that it had a physical odor. "What he doesn't know won't hurt him. What about you? What are you doing out here so late?"

"Someone's after me," said Yehuda Leib.

Issur laughed. "Who'd want anything to do with you?"

Yehuda Leib shrugged past the insult. "Someone called Avimelekh."

Now Issur's face fell. "Avimelekh?"

"Yes," said Yehuda Leib. "Do you know something about him?"

Issur shook his head. "No," he said, both too quickly and too loudly.

"Are you sure?" said Yehuda Leib.

"I'm not supposed to say," said Issur. He was suddenly very uneasy. "What are you going to do?"

Yehuda Leib gestured to the forest at large as if to say, *What else is there?*

There was a long, heavy silence.

"Well," said Issur. "I hope you survive."

"Yes," said Yehuda Leib. "So do I."

"Best of luck," said Issur, and, turning to the path, he gathered his reins.

"You know," said Yehuda Leib, "if you really want me to survive, you could give me a lift. Just as far as Zubinsk."

Issur rolled his eyes. "Oh, sure. So you can steal my cart when I'm not looking?"

This was incredibly stupid. There would only be cause for Yehuda Leib to steal the cart if Issur *didn't* give him a lift.

"I promise I won't do that."

But now Issur was beginning to enjoy his power, and a little smirk curled at his lip. "What, I'm supposed to trust you? You attacked me, just yesterday, like a vicious animal."

"Yes," said Yehuda Leib, clenching his jaw rhythmically. "I did. And I'm sorry."

"Oh-ho-ho!" laughed Issur Frumkin. "Now you're sorry! Would you have been sorry if I were on foot?"

Of course he wouldn't. "Of course I would."

"Well," said Issur, "I don't believe you."

Yehuda Leib was becoming desperate. "Issur, please," he said, and then, impulsively, "I can pay?"

Issur lifted his lantern high and peered down as Yehuda Leib rifled through his pockets.

"Ha," said Issur, entirely without humor. "Keep your money. You'll need it if you ever make it to Zubinsk."

Yehuda Leib was growing frightened. The donkey cart was his best chance, and if he didn't manage to get on it, who knew what might happen?

"Issur," he said. "Issur, I'm sorry. Please."

Issur scoffed. "You're not sorry. You hate me."

He couldn't quite believe it, but once again, Yehuda Leib had been caught off guard by just how awful Issur Frumkin really was.

"I'll say it again, Yehuda Leib: I wish you the best of luck."

And then, softly at first, then louder and louder, a drumbeat of snowy hooves.

Someone was coming down the path.

Someone on horseback.

Someone big.

The drumming of the hooves slowed first to a trot and then to a walk.

Yehuda Leib crouched low in the snowy brush, his own breath deafeningly loud in his ears.

The horseman was huge, his long, dark coat spilling down on either side of the saddle. His thick beard was black with patches of gray, and his cloudy eyes hid something sharp and angry, like needles secreted into soft, gauzy cotton.

"What's your name, boy?" he said to Issur, busying himself with his saddlebags. His voice was rough, ragged, like it had been torn apart and stitched together a thousand times.

"Missursur," murmured Issur.

In a swift, violent scuffle, the horseman seized Issur by the front of his shirt and dragged him in close. "You speak clearly when you talk to me."

"Issur! My name is Issur!"

With a heave, the horseman returned Issur to his seat. "Good."

"What's yours?"

At this, the horseman began to laugh.

It wasn't a friendly sort of laugh.

"Avimelekh," answered the horseman. "You come from Tupik?"

Issur nodded. "Yes, sir."

"I'm looking for a boy there called Yehuda Leib. You know him?"

"Yes," said Issur. "I do."

Low in the bushes, Yehuda Leib stiffened, his muscles tightening in preparation to run.

Avimelekh was busy packing sticky black tobacco into a long, knobbled pipe. "Know where I might find him?"

Beneath its hulking rider, the dark horse snorted, stamped, tossed its head.

"Last I saw him," said Issur, "he was down by the river. But that was hours ago."

Yehuda Leib nearly jumped out of his skin.

Slowly, deliberately, the horseman leaned forward, thrusting a thin kindling taper into Issur's lantern.

Issur swallowed. "And he's always running around town down there. There's no knowing."

The horseman lit his pipe, puffing three or four times, and then blew out the taper in a long gout of smoke.

"Maybe at his mother's house?"

"Issur," said Avimelekh, and then, pulling his horse to attention, he looked Issur straight in the eye. "I'll remember you."

It was not until the rattle of his spurs had faded back down the path that Issur let himself exhale. "Well," he said. "I guess you'd better get in, Yehuda Leib."

In the glow of the lantern, the velvety darkness on either side of the path looked thicker, fuller than before.

How could the stillness feel so crowded?

Issur had demanded the payment he had been offered before letting Yehuda Leib up into the cart, and though Yehuda Leib couldn't help but think this petty, he'd gladly yielded up one of his two cold coins.

He would've given almost anything to be in that cart, and he was more grateful than he could say not to be alone in the darkness anymore.

But he did wish the donkey could move a bit quicker.

And the ride was hardly luxurious—there was barely enough room for both boys at once, to say nothing of all the junk that had been piled beneath the tarpaulin in back: rusty tools, dented pots and pans. This was all intended for sale or trade in Zubinsk, Issur explained.

Issur had a lot of explaining he seemed to want to do—he babbled when he was nervous. Yehuda Leib had always taken it for showing off, throwing his knowledge around.

Maybe he was just nervous all the time.

Either way, he was certainly nervous now, and he'd chosen the single worst topic to babble about:

The demons in the darkness.

"They congregate in ruins, in cemeteries, in the wilderness," said Issur, "because they can't pass into areas of civilization except under very special circumstances. Which is why they're so eager to get you when you're in the forest."

All this talk was putting ideas in Yehuda Leib's head—tiny, gnashing things, clinging onto his collar, working into his hair.

". . . even, Yehuda Leib, even in the holy Talmud. *Far* more of the demons than there are of us: eleven thousand to one. That's in the Talmud! And they're particularly dangerous at night."

Avimelekh had been moving twice, perhaps even three times, as fast as they. How long would it take him to determine that Yehuda Leib was not in Tupik?

"Only three things can protect us from them," said Issur, counting them out on his fingers. "Salt, cold metal, and red thread."

Yehuda Leib sighed. "*Salt?*" What on earth was he prattling about?

"Salt. When you build a new house in an unsettled area, you're supposed to mound salt in the corners of each room before you sleep there the first night. The demons' magic can't pass beyond boundaries of salt. And because cold metal comes from civilization, they can't stand the touch of it." Here Issur flipped up the collar of his coat to display a thin sewing needle threaded through the fabric.

"As for red thread," he said, "I don't know how it works, but it's the strongest. They tied some onto my bassinet when I was a baby."

This was intolerable. If Issur was going to be prattling, at least he could share some useful information.

"Issur," said Yehuda Leib. "What do you know about Avimelekh?"

Issur looked over at him, his face suddenly drawn with concern. "I'm not supposed to say."

"No," said Yehuda Leib. "But you're not supposed to run off with the donkey, either."

For this, Issur had no answer.

"Issur," said Yehuda Leib. "If he's dangerous, then what you know might help keep me safe. It might—"

But before he could say another word, Issur's voice came bursting forth like water from a dam.

"He beat my father up, once. It was really bad. They were afraid he might die."

Yehuda Leib swallowed hard.

"He'd gamble, he'd get drunk. People were scared. So when the constable came to town saying we had to send conscripts for the Tsar's army . . ."

"They sent Avimelekh."

"Right," said Issur. "Without even warning him. And as scary and angry as he was before . . ."

"Issur," said Yehuda Leib with a sigh. "You don't think your donkey could move a bit faster, do you?"

"What's the matter?"

There was someone—or something—rattling between the trees.

"There," he said. "Don't you hear that?"

Issur shook his head. "I don't hear anything."

"Issur," said Yehuda Leib, rising to his feet. "Issur, stop the cart."

"What?" said Issur. "Just a second ago, you wanted me to go faster."

Yehuda Leib was growing frantic. "Stop the cart. Stop the cart!"

"Fine, fine," said Issur, reining in the donkey.

Yehuda Leib leaned out into the cold and dim and listened with all his might.

But it was the aroma that gave him away.

Thick, sticky black tobacco.

Yehuda Leib had barely managed to dive beneath the tarpaulin before the horseman drew up and began to speak.

"Issur," he heard the man say. "You seem nervous."

"What?" said Issur with a forced laugh. "Me?"

"You know the boy Yehuda Leib—"

"No," said Issur, and then, "But of course, yes, I mean. *No*, I haven't seen him. But *yes*, I know him. As you said. And as I said. Before."

Yehuda Leib fought not to sigh aloud.

"When did you say you last saw him?"

"Earlier," said Issur.

"Yes," said Avimelekh. "*When?*"

"Oh, hours and hours," said Issur Frumkin. "Back in Tupik. Down by the synagogue."

The cart jostled as it went over a thick tree root.

"The river, you mean," said Avimelekh.

"Hmm?" said Issur, just a bit too loudly.

"You said you saw him by the river. Not by the synagogue."

Issur was silent.

"The reason I ask, Issur, is that I dropped something near where we met last, and when I tracked back to retrieve it, I saw the strangest thing: a pair of footprints, small, like a boy's, leading out from between the trees and ending right next to your cart ruts. How do you explain that?"

Softly, foolishly, Issur Frumkin murmured, "Demons?"

Yehuda Leib could feel his heart beating in every extremity of his body.

With a jangle and a clank, the horseman cut in front of the donkey, and Issur was forced to pull his cart to a swift stop. "Hey!"

"You're Moshe Dovid Frumkin's boy, aren't you?"

Again, Issur failed to speak.

"I know your family, Frumkin. I know what kind of people you are. So why don't I make this clear: I came looking for one boy, but I could be perfectly happy leaving with another."

"Ah," said Issur.

"I'll ask you one more time," said Avimelekh. "Where is Yehuda Leib?"

It was over.

He was caught.

Yehuda Leib drew in his breath, tore back the tarp, and launched himself into the trees.

CHAPTER FOUR

Into the Darkness

Branches, needles, thorns, tearing at his coat and cap and face, and he raised his arms to keep them away from his eyes, and the horse was crashing through the brush behind him, and it would be upon him now if he didn't move, move, *move*, and he leapt sideways, putting the trees between them, but the horse was deft and dodged, and he would never outrun this man, never, never, never, and he could not see into the dim, and he had to do something, had to think, but his heart was banging and his jaw was tight and he was afraid the pounding hooves would trample him into the loam and he dove down into a low copse and the hooves pounded past.

What could he do?

Soon the horse was reined in, turned around.

Gradually, it began to pick its way back toward him.

He had to do something. The longer he waited, the closer the horseman would come.

Far off, in the direction of the path, he could still see the flicker of Issur Frumkin's lantern.

Slowly, the horse's padding came to a stop. Avimelekh slid from his saddle, crouching low to the brush.

"Boy!" he called.

Now.

In one motion Yehuda Leib was up and flying, racing through the trees toward the lantern light, and he could hear Avimelekh cursing, fumbling to get back into the saddle, and Yehuda Leib was nearly to the path when the crash and thunder of pursuit rumbled out from the trees behind, and he was desperate, tears in his eyes as he tore across the brightened track, and he yelled to Issur to *help him help him*, and he was back into the brush and the black and running, and the horseman was with him, but suddenly he was running alone and there was stillness behind him and he slid and found himself beneath a branching bush and there he stayed.

This time Avimelekh remained mounted. The flickering lantern light seeped out around the edges of his broad silhouette.

"Come on, son," he called, urging his mount into a measured walk. "You're wasting my time."

And the terror of it was that he was right. What could Yehuda Leib do? Hide in the brush forever? How long could he keep running back and forth across the path?

"I'm not letting you get away," said the horseman.

"Yehuda Leib!" Issur's voice split through the still night, and Avimelekh was startled, swiveling in his saddle.

Yehuda Leib saw, and almost without thinking, he took his opportunity, running, running, running toward the sound, and the horseman heard his feet, and he twisted back just as Yehuda Leib passed by the shoulder of his horse, and he reached down and grabbed, and Yehuda Leib felt long, ragged fingernails rake the back of his neck, and the man had him by the collar, and he twisted and he struggled and he pulled, and for a moment his feet were off the ground, but then he was away, he was going, and his neck was cold and bare, and he turned back to see the horseman charging out of the darkness with the red woolen scarf in his hand, and he turned to the light and Issur was standing in the back of the cart and there was something in his hand and—

With a sound like a ringing bell, Avimelekh fell hard from his saddle.

His horse charged on into the forest, never looking back.

Yehuda Leib stilled his legs.

There, in the back of the cart, was Issur Frumkin, holding one of the dented pots from beneath the tarpaulin.

He had hit the horseman.

He had hit him in the head.

Hard.

From where Yehuda Leib had come to a halt, he could see the horseman's boots twisting, squirming in the snow. Slowly, he made his way around the side of the cart, careful to stay out of arm's reach.

Avimelekh was flat on his back.

His eyes were wide open, his jaw flopping wordlessly.

In his hand he held Yehuda Leib's woolen scarf, and beneath his head the pure white snow was turning the exact same color:

Blood red.

"Issur," said Yehuda Leib. "Issur."

"I don't—I didn't mean—"

But now a low croaking sound was filling the air.

Avimelekh was laughing.

"Frumkin," he said, his eyes flashing, and then, "Yehuda Leib." His laughter broke off. "Yehuda Leib."

The horseman's legs stopped moving.

Beneath his head, the pool of red in the snow had grown as wide as the path.

"Oh my God," said Issur Frumkin. "Oh my God."

And there was a new kind of stillness lying on the path.

"He would've gotten me," said Yehuda Leib. "He would've taken me."

"I know," said Issur.

But neither of them felt comforted.

It is difficult to say how long the two boys stood in silence over the body of the dead horseman. But the sound that broke the silence is sure:

Footsteps. Footsteps in the snow.

All of a sudden, the wind grew restless.

Issur's donkey began to stamp and snort, straining against her tackle; high above, the birds took wing for safer territory.

And then he came around the bend, his coat blacker than the night, blacker than the darkness hidden inside your eyes—so black it seemed to eat up the light. At the sight of him, the donkey began to scream and pull, nearly tipping the little cart in her terror.

"Whoa," said Issur. "Whoa, girl!" But there was no calming her, and, buffeting her body against the shafts of the cart, she turned it around by sheer force of fear and bolted back up the path toward Tupik, dragging Issur, cart and all, behind her.

And what he saw as he turned to look over his shoulder would haunt his eyes for the rest of his life:

A small patch of moonlight.

A dead man.

A pool of blood.

Yehuda Leib, looking very small.

And a stranger, dark and tall, closing in along the path.

"We meet again," said the Dark Messenger.

He seemed very tired.

"Hello," said Yehuda Leib.

"You must forgive me, Yehuda Leib," said the Dark Messenger. "I am not best suited for *comforting*." He said the word roughly, oddly, as if it were in a language he did not understand.

But Yehuda Leib was confused. His flight from Avimelekh had been frightening, but it was over now; he couldn't see that he needed comforting.

"What?"

The Messenger cocked his head to the side. "Ah," he said, "I see," and then, "Oh dear."

"What?" said Yehuda Leib again. "What is it?"

The Dark One sighed. "Have you never seen this man before today, Yehuda Leib?"

Yehuda Leib shook his head. "No."

"Are you sure?"

Yehuda Leib nodded. "Of course I'm sure."

But the truth was that, as yet, he had not taken a careful look at him.

Softly, wearily, the Dark Messenger beckoned Yehuda Leib to move closer.

Now that he looked, Yehuda Leib thought perhaps he *had* seen the man before. There was something—something familiar.

"I don't . . . ," he said. "I'm not . . ."

The blood had spread wide, a huge red halo beneath the horseman's head, extending halfway down his rib cage by now, and Yehuda Leib was careful not to let it touch him as he came nearer.

That face.

Whose was that face?

"Who is he?" said Yehuda Leib.

The Dark One spoke softly. "Unknit the silver from his beard; smooth down the wrinkles of his face. Do you not know him?"

Yehuda Leib shook his head in frustration.

He didn't.

But he thought he almost might.

There were two large patches of gray in the man's beard. Despite his best efforts, Yehuda Leib couldn't quite manage to ignore them, and so he reached up his hands to block them out.

And just like that, he knew.

His hands.

His little hands in the beard.

The ghost of a smell: wax and wood and sweat and wool.

Yom Kippur.

His little hands at the edges of his father's beard.

His father's beard.

His father.

This was his father.

"Oh," said the Messenger of Death. "Oh dear."

Nothing.

There was nothing else in the world.

His father—his father—the vacant face of his father, staring up at the scattered stars.

Oh, it hurt.

He had been waiting, every day, every day, every empty, boring minute of his stupid little life, to see this face split into a smile again.

And he had missed his chance.

He had run away.

Why had he run away?

It hurt.

Oh, it hurt.

The world began to bleed out now into a streaky wash of tears.

He had asked for help. He had called out aloud.

He—he—had asked for this. It was his fault.

His fault.

There was something in his chest, something hard and heavy that felt as if it would crack his ribs, and it reached up into his throat and took hold of him and squeezed, and it hurt, and he hurt, and he could hear a sound nearby, a wounded sound, an animal sound, and only when he began to feel a ragged ache in his throat did he realize that the sound was his own.

He didn't care about the blood anymore.

He didn't want to be careful.

He buried his face in his father's chest, and he sobbed.

It hurt.

Oh, how it hurt.

But there are protocols in these moments; there are necessities to think of.

"Yehuda Leib," said the Dark Messenger. "I must ask you to move aside."

"What?" said Yehuda Leib. Something deep inside him felt suddenly broken, and he almost feared to move lest the pieces be irretrievably scattered.

"It is time."

The Dark Messenger stepped forward, and, instinctively, Yehuda Leib scuttled back. The Messenger reached deep into his black coat and brought forth—

Brought forth nothing.

"Ah," he said, patting at his pockets. "Forgive me. Forgive me, I—I seem to have mislaid . . ."

Yehuda Leib gazed silently up at him past red, tear-streaked cheeks.

"I'm afraid I cannot . . . without my . . ." The Messenger sighed hard. "No. No matter," he said, pushing up his sleeves. "We shall simply have to improvise."

Carefully, Yehuda Leib inched forward, craning to see what would happen.

Taking firm hold of his right pinky between the thumb and forefinger of his left hand, the Dark Messenger grimaced and pulled.

The nail grew longer.

Twice more the Messenger grasped and pulled, grasped and pulled, until he had made, protruding about an inch from his little finger, a sharp, rounded trough of his smallest nail.

"Stand back," he said, and moved forward to plant a foot on either side of the dead man's chest. Bending low, the Messenger dipped his nail deep into the eyes of Yehuda Leib's father—first the right and then the left—and, delicately, he scooped out a small point of light from each and tipped it into the palm of his left hand.

And, just like that, the body in the snow was vacant—nothing more than cooling meat.

His father, however, was still there: a pair of faint, glimmering lights in the left hand of Death.

If only he could reach them . . .

Slowly, Yehuda Leib began to creep forward.

"Stay back," said the Messenger with a voice of ice.

Carefully, the Messenger rolled the two points of light into one between his palms, and he began to look about on all sides as if searching for a convenient place to put it down.

"But how?" he muttered to himself. "How to safely contain . . ."

"What is that?" said Yehuda Leib.

The Messenger seemed annoyed. "Oh, nothing. If I had my . . ." And here he sighed. "This is truly . . ." And, looking deep into the trees, he called out sharply: "You there!"

There was a skittering in the darkness, and a honking caw.

"Yes, you. Come forth." It was a long moment before he repeated, "Come forth, I say!"

Finally, what seemed to be an ordinary if startlingly large crow came flitting out of the darkness.

But there was something odd behind its eyes—something dark. Something intelligent.

The crow bowed its head toward the snowy path and spoke in a crackling voice. "Most Reverend Regent."

Yehuda Leib recoiled at the sound. Were crows meant to speak? He thought not. But then nothing seemed more impossible than what had just happened: his father given and taken away in a single moment.

The Messenger did not bother to look at the crow. "Whom do you serve, demon?"

The crow hopped forward and blinked. "I am the Right Deplorable Carrion of the Cracked and Blasted Wastes of Tehom, Master of Ragged Flesh, Bringer of—"

But the Messenger held up his empty palm. "Spare me."

The crow preened lightly.

"I asked whom you serve."

"I am counted, Most Reverend Regent," said the crow, "among the legions of Lord Pazuzu."

"Good," said the Messenger. "Then I charge you, Crow of Pazuzu, in the name of your master, to carry this cargo into the Far Country, to the very gates of my house, and there to wait for me until such time as I shall return to collect it. You shall not tarry in your errand, nor shall you turn to the left or the right. Do you understand?"

The crow nodded. "Yes, Most Reverend Regent."

"Good," said the Messenger. "Then approach and take your charge."

With a flitting hop, the crow rose to perch on the Messenger's wrist.

And what it did there appalled Yehuda Leib.

With a sharp peck and a toss of its head, it swallowed the bright point of light in the Messenger's palm.

"No!" cried Yehuda Leib.

The Dark One flinched, as if he had forgotten Yehuda Leib was even there.

"No!" called Yehuda Leib again, and, darting forward, he reached out for the crow, which, with an angry croak, rose from the Messenger's wrist.

"Come back!" cried Yehuda Leib, but the crow beat the air with its wide wings, rising high up into the sky.

Yehuda Leib could still see the glimmering light, just barely, lodged in the crow's throat, racing away into the night.

He could not bear to let it disappear.

"Wait," said the Dark Messenger feebly, but Yehuda Leib leapt off in pursuit. "Wait!"

But it was too late.

The sound of the boy's thumping feet was swallowed quickly by the thick, skulking trees.

Silence fell on the path.

The Dark One turned and let go a heavy sigh. He was tired—so terribly, terribly tired.

He had meant to be in Zubinsk by now. One sweet day of anonymity, one day to walk among others, to join in their celebration and not be reviled for simply existing—was that so much to ask?

And now, on top of it all, he had lost his instrument.

Trusting Avimelekh to a common demon was dangerous—perhaps even foolish—but his light had to make its way into the Far Country, all the way to the House of Death, and without his instrument, he simply could not contain it safely.

He could've borne it back himself, it was true. But it was always such a long journey. And he was so tired already.

Besides, he would not have risked missing the wedding in Zubinsk for any price.

All the same, though, he was afraid there was one more stop that he could not possibly avoid. He thought he knew where he might've left his instrument.

But it meant going in the wrong direction.

It meant going back to Tupik.

What took Bluma by surprise was how wearying the sadness was.

When the crowd of guests and neighbors began to leak back out the front door, all the energy in the house seemed to go with them.

The food was left where it sat, laid out in half-eaten array on the front-room workbenches. The candles were allowed to gutter and smoke.

Slowly, her parents mounted the staircase.

Slowly, sighing, they climbed upstairs.

There was no chatting, no baking, no activity of any kind. It seemed as if the order of the day was just to sit and wait for the aroma of death to pass from their nostrils.

And it took its time in going.

But it wasn't just the fatigue that weighed so heavily—it was the boredom, too.

No one had energy to do anything.

For a little while, Bluma thought she might pass the time in reading, and she flopped down atop her bedclothes in the late-afternoon twilight to do so, but her mind was slow and thick.

So instead, she just lay.

From time to time, someone would move. Around suppertime, her mother went downstairs to pick at the leftovers in the front room. Now and then her father would cry softly.

Before long, Bluma's eyelids began to drift.

Sleep, it turned out, was the only thing that made any sense.

Bluma opened her eyes. Time had passed. One short, smoldering wick burned in a wide puddle of wax, and outside, darkness had fallen. In the next room, her mother and father were snoring softly.

And above, in the attic, there was nothing.

Her bubbe was gone.

Her bubbe was dead.

Nothing would ever be the same.

She had never meant to come to bed—she was still dressed

there, atop the bedclothes, all the way down to her boots. And now it seemed as if she'd never escape the bed again. She couldn't even muster the inclination to rise and change into her night-gown.

Grief and boredom pecked at her brain like a pair of starving birds.

She longed to sleep, but she had squandered her fatigue on the boredom of the afternoon.

The time scraped.

The time scraped slowly.

The time scraped slowly by.

And she had just finally begun to doze again when a familiar sound groaned out through the house.

The front door was opening.

Before she had time to remember why her heart was so heavy, Bluma was on her feet.

Bubbe has come home.

This, of course, was not true. If there is one thing that unites the multifarious dead, it is the fact that none of them ever come back.

But someone had returned. Someone in a dress blacker than the night, blacker than the darkness hidden inside your eyes.

And where, ordinarily, the face of the Dark One remains hidden—inside the folds of her mantle, beneath the brim of his hat—Bluma happened to reach the top of the stairs just as the ascending Messenger passed through a falling beam of moonlight.

She saw the face.

She saw it very clearly.

Her insides squirmed into a twist of panic. It could've been no other face in the universe.

"You," said the Messenger of Death.

And Bluma fled.

Tired as she was on that night, still the reach of Death was long.

It began with the water barrel in the corner, stolid and immovable in its spot for years, never once to wobble.

Until Bluma began to run.

And suddenly, the barrel tipped and fell. Water covered the floor, and if Bluma had not neglected to take off her boots before lying down on her bed that afternoon, then her feet would surely have slipped and slid; she would've broken her neck.

But Bluma splashed away, the water lapping at her ankles, and she fled in the only direction she could go as the Dark One's slow, aching feet followed behind:

Up.

Up toward Bubbe's bedroom.

And as she pounded up the stairs, her breath short and shallow, the sole of Bluma's boot fell hard in the center of a step—a step that had never before shown any sign of weakness—and it splintered and cracked and gave way as if the rot had been eating at it for a century.

If Bluma had been just a moment slower, then she would have fallen; she would've cracked her head open on the workbench below.

Behind her, Bluma could hear the Dark One leaning against the wall to cross over the splintered gap where the stair had been, and Bluma pushed through the door of her bubbe's room and slammed it so hard that several of the chimney stones shifted and fell in a sooty avalanche that strained the beams and rafters of the house below.

Surely, surely, her parents would wake at this racket, would come and save her, chase the Dark Lady away, make her safe.

But the sleep of the grieving is a heavy thing, and Death has a way of passing lightly where she wishes not to be seen.

Bluma pushed open the bedroom window.

Everything outside was terribly still.

The cold wind turned over in its sleep.

It was a long way down.

The fallen stones were blocking the bedroom door, and she could hear it shaking rhythmically at the *shove-shove-shove* of the Dark One.

There was no time.

Quickly, Bluma lifted herself up to sit on the windowsill and reached her foot out onto the ledge below. If she was careful, she might just be able to climb down. . . .

But her heel slipped on a patch of ice, and with a lurch, she slid and began to fall, her heart plummeting before her.

Surely Death had caught her at last.

Bluma landed hard in her neighbor's haystack, shattering the wooden undergirding below. Her heart was pounding. She couldn't catch her breath, and her head ached terribly.

But only the wood had broken. She seemed—yes, she seemed to be intact.

Far above, the Messenger of Death leaned out of her bubbe's window, searching the ground.

Bluma had to go.

Now.

But no sooner had Bluma climbed to her feet and made her way out of her neighbor's goat stall than there she was: the Dark Lady, pushing her way out Bluma's front door.

Without sparing a thought for her route, Bluma turned on her heel and fled, running directly into the cemetery.

And this was a terrible mistake.

If the world of the living were a suit of clothes and the world of the dead the bony flesh beneath, then at each elbow there would be a cemetery gate.

Here the dead rub up against the living world.

Here the living world wears thin.

Bluma had spent her entire life within a stone's throw of this graveyard, but she was immediately disoriented upon entering it that night. The graveyard no longer seemed centered on the path that ran down its middle: suddenly it revolved around the tidy black blanket of fresh-turned earth beneath which they had buried Bluma's bubbe.

The young grave drank up all her attention. And for this reason, Bluma was twisted back to look over her shoulder as she ran into the cemetery.

By the time she came to a halt, she had already strayed from the path.

And you must never stray from the path in a cemetery once darkness has fallen.

But where was her pursuer?

Bluma's slowing footsteps in the crunching snow seemed as loud as rumbling thunder. The night was cold and still. Snow had begun idly to fall, as if it had nothing better to do.

Had she outrun the Dark Lady?

But she had not.

There are certain ancient protocols that restrict the behavior of the Messenger of Death in the world of the living. But once cemetery borders have been crossed, an entirely different set of rules applies.

She came from the direction in which Bluma had been running, blossoming up cold and heavy out of the deep shadow of a moonlit grave: a cloud of frothy darkness, reaching out with long, choking tendrils.

She did not look the same now. But to those who know her, the Dark One is unmistakable.

In a flash, Bluma was running again, fleeing, weaving between gravestones.

Death was everywhere, hanging a black cloud in front of the moon, giving chase on swift paws, screeching, lowing, roaring, but Bluma would not give up, would not stop, and every time the Dark One loomed up from a different angle, she turned and fled, farther and farther and farther into the cemetery, and she took a swerving side step around a low marker, and her toe caught and she slid and fell on her hip and landed on something cold and hard in her apron pocket, what was it, and as she rose and ran, she put her fingers into her apron and there it was:

The spoon.

Something behind her was whispering her name, and without dropping a step, she shouted, "Take it!" and threw the spoon away, and she ran and ran and kept on running.

But it was different now.

Something had changed.

The Dark Lady was no longer behind her.

She had followed after the spoon like a hungry dog after a bone.

Bluma collapsed behind a crumbling headstone, pressing her eyes into her knees. Softly, she began to sob, and each ragged breath pumped her little chest like an ancient bellows.

But scarcely had she allowed herself the latitude to cry when, again, she heard the terrible sound on the other side of the gravestone:

Footsteps.

Footsteps in the snow.

Oh, the Dark One was tired.

Her feet ached. And her hips. And her back. She ached in places that people do not live long enough to learn can even ache in the first place.

That idiot girl. Why had she run?

But this was a foolish question. They always ran if they had the chance.

Where was her instrument? She had seen the girl throw it aside. She had seen it land in the snow. It should've been right here, shining darkly in the moonlight.

But it wasn't. She couldn't find it anywhere.

Back and forth she tracked among the gravestones, time and time and time again, searching in circles ever wider and wider.

Where had it gone? She could not do her job properly without it. She certainly could not continue to entrust the transmigration of souls to whatever petty demons happened to be at hand. In fact, the more she thought of it, the more it seemed a monumental mistake that she had done so even once.

She was so tired that she had begun to make mistakes.

And in her business, mistakes could not be made.

This was nonsense. Her spoon was not here. And now she had lost track of the girl as well.

"Girl!" she called to the silent gravestones. "Bluma!"

But there was no answer.

There was never an answer when she called.

The Dark One muttered a heavy oath.

As far as she could see, tramping back and forth like this, making herself wearier and wearier, was only likely to cause more accidents, more mistakes. If she hadn't been so tired—so very, very tired—she wouldn't have left her spoon behind in the first place.

No.

She couldn't do her job properly without the instrument, but where she was going next, she had no plan to do her job at all.

Perhaps if she just allowed herself a little break, things would become clearer.

Yes.

And once the wedding was over, she would come back and retrieve her spoon.

It was the only responsible thing to do.

And so, throwing her hands in the air, the Dark One turned and, with a newly brightened step, began to make her way toward Zubinsk.

Slowly, slowly, as the heavy footsteps faded into the soft hush of the snow, Bluma lifted her head to peek out over the top of her gravestone.

The Dark Lady was nowhere to be seen.

She was alone.

But only now did she truly perceive the depth of the trouble in which she found herself.

If she had stopped to think about it along the way, Bluma would've quickly come to the conclusion that she had run much farther than the length of the tiny Tupik cemetery. And yet she had not come out the other side. And, more troublingly, there was no sign whatsoever of Tupik to be seen: no houses, no chimneys, no candlelit rooms.

But how could this be? She had lived beside the Tupik cemetery her whole life long, knew every plot and corner of its extent.

And yet, somehow, she had carried herself farther inside it than should've been possible.

Silver moonlight sifted down between the falling flakes of snow.

Gravestones.

Gravestones as far as the eye could see.

Where was she?

The snow continued to fall, soft and fine, almost clandestine, and by the time Bluma rose from her hiding spot, there was no sign of a single footprint behind her.

How could she say which way was home?

But Bluma was not foolish. The surest way *not* to make her way home was to stay where she was.

And so she rose and began to walk among the graves, looking for something familiar.

In the little cemetery back home in Tupik, the tombstones all shared a certain family resemblance: each stone in a generation had been carved by the same pair of hands, and that pair had been taught by the pair that came before it.

But in this cemetery there were very different sorts of memorials.

Here, laid out in the snow, was a square wooden table and a sturdy wooden chair. On the table was a bowl of barley gruel in which Bluma could make out the individual grains, and it was only once she laid her hand on the back of the chair that she realized the entire arrangement had been carved from a single block of gray stone.

Up until that moment, Bluma had been convinced she could smell the aroma of the warm porridge.

And there were other such markers: a top hat of obsidian lying as if abandoned on its side in the snow, an open book with letters so delicately hewn that they were scarcely distinguishable from real ink on the stone page.

The moon above bled forth cold, clear light like an open wound in the sky.

Farther and farther Bluma went. Her fingers and toes began to grow chill, her legs and feet to ache. She searched and searched and searched and searched, but she could not find any hint of home.

There seemed to be no end to the dead, no wall or fence or boundary to hold them in.

They seemed to go on forever.

It was when she stopped, just for a moment, just to stretch her back and roll her shoulders, that she felt it there, cool and heavy against her thigh, and she knew immediately, somewhere in the moldy basement of her mind, that it had made its impossible way back to her.

What she didn't know was why.

But as soon as she put her hand into her apron pocket, she found out.

"Ah!" she cried, pulling her fingers out as quickly as she could.

Ahhhhhhhhh, replied the echoing vastness of the graveyard.

Tiny droplets of blood budded from Bluma's fingertips.

The spoon had come back because it was hungry.

The spoon had come back because it wanted another taste.

CHAPTER FIVE

Rules of Acquisition

Everyone knows: you must never stray from the path in a cemetery once darkness has fallen.

But there is no particular wisdom to straying from the path in a midnight forest, either.

The crow flew far overhead now, so far that, between the gloom and the treetops, Yehuda Leib could scarcely keep track of it. When the trees thinned enough to allow him a peering vantage through the pine-needle canopy, more often than not he recognized the bird above by the darkness it produced in blocking out the stars.

On they went, and on and on, Yehuda Leib struggling to see, struggling to make his way forward. The cold did not matter, nor did the dark: the crow flew on.

The snow grew thicker, and the night in between.

Yehuda Leib's eyes were turned skyward nearly the whole way, and he did not have the presence of mind to take notice when the gravestones first began to loom up between the trees. It was only when he put his foot through what felt like a basket of brittle sticks that he looked down.

He had stepped, up to the knee, into an ancient gray rib cage.

Suddenly Yehuda Leib was aware: the stones were all around him, their names and dates and remembrances worn away by time and weather. Some were choked in dormant creepers, some covered over entirely with snow.

But Yehuda Leib could not afford to stop.

The crow flew onward, and Yehuda Leib pursued.

Slowly, the balance began to shift, the trees falling off, the stones growing thicker. One of the last trees Yehuda Leib passed beneath was an ancient, knobbled, reaching oak, bare of leaves, that spread its boughs and fingers wide across the thinning forest. Even before he was beneath its branches, Yehuda Leib knew there was something odd about it: he could hear its long, twiggy extremities clacking against one another in the breeze, and they were not of wood—they were of bone.

Yehuda Leib swallowed hard. Only hours ago, he would have scoffed at talk of a tree of bone.

But he would have scoffed at the notion that he would meet his father, too, and stand above him as his lifeblood trickled out into the snow.

And yet beneath him his father had lain, and above him stood the tree of bone.

It seemed to matter very little whether or not he was willing to believe it.

On the crow flew, and Yehuda Leib followed after. The trees gave way to open fields, hills, valleys full of gravestones, and the fall of snow grew thicker and thicker, until all Yehuda Leib could see in the swirling obscurity was the tiny ball of light, lodged far above in the throat of the crow.

And then—just when the world seemed to be swallowed in snow and darkness—shapes loomed up from the gloom.

And they were close.

Yehuda Leib darted back, taking cover behind a low crypt wall.

There were so many that the column seemed endless—soldiers upon soldiers upon soldiers, marching wearily through the night. Their uniforms were soiled and torn, bloody, mismatched. Some were missing things—fingers, hands, even whole legs. Others had been slashed open with sabers or peppered with grapeshot. Yehuda Leib saw one soldier whose belly had been blasted clean through with a cannonball, and still he slogged forward through the snow.

This was no ordinary army.

For some time, Yehuda Leib crouched in the snow, watching the Army of the Dead go by. Their numbers never dwindled, and the rhythmic marching of their feet seemed to match the beating of his heart.

This was no coincidence.

It was the simplest, most beautiful thing to him—one foot and then the other. It could go on through everything.

It could go on even on the far side of death.

With a start, Yehuda Leib raised his eyes to the sky. He'd become so distracted by the trooping dead that he'd lost track of his father. A little panic began to gather in his gut.

Before long, though, his keen eyes picked out the muffled light, turning and wheeling far above. The crow was descending now, and as it came, its aim materialized in the gloaming:

A great, rambling, shrug-shouldered house, not five minutes' march from where Yehuda Leib stood.

The Treasure House of Lord Mammon.

Bluma couldn't get rid of the spoon.

No matter what she tried—throwing it away, placing it deliberately atop a grave marker, even digging a hole and burying it—as soon as her eyes left the dim glimmer of its surface, there it was again, back in her apron pocket.

Before long, Bluma grew discouraged. Her discouragement put forth buds of frustration that bloomed into fury, and one last time, Bluma flung the spoon away, so hard that it tore an echoing yell from her as it went. She heard it clang against a headstone some ways away, but as she fell to the cold, wet snow, sure enough, there it was, hard and sharp, in the crease of her hip.

Bluma's eyes filled with tears. Her fingertips smarted. Droplets of blood flecked the snow beside her.

What could she do? What on earth could she do?

She was rising when her eye was drawn to a carving she had not noticed before—there, on top of a plain headstone, perhaps three or four rows away, an incredibly lifelike gray cat sat upright, staring at her.

Only when its tail began to twitch did Bluma see the captive moonlight in its eyes.

Carefully, she made her way in the opposite direction, but when she looked back, the cat was nowhere to be seen.

A knot was rising in Bluma's throat.

It's just a cat, she told herself. *Just a stray cat.*

But the eyes shone again out of the darkness, and there it was, high above, perched on the roof of a little crypt, staring down at her: a lurking gray cat.

Again, Bluma moved away, her feet beginning to step more quickly now, and, turning to look behind her, she saw the cat take a silent leap to the head of a nearby obelisk.

It was following her.

Bluma wheeled about, searching for a safe way to go, but here were two more cats, and a fourth hopping lithely up onto a gravestone.

Their eyes shone out like dead stars. Bluma tried not to notice the thin razor claws at their paw ends, the sharp needle teeth in their heads.

What did they want?

Slowly, quietly, Bluma edged away, heading in the only direction the cats had left open to her. When she looked back, still they sat, staring, waiting, their cold, bright eyes shining out in the darkness.

They were herding her.

Twice more a cat loomed up beside or before her, correcting her course, keeping her moving in the direction they desired. Only when Bluma finally arrived in the moonlit clearing could she count their full number: six gray cats on six crumbling headstones.

And in their midst stood a woman all in white, neither old nor young, short nor tall, plain nor beautiful. Her thick curls hung loose and free, studded with flakes of fallen snow, and her cheeks were rosy with the cold.

Her eyes never once blinked.

"Hello there," said the woman.

All around her, the cats began to smile.

"H-hello," stammered Bluma.

The lady's gaze seemed endless. It made Bluma feel very warm and very cold at the same time.

"My Sisters told me there was someone abroad in the cemetery," she said. "But I did not imagine it would be someone like you."

Bluma wanted to swallow but couldn't manage it. What did she mean, *someone like her?*

"You must take care," said the lady in white. "It is long after midnight now, and the cemetery is a dangerous place for even the best prepared of us. How did you come to be here?"

Bluma's mouth felt impossibly dry. "I—I was chased."

The lady in white sighed, stepping forward, and for the first time, Bluma noticed that her feet were bare in the snow. Bluma's own feet felt completely frozen, and they were safe within boots and thick knit stockings.

Now the lady in white took a moment's silence, tilting her head to the side. Her unblinking eyes traveled down to Bluma's toes and back up again. The tails of the cats behind her twitched in the moonlight.

"Yes," said the lady in white. "Yes, there are many things in the cemetery that might like to get their claws into you."

Now she turned to face the cats. "Sisters," she said, and in the blinking of an eye, the six gray cats were six gray ladies, each leaning back against a headstone. "I do not think it right to allow this girl to wander the cemetery alone. How say you?"

And now the gray ladies began to consult one another in silence, a system of blinks and glances passing between them so complex that Bluma could not begin to follow it.

But Bluma found herself distracted. There was a cold, lurking thing in the pocket of her apron, something that would not go away, would not leave her alone.

She wanted nothing more than to be rid of it.

But if she could not be rid of it, then she was desperate that it should remain hidden.

And, to her horror, she thought she felt it moving.

Carefully, she dipped her hand into her pocket, closing her fingers gently around the frosty handle of the spoon, as if to calm it.

There, there, she thought, her breath beginning to slow. *There, there.*

And, looking up with a start, she discovered seven pairs of eyes trained upon her in the dim.

The lady in white was gazing at the pocket of her apron.

Without lifting her eyes, she spoke. "Come," the lady in white said. "It is decided. You will travel with us."

And she turned and walked into the darkness.

All around, the gray Sisters fell into step, foot and paw, now striding between stones, now hopping lightly from grave to grave.

Bluma was by no means certain that she would be safer with them than she had been walking alone, but two of the cats had remained behind to make sure that she followed.

And Bluma had no desire to find out what they might do in order to encourage her.

This is how Bluma came to travel with the ancient demon Lilith and the Sisters of the Lileen.

The Treasure House of Lord Mammon is a wide, rambling jumble of walls and buttresses, porticoes, arches, and columns. By the time Yehuda Leib came near, the crow had long since gone in through a window casement many stories above.

Yehuda Leib was eager to follow.

But the doors of the Treasure House are many. Those who wish to walk in unopposed find open archways; those who wish to ask and be invited find doors that swing inward at the tapping of a knuckle.

And boys like Yehuda Leib—who are as certain that they deserve to be inside as they are that they will be turned away—find locks and barriers, chains and deadbolts, and, eventually, a single, low, out-of-the-way door with a knob that turns smoothly.

As much out of habit as out of caution, Yehuda Leib left the door ajar behind him.

Everyone knows: it is unwise to shut yourself in where you ought not to be.

The room in which Yehuda Leib found himself now was low and dim. All around him, rough-hewn shelves crowded in close, reaching from the floor—which was either made of dirt or so thick with dust that it might as well have been—up to the bowed and buckling ceiling.

No one is meant to see Lord Mammon's Hoard itself.

In accordance with the terms of a treaty once set out between Lord Mammon and Lord Dantalion, Master of Whispers—another great and noble demon—a cataloging was undertaken long ago to make a record of the Hoard's vast holdings.

As of this writing, the project is still ongoing.

As an example, among the catalog's nearly innumerable volumes, there are fully twenty-seven (five hundred pages each, with every page accommodating between twenty-five and thirty entries) describing *only* Lord Mammon's collection of porcelain cups. None of these twenty-seven volumes touch upon his porcelain bowls (of which there are many), or his stone cups (of which there are more), or any other vessel of porcelain or any other substance.

At first Yehuda Leib thought the Hoard was entirely without organization, but as he made his way through room after low-ceilinged room, he began to notice affinities in the chaos. Here were several shelves containing dulled sharp things—kitchen knives, needles and pins, shards of glass. On his right was a shelf of writings that had once been legible but were no longer, and up ahead the marks of dirt and clay identified shelves of things dug up from the ground.

Things, things, things—there seemed to be no end to them.

Out of curiosity, Yehuda Leib took an old map down from a high shelf, but the accumulated mass of angry, feathery dust on its surface threw him into such a paroxysm of sneezing that he resolved, as much as possible, to leave things where they were.

On and on Yehuda Leib went. Where was the crow? Where was his father? There were no lamps or windows here—at least none that were operational—and the shelves began to close in, bringing the thick darkness close to his skin.

Before he knew it, Yehuda Leib could no longer see where he was going. Soon he was navigating by touch alone, running his fingers along the rough wooden shelves until his hands were full of splinters.

Carefully, he made his way onward, his nerves fraying further and further by the moment.

But in the thick, silent darkness, time had come to spin in anxious, meaningless circles.

Who could tell a moment anymore? Was there even such a thing?

And just as this notion occurred to him, Yehuda Leib put his boot directly into a large burlap sack of what were unmistakably human teeth.

He cursed and stumbled backward, brushing hard at his pant leg.

And it was only at this precise angle, bent and backward, that he happened to see something far off through the clutter:

A hint of glimmering light.

A door.

And, behind it, a fire burning.

Lilith walked alone through the cold blue moonlight. Her attendant cats left small marks in the snow—here the scraping of a claw, there the brushing of a tail—but her bare feet left none.

For a long while, Bluma followed in silence, unsure if she wanted to continue, unsure how she could stop. From time to time, one of the Sisters of the Lileen would join Lilith—a gray cat alighting on her shoulder, a gray lady falling in beside her—and they would walk together briefly, talking quietly or not at all. It seemed to make no difference to Lilith if she was accompanied.

Or, rather, she seemed to be accompanied whether there was anyone beside her or not.

The path they took between the graves was long and winding. Soon Bluma began to wonder if it would lead them anywhere at all. It seemed totally capricious: back and forth, back and forth, as if they were following only Lilith's whim.

But as soon as this thought had cut into her head, there, beside her, a gray lady spoke.

"It's not like in the living world," she said. "The direction matters less than you think."

Bluma's gut lurched. If this was not *the living world*, then what was it? She turned her head, and there was a skulking gray cat.

"But we are going *somewhere*, aren't we?" said Bluma into the darkness.

"Oh yes," said a voice from over her shoulder.

This was less than convincing to Bluma, and she muttered in a voice so small that she could barely hear it herself: "Well, then, where?"

Without looking over her shoulder, Lilith spoke, far ahead: "To Zubinsk. To receive the bride."

But this didn't make sense. Everyone in Tupik knew the quickest way to Zubinsk—through the forest—and this was surely not it.

And then, again, so soft that she could not say if it was in her ear or in her mind, a voice:

The direction matters less than you think.

On her other side, another gray lady was speaking.

"It must be hard to understand. Where you come from, the people move around the earth. Here, the earth moves and the people are still."

Bluma shook her head to clear the sudden vision of her bubbe sunken in the cold dirt.

"But I know a faster way to Zubinsk," she said.

A gray lady shook her head. "Not for us."

"There are rules," said another.

On her other side: "The Cemetery is a hall with many doors— one can enter from wherever the living die."

"But to come back out again—that is a rarer trick."

Ahead, Lilith paused to examine the passage between two tall obelisks.

"But there is a wedding in Zubinsk."

"Have you heard?"

"All are invited."

"Without exception."

"Neither the living nor the dead shall be excluded."

"Nor any other besides."

"And for those of us normally barred from the living world . . ."

"A living invitation can bring us through."

Bluma's head was swimming.

"Watch."

"And follow."

"One can enter the Cemetery from wherever the living die."

"But follow."

"And watch."

"And with the guidance of our Sister Lilith . . ."

"We may come back out again," said the Sisters of the Lileen, "wherever the dying live."

There was something wrong. This room was not as it should've been.

Yehuda Leib had lost track of time in the Hoard, but he didn't think he could've passed entire seasons among the shelves. And yet, right in front of him, with his own two eyes, he could see a window letting in the gray light of an overcast summer evening.

How could this be?

Cautiously, he crept forward.

It was a billiards room with thick velvet drapes and dark wood-work. A fire had been left to dwindle in the grate, and a glass of brandy sat on the edge of the table, which—cues and all—had been abandoned mid-game.

The room felt as if its occupants had just departed and equally as if they had not been here in years.

And both were true. For Lord Mammon trades not only in things but in places, as well, and thoughts, and memories.

And many other things besides.

Yehuda Leib felt himself simultaneously comforted and disquieted as he pushed through the door on the far side of the room. It was a second billiards room—blue, where the first one had been red.

But, more importantly, outside the window of the second room a gentle rain fell through brown autumn leaves.

Yehuda Leib looked back. Still, through the window of the first room, he could see a thicket of sunlit summer leaves.

Yehuda Leib swallowed hard.

The rooms in this place seemed to keep their own time.

He was about to go through into the blue room when a loud cracking made him jump. Spinning around, Yehuda Leib saw that a shot had been taken on the red billiards table—the balls were no longer in the same position—and, what was more, the level of the brandy in the glass had sunk precipitously.

But there was no one here.

"H-hello?" called Yehuda Leib.

No answer.

Yehuda Leib was uneasy. Perhaps he ought to find his way out.

But at precisely this moment, a sound echoed from far within the Treasure House.

A sort of honking caw.

The crow.

His father.

Yehuda Leib pushed forward.

At first they were all billiards rooms—some pristine and unused, some choked in cigar smoke, one even missing half its ceiling—but before long, the theme began to vary:

Here was a room dotted with card tables, the hands dealt out before pushed-back chairs. As Yehuda Leib picked his way through to the far door, he saw all the suits he was familiar with—hearts, spades, diamonds, clubs—but there were new and strange suits as well:

Hats.

Clocks.

Planets.

Ears.

There was a small stone chamber containing nothing but a midgame chessboard, and at one point, Yehuda Leib pushed through a door to find himself in a long wooden hall with a net slung down the middle: an old wooden tennis court.

And, all the while, the squawk of the crow echoed out through the Treasure House.

Finally, Yehuda Leib went through a heavy white door into a rich corridor lined with thick carpeting.

Here. The sound was here.

The corridor was, in fact, part of a massive stairwell, and, peering down its long shaft, Yehuda Leib could see the crow, squawking and hopping, flapping furiously, trying to get off the floor at the very bottom of the staircase.

But no matter how hard it tried, the attempt was doomed to fail: the crow had been weighted down with treasure—heavy jeweled chains, bulky gold rings, even a little crown atop its feathered head—and under all this weight, it had no chance at all of flying away.

In a flash, Yehuda Leib spun down the stairs, flight after flight, turning and turning until he had it, a handful of dark, croaking feathers that squirmed and squalled in his grasp.

"Give him back," cried Yehuda Leib, suddenly on the verge of tears. "Give him back!"

But to his horror, the crow was laughing. "Too late!" said the bird.

"What?" said Yehuda Leib. "What do you mean?"

But already Yehuda Leib was beginning to understand: there was no light in the bird's throat.

With a sound like the snipping of heavy shears, the crow's great beak snapped at Yehuda Leib's fingers; with a crashing thud, he let the demon fall to the floor.

"What did you do?"

"I sold him."

This was incomprehensible to Yehuda Leib. "You what?"

"I had something," croaked the crow, "and I wanted something. That's the way the world works."

Yehuda Leib was furious. "He wasn't . . ." It took all the strength he had left in him not to punt the little demon across the hall. "He wasn't yours to sell!"

"Ha!" said the crow. "At least I gave him up *for* something. What would *you* have given me?"

Yehuda Leib felt hot embarrassment spread across his cheeks. "Just tell me where he is."

Another grunting laugh. "You'll have to talk to Lord Mammon."

Yehuda Leib grimaced. "Where?"

The crow gestured across the hall with its beak: a pair of grand double doors, one ajar.

Yehuda Leib was in a hurry to retrieve his father, and so he turned and left the crow to its vain hopping without asking the details of its bargain.

But it would've served him to learn:

Lord Mammon is cunning.

And everyone knows: he rarely deals plainly.

Even having come through the Treasure House, Yehuda Leib found the room behind the double doors strange.

At the far end, a gilded throne sat empty on a high dais. Before the throne, there was a table of pure marble, intricately figured, with innumerable instruments of inspection branching out on thin, swinging arms: a gas lamp, a jeweler's loupe, probes and saws, chisels, gouges, and syringes.

"My lord?" a choked voice crackled out of the dim beneath the altar. "Lord Mammon?"

"Don't be an idiot," said another voice. "That's not him."

It took Yehuda Leib long moments of blinking to discern who had spoken.

At the foot of the dais, rows of rough wooden chairs stood in parallel, and among them, several figures sat waiting.

"Are you sure?" said the first voice again, a wide, anxious man with big, watery eyes. "Is it you, my lord?"

"No," said Yehuda Leib.

A derisive snort came from a spindly woman slouching over two chairs at once. "I told you."

"But when?" cried the man. "When will he come?"

"You must be patient," said a third voice, a little fellow with a perfectly round head.

Yehuda Leib chose a seat near the third fellow. As he sat, he felt the wood beneath him squeal and complain.

"Psst," said the round-headed fellow, beckoning, and Yehuda Leib leaned near. "You see him?"

The third fellow pointed at the anxious, portly man, who had begun to pace.

Yehuda Leib nodded.

"He's come for a loan."

"A loan?"

"Yes. And he hasn't yet decided what to offer as security. If you listen closely, you can hear him bargaining with himself."

At just this moment, the anxious man paced by, and Yehuda Leib heard a snippet of his muttering: "How long? Thirty, forty thousand years? But would he even accept that?"

The round head of the third fellow shook softly. "It's no wonder we're still waiting. Why enter into negotiations when your opponent is already doing the work for you?"

This made a certain kind of sense to Yehuda Leib: with every passing moment, the man's own anxiety was stripping off layer after layer of resistance.

"Now, over there," said the third fellow, gesturing with his domed forehead, "is a demon who's come to buy something back that she sold off long ago. But she's by no means certain that she'll be able to afford it."

Through the gloom, Yehuda Leib could see the spindly woman chewing idly on her lower lip.

"She came prepared," said the round-headed fellow. "She had a price in mind when she walked through the door. But the other one's anxiety is wearing away at her. Little by little, the highest price she's willing to pay is rising."

Yehuda Leib was disquieted to see that the round-headed fellow was smiling.

His teeth were very small but very, very sharp.

"She's ripening," he said. "Like fruit on the vine. And so my question is this: Do you bring any pressing business to tempt Lord Mammon? Or shall I have a nap?"

Yehuda Leib nodded eagerly. "My business is urgent."

The round-headed fellow turned his beady black eyes on Yehuda Leib. "Oh?"

"Something was taken from me and sold to Lord Mammon without my permission."

"Ah," said the little round-headed fellow. "I see. And how do you propose to get it back?"

"I thought," said Yehuda Leib, "that if I explained the situation ..."

"Ha!" He seemed to be genuinely amused. "You won't get anything from Mammon without paying, I can promise you that—no matter what the situation is."

"Well, then," said Yehuda Leib, "I'll offer him a trade."

Thin lips curled into a smirk, showing the yellowed arrowheads of the fellow's teeth. "You? What could you possibly have to trade?"

Yehuda Leib was at a loss. He hadn't come with a plan, and he had little of value. A spare cap? A few potatoes? "I don't know."

The fellow's round head wagged back and forth. "This business is seeming less and less urgent by the moment," he said.

A warm flush was spreading across Yehuda Leib's face. It *was* urgent, whether this tiresome old fellow thought so or not.

"But—"

"I think I shall have that nap after all," said the fellow.

"But—"

"Do wake me when Lord Mammon arrives, won't you?"

"But—"

The little fellow began to snore with a sound like a thousand billiard balls cracking together at once.

Yehuda Leib sat back and let out a tight sigh. He did not much savor the idea of sitting and waiting.

When his eyes fell on the crowded little table by the foot of the dais, then, he greeted it gratefully: a distraction from the wait.

Lightly, Yehuda Leib hopped to his feet and ambled over to look.

If the Hoard at large were a very long list, then this table could've been a summary. It was crowded with all sorts of things: an old cracked pitcher, several disembodied harpsichord keys, a collection of dry autumn leaves. Near its center was a small leather pouch bound with twine that Yehuda Leib tried to ignore—it was twitching and squeaking.

And then, in the midst of the detritus, as if it were no more important than any other thing, there it was:

A small glass bottle containing the unmistakable light of Yehuda Leib's father.

It could've been nothing else.

With a thrill, Yehuda Leib stole a glance over his shoulder. The anxious man was busy pacing, the thin woman facing away. The rattling snore of the third fellow filled the air.

No one was paying attention.

Slowly, Yehuda Leib reached out his hand. It was strange—as if he were meeting his father for the very first time. He felt awkward, abashed, but as soon as his fingers closed around the little bottle, all of that melted away.

It was warm. He had thought that the glass would be cool to the touch, but it was warm. And not just on his fingertips—the warmth seemed to seep into his bones, traveling up his arm, through his shoulder, branching into his clavicle and ribs until Yehuda Leib was filled with an impossible radiant warmth.

His eyes began to fill with tears.

It was as if there had been within him a chill so long-standing and insidious that he had never taken notice of it before.

It was very beautiful, this light.

And yet it was waning.

Yehuda Leib gave a little sniff, which echoed loudly in the silence of the throne room.

The light was waning. But he had it now. And he would find a way to bring it back to its full brightness.

Softly, swiftly, he slipped the small bottle into the pocket of his coat.

But something was wrong.

The throne room was silent.

Too silent.

What had happened to the snoring?

Turning, he found the little round-headed demon wide awake, his beady eyes fixed on Yehuda Leib.

He was smirking.

Yehuda Leib did not understand.

Slowly, the smirk grew into a smile, and then into a grin.

His teeth were very, very sharp.

Loud and shrill, the demon shrieked, "Steward!"

The round, pacing demon jumped in surprise.

For a long moment, there was a tense silence in the throne room, and then the door opened wide.

A tall demon in velvet breeches stepped inside. "My lord?" he said.

"What," said the little round-headed demon with glee, "is the penalty for burglary in our realms?"

The steward bowed his head slightly and spoke as if reciting: "The burglar abdicates ownership of everything he carries, including but not limited to his possessions, his clothing, his body, his past, and the sum of his eternal potential, my lord."

"Splendid."

Everyone in the room was staring at Yehuda Leib, who was barely able to keep up.

"But," said Yehuda Leib. "But—"

"Now, now," said the little demon. "You cannot ask me to tolerate thievery within my own throne room."

And suddenly, Yehuda Leib realized to whom he was speaking.

"Take him," said Lord Mammon.

CHAPTER SIX

The Swarming

It happened without Bluma noticing: one moment, she was walking well behind Lilith, caught up in a loose constellation of cats, and the next, she was alone at the lady's side.

"Bluma," said Lilith softly, without looking.

Immediately Bluma was disarmed. Had she given her name?

"Have you ever been to a wedding?"

Bluma stuttered senselessly, though the answer ought to have been a simple no.

"I think," said Lilith, "that you will find it very interesting. It is quite powerful sorcery."

"S-sorcery?" said Bluma.

"Oh yes," said Lilith. "Two cannot become one and both remain without a little bit of magic. Of course, these days, it is rare for the operation to succeed—one or the other inevitably perishes somewhere along the way—but if executed properly . . ."

Here Lilith trailed off, bending to chart their path by the angle of a moonlit shadow.

When she spoke again, she didn't even bother to look back.

"Bluma," she said into the darkness, "what have you got in your pocket?"

Bluma felt a warm blush spill across her face. The spoon hung low and heavy in her apron.

"I—I'm sorry," said Bluma.

Now, for the first time since Bluma had joined her company, Lilith turned the full force of her unblinking gaze on her, and the world seemed to drop away.

"Whatever for?" said Lilith.

Bluma had no answer for this question.

Slowly, her eyes never shifting from Bluma's own, Lilith crossed the snow between them, raised the fingers of one thin hand, and dipped them down into Bluma's apron.

Bluma felt disinclined to breathe.

Lilith smiled as she drew the spoon from Bluma's pocket. There was something right, almost symmetrical, about the sight of it between her fingers—they seemed to catch the moonlight in the same way.

"Yes," she said. "It is very beautiful."

Perhaps this was the answer. Perhaps the spoon would leave Bluma and go to Lilith instead.

But as right as it felt to Bluma to see the spoon in Lilith's hand, it felt just as wrong that it was not in hers.

Something dark and confusing began to blossom in Bluma's chest.

Something like jealousy.

"I do not generally relish the feeling of cold metal on my skin," said Lilith. "But this is different: metal and not metal all at once."

Lilith lifted the spoon to examine it more closely, and Bluma saw her eyebrows rise.

"The reflection," said Bluma.

"Yes," said Lilith. She held the spoon up to Bluma's face like a looking glass. "What do you see?"

At first the reflection showed what Bluma expected—the empty moonlit cemetery and, before long, Bluma tramping up, surrounded by a corralling knot of cats.

But Bluma's blood ran cold.

There was someone else in the reflection too.

An old woman in black, hunched, shrunken, empty, looming up behind her.

She was reaching out, as if to seize Bluma by the hair.

Swiftly, Bluma wheeled about.

There was no one behind her but the cats.

Turning back, she had just enough time to catch sight of herself startling and wheeling in the reflection of the spoon. But already she could see there was no one behind her. Or at least no one who meant to be seen.

"It is an altogether uncommon object," said Lilith, withdrawing the spoon. "Very old. In truth, I do not believe it to be a spoon at all."

Bluma swallowed hard, trying to calm her pounding heart.

"Why do you think that?"

Lilith fixed Bluma with her eyes.

"I wonder . . ." Now she cast about, left and right, her gaze eventually settling on a small, smooth stone atop a grave marker. This her long fingers plucked from its place, and, light on her feet, she made her way behind Bluma.

"Here," said Lilith softly into her ear.

Carefully, she threaded the cold spoon between Bluma's fingers. Then, having deposited the little stone in its basin, Lilith wrapped Bluma in her arms, hands atop Bluma's own. Bluma could feel the mound of Lilith's dark curls brush against her cheek, and for a moment she herself felt like the small, dark stone there, nestled in the cold basin of Lilith's arms.

And then, with a deft motion of her fingers, firmly, gently, Lilith inverted the spoon, swung it all the way around the top of the stone, and brought it swiftly back down again. Bluma could feel a kind of friction through the handle, but all the same she was shocked to see what had happened:

The stone was nowhere to be seen—neither in the basin of the spoon nor in the clean white snow beneath.

But the empty spoon felt just as heavy as it had earlier.

"Never before," said Lilith's soft voice, "have I encountered a spoon that *eats*."

Lilith moved smoothly away, leaving the cold spoon between Bluma's fingers.

"You are very warm, Bluma," said Lilith.

This surprised Bluma; she certainly didn't feel it. "I am?"

"Your arms, your hands, your body—far warmer than mine. And far warmer than any of my Sisters have been in a long time."

Bluma's heart was beating quickly.

"You are still living."

Bluma's stomach lurched.

Lilith raised an eyebrow. "Are you not?"

Bluma swallowed hard.

Lilith was walking away.

"What benefit," said Lord Mammon, "could I possibly derive from slumming around the Zubinsk cemetery with a bunch of tiresome little imps and devils?"

Mammon was seated before his altar, taking up only a small portion of the throne's wide golden seat. His feet dangled, unable to reach the floor, and he wore three pairs of spectacles in various positions—on his nose, beneath his chin, atop his bald head— which he switched rapidly as he scrutinized his new acquisitions.

Yehuda Leib—the newest of these—had been compelled to join the rest, sitting on the edge of the small table at the foot of the dais. There the velvet-breeched steward had given him something to drink that—to all appearances—seemed to be rich, warm milk.

Soon Yehuda Leib's belly began to grumble. When was the last time he'd had anything to eat or drink? His throat felt suddenly parched, and the aroma seemed impossibly sweet.

One little sip couldn't hurt him, could it?

Just one little sip.

But he was revolted to find that what had seemed warm and rich was, in fact, tepid and fusty, like ancient green pond water, and it neither filled his belly nor soothed his throat.

And yet, time after time, he found himself going back for more. The aroma was unbelievably tempting.

Gradually, his head began to swim.

What was happening?

Where was he?

What was all this?

"But the swarming in the cemetery is hardly the reason to go, my lord," said the steward. "Just think of what might be accomplished if one managed to capture the Rebbe! Why, if you could corrupt him in place, he could spread your avarice among all his followers. You might even be able to accumulate property in the living lands. Or you could choose to hold him as a commodity, my lord! I needn't tell you how many others desire the advantage of the Rebbe. What price might he command?"

Lord Mammon held up the palm of one clammy hand as if to say, *Spare me.*

At just that moment, he was half occupied with the small, squirming leather sack that only moments ago had lain on the table. This turned out to contain a tiny, protesting Englishman in a neat frock coat and top hat. How he had come to be here—or come to be this size, for that matter, no larger than a chicken drumstick—was unclear.

What was abundantly clear, however, was that he was *rather displeased.*

He said so as Lord Mammon knocked the hat from his hand and absently seated it on his thumb like a thimble; he said so as Lord Mammon pinned him to the altar like a captive butterfly; he said so as Lord Mammon took the gentleman's intricate measure (from *circumference, head* all the way down to *width, shoe*); and he was still saying so—albeit significantly more frantically—as Lord Mammon dangled him by the leg high above his toothy maw, dropped him in, and began to munch.

This accomplished, he turned his attention back to his steward.

"Of *course* the swarming is not the reason to go," said Mammon, his mouth full of Englishman. "But in order to get to the Rebbe of Zubinsk, it is necessary to make one's way through all the accumulated scum in the cemetery. And once the day of the wedding dawns, it shall be, what, a footrace to reach the old man first? I am no good in a footrace, Steward, and I don't like losing."

The steward gave his head a tight little shake. "No, my lord."

"This tastes *awful*."

"Yes, my lord."

The Rebbe of Zubinsk. Yehuda Leib had heard him spoken of many times before—a great miracle worker. If only he could manage to make it out of Tupik and through the woods, perhaps the Rebbe could help him stoke the dwindling fire of his father back to life.

But Yehuda Leib wasn't in Tupik.

Where was he?

What had happened?

Idly, he sipped from the cup of warm milk in his hand and was disgusted to find that it tasted like algae and muck.

"And all this is to say nothing," said Mammon, still chewing with mild displeasure, "of the expense involved in mounting a suitable procession to convey me to Zubinsk in the first place. I tell you, I won't be seen in public without the appropriate display."

"Why, no, my lord," said the steward. "But isn't the pageantry reward enough in itself? To be seen?"

Mammon sighed. "You are a fool, Steward—a terrible fool. It is advantageous to be seen in glory, to be sure, but without some rich acquisition to balance out the expense, why, it is hardly worth the effort. No, I shall stay at home, and that is my final word in the matter."

"Yes, my lord," said the steward.

With a loud, phlegmy crackle, Mammon cleared his throat. "What remains, Steward?"

The steward looked down at the table beside him, empty now but for Yehuda Leib.

"The boy," he said. "And the point of light."

"Ah, splendid! Bring them here," said Mammon, sucking a shard of skull from his molars.

"Would my lord care to see the boy and the point of light separately or together?"

Mammon rolled his eyes and gave a demonstrative groan. "You are such a tiresome fool, Steward. If you separate the thief from what he has stolen, then the set is incomplete. Would I have you separate the wine from the goblet before I drink it?"

"No, my lord," said the steward, as if he were very, very tired. "Of course not."

"Of course not," said Mammon, and with a florid gesture he beckoned Yehuda Leib up.

The steward led Yehuda Leib, dizzy, stumbling, to the stairs. They were steeper than they seemed from below, requiring him to lift his foot up to almost hip height with each successive step.

Roughly, Yehuda Leib was made to sit down on the marble altar. His vision couldn't seem to hold focus, but Mammon's beady little eyes cornered him through the haze like a pair of pistols.

"Splendid," said Lord Mammon, and, licking the sharp points of his little teeth—still lightly pink with Englishman—he moved his eyes from the brim of Yehuda Leib's cap to the toes of his boots and then slowly back up again.

Yehuda Leib swallowed hard.

Mammon began his measurements with *circumference, head*.

Yehuda Leib's heart began to pound. Mammon had measured the little Englishman as well. Was he, too, destined for the demon's maw?

Sharply, Mammon looked up. He had been busy working a tiny pair of calipers in the measurement of Yehuda Leib's fingernails, but now his eyes narrowed, and, cocking his head to the side, he frowned, listening intently.

"Steward," said Mammon. "Do you hear that?"

The steward raised one eyebrow. "Hear what, my lord?"

"Like a drum," said Mammon. "*Bum-bum, bum-bum, bum-bum.*"

Yehuda Leib cast his eyes quickly downward to avoid Mammon's gaze.

The steward shook his head. "I hear nothing, my lord."

"Never mind," said Mammon, turning his attention back to the calipers.

But then he stopped.

"Huh," he said. "That's strange."

"My lord?" said the steward.

"Only by the barest increment, but . . ." Mammon switched spectacles and peered down at his calipers. "Why, yes: this nail is longer now than it was just a moment ago."

Mammon's eyes began to widen.

"Longer?" said the steward. "I don't understand."

But Mammon did.

"Steward?" called Mammon, a sharp smirk on his lips.

"Yes, my lord?"

"We've had a change in plans."

"Oh?" said the steward.

Mammon stretched his smile wide, showing more teeth in one place than Yehuda Leib had ever seen.

"Oh yes," he said. "This boy is alive."

W

It is often repeated that the night is darkest before the dawn. This is plainly false. The night is darkest in its precise midst.

What is true, however, is that it is hardest to breathe just before one surfaces from the deep, and in the same way, it is hardest to bear the cemetery as one draws closest to the territory of the living.

Zubinsk was near, and the demons were swarming.

The first came up slowly, heavily, from behind: a looming thing, a shadow shaped like a man, dark and ragged, three times as high as the tallest tree Bluma had ever seen, and as it came striding over them with its long legs, it peered down and stared at her with eyes like drowning stars.

A stooped old lady with hairy, twitching spiders instead of hands moved to the side of the road when she saw Lilith approaching, curtsied, and lowered her eyes, but as the Lileen went by, she lifted them up again—glossy, perfectly black—to peer at Bluma.

Bluma couldn't be certain, but it seemed to her that the lady was hiding a smirk.

Now more came, and more: a flock of bat-winged creatures cackling and diving, a huge serpent slithering languidly beneath the accumulated snow, the figure of a man so covered in sores and boils that he cracked and oozed with every little movement of his body.

Every one of them turned back to gaze at Bluma's face.

Slowly, nervously, Bluma began to chew on her lower lip.

What were they looking at?

More and more demons crowded in around them—scales and claws, murmurs and whispers—and Bluma grew more and more nervous. Little by little, she began to imagine she could feel something tugging at her hair, and she ran her hand back over its surface to ensure that it was free.

They were all looking at her. Why were they all looking at her?

With every little worry, Bluma gave a gnaw at her lower lip. Slowly, without even realizing, she brought herself to bleed.

And the smell of warm blood has a way of attracting demons.

Soon the fracas began to grow: petty little goblins barking and screaming, hawking their wares at the outskirts of the swarming.

"Come buy!" they squawked. "Come buy!"

Neither Lilith nor the Lileen paused even a moment to listen, but Bluma's ear could not help but catch on their promises:

"You there! I have the smell of mountain stones after a long summer rain!"

"I have a melody without beginning or end!"

"I have a long night's sleep!"

"Come buy!"

"Come buy!"

"Come buy!"

Bluma's feet were slowing, and a chiding gray voice spoke into her ear: one of the Sisters of the Lileen.

"Take no notice," she said. "They are too stupid to deal plainly. And besides, they rarely have anything real to sell: only memories and lies."

"Memories?" said Bluma. "How can one sell a memory?"

The gray lady chuckled. "Why, by picking it up when it falls and trading it for something of value. Loose memories are like autumn leaves in the Far Country—the dead shed them easily."

Bluma found her hands patting nervously at her shoulders and skirts. She had not dropped any, had she?

"And besides," said another voice of the Lileen, "memories such as those rarely last. By the time they've come into goblin hands and made their way to market, they're overripe and fading fast."

"Then who would want them?" said Bluma.

"Oh," said the Lileen. "The demons are desperate for anything that can make them seem more human. The better they can hide their true nature, the more respectable they become—and, eventually, the better able to deal directly with the humans they wish to ensnare."

Bluma swallowed hard. Ahead of her, she could see Lilith's bare feet padding pink through the snow.

The crowd was thick now, demons of all stripes surging toward the little Zubinsk graveyard like a rain-flooded river. If Bluma had been alone, she would've been subsumed, swallowed in the tide for certain, but traveling with the Sisterhood of the Lileen had its advantages: Lilith was known to all, and feared by those with any sense. The crowd had a way of parting to let her through.

More and more, though, as the blood welled up on her lip, the demons' eyes began to pass from Lilith back to Bluma.

Before long, the whispering began.

"Lilith! Why, Lady Lilith!" a demon with slick hair called out from a clique of tittering followers, and after a long moment, Lilith turned to see who spoke.

"Let him through."

The formation of gray cats behind Bluma opened and closed again to admit the smarmy demon.

"What is it, Belial?" said Lilith, without bothering to look at him.

"I must say, Lady Lilith: you cut a very fine figure in this shift of yours. Is it new?"

One of Belial's attendants giggled and rolled his eyes on the far side of the cordon of cats.

"No, Belial. It is the same as ever. What have you come to say?"

"It's only that we're unaccustomed to seeing you attended,"

said Belial. "I was under the impression that you didn't hold with rank and hierarchy. *All are equal in the Sisterhood of the Lileen*, is it not so?"

Lilith sighed. "What are you talking of, Belial?"

"Why," said the florid demon, "this little maidservant of yours."

It seemed to Bluma now that every single eye in the universe was turned upon her.

Her face was burning.

"Bluma? She is not my maidservant."

"No?" said Belial demonstratively. "A prize, then? Or perhaps one of your projects?"

"She is nothing that you need concern yourself with."

"Your Bluma is very fragrant, Lilith. If you are entertaining offers for her . . ."

"That will do, Belial," said Lilith sharply, and like a flash the Lileen had separated the smarmy demon from her. "She is not for sale."

"You surprise me, Lady Lilith," said Belial. "I have always thought you a very reasonable woman—insofar as there is such a thing."

A gout of pretentious laughter rang out from Belial's attendants.

"Goodbye, Belial," said Lilith, but as they made their way forward, Bluma saw him bend to whisper to one of his followers, pointing a long, manicured finger at her face.

Slowly, the word *Bluma* passed from Belial's lips and disseminated itself throughout the little clutch of hangers-on. More fingers were pointed, grins suppressed.

There was no mistaking it.

Her name was racing through the swarm.

Bluma began to chew idly on her bleeding lip.

The closer they drew to the Zubinsk cemetery gate, the thicker the scrum became—and the richer and more prominent the demons.

Near the outskirts of the swarm, the goblins and imps were unmistakable—all slavering maws and leathery wings—but here they'd begun to arm themselves with the leavings of human life: pale, flickering memories at first, of shabby dresses and threadbare coats, and then things that were more substantial. Bluma saw a demon with only one expression to her name—a wide smirk—and she wore it, thick and motionless, everywhere she went. Another demon had managed to lay his hands on a grubby toe-holed sock, and he was busy auctioning it off to a fierce crowd of bidders.

But soon the simulacra became more refined. There were demons here that Bluma might very well have mistaken for living people if, every so often, the moonlight hadn't cut through their skin, showing the ragged, ravenous things beneath.

Before long, the thrumming torrent of demons ran up against a hard barrier: a massive pavilion of crimson and black silk. Inside, an exclusive fete for only the eldest and most powerful demons was being thrown, and burbling chatter could be heard from within. A beguiling, lolloping melody was being played. Demons in the finest apparel went walking back and forth, and a tantalizing aroma floated out on the breeze.

Needless to say, this exclusive reception blocked off entirely the swath of cemetery closest to the Zubinsk gate. No one could hope to approach the town without first finding their way into the pavilion.

There was no more forward progress to be made without passing into the party, and as the riffraff were turned away, the crowd began to roil with a restless, aggrieved turbulence.

Lilith pulled up short, and, herded inward by the Lileen, Bluma drew close.

"Lady Lilith," said the doorkeeper, a hulking saber-toothed ogre in a neat red-and-black livery. "Lord Azazel would be honored to welcome you into his pavilion."

"Yes, he would," said Lilith. "And I have no intention of giving him that honor."

"Are you sure, my lady?" said the doorkeeper. "Lord Azazel has taken care to procure every delight for this occasion."

Swiftly, a gray cat came springing up through the crowd, and without even dropping a step, in the blinking of an eye, she was a squat gray lady.

"The girl is bleeding," she whispered.

Lilith's cold, still face twitched, and she looked down at Bluma as if she were a rip in an expensive new dress.

"Quite sure," said Lilith.

The doorkeeper smiled falsely. "Very well, my lady. If you would, then, do us the courtesy of clearing the entryway?"

Behind Bluma, one of the Lileen spoke softly. "Put your lip in your mouth, girl."

Bluma complied, and quickly her mouth flooded with warm, iron blood.

The crypt was ramshackle and shabby, half collapsed in the snow. Under normal circumstances, even the lowest among demons would've passed it by in favor of more comfortable shelter, but tonight, with the swarming in full force, a large pack of shadowy imps had to be chased out before the Lileen could be sure of any privacy.

Bluma stood corralled against the fallen rock to the rear, Lilith and her Sisterhood gathered about her in a tight semicircle.

"She cannot stay," said one of the Lileen.

"No," said a second.

"I am inclined," said Lilith, "to agree. But the question remains: What to do with her?"

"Can we not disguise her?"

Lilith shook her head. "There are many eyes here. And little time."

"What if," said a glowering cat, "we simply take what we want of her and leave the husk behind?"

Bluma did not like the way she said *husk*.

"No," said Lilith, her eyes gleaming oddly. "No, I think not."

Bluma was beginning to panic. The Sisters of the Lileen were all that stood between her and the mob of hungry demons outside the crypt door.

"The sooner we are rid of her," said one of the cats, "the sooner we return to our business. Can we not simply leave her?"

"We can," said another. "But ought we to? A living girl . . ."

"No," said Lilith, "I do not think it wise to leave her for the taking. She is pursued by Something Powerful."

Bluma swallowed hard. It was true.

"What option, then, is left?"

"Nothing. Nothing is left."

What could she do?

Lilith sighed. "Perhaps it is best to drain her after all."

This did not, to say the least, seem like a good option to Bluma.

And at just this moment, she remembered:

The spoon.

The hungry spoon.

All of a sudden, she knew what to do.

"I know!" said Bluma.

Slowly, the eyes of the Lileen turned upon her.

"What?" said Lilith.

"I say we drain her," snapped a thin, ragged cat.

But Lilith was intrigued; Bluma's hand was in her apron pocket.

"Yes?" said Lilith.

Bluma drew out the spoon.

"Tell me," said Lilith. "What do you see?"

By now, Bluma knew what to expect. After a moment, her face swam into view, and then the Dark Lady rose behind her, seeping up from among the fallen crypt stones, all thirsty lips and grasping fingers.

But Bluma brought the spoon closer, until all she could see was her own face.

Her face.

She was nervous now, and her eyes darted up to Lilith. "Is there any trick to it?"

"Only confidence," said Lilith.

And so, with confidence, Bluma took hold of the spoon's cold handle and, as she had seen Lilith do, turned it all the way around the image of her face that lay in its basin.

And what she saw when the spoon had completed its revolution shocked her.

It was a girl.

Just a girl. No one she knew. And as her eyes slipped away from the reflection in the basin of the spoon, the details of the girl's face slipped from her mind.

An odd grin had begun to crease Lilith's face. "Good," she said. "Very good."

"Her lip," said one of the Lileen. "Her lip isn't bleeding anymore."

With her free hand, Bluma lifted her fingers to her mouth. Sure enough, her lips were smooth and cool.

But something warm dripped onto her finger, and with a shock, Bluma let the spoon fall into the dirty snow underfoot.

A trickle of warm blood.

Swiftly, Lilith bent and retrieved the spoon. Before Bluma knew it, it was in the pocket of Lilith's shift.

"Sisters," she said. "Keep to the plan."

And with that, Lilith backed through the door of the crypt and, smiling, blew away on the wind.

Instantly, Bluma was through the crypt door.

Lilith was nowhere to be seen. Flakes of white danced through the night, but which had been Lilith and which were ordinary snow was impossible to tell.

Bluma was terribly upset.

Lilith had taken the spoon, and Bluma's face with it.

Oh, how she hated that spoon and longed for it, needed it and wished it had never been.

Bluma wheeled about to ask where Lilith had gone, but already the Sisters of the Lileen had dispersed, fanning out about the cemetery like the fingers of a fist spread wide.

They had business to attend to.

Bluma swallowed hard. All around her, the crowd of demons barred from Lord Azazel's fete roiled with restless energy. Before long, squabbles and skirmishes began to break out, and Bluma grew afraid that she might inadvertently be smashed against a gravestone.

No one seemed to notice her.

In fact, none of the demons seemed able to hold her in their minds for more than the few moments they spent looking at her: as soon as their eyes slid away, she seemed to slide from their awareness, as if she had never been there.

And, little by little, Bluma began to wonder how far this new anonymity extended.

Perhaps she no longer needed Lilith's help to outrun what pursued her.

Perhaps she already had.

Heart pounding, Bluma made her way to the hulking ogre at the entrance of the pavilion. If she was wrong about this, she was taking a terrible risk.

But if she was right . . .

"I'm afraid this is a closed gathering," said the doorkeeper.

"Y-yes," said Bluma. "I know."

The ogre sucked in slobber from between his great tusks. "Let me be clear," he said. "It is a closed gathering to which *you* are not invited."

"I know," said Bluma again.

She had to get him to look away from her face.

"But *he* wasn't invited either," she said, pointing at no one. "And you let *him* in."

The doorkeeper smiled condescendingly and turned to look over his shoulder. Bluma could almost see the moment in which he forgot her, and without pause, she trotted into the party.

The light in the pavilion was strange, the blue moon filtering oddly through the red-and-black silk. At the far end of the pavilion were the wrought-iron cemetery gates that held the demons back from Zubinsk. Two liveried goblins stood guard before them, ostensibly to keep the reveling demons from inadvertently coming into contact with the cold metal, but in truth to protect Lord Azazel's privilege: first through when dawn broke in Zubinsk.

Every so often, the voice of the ogre at the tent flap would ring out and someone new would arrive: Lord Uzza the Fallen, sweeping in beneath an impeccably styled powdered wig, each hair of which had been plucked from a different human king or queen; Lady Agrat of the Abyss in a sleek evening gown spangled thick with blinking eyes like rhinestones.

These rich and powerful demons were nothing like their inferiors. Outside, hideous beasts, creepers and crawlers, the slithering and the slimy abounded, but within the pavilion, only if one knew precisely what to watch for would one see the nostrils gaping uncommonly wide, the implausible amount of wrinkles, the ears too large or eyes too far apart.

With a shock, Bluma heard a sharp, familiar peal of laughter stabbing up into the fragrant air.

The smarmy demon: Belial.

As Bluma made her way across the luxuriant scarlet carpeting laid down between the gravestones, Belial's voice grew more and more distinct, like an unpleasantly sweet aroma carried in on the wind. "Of course not," he said to the adoring knot of demons around him. "You don't imagine Lord Azazel would be so gauche as to arrive on time to his own party."

"Of course not!" agreed one of his clique. "How absurd."

"Perhaps," said Belial, "he is hunting the Bluma, like the rest of the rabble out there. I don't know whom I pity more tonight— Lilith, or all the poor devils foolish enough to try her."

At this, the clique gave a shimmering giggle.

"Oh, Lord Belial, Lord Belial!" said a preening young demon, cutting in. "Have you heard the rumor?"

Belial smiled an acrid smile. "I have heard *every* rumor."

At this, the knot about him gave a knowing little titter.

"They say," said the preening young demon, "that Lord Mammon has come to the cemetery."

Now Belial laughed alone, sharp and small, like the cold point of an icy knife. "If Lord Mammon had chosen to inflict his presence upon us, I assure you, we would know."

Belial's clique giggled at this unkindness.

With effort, Bluma pushed her way into the small knot of demons attending Belial, and immediately she thought she had made a terrible mistake. Every single one of them in their turn took special notice of her—her dull, ragged clothing, her wild, untamed hair.

But they were just like the rest of the demons. As soon as their eyes slipped away from her, she might as well have been nothing.

"Besides," said Belial, "I can't imagine what Mammon would want here. Lord Azazel has the clear advantage, and Mammon doesn't tend to play unless he can win."

"But it's true, my lord!" said one of Belial's fawning attendants. "He's been seen! He arrived in the outskirts not long ago, pushed along in a little wheelchair."

"Ha!" said Belial. "I don't doubt that someone saw something that looked like Lord Mammon, but the last time he traveled away from his Treasure House, Mammon went in a carriage the size of a castle, drawn by a team of elephants. He is not, let me tell you, one for *subtlety*."

Scarcely had the dripping contempt of this last word died away when the great braying voice of the ogre at the door shook through the pavilion.

"Lord Mammon the Avaricious!"

Belial's pale face turned bright pink. "Surely not," he said.

A spasm of chatter spread through the pavilion. Mammon had not been expected, and he was a demon of great power and influence. Before long, the crowd was practically surging toward the little old fellow in the wheelchair, each demon eager to have his ear.

"No, no, no," said a high, reedy voice, cutting through the racket. "I shall be more than happy to entertain all offers, but not here, and not tonight. I am only passing through."

Bluma wriggled and pushed her way into the mad press.

"No," said the voice. "No, I cannot stay. You really must visit me at my Treasure House. As I say, I am only passing through."

He was small, Lord Mammon, in the figure of an aged man, shriveled and vaguely yellow, like an old lemon. His spectacles and sharp teeth gleamed in the diffuse moonlight, but Bluma had scarcely any attention to spare for them.

Bluma's eyes were drawn, like water down a drain, to the wheelchair in which Lord Mammon sat.

At first she thought it must've been made of fine wickerwork, and then possibly of intricately carved bone—it was so thin and delicate.

Only when she saw the unnaturally stiff posture of the mittened hands that pushed the wheelchair did she realize:

It was made of fingernails.

Coaxed through the woven fabric of the mittens, they had been carefully trained into the shape of seat and armrest and axle, and it must've taken ages to grow them so long—decades. In fact, Bluma could hardly believe that the ten looping nails that formed the wheelchair had had time to grow out of the young boy behind it.

And then, with a shock, Bluma recognized him:

Yehuda Leib.

She had seen him only yesterday (had it only been yesterday?), and somehow in that short time, he had grown wan, lean, and haggard, his hair long, his jaw set, his eyes deep and searching.

He was looking for something.

Quickly, sharply, Bluma tucked her chin down. It was becoming an instinct now, moving her face away from importunate eyes in order to preserve her anonymity. She felt a small spasm of guilt as she performed the maneuver: Yehuda Leib was in an even more precarious position than she, and she felt bad not leaping to help.

And this is why, when she looked back up again, the guilt and fear in her gut blossomed large.

The keen blue eyes of Yehuda Leib were staring directly at her.

CHAPTER SEVEN

Zubinsk

Even an ordinary wedding would've brought guests and visitors—the family and friends, the hopeful poor, gawkers and pleasure seekers.

But this was not an ordinary wedding. And in addition to all these, there was a large contingent that came to Zubinsk solely to see the holy Rebbe, grandfather of the bride:

His Hasidim.

A Hasid is nothing without his Rebbe, just as a sail is nothing without the wind, dough nothing without the oven. It is said that a Rebbe's holy being contains a fragment of the soul of each and every one of his devoted Hasidim, and for this reason, a Hasid is never quite complete unless he is beside his Rebbe.

And so they came, from far and from farther, however they were able—trains, carts, donkeys, and many, many, many pairs of sore and aching feet—to be near the saintly Rebbe. It was a very auspicious occasion, the wedding, and it was said that the Rebbe himself would be officiating, stretching up his holy hand from beneath the wedding canopy in order to draw down the heavenly cord that would bind the bride and groom together in marriage.

It was an occasion not to be missed.

And so on and on they came, more and more of the Hasidim, until Zubinsk was nearly overrun with threadbare black coats and long, ragged beards. Impromptu prayer sessions formed in streets and alleyways. Mystic whispers and melodies of meditation bloomed out from between the bricks and cobbles. The inn, the boardinghouses, even the private rooms put up for hire were full to bursting, often with three, four, five young men sharing the scant space intended for just one. And this was to say nothing of those Hasidim who came to town without the means to find themselves lodgings; the square was full of them long after sundown, and as the darkness thickened, one by one they made their several ways toward the best shelters they could find: empty market stalls, stables, sheepfolds. The study house had become a sort of makeshift campground, with Hasidim lounging, praying, singing, falling asleep on every available surface.

Even as the night wore on, now and again a straggling pilgrim would arrive at the study house, and a new round of excitement would break out: bottles passed, toasts of l'chaim proposed, hands clapping, voices singing with the joy of the Eternal.

By the time the snow began to wander down from the sky, it was long after nightfall. The steady stream of arrivals had dwindled. More and more of the bearded heads in the study house began to nod, and before long, aggrieved shushing was more likely to be heard than singing or prayer—after all, sleep is sleep.

This drove the last of the ecstatic revelers, four young Hasidim named Fishl, Mendl, Velvl, and Reuveyn, out of doors. It was there that they stood—laughing, smiling, stamping in the cold—when midnight fell.

There was a clatter of bells from the Russian church on the hill; the knot of Hasidim paused to hear.

It had been a long day of reveling and excitement. Each of the young men was overwhelmed with gladness and anticipation, and the bottle of vodka and pipe of tobacco orbiting their circle did nothing to still any of their heads.

All the same, one by one, through the dying hum of the bells, each of them began to think he heard ... footsteps in the snow.

And turning their eyes to the long road into town, they saw one final guest make his arrival:

A young man in a black coat.

Blacker than the darkness hidden inside your eyes.

"Come, stranger, come!" cried Fishl. "Join us!"

The dark stranger paused in the middle of the street.

Softly, through a cloud of pipe smoke, Mendl tsked his tongue. "Come, *friend*."

"Of course," said Fishl. "Come, *friend*, and join us."

The stranger made his way over to the little knot of Hasidim.

"Welcome," said Fishl. "Welcome."

It had been a very long time since the Dark One had been given welcome anywhere; it produced an odd sensation in his throat—something like sorrow, but then again, nothing like sorrow at all.

Slowly, stumblingly, Fishl began to go around the circle. "This is Reuveyn; the fellow behind all the smoke there is Mendl; the one who won't stop singing is called Velvl; I am Fishl. And what is your name?"

Four pairs of bloodshot, smiling eyes turned toward the Dark One.

"It depends who is asking."

The Hasidim burst into laughter.

But this was literally true—the caretaker of the Russian church on the hill would've called him by a different name than the four Hasidim who stood before him now.

"Very well," said Fishl, "very well. We've all felt like we had to run from something before. But you needn't worry. You're among friends."

The Dark One was acquainted with this word, *friend*, but never before had it been spread around with such profligacy in his presence.

"And where do you come to us from, my friend?" said Mendl.

There it was again. Were they mocking him?

"I travel from place to place," said the Dark One. "But my home is always near."

"I understand completely," said Reuveyn. "I spent a couple of years traveling, and at a certain point the road itself becomes your home."

A general murmur of understanding went about the circle.

"Listen, friend," said Fishl. "If something weighs on you, some deed you have done, if you are weary, perhaps you ought to see the Rebbe."

"Yes, certainly," said Reuveyn. "The Rebbe is very wise. And the wonders he works are pure miracles! One poor pilgrim I met walked three full days to sit with the Rebbe and recite Tachanun just once, and when he returned home, he found that all his hens had laid eggs with heavy gold coins where the yolks ought to have been."

"That's nothing," said Fishl. "My cousin and his wife were struggling to conceive, and so he came to see the Rebbe. Before my cousin could even say a word, the Rebbe took one look at him, wrote out a verse from the Psalms, folded up the piece of paper, and told him to put it beneath his wife's pillow. And what do you think? In nine months' time: triplets. *Triplets.*"

"Yes, yes," said Mendl. "The Rebbe is capable of all this and more. When he sits for meditation, he traverses the distance between Zubinsk and the Palace of Heaven in less than an hour's time. But do not be deceived: far and away his greatest gift is the revelation of people to themselves. It is impossible to spend even five minutes in conversation with the holy Rebbe without learning something about yourself, and that something can be so fundamental that it changes everything in your life. It certainly did for me."

Little by little, like snow accumulating on a cold stone, the Dark One began to think:

He *did* feel heavy. He *did* feel tired.

What could the Rebbe show him?

"You ought to see him!" said Fishl.

"Yes, you ought to," said Mendl with a sigh. Of the four Hasidim there assembled, he was the only one who lived close enough to make regular visits. "But it's been a long time since the Rebbe gave private audiences."

"Is the Rebbe ill, God forbid?" asked Reuveyn.

"No, no, no," said Mendl. "God forbid. But surely you heard of the passing of his wife, Fruma Rivka, three years ago?"

"I remember it well," said the Dark One.

"We all expected that the Rebbe would resume his normal activities after a year of grieving, and then again maybe after two, but now it seems more and more unlikely. He never speaks in public except to pray. He rarely eats. When morning prayers have ended, he sits for hours in meditation on the very same chair until the time comes around for afternoon prayers. He grows thinner and thinner, paler and paler."

For a moment, the cold gloom of the night seemed insuperably heavy.

"But the faithful among us are sure," said Mendl. "The Rebbe's fifth and final granddaughter is to be married in the morning. Surely, surely, the holy joy of the occasion will help us to lift the Rebbe back up again, and even higher than before. It is *our* job to encourage, to foster, to grow that joy to as great a height as possible."

"Yes," said Fishl, and "Yes!" said Reuveyn.

"Come!" said Mendl. "What's this dirge you're singing, Velvl? Let's have a dance, a real dance!" And handing his clay pipe to Reuveyn, he began to clap and sing.

Swiftly, gladly, the others joined in, whipping one another around, kicking their legs and throwing their arms in the air, singing and dancing with everything they had—which was mostly vodka.

The Dark One stood at the edge of the circle, stock-still in the falling snow. In the shuffle, somehow, he had ended up with the bottle. Red-faced Fishl looked over his shoulder now and saw it in the Dark One's hand, and he gave a great whoop and a laugh that called down the shushing from five different windows.

"L'chaim, my friend! L'chaim!" And he mimed swigging from the bottle.

It had been quite some time since someone had offered the Dark One a drink, and it took him a moment to figure out how it was done. Soon, though, he swigged and coughed and found himself smiling. The drink tasted like sorrow—but then again, nothing like sorrow at all.

"L'chaim," said the Angel of Death.

To life.

Bluma turned her face sharply toward the ground and shuffled backward, hiding herself in the press of demons all around her.

Something was wrong.

When she looked up again, she could see Yehuda Leib scanning the crowd, his brows low.

He knew he had seen something.

Fortunately, he did not seem to know what.

"Lord Mammon," said Belial, stepping forward. "What a pleasant surprise! We had not expected to see you here."

"Ah," replied Mammon. "Belial." With a motion of his hand, he signaled Yehuda Leib to stop. "I am afraid I cannot say that *your* presence here is particularly surprising . . ."

Or particularly pleasant was the implied conclusion.

Belial stiffened. "I am rather more generous with my time than some, it is true."

"Oh yes," said Mammon. "Nearly as generous as you are with other people's money."

A titillated buzz ran through the crowd. Belial, it seemed, was rather in debt to Mammon.

"Now, now, Lord Mammon," said Belial. "It is not the done thing to discuss such matters at parties. You might've been sensible of that if you'd ever been invited to one."

Mammon let out a demonstrative sigh. "Oh, very clever, Belial. But I shan't deny it—I am, alas, far too often taken up with serious matters of business to spend much time in company. Even tonight, I cannot stay long. I am afraid I am only passing through."

Belial showed his teeth in a smug grin. "*Passing through?* Found the odds a bit daunting, did you, my lord?"

Now Mammon frowned in mock puzzlement. "Hmm? Odds, you say? I do not play the odds. Or, to put it rather better: once I have begun to play, the odds are irrelevant."

At this, Belial gave a derisive snort. "Lord Azazel has surrounded the gates, Mammon. Not even you could be arrogant enough to think that you can beat him to the Rebbe once the morning comes."

Mammon laid a hand on his chest and bowed his head in an exaggerated show of humility. "Of course not."

Belial began to chuckle exultantly, but he was cut short when Mammon continued:

"I shall beat him to the Rebbe tonight."

This sent a flurry of murmurs through the crowd, and it took Belial an undignified amount of effort to raise his voice above the hubbub.

"How, how, *how ever do you think*, Lord Mammon, that you shall be able to make your way into the territory of the living tonight without the help of a mortal's invitation?"

Mammon chuckled, and he leaned toward Belial in his chair with all the condescension he could muster. "I don't need a mortal's invitation, Belial."

"Oh?" said Belial, blundering forward. "And whyever not?"

"Because," said Mammon with a smile, "I have a mortal of my own."

Now the crowd exploded with chatter. A living mortal was a precious thing—perhaps the most precious thing a demon could ever acquire—and immediately, the onlooking fiends and devils began to speculate, craning their necks to see: Who was it?

It was only bare moments before she heard—her name was bouncing about from lip to lip:

Bluma.

The rumor had spread quickly: a living girl loose in the cemetery. She must be the mortal of whom Lord Mammon had spoken.

Bluma, they said. *Bluma. Bluma.*

She could not stay here. Slowly, careful to keep her head down, Bluma began to edge backward toward the tent flap.

In the midst of the chattering crowd, Lord Mammon flicked his hand forward. "On, boy," he called, and without thought, Yehuda Leib began to move, rolling the wheelchair at the end of his hands toward the heavy iron gates. All he had ever known, his whole life through, it seemed, had been to push: pushing, pushing, pushing a wheelchair through the thick clogging snow, dodging and swerving between gravestones.

He had never known anything else, it seemed.

But no.

He had.

He had seen her, there in the crowd—he knew it. She had been off, somehow—skewed, like the right shoe on the wrong foot.

But it had been her.

Only who?

With a clink, Yehuda Leib's fingernail footrest met the iron gates; at a shove, the gates groaned open.

A heavy hush fell over the assembled demons. It was a terribly dangerous thing, to try to pass into living territory: a demon could perish if it went wrong, cease to be entirely.

But all of a sudden, with a shock, Yehuda Leib stopped his pushing and turned to look back over his shoulder. It was as if he had been sleeping, sleeping for an eon, and something was beginning to wake him: an aroma, sweet and clean, like linen dried in the breeze, like the soft toasted smoke of the hearth.

Lord Mammon cleared his throat nervously. "On, boy," he muttered through gritted teeth. "Walk on."

But Yehuda Leib had remembered.

"On," said Mammon again, his voice full and loud.

That frown.

How could he have forgotten?

"On," cried Mammon. "Walk on, or so help me—"

The assembled demons had fallen silent, and when Yehuda Leib spoke, her name floated out to every ear:

"Bluma?" said Yehuda Leib.

His keen eyes seemed to look straight through her vague and dreamy face.

Slowly, all the dark eyes of the cemetery turned to fix upon the girl.

"On, boy!" roared Mammon. "On! Now!"

With a jolt, Yehuda Leib pushed the little demon forward, through the gateway and into the territory of the living.

An excited commotion blossomed through the crowd—this was, after all, a practical miracle.

And then, one by one, as grinning Mammon clattered off over the cobbles into Zubinsk, each of the demons in the crowd began to realize that this miracle had been performed by way of a living human child.

And there—just there—was another.

Bluma.

Afterward, she could not say who had moved first—her or one of the demons.

All she remembered was running.

Gnashing teeth and grabbing hands, long, scraping claws, voices screaming, yelling, pushing, cursing—she had to keep going, she had to keep moving, running, and she dodged and leapt over headstones, and still they were grabbing on to her, touching her, and there were fingers in her hair pulling her back, and she wrenched forward, but there was no end to them, none, grabbing, their hands, and as soon as she had torn herself away, there were more, and there were more, and there were more, and there were more, and their faces loomed up, twisted and furious, and the monsters beneath, fiery eyes, teeth, gullets deeper than the ocean, talons, barbed, stinging tails, and the gate was just ahead, she could see it, and if she could only make her way through, then they could not follow, but she was slowing, the strength sapping from her legs, encumbered, weighted down by the sheer number of grabbing hands, and now they began to pull her in opposing directions, and she began batting at them, kicking and flailing, and she was sure that they would rip her apart, and her throat was ragged and sore and she found that she was screaming, and she pushed hard against a gravestone behind with her feet, and this was it, she was there, the heavy iron gates looming up on either side, and the warm, silky light of the raging pavilion fell quickly away, leaving only the silent, snowy midnight of Zubinsk to receive her.

From this perspective—from the mortal side—there seemed to be no tent, no crowd, no demons: just a still and snowy graveyard at the edge of the slumbering town.

But as she passed through the gates, a cold, clammy hand closed around her ankle.

Something had her—a snarling, rabid, grasping thing—and she fell on the cold cobbles, and it was pulling its way through, hand over hand up her leg, she could see its eyes, alight with desire, and she kicked hard, once, twice, against its head, and with a yelp, it let go.

Bluma skittered back, out of reach of its long arms, and she watched with horror as the demon began to realize its situation:

It was caught halfway through.

Stiff with terror, the demon looked down in the direction of its feet.

But there were no feet to be seen. The demon simply stopped, as if cut in half by the threshold of the cemetery.

For a long moment, tense with fright, the demon barely moved. Bluma could hear its rasping breath echoing out through the dim of the night.

And then, with a light so bright Bluma had to look away, the demon began to burn, yelling, screaming so loud that curtains drew back in nearby bedroom windows.

But it was not the threat of discovery that made Bluma fly, sprinting, down the cobbled lane.

It was the screaming.

She couldn't stand the screaming.

On and on Bluma ran, deeper and deeper into sleeping Zubinsk, the scream ebbing away behind. Zubinsk was much larger than Tupik, all high brick row houses and glassy-eyed storefronts, and in no time at all, Bluma had thoroughly lost her bearings.

Soon the screaming was subsumed in snowy silence. Bluma slowed to a trot, and then to a walk.

The streets were hushed all around her, cushioned with

accumulated snow, and the wind grumbled softly, as if it wanted to go home.

Gradually, Bluma's walk slowed to a creep. It seemed wrong to disturb the heavy silence of the night, and she found herself fighting to hush her panting breath.

Bluuuuuuumaaaaaaa . . .

The sound was anything but certain—hidden behind the moaning wind like frozen earth beneath the snow.

Bluuuuuuumaaaaaaa . . .

Without meaning it, Bluma began to quicken the pace of her steps once more.

She was not running. She didn't need to. There was nothing behind her.

Nothing.

Bluuuuuuumaaaaaaa . . .

As if to throw the sound off her track, Bluma turned sharply down the first road she saw—a broad, cobbled shopping street—and with a stumble, she came immediately back. A stranger was blinking at her from every polished windowpane: an obscure, faceless girl.

Bluuuuuuumaaaaaaa . . .

There was no question. Something was calling her name. And no matter where she went, it grew louder.

She could no longer run—she no longer had the strength. Her legs were weak, wavering atop her ankles with each step.

Bluuuuuuumaaaaaaa, sang the wind.

And then she saw, far down a dim and narrow alleyway, the unmistakable form of a woman in white:

Lilith.

CHAPTER EIGHT

Great Souls

The Rebbe's granddaughter could not sleep.

Tomorrow, her wedding day, was to be the most important of her life, and people had come from far and wide—many, many, many of them—to see her married.

She was sure she would disappoint them.

What if she tripped? What if she said the wrong thing?

Everyone would whisper to their neighbor: *Ah. I always knew.*

She rolled over in bed.

Outside the window, the Rebbe's granddaughter could see flakes of snow rolling through the overcast nighttime sky.

And what if her groom didn't like her? Would he still go through with the wedding? That would be less embarrassing than having it called off at the last minute, under the canopy with everyone watching. But would it be better? What if he went through with it just to save her feelings? Then what? Would he be cruel? Would he divorce her?

And all of this was to say nothing of what *she* thought of *him*. She'd heard plenty about the boy—a good young man, they'd said, the son of a rabbi. He was suitable.

But his suitability was based on other people's expectations—not hers. Come to think of it, she didn't even know how she would begin to evaluate the suitability of a young man.

The Rebbe's granddaughter squeezed her eyes shut for the billionth time that night. She had to get some rest. None of this could be solved by sleep deprivation.

But every time she shut her eyes, the image of her grandfather swam up to meet her.

Her grandfather.

The Rebbe.

Standing beneath the wedding canopy.

Waiting for her.

Waiting.

Her grandfather was perhaps the most daunting part of this whole undertaking. One could feel the holiness in his gaze, and it was not always comforting. He had never been anything but kind to her in the rare moments he could spare, but the way he looked at her—looked into her—made her feel defenseless, like an open book, her pages riffled by the wind.

What would he think? If she was not good enough?

There was nothing for it. She couldn't sleep.

With a sigh, the Rebbe's granddaughter opened her eyes again. While they had been shut, a large gray cat had come to sit quietly on the sill outside her bedroom window. It was an odd thing—her bedroom was on the third floor, and the narrow sill did not seem like a very comfortable place to rest, particularly on a blustery night such as this.

Once, twice, the Rebbe's granddaughter blinked.

The cat was staring intently through the window.

After a moment, the Rebbe's granddaughter began to grow uneasy.

What did it want with her?

And then, softly, unmistakably, like purring, she heard the cat speak her name:

Rokhl.

Rokhl, the Rebbe's granddaughter, sat up in her bed.

Mammon was in a foul mood.

"Unbelievable," he grumbled. "Unbelievable! You completely ruined the effect. Foolish boy. Now all they'll be talking about is that girl."

His petulant little voice bounced and jostled with every bump and cobble they went over.

"Just you wait," he said. "Just you wait. Once we're back in my Treasure House, I'll make you wish you weren't alive."

Yehuda Leib's head was swimming, and no matter how hard he fought to still it, it wouldn't come to rest. Everything was a wide, turbulent nighttime sea, and as soon as he thought he recognized something—a person, a place, even an idea—it slipped away, sloshing into oblivion in the darkness.

Where was he? Where was he going? And for God's sake, who was this sour little beast sitting between his fingers?

The cold wind whipped angrily through the streets of Zubinsk, cutting through the open neck of Yehuda Leib's coat. He wanted to pull his lapels shut, but he couldn't move his hands.

His scarf. If only he hadn't forgotten his scarf.

But he hadn't: that he could remember. He'd gone back to get it.

Where was it?

What had happened?

"Well?" said Mammon. "Where is he?"

It took Yehuda Leib a moment to realize that the little fellow was speaking to him.

"Um?" said Yehuda Leib, bringing the wheelchair to a stop.

"The Rebbe," spat Mammon. "Where is the Rebbe?"

Yehuda Leib's brows wrinkled and creased. Back in Tupik, he knew where to find their rabbi. But a little community rabbi is nothing like a holy mystic Rebbe.

"Where are we?" he said.

With an exasperated sigh, Mammon turned back in his chair to glare at Yehuda Leib.

"Zubinsk, boy," he said. "We are in Zubinsk. And you are to take me to this miracle-working Rebbe so that I may claim him before any of those pompous fiends in the cemetery manage a way through." In a huff, he sat back hard. "Honestly," he muttered.

Yehuda Leib was still for a moment. Murky forms were beginning to emerge in the gloom of his mind.

Zubinsk.

The miracle-working Rebbe.

Yehuda Leib needed a miracle himself. What miracle did he need?

"Well?" cried Mammon.

With a sigh of his own, Yehuda Leib chose a street at random and pushed the wheelchair down it.

"That's more like it," said Mammon.

What miracle did Yehuda Leib need?

He had to think.

Zubinsk.

The road to Zubinsk.

Something had happened on the road to Zubinsk.

But everything was so strange here. The cobbles beneath his feet were firm and unmoving, not a single stone swapping with its neighbor.

Why was nothing in this place like a dream?

Think:

The road to Zubinsk.

Why had he been on the road to Zubinsk?

There had been another boy, a stupid boy in a donkey cart. And a warning—what had it been?

This was getting him nowhere. He needed something still— a landmark in his mind to reckon by.

And, like a lighthouse shining out through the dark, there she was:

Bluma, standing in the doorway. Bluma the baker's daughter. She had given him a loaf of challah—he still had it in his bag.

Because he'd had to go.

Because someone had chased him.

And someone had caught him.

With a rush, it all came flooding back: the Treasure House, Mammon, the march of the Army of the Dead, the cold forest that had become a graveyard.

And like a blazing comet that flew out of the darkness to land warm and flickering in his pocket:

His father.

His poor, awful father.

That was the miracle he needed.

"How much farther?" snapped the ancient demon in Yehuda Leib's hands.

"Not much," said Yehuda Leib. He had no idea where he was going, but still it felt like telling the truth. "Not much at all."

On the night preceding the wedding of his final granddaughter, the Rebbe of Zubinsk retired early. The parents of the groom had insisted upon issuing a completely open invitation to the wedding—a spiritually hazardous proposition, to be sure, but, all in all, slightly less hazardous than the prospect of revoking such an invitation once it had been issued. The result of this was that Zubinsk was full to bursting tonight—of guests, of Hasidim, of spirits and beings of all sorts—and the Rebbe was deeply overwhelmed.

Imagine yourself seated in a crowded train station at the very center of the waiting area. All around you, a hundred conversations are taking place in a hundred different languages. Bells clang. Whistles scream. Outside, arrivals grind into the station as departures rumble and chug themselves into full heads of steam.

Now imagine that you are a sublimely talented musician. Each of these sounds in each of its constituent parts—the rhythm of the engines, the pitch of the squealing wheels, the timbre of the voice of each of the waiting passengers, not to mention its words and intonation—each of these is perfectly clear, perfectly distinguishable, and entirely inescapable to you.

This is much how the Rebbe felt. Every soul that ventured into his orbit, even as far as the farmland surrounding the town, called out to him clearly as if to say, *Help me, help me.*

It was a cacophony. And it was exhausting.

And so the Rebbe retired early, immediately following evening prayers. He had taken great care to disguise the fact, but he had not managed to sleep in the three years since his wife's passing. At first, this had presented him with quite a challenge—sapping his energy, stealing his focus. The Rebbe soon discerned, however, that his fatigue came not from sleeplessness, but rather from fighting against it. Now, once the darkness fell, the Rebbe would retire to his private chamber, don his kittel, a long white robe worn for holy occasions, and, enclosing himself beneath the cowl of his prayer shawl, sit and meditate.

If he could not manage to sleep, at least he might leave his body behind for a time.

When he had still been a young Hasid himself, it had taken him quite a long time to quiet his mind and loosen his spirit. Now he was practiced, skilled.

Scarcely had he shut his eyes before his soul began to rise.

The Rebbe saw himself from above—first the kittel, prayer shawl, and long white beard and then (with a pang of sadness every single time) the half-empty bedchamber in which he sat. Slowly, like smoke, he continued to rise, his entire house spreading out below him: the Hasid dozing outside his bedroom door, waiting to attend him; the little sanctuary on the first floor with its Torah scrolls asleep in their ark.

On and on he would rise, higher and higher, until the shape of the town below faded in the darkness of night, leaving only the shining light of its souls to twinkle like a vast constellation of candles. At the peak of his rising, even the dark spots fell away, and all the lights were revealed to be One.

This was a glorious, holy thing.

But this evening, deliberately—out of a certain weakness—the Rebbe remained rather lower.

That night, Zubinsk looked very different than it normally did. There were far, far more souls within its boundaries than usual, crammed into corners and rooming houses, stables and stockyards, sleeping wherever they might find rest. There was even one excited young Hasid dozing in the doorway opposite the Rebbe's window, desperate to catch a glimpse of him.

But it was none of these new lights that compelled the Rebbe to break off his meditation and rush out into the cold, snowy night.

This he did because of what he saw at his granddaughter's house: a blazing white light, ushered out into the beckoning darkness by a clutch of creeping gray shadows.

"Friends!"

The young Hasid came sprinting around the corner toward the study house, calling out from the far end of the street. "Friends!"

But the Hasidim in the street did not pause in their dancing.

The young man came rushing up. "Friends!" he said again.

Only one of these Hasidim was singing, a man in a coat blacker than the night, blacker than the darkness hidden inside your eyes, and he stood in the very center of their circle, clapping his bony hands in a pulsing, hypnotic rhythm. At his feet, half buried in the snow, was a very large and very empty glass bottle.

"Friends," said the young Hasid. "The Rebbe is abroad!"

At this, the drunken Hasid in the middle of the circle stopped his singing, and his cold eyes grew wide.

But the pulse of his clapping hands never faltered.

"The Rebbe?" said the dark Hasid. All around him, the swirling dance continued unabated, the Hasidim shuffling and stepping to the rhythm of his hands.

"Yes," said the young man.

But something was wrong:

The rhythm of the Dark One's hands, like the finite beat of the heart, like the lurching tick of the clock.

"Where is the Rebbe?" said the dark Hasid, his words slurred with drink. "Can you take me to him?"

The dancers—something in their eyes. Something manic. Something frightened.

"Yes," said the young Hasid. "Yes, of course. He's just—"

But the dark Hasid cut him off. "Then come!" he cried. "Join us!"

The young man found that he was breathing in the dark rhythm:

In-out, in-out.

Clap-clap, clap-clap.

And then, suddenly, as easily as falling asleep, his feet began to move:

Step-step, step-step.

And it all made terrible sense.

The dance was sweet; there was nothing as sweet as the dance. And he could not abide the fear of what would come to pass once it reached its end.

The whole world was the shuffling beat of palm upon bony palm.

"Come!" called the Dark One. "Take us to the holy Rebbe!"

"Lilith?" said Bluma.

The reply came back soft and clear, as if the pale lady were only inches from her ear.

"Hello," said Lilith, and she beckoned from the far end of the alley. "Come."

The way was long and narrow, its squared corners rounded in with snow, and it took Bluma far longer to traverse its length than she had expected.

"Bluma," said Lilith. "What are you doing here?"

Bluma found herself shivering to hear her name spoken aloud, as if it were a piece of cold metal held against the back of her neck.

"You called my name," she said. "And I came."

At this, Lilith frowned. "I did not call your name."

Bluma wanted to argue, wanted to yell that of course Lilith had called to her, but she stopped herself; if Lilith denied it again, Bluma would have to ask herself who—or what—else might have done the calling.

And that was a question she didn't want to consider at all.

"You are troubled," said Lilith. "What is the matter?"

This question seemed unutterably stupid, and Bluma brushed past Lilith as if she were nothing more than an annoyance.

"Bluma?"

Idly, Bluma cast her eyes around the empty plot of land on which they found themselves. High brick walls loomed in on all sides. Here and there, she could see stalks of uncut grass rising through the thick blanket of snow.

What was this place?

"Bluma," said Lilith from behind her, and Bluma flinched. She had begun to hate that word, to hate the inescapable sound of it.

It was like a trap, and she wanted to be rid of it.

"What troubles you?"

Now Bluma felt a hot spike of anger surging up in her chest. "Where did you go?" she said. "You made me think that I was safe and then you just left."

Now Lilith's brows fell, and her jaw set hard. "What happened?"

She wanted to tell Lilith, wanted to say what had happened, but Bluma was afraid that speaking it would bring them back again, the sharp eyes and long fingers, touching her, grabbing her, holding her back, and . . .

Lilith's eyes were cold and hard. "I understand."

This both comforted and angered Bluma: she desperately wanted someone to understand, but she didn't see how anyone possibly could.

Wheeling about, Bluma held out her hand. "The spoon," she said. "Give me the spoon."

Lilith raised an eyebrow. "Why?"

It took a long moment for Bluma to collect herself. All she wanted was to be left alone—by the people in Tupik, by the demons in the graveyard, and, most of all, by the Darkness that Prowls at the End of Everything. "It was my name," she said. "Someone called me by my name."

"Ah," said Lilith.

"I want to cut it away," said Bluma. "Give me the spoon."

With a sigh, Lilith ran her long hand into the pocket of her shift.

But then she hesitated.

Bluma felt the anger stabbing up through her chest once more. "What are you waiting for? It's mine! Give it to me!"

"Very well," said Lilith, producing the spoon. "But I must admit, I am not certain how you mean to accomplish this thing."

Bluma's lips folded into a light, tight frown. "I'll do just what I did with my face."

Bluma took the spoon from Lilith's fingers and gazed into its basin. There was no one there.

"Yes," said Lilith. "But how do you intend to put your name into the spoon?"

The reflection above was cold: only snowflakes and the thick sheet of cloud that smothered back the stars.

"Maybe . . . ," said Bluma, and, bringing the spoon up to her lips, she whispered a puff of steaming breath. "*Bluma.*"

But even before she flipped the handle of the spoon, she knew it hadn't worked.

"No," said Lilith. "What you wish to shed is not simply a sound—it is something beneath, is it not? A handle, a bellpull?"

Bluma nodded. This was correct.

"Here," said Lilith, placing a hand on the small of Bluma's back. "Come and stand where I am." Lilith's hand was so cold that Bluma could feel it there, frigid through the thick fabric of her coat.

"Now raise the spoon and watch over your shoulder," said Lilith. "Shortly, you shall see yourself coming down the alleyway, and when you recognize yourself . . ."

"Then I can call out my name," said Bluma.

"Just so," said Lilith with a smile. "You are very clever."

But with a lurch, gazing up at Lilith above her, Bluma realized something.

"Wait," she said. "You're not supposed to be here."

"Oh?" said Lilith.

"I thought you couldn't cross into the town."

"Ah." Lilith nodded. "Shrewd as ever, Bluma. And you are correct, of course. I cannot pass into mortal territory uninvited. But, as I am sure you know by now, there are places that belong to both the living and the dead."

Bluma's eyebrows fell. There were no headstones or graves here, no crypts or markers to be seen.

"This is a graveyard?"

Lilith's jaw twitched, once, twice. "There are deaths that occur in secret, Bluma," she said, "and burials attended by one alone. Not every grave is marked."

Slowly, languidly, like a wooden spoon in a pot of cold soup, the wind stirred the air within the four brick walls of the second cemetery of Zubinsk.

Bluma swallowed. "A secret cemetery," she said.

"Forgotten," said Lilith. And then, with more than a little bitterness: "Men have a way of forgetting."

"You are clever too," said Bluma, and Lilith began to smirk.

"Is that so?" she said.

"This cemetery is closer to the center of town," said Bluma. "Nearer to the Rebbe."

"Oh," said Lilith with a wave of her hand. "I have no interest in the Rebbe."

This was a surprise. "Really?" said Bluma. "All the others seem to want him."

"I am not," said Lilith, "like all the others."

"What do you mean?"

Now Lilith's eyes narrowed. "You saw them, Bluma—all grasping for advantage, desperate to be the richest, the strongest, the most powerful. They clamor for the Rebbe, but only because the others desire him. No, I have no time for such nonsense."

"But you are here," said Bluma. "In Zubinsk."

Lilith nodded. "We are."

"Why?"

"Because a great soul is about to perish," said Lilith. "And we wish to save her."

Bluma's heart began to beat faster. Was Lilith speaking of her?

"Who?" said Bluma. "Who is she?"

And at just this moment, in the reflection of the spoon, Bluma saw the dark silhouette of a girl stumble into the thin frame of the alley's entryway. Out of habit, she turned, looking over her shoulder to see the girl in the flesh.

But there was no one there.

"Carefully, now," said Lilith. "Wait until you recognize yourself. Only then can you call out and catch your name in the basin of the spoon."

Slowly, the silhouetted girl began to come nearer, closer and closer down the alleyway. Bluma was prepared, ready to speak her name as soon as she recognized the girl in the reflection.

The word was on the tip of her tongue.

And this is why it was such a shock to Bluma when she found, as the girl stumbled out of the shadowy alley, that she did not recognize herself at all.

"What is it?" said Lilith.

"Her face . . . ," said Bluma. "I don't know her."

"No," said Lilith with a sigh. "No, of course not."

Bluma dropped her arm. "Then what can I do?"

Lilith's brows fell. "We must put your name into the spoon. Which I suppose means that we must find your name somewhere."

"But where?" said Bluma.

"It is a difficult question. Perhaps, once we have whom we have come for, we should return to the Far Country and consult Lord Dantalion. . . ."

"Who have you come for?" said Bluma, her hope rising.

Now Lilith raised her eyes to the end of the alleyway—odd, almost hungry eyes.

"We have come for Rokhl," said Lilith. "The Rebbe's grand-daughter. Hers is a very great soul, Bluma—very great indeed. Why, if she were a grandson instead of a granddaughter, she would be in line to replace the Rebbe already. But as it is, in the morning, they mean to bind her to some blundering fool of a groom for all eternity. It is a crime, Bluma, a waste, like binding a soaring eagle to a plodding rhinoceros. I will not permit it. Even now my Sisters are inviting her here to speak with me."

"But," said Bluma, "what if she wants to get married?"

"She will join our Sisterhood, one way or another," said Lilith.

This surprised Bluma.

"But," said Bluma, "she's a living girl, isn't she? Not a . . . Not . . ."

"Not a demon?"

Bluma blushed.

"None of my Sisters are," said Lilith. "And I do not care for that word."

"Then," said Bluma, "what are they? Your Sisters."

"What they were," said Lilith, "was mortal women. Just like you. And when their time came to die, they looked back on their lives and saw how they had been compelled to live: subservient, second, Sisterless. And so, one by one, they joined me, in the hope that things might change. Now, for the first time, we mean to enlist a living Sister—for nothing changes in the realm of the dead. But once we are bound into Sisterhood with the living . . ."

This was all very exciting to Bluma. It meant that she, too, might join the Sisterhood.

But something nagged at her.

Why couldn't *she* be the first of Lilith's living Sisters? Surely her soul was great enough.

Wasn't it?

"But," said Bluma, "what if the Rebbe's granddaughter really *does* want to get married? If she—"

Bluma was just about to offer herself as a replacement when Lilith cut in.

"She will join our Sisterhood," said Lilith again. "One way or another."

And at precisely this moment, out of the corner of her eye, Bluma saw a hungry gray cat alight upon the far wall of the second cemetery.

"Ah," said Lilith. "She comes."

Swiftly, the Lileen assembled, crouching, perched, gazing down from the high brick walls: one, two, three, four, five Sisters, spread out about the second cemetery like the fingers of a fist, waiting to snap shut.

But *six* of Lilith's Sisters had come along to Zubinsk.

Where was the final cat?

Lilith's eyes were fixed on the alleyway. "Yes," she breathed, so tightly and so soft that Bluma thought it must've been an accident.

And turning to look over her shoulder, Bluma saw why.

The sixth Sister, tail upraised, was there at the far end of the alley, and as she began to stalk her way into the second cemetery, the Rebbe's granddaughter appeared, silhouetted in the road behind her. She was skinny, shivering in her nightgown, nervous, and she hesitated at the end of the long alleyway.

The sixth Sister of the Lileen arrived in the second cemetery and sat softly down at Lilith's feet.

All was still. The snow had begun to thicken, but in the absence of any hint of wind, the flakes crowded the sky, taking their time swirling down to the ground.

It felt to Bluma as if all the world were holding its breath.

Lilith raised a long finger and beckoned. Somewhere nearby, the wind began to stir.

"Come," said Lilith.

Bluma could see the Rebbe's granddaughter stiffen.

In a spasm of light, behind the clouds, behind the veil of shimmering snow, sharp blue lightning split the sky.

And then, from the street beyond the alley, a deep, round voice rang out. Bluma had never heard or even seen the man before, but instantly and without doubt she knew the voice of the Rebbe of Zubinsk.

"Rokhl!" Sharply, the Rebbe's granddaughter turned her head toward the sound of her grandfather's voice. "Run!"

Thunder rolled through the sky, low and round, as if in echo of the Rebbe.

"No," said Lilith, in a voice so sharp and cold that Bluma wanted to check her ears for blood.

Again, the girl at the end of the alleyway stiffened.

And then she turned and ran.

"No!" called Lilith again, like a screeching gale. Bluma looked up. Lilith's face was terrible and furious and beautiful.

"Go!" cried Lilith. "Bring her back to me!" And with a lurch, Bluma was running again, her feet falling hard and fast against the packed snow, and, all around her, the bounding shadows of six gray cats tore into the town of Zubinsk.

CHAPTER NINE

The Flight and the Fall

Yehuda Leib was exhausted. Round and round the streets of Zubinsk they had gone, Mammon growing more and more impatient, Yehuda Leib growing sweatier and sweatier. His hands in their mittens were swamped, and he hated sweating under woolens—nothing made him feel more constrained.

"Faster, boy," snapped Mammon. "If I fail to secure this Rebbe after having made such a show of crossing over . . ."

Yehuda Leib stopped listening as soon as possible.

He had to think.

If there was anyone who could help him bring back his father, it was the Rebbe of Zubinsk. But how could he manage to consult the holy Rebbe with this little lump of a demon in his hands?

He had to ditch the demon. But how?

He wished his hands weren't so sweaty—it was just one more distraction, and time was running short.

If he could only remember how they had made the wheelchair grow from him, perhaps he could figure out how to rid himself of it. But his memory was still so hazy, and every time he began to think back, he found himself remembering further than he meant to:

The road in the forest. The smell of pipe smoke. His father's empty face. The blood in the snow.

This wasn't helping. His hands were so sweaty. He just wanted to wipe them, just once against his coat. And to make matters worse, there seemed to be some grit in his mittens, sand or gravel, that had begun to cling to his sweaty fingers.

"Wait," said Mammon. "Haven't I seen that shop before?"

Swiftly, Yehuda Leib turned the wheelchair up a steep hill.

He had to concentrate.

He had to think.

The forest road. A donkey cart. Issur Frumkin.

Here was something useful: Issur had told him three ways to ward off demons.

What had they been?

"Ugh," said Mammon. "Can't you go any faster? We're hardly moving at all."

And it was true: Yehuda Leib was making barely any headway, and the heavy load in the wheelchair pressed backward painfully against his fingernails.

He had to think.

Three protections against the demons, Issur had said. What had they been?

Red thread—that had been one. If only his scarf hadn't been torn from his neck . . .

But that wasn't a useful thought.

What were the other two protections?

Cold metal. But even had Yehuda Leib carried any metal with him, how could he have accessed it with his hands bound up in the wheelchair?

No, there was no help there.

What was the third?

Cold metal, red thread . . .

"Come on, boy," said Mammon. "Put forth a little effort!"

They had stalled, a raised cobble in the steep road presenting a nearly insuperable obstacle to Yehuda Leib and the fingernail wheelchair. Once, twice, he shoved against it, but he couldn't pick up enough momentum.

"Don't make me use the whip, boy."

Yehuda Leib's fingernails ached painfully with the weight of the wheelchair they had formed. Inside his mittens, the grit had begun to sting, abrading his fingers.

Why on earth had he put on these mittens?

"Move, boy! Move!"

With a great shove, Yehuda Leib forced the wheelchair up and over the cobble.

And the oddest thing happened.

Inside his right mitten, one of his fingernails—the third—snapped.

It was free. He could bend the finger alone. And when he did, he felt quite a bit more grit in his mitten than he had anticipated.

What was this in his mittens?

And in a rush of illumination, it all came flooding back:

Salt. The demons' magic can't pass beyond boundaries of salt.

He had filled his mittens in Tupik, a lifetime ago—before his fight with Issur, before he met his father—in order to replenish the saltcellar at home. That explained why he was wearing them in the first place. He must've remembered just in time.

Yehuda Leib swerved wildly to drive the wheelchair over another protruding cobble, and, just as he'd hoped, a second nail broke— this time in his left mitten.

The salt was eating away at his magically grown nails.

"Careful, boy!"

"I'm sorry, my lord," muttered Yehuda Leib through a wide grin.

Far above, behind the snow and the clouds, an arc of blue lightning split the sky.

"My," said Mammon. "What a night."

And then, as if in anticipation of the thunder, the sound of a deep, obscure voice called out through the streets below.

They could not hear the words, but its tone was clear: commanding, dire, almost frightened.

Mammon turned his head sharply, and before he even spoke, Yehuda Leib knew.

"That," said the demon, "is the Rebbe."

Thunder rolled through the sky, low and round, as if in echo.

"Go," said Mammon. "Go!"

Bluma burst from the alleyway, her legs pounding, and just when she thought she had exhausted her reserves of strength, she was bolstered by the Lileen leaping and bounding all around her.

It was as if their strength were hers.

It was thrilling.

Far ahead she could see Rokhl, the Rebbe's granddaughter, slipping on the wet snow as she ran. There was no question: they would catch her.

Bluma's heart swelled with dark pride.

And then, behind her, like deep thunder, she heard his voice roll out.

She could not help but turn around. The Rebbe was there, robed in white. His eyes were obscured from Bluma's view beneath the cowl of his prayer shawl, but still, she could feel them fixing on her, flipping her open like an old book.

The Rebbe's hand was raised, and he was speaking.

"וַאֲפֵלָתְךָ כַּצָּהֳרָיִם" intoned the Rebbe. "וְזָרַח בַּחֹשֶׁךְ אוֹרֶךָ".

The Rebbe had spoken to each candle, lamp, and hearth in the street, and as the final word escaped his lips, he dropped his hand, and they heard and obeyed: from every window, blazing light spilled forth into the road.

The Lileen had outpaced Bluma when she turned around, and ahead of her now, they yowled and spat, swerving, leaping, corralled into the shadows at the center of the street by the sudden flood of light.

Something had happened: there were only five cats now, instead of six. One of them had been caught, banished in the illumination like a shadow in the sun.

Hissing madly, three of the remaining Sisters wheeled about and sped back past Bluma toward the Rebbe, their claws unsheathed, their coats bushy and tall, and Bluma heard the Rebbe speak again.

"רְפָאִים, בַּל-יָקֻמוּ" he said. "מֵתִי, בַּל-יִחְיוּ". And, before Bluma's very eyes, the three attacking cats, mid-leap, wore thin and, screaming, vanished. She saw the remaining two Lileen trip and stumble, stunned, their eyes wide with anger and fear.

But beyond them, Rokhl continued to run, sliding into a wide intersection, scrambling as she turned.

Bluma couldn't allow the girl to get away.

Reaching deep within herself now, she found a final well of strength and raced on, past the stunned Lileen and into the cross-roads. Ahead, she could see the Rebbe's granddaughter, fleeing, running, every window she passed on either side bursting forth with sudden, brilliant light.

"Stop!" she called out. "Wait!" But the Rebbe's granddaughter continued to run, sliding around the next corner.

Bluma followed close behind.

This street was narrow—barely even a street at all—and it was suddenly dark by contrast with the bright street behind. Bluma blinked, trying to acclimate her eyes to the dim.

Was there something up ahead?

The Rebbe was far behind Bluma now, and she was surprised to hear his voice again, as if he spoke from the mouth of every door in Zubinsk.

"עֵינֶיךָ, לְנֹכַח יַבִּיטוּ," whispered the voice of the Rebbe. "וְעַפְעַפֶּיךָ, יַיְשִׁרוּ נֶגְדֶּךָ"

Bluma stopped.

It was as if, by the power of these words, her eyes had changed: still she saw where the darkness lay, but it no longer had the power to hide things from her.

Now she could see, fast approaching in the dim, a small knot of Hasidim dancing along the narrow road, and, in the very center of their circle, a horrible, familiar figure, clapping her hands in time with the dance:

Death was coming down the street.

She was singing, singing a melody to which there were no words, and yet Bluma could not stop herself from hearing a single word, like a shadow of the melody, floating down the alleyway:

Bluuuuuuumaaaaaaa . . .

Something twitched between her fingers, and Bluma looked down.

The spoon. She still held the spoon.

And it was starting—slowly, of its own accord—to spin around its empty basin.

The edges of Bluma's vision began to blur. She could not catch her breath, could not slow her pounding heart. There was something, something heavy, pressing down on her chest, and she felt as if her mind might simply flee in fear.

She was coming.

The Dark One was coming.

And ahead, oblivious, Rokhl ran toward her.

Now Lilith's words rose back up in Bluma's ears:

She will join our Sisterhood, one way or another.

What was Bluma doing? Chasing another girl toward Death?

"Rokhl!" she called out, and far ahead of her, the Rebbe's granddaughter turned back, breath misting in the chill air.

What could Bluma say to her? Where could they be safe?

Rokhl's eyes grew wide. "Who are you?" she said.

Bluma shook her head. "I don't know." Death was drawing near—there was no time. "It doesn't matter."

In the back of her head, Bluma remembered the song sung in synagogue every Sabbath as the Torah scrolls were laid in their ark:

It is a Tree of Life for those who cling to it. . . .

"The synagogue! Come on!"

"Faster, boy," cried Mammon. "Faster!" And, obligingly, Yehuda Leib put on a little burst of extra speed. Only two of the fingernails on his right hand were still attached to the wheelchair; his left hand was completely free.

But time was running short.

Just as they rolled into the intersection, a shock of bright lightning cracked through the sky, and there he was, not half a block distant:

The Rebbe.

There was the Rebbe.

"Stop!" said Mammon in a hoarse whisper. "Stop, stop, stop, stop, stop!"

Now Yehuda Leib fought to still the wheelchair, wrenching its wheels perpendicular to the slope of the hill, slipping, sliding, digging his heels in between the cobbles. He had to squeeze onto his jagged nail ends with his left hand to keep from losing control of the chair, and with a thrill, he felt the brittle nail of his right little finger snap in its mitten.

Only one left now.

"Listen to me carefully," said Mammon. "We must approach slowly, decorously, as if we were only out to take the night air and happened upon him by chance."

Yehuda Leib could not imagine anyone venturing out to take the air in weather such as this, but it hardly mattered. His father's light was there in his coat pocket, warm against his thigh.

He had to sever his last nail, and he had to do it now.

"You will not speak," said Mammon, "under any circumstances. Even if he addresses you directly. Even if *I* address you directly. Is that clear?"

"Yes, my lord," said Yehuda Leib, nodding, but he had barely even heard what the demon had said.

This was the moment.

"Splendid," said Mammon. "Walk on."

He was out of time.

There was no other choice.

"Yes," said Yehuda Leib. "Let's go." And, turning the wheels of the chair to face back down the hill slope, he swung his freed left hand madly, bashing it against his right, once, twice, three times.

"What are you doing?" said Mammon, tension stealing into his reedy little voice. "What, what, what is this?"

With the third swing, Yehuda Leib felt his final fingernail crack and break. The weight of the chair was lifted from him.

He was free.

With a great shove, Yehuda Leib launched Mammon away, confusion, panic, fury rising in the demon's voice as, shaken by the cobbles, he rolled off into the falling snow.

No time to lose.

Yehuda Leib tore the mittens from his hands and drove his fingers into his pocket.

The beautiful warmth of his father filled his bones.

He hadn't imagined it.

He was still here.

With care, Yehuda Leib drew the little glass bottle forth, bright and clear in the snowy night, and, clutching it against his chest, he began to cry softly.

He had to get to the Rebbe.

The Rebbe stood in the middle of the road, breathing hard.

On all sides of him, the blazing hearths and lamps of the street began to gutter and dim.

The smell of dying candles crept into the air.

Something strange was afoot, and the Rebbe did not understand. Once this wedding was done and put behind them, he resolved to question certain Ministers and Messengers of his acquaintance. He resolved to find out.

For the moment, though, things seemed to have been set right—the dead who walked abroad had been banished or chased away; his granddaughter was unpursued, nearly to the safety of the synagogue. It would not do to abandon his vigilance this night, but for now the Rebbe thought he might again retire to the comfort of his rooms.

And yet something was happening. Something was strange.

Even the wind was behaving oddly: now crouching, taut, still and waiting, now thundering, whipping, tearing by.

As if in flight.

As if afraid.

What did the wind know that he did not?

With a sigh, the Rebbe turned. It had been a long time since he had exerted so much effort in one night, and he was not as young as he once had been. His footsteps faltered lightly as he trudged toward bed.

He really must get some rest.

The snow had begun to thicken, the flakes fatter and more numerous than before, and soon the Rebbe could barely make out the shapes of the houses on either side of the road.

For this reason, he heard before he could see: stamping, shuffling feet coming up from behind, a pair of thin, bony hands clapping along in time, and, high above it all, a single voice, singing a wistful, stumbling melody.

The Rebbe was sure he recognized the tune, but he could not for the life of him say what it was.

He turned now and blinked into the snow.

"Hello?" he said.

Through the thick veil of white, he could see obscure shapes, figures: a clutch of young men dancing in a trudging circle, each of their feet falling in time with the clap of the bony hands.

And Someone—Someone in the midst of the dance.

The Rebbe could not see through the snow.

"Hello?" he said again.

The clapping and dancing continued unabated, but with the sound of sudden sighing, now the song broke off.

"Oh," said a voice from the center of the circle. "Oh, holy Rebbe, help me. You must help me."

The Rebbe took a step forward, squinting to see through the snow.

And at just this moment, blue lightning came forking through the sky, and there was a sudden illumination in the street.

In the center of the circle, the Rebbe of Zubinsk saw him: long, thick beard blacker than the night, caftan blacker than the darkness hidden inside your eyes.

The Rebbe of the Dead.

"Rebbe?"

Yehuda Leib was enfolded in snow that fell thicker and thicker by the minute. "Rebbe, I need your help."

He could see so little now. The street seemed like a wash of featureless white. Was he even headed in the right direction?

"Rebbe, please!"

But there was no answer.

Carefully, foot over foot, Yehuda Leib moved forward. Every

now and again he heard a hint from the road ahead: murmuring voices, shuffling feet, snatches of a bony rhythm.

"Rebbe?" he called, his voice no more than a hoarse whisper.

He had seen the holy man. He knew he had.

Gradually, his tenuous steps slowed and then stopped.

Now that his feet were still, he was sure he could hear something else—something ragged.

Something near.

Yehuda Leib turned his head and squeezed his eyes shut. Sure enough, there it was, clear and close:

Breathing. Raspy, reedy breath.

"Hello?" said Yehuda Leib into the gloom.

For a moment, the breathing broke off.

And then, all of a sudden, Mammon struck, a furious, snarling tangle of sharp teeth and tearing fingers, and he was on Yehuda Leib's back, smashing him into the ground, bashing his face against the snowy cobbles, twisting and tearing at his hair, spitting venomous words like *cheating* and *thief* and *show you* and *pay*, and Yehuda Leib elbowed and pushed and kicked, and somehow he managed to throw the demon from his back, but the little glowing glass bottle slipped from his fingers and flew across the snowy street, and he was scrambling, he was so cold, chasing its light into the darkness, but again Mammon pounced and hit him hard, and his sharp teeth drove into Yehuda Leib's shoulder, and the boy cried out and rolled, throwing his weight atop the demon, and he was free again, and the light, the light, he had to get to the light, but now Mammon saw it and recognized it, and in a tight, rasping snarl, "Mine," he said, "it's mine, it's mine!" and swiftly he scuttled over the snowy road to scoop it up in his grasping fingers.

And at the sight of Mammon's sick little smile, his dark eyes glowing in the light of his departed father, Yehuda Leib's fury stirred and rose.

"Get your hands off him," he said.

And Mammon began to laugh.

Yehuda Leib launched himself across the street, grabbed the little demon by the lapels of his coat, and slammed him again and again against the snowy ground, and all the while, crazed, manic, the demon was repeating it—*it's mine, it's mine*—and with the third impact, the glowing glass bottle slipped from his clutching fingers, and Yehuda Leib hurled the demon aside and began to crawl toward it, but in a flash, Mammon was on top of him, laying all his weight between Yehuda Leib's shoulder blades, twisting his reaching arm painfully back, smashing his face down into the snow, and "Oh no, you don't," he said, "that's not yours, you dirty little thief," and Yehuda Leib couldn't move him, couldn't budge, couldn't even turn his face toward the light, and he thought his arm would break, and he called out:

"Rebbe, Rebbe, please!"

And then he saw it, lying just where it had been dropped, only an arm's length distant, crumpled, dark, trampled over in the snow: his mitten.

His salt-filled mitten.

Mammon was exultant, laughing, twisting his arm, reaching for the light with his long, bare toes, and he failed to notice Yehuda Leib's other arm stretching out through the snow.

With a buck and a flip, Yehuda Leib threw Mammon from his back, and, grabbing, sprinkling, he sent a hail of salt raining down on top of him.

There was a sudden stillness.

Slowly, Mammon began to sizzle, and then to smoke. Large

splotchy burns materialized in a spray across his skin where the salt had fallen. Clawing at his face and rolling in the snow, Mammon retreated backward into the snowy night with a bloodcurdling screech.

And, just like that, his terror and anger echoing behind him, Mammon was gone.

Yehuda Leib wasted no time. In the barest moment, he had the light in his hands again, and he called out once more:

"Rebbe!"

The snow fell softly, and the Messenger of Death drew near the Rebbe of Zubinsk. Slowly, the dancing Hasidim began to circle them both.

"Holy Rebbe," said the Dark One with a sigh. "Oh, holy Rebbe. They have taught me a new and cruel sorrow."

"Who?" said the Rebbe of Zubinsk.

"Your Hasidim," said the Dark One. "They have given me *welcome*. They have called me *friend*. And only I know that they are mistaken."

The Rebbe frowned. "How?"

The Dark One shook his head as if to dislodge this question from his ear. "Hmm?"

"How do you know that they are mistaken?"

"Why, I know it."

The Rebbe's frown deepened. "*How?*"

There was a cry from the darkness—somewhere, nearby, a boy in distress—and the Rebbe turned over his shoulder to look.

There, beyond the dancers, in the gloomy fall of snow, could he see a shining light?

"I shall tell you," said the Dark One, and the Rebbe turned

back. "I have met every man, every woman, every child whose time has ever come to pass. Sometimes the suffering are gladdened by my approach, but when the moment finally comes to look me in the face, no one, not one of them, has ever greeted me as a friend."

Now the Rebbe chuckled, and he shook his head softly. "You, my friend, are a fool."

And again, a sound from over his shoulder: a bloodcurdling screech. The Rebbe turned swiftly. There was danger in the darkness, and someone had called for his help.

"Then teach me, Rebbe," said the Dark One. "Teach me to be a fool no longer. I cannot bear this *sorrow*."

"Time is short," said the Rebbe with a shake of his head. "I cannot teach you. Only consider this: Two are required to meet in friendship. And to decline to shake the outstretched hand because someday it will no longer be there is as foolish as to decline to eat dinner because someday the plate shall be empty. Nothing at all is permanent. Not even you."

"Then what ought I to do?"

The Rebbe had just opened his mouth to answer when again, from over his shoulder, Yehuda Leib's voice came cutting through the night:

"Rebbe!"

It was certain. There was a flickering light in the darkness. The Rebbe was needed.

But the Dark One needed him too.

As the Rebbe turned to go, Death reached out with his bare bony hand.

And no man—no matter how holy—may feel the hand of Death and live.

The moment the bony hands ceased their clapping to reach out for the Rebbe, the dance was at its end. As if waking from a dark dream, the five Hasidim blinked their woozy eyes in the snowy gloom.

And what they saw was terrible.

Death stood in their midst, ancient and ragged, reaching out with twiggy thin fingers, grasping desperately for their holy Rebbe.

The Rebbe was turning, turning away, his face drawn with concern, turning away to help.

As one, the bewildered Hasidim called out in terror and in warning.

But it was too late.

The long fingers of Death caught on the hem of the Rebbe's prayer shawl, and he fell.

Until this moment, the wind, as a mark of respect, had observed the custom of parting on either side of the holy Rebbe, but now, as if crying out in grief, the full force of its strength went tearing indiscriminately through Zubinsk, and as the five young Hasidim dashed forward, forward to catch their Rebbe, the gale tore screaming past them on every side.

When the swift storm passed, there was stillness in the road. The clouds above had been washed away, taking the falling snow with them. Only the stars were left to twinkle coldly, high above.

The Hasidim were consumed in their distress, cradling the holy Rebbe where he had fallen in the street, checking for breath, for warmth, for a beating heart, calling out to *anyone, anyone* for help.

And several feet away, all but forgotten, was the Dark One, lurking, grief-stricken, beneath the shadowy eaves of a house.

What had he done? He had not meant to harm the Rebbe—nothing could've been further from his heart.

"He's breathing," said one of the Hasidim. "He's still breathing. Someone, anyone, help!"

The Dark One had been foolish. He should never have come to Zubinsk, never have taken up with these rejoicing Hasidim. His head was swimming—with drink, with shame, with sorrow, with rage.

Before him in the street, he could see the holy Rebbe, still and stony, cradled in the arms of one of his Hasidim.

Why had he turned away?

Why?

And then the Dark One lifted up his eyes, and at the far end of the snowy street, clear in the knife-sharp starlight, the Dark One saw the reason:

Yehuda Leib.

"You," said the Dark One. It was only a whisper, but Yehuda Leib heard it loud and clear from across the crowding road—a charge, a prosecution:

You.

His heart lurched, and without looking back, Yehuda Leib turned and tried to make himself scarce.

But he had been seen, and he knew it.

"I see you there," said the voice behind him. "You cannot run from me. I see you, Yehuda Leib!"

Yehuda Leib swung around a narrow corner, and his feet skidded and came to a stop. In front of him, a short alleyway ran no more than six feet deep before ending in a solid brick wall plastered over with faded handbills and torn advertisements. All around him, the buildings rose, two, three stories into the sky.

Yehuda Leib wheeled about.

The Dark Messenger was closing in. There was no escape.

"You," said the Dark One.

"Stay back," said Yehuda Leib.

"Why did you call out to the Rebbe?"

"What business is it of yours?"

"It was not his time," said the Dark One. "What have you done?"

Yehuda Leib was flabbergasted. "What have *I* done? What have *you* done?"

The Dark One scoffed. "You know nothing, boy."

"Oh no?" said Yehuda Leib. "I know this: if I'd called out to the Rebbe and you hadn't been there, I'd be talking to *him* right now instead of *you*."

"But if you hadn't—"

"Then what?" said Yehuda Leib, taking a lunging step forward. "What wouldn't have happened? Finish the sentence."

"You are nothing, boy," said the Dark Messenger. "You are a buzzing gnat. I shall be talking with kings when the dust that was your bones has all blown away."

"That changes nothing," said Yehuda Leib. "When my bones have blown away, you will still bear the guilt for what you've done."

With a growl, the Dark One lifted his hand to wipe the little gnat away, and Yehuda Leib, shying back, found himself clutching instinctively at the light in his pocket.

The Dark One stopped, his hand high in the air. "What have you got in your pocket?"

Yehuda Leib swallowed. "Nothing."

The Dark One's cold eyes twinkled like stars in the frigid sky. "Don't lie to me."

Yehuda Leib shook his head quickly. "It's nothing."

"Do you wish to know what happened to the Rebbe, Yehuda Leib?" said the Dark One, the sound of a sick grin creeping into his voice. "My bare finger—this one here—caught on the hem of his prayer shawl. That alone was sufficient to fell a man as holy and as potent as he."

Yehuda Leib was still clutching at his glowing pocket. "You can't have it."

"You are meddling with powers you cannot possibly comprehend," said the Dark One, shaking his head. "Give him to me, boy. Now."

Yehuda Leib could feel the cold brick wall against his back. There was nowhere to go, nowhere to run.

"You'll have to kill me first," said Yehuda Leib.

"Ha!" said the Dark One. "Do not tempt me."

"I mean it," said Yehuda Leib.

The Dark One shook his head. "Perhaps you do," he said. "But you have no idea what it is that you mean."

All of a sudden, Yehuda Leib found that he could not speak without screaming. "I know perfectly well!" he said, tears stinging his eyes. "I watched him die!"

Now the Dark One lost all patience. "And still you continue to meddle! Do you realize that if you hadn't run from Tupik, your father would still be alive? Do you not realize that he died because of *you*?"

"Liar!" Yehuda Leib lunged forward, fists swinging blindly in the swimming of his tears.

If, in taking hold of Yehuda Leib, the Dark One's bare hands had come into contact with even so much as a thread of his clothing, our story would've ended here; it was only by Yehuda Leib's very good fortune that the Dark One managed to cover his hands with his sleeves in time.

But it did not feel like good fortune at all.

With icy fury, the Dark One lifted Yehuda Leib from the ground and slammed him hard against the brick wall. His mouth was beside the boy's ear, his body close and cold, and Yehuda Leib could smell him: rot and vodka, and a million years of open road.

"I never lie, Yehuda Leib," he whispered. "*Never*. And I shall prove it to you. These shall be your final moments: You will be alone. And you will be frightened. Nothing and no one will come forth to save you. And when your time comes, you shall look me in the face, and you shall tell me that I was right."

One of the Dark Messenger's strong hands was sufficient to pin the boy there against the wall, feet dangling in the winter night, and he reached the long, twiggy fingers of the other into Yehuda Leib's glowing pocket and took back the light, which sputtered, flickering in his grasp.

With disgust, the Dark One dropped Yehuda Leib to the ground and tucked the little bottle deep into the blackness of his coat.

"Take my advice, boy," he said. "Go home. Do what you're told."

And, leaving Yehuda Leib in a sobbing heap on the cobbles, the Angel of Death turned and began to stumble away.

"Nothing at all is permanent," said Death into the night. "Not even you."

CHAPTER TEN

The Next Mourning

That night, Yehuda Leib slept where he'd fallen, crumpled at the foot of a dead end. Bluma slept beside the Rebbe's granddaughter on the rostrum of the Great Synagogue of Zubinsk, and even the Messenger of Death, accustomed as it was to remaining awake for millennia, stumbled into the cemetery and passed out in an empty grave, scattering imps and goblins in its wake.

But on the other side of the forest in silent Tupik, warm beneath the blankets of his own bed, Issur Frumkin could not sleep a wink.

A small patch of moonlight.

Yehuda Leib, looking very small.

A pool of blood.

A dead man.

He tried to forget, tried to push the memory out of his mind, but no matter how he tossed and turned and squeezed his eyes shut, still, there he was: Avimelekh, bleeding, flat on his back, boots squirming in the churned and slushy snow.

The look in his eyes: knowledge—understanding.

Issur could still feel the reverberation all the way up to his elbow, the way the pot had buzzed and hummed at the impact, and as he lay in bed trying to force his memory to look away, he kneaded the flesh of his arm as if trying to blot the sensation out.

He had never meant to hurt the man.

He'd just wanted to help.

He had to stop thinking about it, had to replace the memory with something else, something pleasant, something that would allow him to drift peacefully off and get some rest.

The smell of Sabbath preparations: warm bread and roasting meat.

The glow of candles.

Light.

With effort, Issur slowed his breathing. Bit by bit, his muscles slackened.

After a short time, he began to doze.

But outside the hallway window stood a bare tree, and when the wind stirred, the knobbled knuckles of its twiggy fingers brushed against the window glass. And from the inside of his bedroom, this sounded very much like rattling spurs.

Issur tore back his bedroom door and peered out into the empty corridor.

No. There was no one here: only the shadow of the tree on the wall, shifting and shuckling in the moonlight.

There was no one.

But at the far end of the corridor, where the stairs descended into his father's shop below, darkness gathered thick like dust in the corner.

He couldn't see.

Back into his room he went, fingers shaking at the matchbox, eager to make a little light, to throw back the curtain of darkness and see what hid beneath.

There was nothing, of course, nothing and no one to see: not in the hallway, not on the stairs, not even in his father's butcher shop below.

But somehow he didn't believe his eyes.

In the stillness, the candlelight flickered and danced on the cool, clean blades of his father's knives.

He began to feel it before he even turned back to the staircase: the lurking certainty that he would find no rest until he *did something*.

But what? What could he do?

Tears began to sting his eyes.

"I'm sorry," he whispered, as much to himself as to anyone else. "I'm sorry."

But this was not to be enough.

The flame of Issur's candle flickered, guttered with sudden movement as he turned to climb back up the stairs. In the narrow passage of the staircase, jumping shadows leapt up on all sides, and he was there, Avimelekh, as clear as could be, looming up on his rearing black stallion, his black coat filling the stairway, his dark eyes shining behind his bushy beard, and Issur cried out and stumbled back, and he fell and dropped his candle to the floor, and it died out in a narrow plume of smoke.

Shadows.

Only shadows.

This couldn't continue. He had to do something.

And so Issur climbed to his feet, went outside, and began to harness the poor, weary Frumkin donkey once more.

It took him nearly two hours to make his way back to the place where it had happened, and by the time Issur arrived, the chill of the night had soaked into his bones.

This was it: the place was unmistakable.

But the body was gone.

It wasn't clear what had happened. Everything was covered over in the creeping obscurity of fresh-fallen snow. The wide pool of blood was rosy and faint, the ruts and footprints thickened, filling in. Issur could see where Avimelekh had lain, that his body had been moved, turned, lifted.

But what had been done with him, he could not say.

Once more, Issur's eyes began to brim with tears. He didn't know precisely how he'd thought to accomplish it, but on his long journey into the forest, he'd come to hope that he might give the man a proper burial.

He certainly couldn't do that now.

With a sigh, Issur hopped down from the cart and set about turning the donkey back toward Tupik.

What else was there to do?

He was just about to climb up and make his unhappy way home when, glancing over his shoulder for one last look at the fateful spot, his eye caught on an unevenness, a strange, protruding wrinkle in the rosy snow.

Drawing close, he reached out and pulled it up, rough and stiff with blood:

Yehuda Leib's red woolen scarf.

And this is how it came to pass that Issur Frumkin stood, chilled to the bone, over a shallow hole he had dug in the Tupik cemetery as the first glimmer of dawn stole into the village.

Carefully, with ceremony, he folded the scarf and laid it in the ground.

"I'm sorry," whispered Issur Frumkin, choking back a sob, and because he didn't know what else to do with them, he put his hands into his pockets.

What was this? Something cold against his fingers: a little disc of metal.

Yes, yes, of course. The coin Yehuda Leib had given him. It was strange, like no other coin he had ever seen: an open eye on one face and a closed eye on the other.

It didn't seem right to keep it.

And so, with care, Issur Frumkin bent low and placed the battered gray coin on top of the scarf, closed eye up. That felt right.

But it was very hard to look at—the blood and the scarf, the unchangeably closed eye—and quickly, impulsively, he pushed dirt in on top of them, filling the little grave.

There. That was it.

Nothing more to be done.

Without looking back, Issur Frumkin made his way down the hill toward his bed.

The sun was beginning to rise.

The creak of a heavy door. The murmuring of voices.

Morning sun.

Inside Bluma's eyelids, everything was warm, a cocoon of amber blush, and when she finally forced herself to open her eyes, she immediately regretted it.

The Great Synagogue of Zubinsk was nothing like the homey little prayer house at the center of Tupik. There, the synagogue walls were of painted wood—they seemed to drink in the warmth of the breath spilled in prayer, as if holding it safe for later—but here, everything was cold polished stone and figured metal.

Bluma shivered and rolled over.

She was alone. The pew upon which Rokhl had slept was empty.

She was alone.

But not quite.

The sharp spoon dug painfully into her hip.

With a wince, Bluma pulled the spoon up from her apron. Resting the handle in her palm, she ran the pad of her thumb through its cool basin and up across its edge.

It was almost—almost—beautiful.

A deep yawn bubbled up inside Bluma. She was terribly, terribly tired, more tired than any single night's sleep could ever wash away. Of all things in the world, she wanted most just to go home—home, where the air was fragrant with the warmth of baking, where she could rest in a bed that knew her shape.

But it was not safe in her bed. It wasn't even safe beneath it.

That was where Death had found her.

And as hard as she ran, she was beginning to understand, Death would always follow.

She always came back.

Bluma's fingers began to tremble, her breathing growing shallow.

She didn't want to see the Dark Lady ever again.

Ever.

She had taken a good first step in doing away with her face, but it was not enough. Still the Dark Lady came, calling out her name:

Bluuuuuuumaaaaaaa . . .

But Lilith had mentioned someone in the Far Country who might be able to help.

Who had it been?

With a start, Bluma realized: the sun had risen above the rooftops, but the synagogue was completely empty. And, today of all days, it should've been packed with worshippers at their morning prayers.

Where was everyone?

Softly, as if loath to disturb the thick silence of the sanctuary, Bluma crept out the front door.

There were people everywhere, and it was early still—on a regular day, only a small number would have been abroad at this hour, aside from those at prayer.

At first Bluma thought it must've been the wedding that was causing the excitement, but before long, it became clear that this was not the case.

Something had happened in the night.

Something bad.

From all corners of the city, feet seemed to rush toward one central spot like bathwater to the drain, and soon Bluma was caught up and carried in the flow. By the time they spilled out into the wide, crowded road to which they were headed, she'd heard words like *Rebbe* and *fell* and *very serious* spoken in enough voices to have a guess at what had happened.

But nothing could've prepared her for the scene that met her eyes.

The street was packed, shoulder to shoulder, the press of people filling the road, passing through the Rebbe's front door, cramming the sanctuary in the front room, climbing the stairs, extending all the way up to the very threshold of the bedroom where he lay.

Everywhere, there were Hasidim, swaying back and forth, cycling manically through the Book of Psalms, praying for a full and speedy recovery; everywhere, long beards were wet with tears.

Bluma began to shove and shimmy her way through the crowd, and once she managed to make her way past the Rebbe's door, she had become so used to everyone facing in one direction—toward the Rebbe's house—that she spotted him immediately.

He was facing the other way, several doors down, his arms folded, his eyes fixed firmly on the shadowy windows above a well-appointed general store on the other side of the street:

Yehuda Leib, wan and sharp-edged—just as he'd been the night before.

By the time Bluma reached him, Yehuda Leib had taken notice of her staring. For a long moment, they stood regarding one another, their ears flooded with a cacophony of psalms.

Finally, "Yehuda Leib?" said Bluma.

And "Bluma," he replied. "So it is you. What happened to your face?"

"What happened to your face?"

Bluma and Yehuda Leib stood in a nearby backyard to which they had retreated for a bit of privacy.

"You wouldn't believe me if I told you," said Bluma.

"I think I might," said Yehuda Leib.

Bluma sighed. Maybe he would—but everyone knows: believing is not the same thing as understanding.

"I traded it, I suppose," she said.

"For what?" said Yehuda Leib.

"For not having to have a face anymore," said Bluma. "A face that people recognize."

She expected Yehuda Leib to scoff at this, but he didn't—he frowned, as if considering the value of this price, and then nodded lightly.

"And what about you?" said Bluma. "What happened to you?"

There was a faraway look in Yehuda Leib's eyes. "I don't quite know," he said.

"Your hair's grown long," said Bluma.

"Has it?" said Yehuda Leib, feeling at the nape of his neck. "I slept for a long time, I think."

This seemed perfectly reasonable to Bluma, for though only a day and a night had passed since they'd stood together at the threshold of her parents' house, she had learned well the ways in which the Far Country can warp and stretch time. One day could be a moment, one night an eternity.

"There was a demon," said Yehuda Leib, but Bluma spoke up sharply. "I don't care for that word," she said. It was Lilith's phrase, and it was out of her mouth before she'd even managed to consider whether or not it was true.

Yehuda Leib shrugged. "Maybe we've met different kinds of demons."

"I expect we have," said Bluma.

But Yehuda Leib was preoccupied. His eyes, beautiful and sharp, were glazed, fixed, as if he were staring at something very, very far away.

"Bluma," said Yehuda Leib. "I met my father."

"Your father?" said Bluma. "I always thought he was dead."

Yehuda Leib shook his head insistently. "He isn't. Well, he wasn't." And then, quietly: "He won't be."

"What was he like?" said Bluma.

"Scary," said Yehuda Leib. "Terrifying. But also warm. Familiar. And strange. I don't know. I didn't get enough time."

"I'm sorry," said Bluma.

And suddenly, Yehuda Leib's faraway gaze was sharp and near again. "Why?" he said.

Bluma shrugged. "Because if you wanted more time with him, I think you should've gotten it."

Yehuda Leib averted his eyes and began to chew at the inside of his lower lip. "Bluma," he said. "I'm going back."

"What?" said Bluma. "To Tupik?"

"No," said Yehuda Leib.

For a moment, she considered asking him where, then, he meant to go.

But they both knew.

"Why?"

"Because," said Yehuda Leib, "he's a bully. And a tyrant."

"Who is?" said Bluma. "Your father?"

"No," said Yehuda Leib. "The Dark One."

"Oh, I know her," said Bluma.

And though they spoke of Death with different words, neither noticed. For everyone knows: those who walk in the shadow of Death can see only its nearest face.

"You do?"

"She tried to catch me in Tupik."

Yehuda Leib's expression fell.

"Oh," said Yehuda Leib. "Oh, Bluma, I'm so sorry."

Bluma shrugged and slotted her hands into her pockets.

"What are you going to do?" said Yehuda Leib. "Keep running?"

She shook her head. "There's no running fast enough."

At this, Yehuda Leib nodded.

"And what about you?" said Bluma.

"I'm going to get my father back," said Yehuda Leib. "I'm going to fight against the Dark One. And I'm going to win."

Yehuda Leib's eyes were blazing. Bluma had never seen such determination in her life. Idly, hand in her pocket, she ran the pad of her thumb through the basin of her spoon.

"Good," she said. "Then I'll come with you."

Yehuda Leib grimaced, and then, after a moment, he spoke. "All right."

This took Bluma by surprise. She'd been prepared to argue, to explain how no one on their side of the Cemetery had ever managed to evade Death before, how she had reason to believe there were beings in the Far Country who had the resources to help her.

"Aren't you going to try and talk me out of it?" said Bluma.

Yehuda Leib shrugged. "Do you want me to?"

Bluma shook her head.

"Then what good would it do?" said Yehuda Leib.

And softly, in the empty aloneness the spoon had begun to carve out inside her, something warm began to flicker and glow.

Yehuda Leib was not yet prepared to leave—his thoughts were fixed on a set of shadowy windows above a nearby general store—but daylight was in short supply in that season, and neither he nor Bluma relished the thought of setting out after dark.

At first Yehuda Leib suggested meeting back up by the wrought-iron gates of Zubinsk's main cemetery, but Bluma was resistant—that place made her skin crawl.

"No," she said. "I bet it's still packed with them."

Yehuda Leib was not so sure, but Bluma was adamant.

"But how else can we get back in?" said Yehuda Leib.

Bluma swallowed. "There's a second cemetery," she said. Her stomach squirmed as she told Yehuda Leib how to find the entrance to the narrow alleyway. What if Lilith was still there?

"Why don't I just come with you now?" said Bluma, but Yehuda Leib shook his head.

"There's something I've got to do," said Yehuda Leib. "Alone. I'll meet you there."

Bluma began to chew on her lower lip. "And you're sure we'll be able to get through?"

"Not yet," said Yehuda Leib. "Give me an hour."

But as Bluma turned to go, something made her freeze in her tracks.

"Oh no," said Bluma, her teeth gritted hard. "Oh no."

"What is it?" said Yehuda Leib.

Bluma turned back. "Don't look," she whispered, "but up there on the rooftop—"

"The cat?"

"Yes," said Bluma.

"It's been there since we arrived."

"Yehuda Leib," said Bluma as quietly as she could, "I think I'm being followed."

This was trouble. Bluma's breathing began to quicken.

"Oh no," she said again. "Oh no, what do I do?"

"It's all right," said Yehuda Leib softly. "Do you think you're in danger?"

"No," said Bluma. "No, I think there would be more if they meant to attack."

"Good," said Yehuda Leib. "That's good. Can you lose her?"

Bluma swallowed. "I'll try."

"All right," said Yehuda Leib. "One hour."

"One hour," said Bluma.

"Go."

The light in the street was cold and gray as Yehuda Leib made his way behind the backs of the fervently praying Hasidim toward the entrance of the general store. The front windows were large, the glass so clean it sparkled, but little of the diffuse, cloudy sunlight managed to penetrate the gloomy shop.

Yehuda Leib tried the doorknob, and it turned smoothly in his hand. He stepped inside, swinging the door shut behind him, and in the sudden quiet of the still shop, the tinkle of the small entrance bell above seemed deafening.

"Hello?" said Yehuda Leib, in as loud a whisper as he could muster.

There was no answer.

Lightly, he began to move farther into the shop. It was clearly a prosperous establishment: despite signs of heavy wear on the floor-boards and countertops, the fixtures were in fine repair—dustless, polished to a high sheen.

The merchandise, too, was of good quality: sturdy suits and stylish dresses, fragrant coffee beans and teas. There were jars full of preserved fruit, dry goods in sacks and barrels, the finest hand tools and farm implements that money could buy, their hafts and blades gleaming. Yehuda Leib had never seen so many new things in one place before: crisp umbrellas, cushy baby carriages, shelves and shelves full of stiff-spined books, magazines, newspapers. His stomach moaned loudly as he passed a display of sweets in brightly colored packages, but he moved swiftly on.

He'd just seen it: a gash of bright light leaking from the back-room door.

Carefully, Yehuda Leib approached and pulled it open.

At first he thought the room was empty, the warm lamplight spilling out over a sturdy desk strewn with ledgers and account books. There was a cast-iron stove in the near corner, its door hanging open to reveal a fire at the very furthest extremity of its life. The chair behind the desk was shoved away on the diagonal, its backrest filling the shoulders of a man's suit jacket, and, beyond, on the rear wall, a set of stairs climbed up to the apartment above the shop.

With a deep breath, Yehuda Leib stepped in, crossing rapidly toward the stairs, but as he came around the desk, he jumped:

There, on the floor, cross-legged before the open maw of a large safe, was a man, feverishly working, sodden with sweat. His tie was undone, his sleeves pushed up, and all around him on the floor were dozens of piles of cash.

Yehuda Leib's gasp awoke the man from his frantic counting, and with a start, he reached deep into the safe and pulled out a wicked-looking pistol, which he pointed straight into Yehuda Leib's face.

"It's mine!" he yelled, spittle flying from his lips. "It's mine! You can't have any of it!"

His eyes were bloodshot and wide, and Yehuda Leib had no doubt at all that the man would pull the trigger if he felt the need.

"I don't want it!" said Yehuda Leib. "I don't want anything!"

The mad merchant laughed as if he couldn't possibly believe this, and with his free hand he began raking up wads of banknotes and shoving them into his pockets. "Sure," he said. "Sure you don't. Then why are you here?"

What could he say?

"I . . ."

He couldn't tell the truth—that much was certain.

"I have a delivery," said Yehuda Leib.

"A delivery?"

"Yes," said Yehuda Leib. "Complimentary samples."

At this, the merchant lifted his pistol away from Yehuda Leib.

"Complimentary?" said the merchant hungrily.

Yehuda Leib nodded.

"Fine," said the merchant, and he laid the pistol back inside the safe. "Bring it around back. I'll look through it later."

And with that, he began to smooth and unfurl what he'd wadded into his pockets, counting as he went.

Slowly, Yehuda Leib exhaled. The cracked lips of the merchant fluttered and mumbled as he counted and recounted his bills.

Nothing else in the world seemed to matter to him.

Carefully, quietly, Yehuda Leib made his way up the stairs, and when he emerged into a dim corridor above, he was immediately on his guard.

A rich crystal chandelier hung overhead; all but one of the candles it bore had burned out. A tall young woman in an evening dress of pale blue satin stood beneath it in the flickering light, bare inches away from her image in the mirror. She turned sharply at the sound of Yehuda Leib's arrival, her eyes staring, bloodshot, just like the man's below.

"Is it enough?" she said. Her voice was tight with panic. "I don't think it's enough."

She was wearing fine white gloves, and there was at least one ring on each of her fingers. Bangles and bracelets of gold and silver lined her arms up to the elbow, and her neck was laden with layer upon layer of pearls and pendants, beads and lockets, ribbons and chains. Her face was caked with rouge, and the rivulets of black that dripped from her eyes showed that she had been crying.

"Do you think it's enough?"

Her eyes were locked frantically on Yehuda Leib's. Three different tiaras were plaited into her hair.

Yehuda Leib swallowed hard and gestured over her shoulder with his chin. "Look again."

This did the trick. With a swift shushing of satin, the young woman turned back, surveyed herself in the mirror, and resumed her soft sobbing. Yehuda Leib was forgotten.

Quietly, Yehuda Leib pushed his way through the front door of the apartment and into the well-appointed sitting room.

There was a fire crackling in the hearth. Someone was seated in a high-backed armchair, staring into the flames.

Slowly, Yehuda Leib made his way around the edge of the room, keeping his distance, until he could see the little man.

Yehuda Leib's stomach dropped. His heart began to race. The spectacles were cracked, and the face was covered in a spray of splotchy red burns, but he had been right.

It was definitely him.

Yehuda Leib cleared his throat softly. "My lord," he said.

The beady black eyes flashed with reflected fire as they turned toward Yehuda Leib.

"*You*," said Mammon.

It was long before and far away that Private Yankev Pasternak of the Tenth Division of the Imperial Army, Tomsky Regiment, met his end.

It happened on an early November morning in a foggy ravine outside Sevastopol. Having been garrisoned in the city, the Tomsky men set out before dawn, taking up their positions under cover of darkness. Pasternak was nervous, but he was always nervous before an engagement—it was a kind of preparation, like laying a fuse.

The ravine was narrow—so narrow that Pasternak wondered if there would be room to maneuver—and the combined nerves of the six thousand or so men filled it to its brim like a tin cup with acrid sweat.

Pasternak checked and double-checked: musket primed and loaded, bayonet firmly fixed. Some men chattered, whispering about everything and nothing to tamp down their fear, but Pasternak didn't say a word; Pasternak checked and double-checked.

Primed and loaded.

Fixed.

The order finally came to advance as dawn spilled into the foggy morning. Behind them, far away, all the churches of Sevastopol began to toll out their bells in a fury of pealing to spur them on.

Forward.

But Pasternak had been right. The ravine was very narrow, and the British had set pickets ahead. They were firing by the time Pasternak reached the choke point. There were already bodies underfoot.

The fog was very thick. All he could see was blossoms of musket fire flaring out in the gloom.

Now his nerves were truly ablaze. Now he was ready to kill anything that moved.

In his final moment, Yankev Pasternak thought he saw one of the Brits rushing forward through the fog—a soldier in a black, black uniform, blacker than the darkness he would soon find hidden inside his eyes—but before the figure resolved, a musket ball rang through his helmet like a bell.

His eyes closed.

And this was the end of Private Yankev Pasternak.

But Pasternak didn't know that. As far as Pasternak knew, he woke again in the aftermath of the battle, rising up from the morass of corpses into an empty ravine.

Everything was still.

His head ached terribly.

But the fog smelled sharply of spent powder, and somewhere nearby—he couldn't quite say where—he could still hear the popping of gunfire, the grunt and the groan of striving men.

Pasternak had died with nerves ablaze, and so that was how he remained: embattled, terrified, bloodthirsty.

He was alone on the battlefield. He had to find the others.

And so he retreated through the fog, bayonet at the ready, prepared to kill anything that moved.

And in this manner, he made his way into the Far Country.

"You there!"

Pasternak wheeled about, his bayonet forward, as an officer on horseback cantered up through the fog.

"What are you doing skulking around out here?"

Pasternak stared. Speech was supposed to fire from the barrel of his mouth, but he could not quite recall how it was done.

"You're not a deserter, are you?"

At this dangerous and insulting insinuation, Pasternak let out a percussive "No, sir!"

"Well, come on, then," said the officer. "The muster point's just beyond the ridge."

The officer turned his mount sharply and made to spur it on. "What are you waiting for, soldier?"

The noise of battle—thudding artillery, screaming horses—seemed to be growing louder in Pasternak's ears with every second.

But something was strange.

Pasternak had never seen an officer with slit-pupil eyes before. The cockade in the officer's hat was made not of ordinary ribbon, but of badly bloodied bandaging knotted into a rosette, and what was more, the mount beneath him was in an extreme state of decay, its bleached white ribs exposed beneath the saddle on its back.

What army did the officer belong to? What army did Yankev belong to? These were indispensably important questions.

But it is impossible to think clearly when your nerves are ablaze.

"Move!" roared the fox-eyed officer. "On the double!" And Pasternak began to scramble up toward the muster point beyond the ridge.

In this way, Yankev Pasternak was absorbed into the Magog Regiment of the 779th Division of the Army of the Dead, under the command of Lord High General Dumah, Whose Name Means Silence.

And it was in this capacity that, years and years after his death, Pasternak would emerge from the gates of the cemetery of Zubinsk, still wearing the tawny overcoat and black spiked helmet in which he had died, the wound that had killed him still leaking turbid brown blood.

Beside Pasternak were two other dead soldiers—a small detachment of scouts with very specific orders:

To find, and at all costs to obtain, the girl named Bluma.

CHAPTER ELEVEN

Onward and Inward

Unless you were looking very closely, you wouldn't have seen her.

The cat had come to rest at the very peak of the roof, her ragged gray coat blending in with the dull sheet of heavy cloud above. She would not normally have allowed herself to sit out in the open like this, but everyone's eyes were cast low this morning.

There was an atmosphere of despair weighing on the heads of the Zubinskers. No one would be looking to the rooftops today.

It did not precisely please her, this despairing; that would not have been right to say. After all, last night's events had been nearly as disastrous for the Lileen as they'd been for the Hasidim. But there was something she appreciated in seeing the shock on the faces of the living.

They were always so surprised when things didn't go their way.

She'd had to get used to that feeling long, long ago.

The cat tightened her crouched legs, preparing to jump— Bluma was moving fast—and she leapt down from the roof, landing lightly in the snowy street below. She was bounding quickly, determined to keep sight of Bluma as she made her way around a corner, when the darkness fell.

Immediately her claws were bared, and she yowled and spat, her teeth lashing out in whatever direction they could, but the heavy burlap sack was cinched tight.

She'd been caught.

Presently, a voice spoke, and she stilled her thrashing rage just long enough to listen.

"Now, now," said the voice. "Don't worry. All we want is a little information, and then we'll happily send you back to Aunty Lilith."

With a scream, the cat bit out at the hand that held the burlap, and she fell awkwardly, dropped hard onto the frozen ground.

"Well, that wasn't very nice," said the voice above, and with a swift kick, one of the soldiers sent the sack, cat and all, glancing hard against a brick wall.

"Let me out!" screeched the cat.

"Answer one question for us, and we'll be happy to."

"I have nothing to say to you."

"Oh," said the soldier's voice. "I'd reconsider if I were you. Lord High General Dumah of the Army of the Dead is always very grateful for useful information."

"Your general is a cadaverous hooligan bastard, and the Sisterhood of the Lileen want nothing that he has to offer."

One of the soldiers gave a long, disappointed sigh.

"That," said the voice, "doesn't seem like a wise position to take under these circumstances." And he lifted the burlap sack from the cold ground and flung it against the wall with all his might.

"Now tell me," said the voice of the soldier to the dazed cat in the bag. "Where is the Bluma girl?"

"You," said Mammon, his beady black eyes ablaze with reflected firelight. "I ought to rip your throat out with my teeth. I ought to bury you beneath an outhouse. I ought to skin you alive and sell you for rat food."

Despite his threats, Mammon had shied back into the wide arms of his chair.

The salt must've made quite an impression.

"Yes," said Yehuda Leib. "Yes."

"What do you mean, *yes?*" spat Mammon.

"I mean," said Yehuda Leib, "that I can understand why you feel that way."

"You can understand?" said Mammon incredulously. "You assaulted me!"

Yehuda Leib sighed. "I think you'll find, my lord, that it was you who assaulted me. I defended myself." It was just like making excuses for brawling back home in Tupik: *He started it.* "And, in fairness, if I hadn't fought back, you likely would've killed me."

Mammon snorted derisively. "You can't prove that."

"No," said Yehuda Leib. "But I don't need to, because you know it's true."

"What are you doing here?" said Mammon.

"I think the more interesting question," said Yehuda Leib, "is what *you're* doing here."

Mammon snorted again and rolled his eyes.

"No," said Yehuda Leib. "Truly. If it were me, I would've made my way back home by now. Why haven't you?"

"Perhaps I'm just biding my time," snapped Mammon.

Yehuda Leib nodded. "Perhaps."

"There's a lot of plunder to be had here," said Mammon. "Good things. Worth having."

"That's certainly true," said Yehuda Leib. "And you seem to have dealt with the shopkeeper and his wife nicely. Why don't you take what you'd like and head back to your Treasure House?"

"Maybe I will," said Mammon.

Yehuda Leib nodded. "Maybe. But I think you'd have done it by now if you'd been able."

"Oh, I'm able," said Mammon. "I'm able."

"I'm not so sure," said Yehuda Leib. "I was standing outside waiting for you to make your move for quite some time. But now I don't think you're planning to make a move. Now I think you're just hiding out."

"I am *not* hiding out," said Mammon swiftly.

"No?" said Yehuda Leib. "There's an awful lot of money in the safe down there, and you seem to think it's more useful occupying your host, the shopkeeper, than it would be lining your pockets."

"Money," said Mammon dismissively. "Paper, you mean."

"Paper money, yes," said Yehuda Leib. "But the jewelry on your hostess is hardly paper."

At the thought of the jeweled lady, Mammon couldn't stop his eyes from glittering.

"What's your point?" said Mammon.

"My point," said Yehuda Leib, "is that either you can't get home on your own or, for some reason, you don't want to."

Mammon huffed dismissively.

But he was still listening.

"Actually," said Yehuda Leib, "I think it's both."

"Oh?" said Mammon. "You know me so well, do you?"

"I was standing out there a long time," said Yehuda Leib. "Eventually I started asking myself why you weren't moving—what might be stopping you."

"And?"

"Well, the most obvious reason is all the Hasidim out in the street: psalms as thick as rain in a storm. That can't be pleasant for a demon."

"It isn't unpleasant," said Mammon. "It's incredibly dangerous—like a forest fire, not a rainstorm."

Yehuda Leib shrugged. "To you, perhaps. But not to me."

Mammon was beginning to connect the dots—behind his cracked spectacles and beady eyes, a desire was beginning to brew.

"I wonder . . . ," said Yehuda Leib. "You were able to use me as a vehicle to cross into town. Could I take you safely through the psalms, too?"

"Why would you want to do that?" said Mammon.

Yehuda Leib hopped over this question as if it were a muddy puddle in the road.

"I really was out there some time, though," he said. "Long enough to think twice, and I thought: Even if there were no psalms, how could Lord Mammon possibly go back now? After the commotion he made at the party? After boasting that he'd take the Rebbe so easily? You never even got close enough to speak to him, even with a head start. That's a failure. That's a humiliation. I'd probably hide out and lick my wounds too."

"I am not *licking my wounds*."

"I'm sure that smooth demon will love hearing all about it—what was his name? Belial?"

This shot hit home: "Belial," Mammon muttered to himself.

"But it occurred to me," said Yehuda Leib, barely even pausing. "Maybe we can be of use to one another."

"Oh, what a shock," said Mammon.

"You," said Yehuda Leib, "can't get through the crowd without me. And even if you could, you'd be embarrassed to return home like this. Or at least you should be."

"Yes, yes," said Mammon, "enough already. You've made your point. What's your offer?"

"The Rebbe was a rich prize," said Yehuda Leib. "But I'm planning on aiming even higher. And if you help me, there will be spoils for the taking like you've never even imagined."

At this, Lord Mammon laughed. "I've got quite an imagination," he said.

"Oh," said Yehuda Leib, "I know."

"Very well, then," said Mammon. "Who's the target?"

Now Yehuda Leib took a strong step forward. "The Dark One," he said. "The Angel of Death."

Slowly, Mammon began to smile.

"My," he said. "You *are* ambitious."

"Yes," said Yehuda Leib, "I am. And with your resources, I can defeat him. We can raise an army and storm his house and overthrow him. And everything he has will be yours."

"Everything?" said Mammon.

"All I want is my father back," said Yehuda Leib. "The rest is for you."

Mammon raised an eyebrow. There was a throbbing, greedy excitement behind his eyes.

"That's quite an offer," said Mammon. "But it's very risky."

Yehuda Leib shrugged. "What is it they say? *Nothing ventured . . . ?*"

Mammon tsked his tongue in annoyance. "Don't quote my own scriptures at me. What I mean to say is that I'm not certain it's even possible to accomplish what you suggest."

"Well, I'm going to try," said Yehuda Leib. "With you or without you. If you'd prefer, I suppose, you can just hide out here until your failure's blown over, but I feel I should warn you: They'll be saying psalms as long as the Rebbe's in bed across the street. And if he should die, God forbid, the mourning prayers will be even worse."

At even this innocuous mention of a Holy Name, Mammon flinched.

"Yes, yes, yes," said Mammon. "You needn't lay it on so thick. I know my situation."

Yehuda Leib folded his arms and nodded. "Then partner with me."

Mammon shook his head tightly. "I really don't know. It's a big risk. Why don't you just take me through the crowd, and then . . ."

But Yehuda Leib was already shaking his head. "No," he said. "No. It's all or nothing. I won't take you through unless you agree to support my campaign."

"Easy now," said Mammon. "Don't draw lines in the sand you'll just have to back over. I'm not signing on to a venture as risky as this one without some assurance of the possibility of success. You're a fine negotiator, boy, and you can fight well enough, but in the end, you need my support, so here's what we'll do: You'll conduct me through the crowd, which you're right that I need you to do, and I'll take you back into the Far Country, which you know as well as I do that you can't manage alone. Once we're through, I'll take you to Lord Dantalion, Master of Whispers. We have very old and very strong treaties, the two of us, and if there's any possibility of success in what you propose, he'll know of it."

"And then?" said Yehuda Leib.

"Well," said Mammon, "it depends on what Dantalion has to

say. But if you truly plan to make the attempt one way or the other, then I'll already have assumed much of the risk of supporting you just by bringing you through."

Yehuda Leib clenched his jaw.

This was not the outcome he'd wanted.

But it was hard to argue with Mammon's logic.

"So," said the smiling demon, extending a small, clammy hand. "Do we have a deal?"

It was undignified, but there was no better option. Yehuda Leib had to be the one to move Mammon through the crowd, and so, with bare minutes remaining in the hour, Yehuda Leib pushed Lord Mammon out into the street in a baby carriage.

There he was, the great evil one, swaddled in blankets, his ears stopped up with wadded cotton, bouncing along over the snowy cobbles.

He was just about the right size for the pram, too.

It was a little bit perfect.

But Yehuda Leib's amusement fell away quickly. People did their best to move aside, but there was so little space in the crowded street that moving aside rarely made way, and he had to angle and nudge and *excuse me* for all he was worth. And, to make matters worse, Mammon had started to moan slightly. Yehuda Leib couldn't be sure if it was nerves or if the roiling psalms had started to affect him, but either way, Yehuda Leib wanted to get through the crowd as quickly as he could—he needed Mammon, and what was more, he needed Mammon's goodwill.

And then, cutting through the sound of the psalms like a heavy cleaver through bloody meat, he heard it.

"That's the boy," said a rough voice. "Long hair, cap too small, old knapsack—just like she said."

Yehuda Leib swung his head back over his shoulder, and his gut knotted up tight in fear.

Three mismatched soldiers, ragged and war-stained, were making their way through the crowd. The Hasidim were parting, giving them a wide berth, and though none of them seemed to notice, it was clear as day to Yehuda Leib:

They were long dead.

Yehuda Leib turned away. He was near the end of the street now, near enough that he thought he just might make it out before they got to him.

But it was going to take some doing.

With a deep breath, Yehuda Leib bent low over the pram and said, "I'm sorry about this."

The bundle of Mammon stirred uneasily.

And in a flash Yehuda Leib was going, dashing, jostling and bumping and pushing people aside with the bumper of the baby carriage. Behind him, he heard one of the soldiers curse roughly. A commotion and then a panic sprang up as the soldiers began to push and throw Hasidim aside, and before Yehuda Leib was halfway to the end of the street, there was a full-blown stampede under way, people shoving and running in order to get as far away from the angry soldiers as they could.

The confusion bought Yehuda Leib valuable seconds. By the time he was through the thickest part of the crowd, the soldiers had been swallowed up behind him, and he turned a corner and charged ahead, racing down the long street. He wasn't far from the meeting point now—just another turn and it would be in sight.

Mammon threw back his blankets and sat up, reeling, in his pram.

"What's happening?" he said. "What's going on?"

"Soldiers," panted Yehuda Leib. "But I think we lost them."

Mammon's gaze was fixed over Yehuda Leib's shoulder, and his beady eyes were growing wide. "No," he said. "No, you didn't."

Yehuda Leib turned back just long enough to glimpse the three dead soldiers pounding around the corner behind him.

"No, no, no," said Mammon. "Don't look—go! Run!"

Yehuda Leib tore around the corner as quickly as he could. There, down in the distance, he could see the figure of a girl waiting for him at the entrance to a narrow alleyway, and he flew toward her as quickly as he could go, feet slipping in the slushy snow.

The girl called out as soon as he was near enough to hear. "What's going on?" she said. "What happened?"

It was a long moment before Yehuda Leib remembered that he wouldn't be able to recognize her, his eyes adjusting to her vague features as if to the darkness in a cellar.

"No time!" he said. "Go!"

They had just piled into the long alleyway when the heavy foot-falls of their pursuers came crashing around the corner into the street behind them, drawing nearer and nearer with every moment.

Bluma turned back, her eyebrows high. "What's going on?"

The alley was narrow, so narrow that they were forced to go in single file, and Bluma was stopping up their progress.

Yehuda Leib lifted a finger to his lips and frantically waved her forward.

Cursing rang out in the street, and then angry voices.

"Where is he?"

"Little bastard."

"Shut up! Keep moving!"

Bluma had nearly made it to the end of the alley when the soldiers clattered by in the street, and their racket was just beginning to fade away into the snowy distance when Bluma's sharp scream split the air.

A man had loomed up at the end of the alley, blocking the way.

Bluma stumbled backward, hand clapped over her mortified mouth, and sure enough, out in the street behind them, they heard a soldier call out:

"What was that?"

The man at the end of the alley staggered forward with a growl.

They were trapped.

"What are you waiting for?" hissed Mammon from his pram. "Pay the man!"

Bluma's face crinkled in fear and confusion. "Who is *that*?" she whispered.

Yehuda Leib shook his head impatiently. "Lord Mammon the Avaricious," he said. "Don't worry about it."

"*What?*" said Bluma.

"I'll explain later."

Again, the man at the end of the alleyway moaned. He smelled terrible.

"What do we do?" said Bluma.

"This way!" called the voices in the street, and the clattering footsteps began to grow louder again.

"I told you!" said Mammon. "Pay him!"

It was in this moment that Yehuda Leib identified the stench of the man at the end of the alleyway. It was Mottke the drunken ferryman. From back home. From Tupik.

"Mottke?" he said.

And Bluma stifled a little gasp. "How did you get here, Mottke?"

Mottke made a noise that might've been an explanation or an extended throat clearing.

"There's no time for this," said Mammon. "Pay him so we can pass."

And as if in agreement, Mottke held out an open palm.

"I don't have any money!" said Bluma.

"What?" said Yehuda Leib. "Well, neither do I!"

This, of course, was not true: deep in Yehuda Leib's pocket, entirely forgotten to him, was a strange coin given to him by a dark stranger at the beginning and the end of a journey.

"Oh, *splendid*," said Mammon.

The feet in the road were drawing very near now.

"What about you?" said Yehuda Leib to Mammon. "Surely you've got something."

"Not here," said Mammon. "And he won't defer payment."

Three shadowy figures ran past the alley entrance, but one turned and came back.

Yehuda Leib's mind was racing.

"Hey!" called the soldier in the street. "Hey, over here!"

He was too wide to fit down the narrow alleyway head-on, but, turning sideways, he reached his thick fingers out and began to shimmy forward.

Ahead, an open palm; behind, reaching fingers.

"Mottke," said Yehuda Leib in a panic. "Mottke, we're from Tupik."

"Toopiggh?" said Mottke.

Behind them, they could hear the other two soldiers pushing, shoving their way into the alley.

"Get them! Go!"

"Yes, Mottke," said Yehuda Leib. "Tupik. The community there, we pay you a salary."

"Hrm?" said Mottke.

"We've already paid."

"Ah!" cried Mottke with delight. "Aha! Too-pikh!"

And, turning to the side like a door swinging on its hinges, he bowed low and cleared the way.

Bluma shot out into the second cemetery, Yehuda Leib and the pram following close behind. It was exactly how it had been the night before—cold, barren, empty—except that where the brick wall ought to have been, the Cemetery stretched on as far as the eye could see. In the distance, a few small headstones peeked up through the snow, and high above, the color of the sky passed from cloudy gray through the bruised purple of dusk and, finally, into the black night of the Far Country.

Bluma turned to look over her shoulder, sure that the dead soldiers would be hot on their heels, but they were nowhere to be seen: the soldiers, the alley, even the ferryman himself, had all been left behind in their crossing.

Yehuda Leib heaved a deep sigh.

"We shouldn't tarry," said Mammon. "I don't know what you've done to make an enemy of Lord High General Dumah, but he'll catch up with you sooner or later."

Two pairs of eyes, keen and obscure, met over the little demon in the pram. The wind was blowing, cold and sharp, and it seemed to scrabble at Yehuda Leib's neck like a pair of sharp claws.

Where had he left his scarf?

"Well, then," said Yehuda Leib. "Shall we?"

Bluma took a deep breath and turned her eyes into the darkness. "Yes," she said. "Let's go."

They trudged forward into the purple dusk, and the bells of the town tolled out behind them.

It was beginning to snow. The bells of the old church on the hill were ringing, and in the first cemetery, deep inside an open grave, something was waking.

With a groan, the Dark One rolled onto its back and blinked its eyes open. It had been millennia since the Dark Messenger had had a full night's sleep, but it hardly felt refreshed. The pale gray light of the dying day seemed to cut straight into its head, and the tongues of the pealing bells might as well have been clattering in its own skull.

Headache was altogether too polite a word.

What had happened?

As the Dark One lay moaning in the grave, the dusting of snow filling the folds of its black, black raiment, flashes of memory came swimming back:

A cold glass bottle. Burning liquor. Smiling faces. Dancing and song.

But something else, too: a feeling of dread, of foreboding.

Of guilt.

What had happened?

With difficulty, the Dark One stood and pulled itself woozily from the grave. It was dizzy, its head pounding, and just as it began to find its balance, an oily voice rang out from across the graveyard.

"Most Reverend Regent!"

The Dark One raised a hand to its head. If no one at all ever yelled again, it would have no objection.

"Oh, Most Reverend Regent," said Belial, dodging lightly between the headstones to make his way nearer. "I am so pleased to have caught you. I was just—"

"Belial," said the Dark One. "I must beg you to lower your voice."

"Yes, Most Reverend Regent," said Belial. "Yes, of course. But I must tell you—"

The Dark One sighed. "Perhaps later, Belial. I am in no mood—"

"Ah," said Belial. "But there has been terrible misbehavior. *Terrible*. And—"

"Yes," said the Dark One. "And I am sure that you shall be only too happy to tell me about it when I return home."

All around them, scampering goblins were hard at work striking Lord Azazel's grand pavilion, packing the pieces onto carts and sledges. With a lurch, the Dark One realized how late it was.

Had it missed the wedding?

"But," sputtered Belial. "But, Most Reverend—"

"That will do for now," said the Dark One, and, wobbling slightly, it lurched toward the iron gates of the cemetery.

There was no question: Zubinsk was not in celebration today. There were scarcely any people about, and the few who moved through the streets wore drawn, mournful expressions.

How long had it been? Was it possible that the Dark One had slept two full nights? Or even more?

But no. The wedding celebration had not simply passed through Zubinsk and gone again—something had replaced it, something heavy and mournful.

What had happened?

The dusk huddled in close as the Dark One's feet turned down the Rebbe's broad, empty road. Last night's snow had been trampled into the cobbles by many people, but rumors of angry soldiers had torn through the town, and, fearing a violent pogrom, the Jews of Zubinsk had taken shelter.

Now the place was deserted.

A memory was stirring in the Dark One's pounding head. It had been here last night. It had done something.

Clapping hands. Dancing feet.

What had happened?

With a sigh, the Dark One slotted its hands into the deep pockets of its black raiment.

They were empty.

Whatever else had happened, it needed to recover its instrument—of that it was sure.

It had waited too long.

Halfway down the road, the plate-glass door to a richly stocked general store hung ajar. The Dark One could not abide such things—doors left open, chairs pushed out, candles burning down in emptied rooms—and so, moving swiftly and softly, it grasped the frigid doorknob and pulled.

The little bell inside jingled lightly as the door met its jamb.

"Excuse me," said a voice, and the Dark One turned to look over its shoulder.

A young Hasid was standing in a doorway across the road, warm light streaming past him into the street.

"I'm sorry to bother you," he said. "But we need a tenth man for our prayers."

The snow was thickening now, and with horror, the Dark One began to remember.

"Psalms," said the Hasid, and then, gesturing upward to the bedroom window above: "For the Rebbe."

Like a flash of blue lightning through the thick evening snow, memory shot through the Dark One's mind:

The Rebbe.

His kindness.

His friendship.

His fall.

It was all the Dark One's fault.

"Will you join us?" said the young Hasid.

"Please," said the Dark One. "Please, lead the way."

CHAPTER TWELVE

Strange Navigation

Lilith was displeased.

The Lileen were huddled close around their injured Sister—licking, purring, condoling—but Lilith stood aside, staring deep into the forest between Tupik and Zubinsk.

She was terribly displeased.

In the blinking of an eye, an old gray lady rose from the knot of cats and settled in beside her.

"Will we go to war?" said the old lady.

Lilith sighed. "Something ought to be done," she said. "If Dumah is permitted to treat our Sisters in this manner without fear of repercussion . . ."

"Yes," said a second Sister, rising also from the huddle of comfort on the snowy forest floor. "We must teach him a lesson."

"Indeed, we must," said Lilith.

"But it would be foolish to make war with Dumah," said a third Sister. "One might as well gossip with Belial, or bargain with Mammon."

"It would be difficult, yes," said Lilith. "Perhaps even foolish.

But is there any stronger rebuke than that spoken in the native tongue?"

"Dumah is Silence," said the first Sister. "What language does Silence speak?"

"She means war," said another. "War is Dumah's tongue."

"It is," said Lilith. "And he is eloquent."

"If only we had taken Rokhl in Zubinsk. . . ."

One of the gray Sisters spat. "We should have taken the Bluma girl when we had the chance."

"Perhaps," said Lilith softly. "But she may yet be the solution to our problem."

"Oh?" said a gray lady. "How's that?"

Lilith was silent.

After a long moment's thought, she turned back toward the grove and spoke:

"My Sister."

The knot of comforting cats parted to reveal a lady in a torn gray shift, bruised and battered, lying in the snow. Her eyes were red with tears, and one of her legs was badly broken. "Yes?" she said.

"Why do you think they want the Bluma girl?"

The broken Sister sat up, wincing. "I do not know for certain. One of them spoke of a great weapon."

Lilith's eyes narrowed. "What weapon?"

A Sister spoke: "Perhaps they mean to use Bluma as we meant to use Rokhl—as a living vessel."

Lilith grimaced. "Perhaps."

"With respect to my Sister," said the broken one, "I believe they mean a blade, and not a vessel—the boy who travels with her."

"Oh?" said Lilith.

"His eyes," said the broken Sister, lost in memory. "His eyes are very sharp."

Lilith turned away.

There were many questions. Too many.

She needed to strike back at Dumah—that, at least, was clear. But Dumah was a terrible foe. And there was talk of Mammon's involvement in this affair as well.

Many powerful players. No room for rash decisions.

Perhaps it *was* the boy they were after. And if that was the case, then Lilith might very well be able to take Bluma; it would be just like Dumah and Mammon to look past her potential.

But there was, of course, another possibility, something so incredible and strange that Lilith could barely bring herself to consider it directly:

The spoon.

She couldn't stop thinking about the spoon.

"Very well," she said, and, as one, the Lileen raised their heads. "This is my will: You shall conduct my injured Sister back to our Haven for succor and healing. When you have arrived there, you shall muster the full strength of our Sisterhood, and you shall await my return."

"Yes, Sister," said the Lileen, as one.

"And where will you go?" said the broken one.

"I go to find answers," said Lilith. "I go to consult Lord Dantalion."

Lord Dantalion.

Bluma had heard that name before.

"Who is that?" she said.

"He is called Master of Whispers and Steward of Secrets," said Mammon, his voice bouncing as the pram jostled its way over the snowy ground. "Every concealed thing is written in his ledgers, and if it is possible to overthrow the Angel of Death, he will know of it."

Dantalion. Where had she heard that name before?

"But surely," said Yehuda Leib, breathing hard with the exertion of pushing, "this Master of Whispers won't be eager to reveal what he knows."

"No, indeed," said Mammon. "Dantalion defends his secrets jealously. But our treaties are strong—he alone is privileged to know the contents of my Treasure House, and in return, on rare occasions, I am entitled to consult him. But it is a very delicate thing: his answer is often obscure."

"I see," said Yehuda Leib. "In that case, I must go with you to consult him—two sets of ears will be better than one."

At this, Mammon let out a hearty laugh. "Oh no," he said. "By his own law, one consults Dantalion only alone; secrets cannot be spoken in company."

"All right," said Yehuda Leib. "Then you must promise to ask him for clarification if you don't understand what he says."

"Again, no," said Mammon. "Dantalion will entertain only one question on any topic from any questioner. For this reason, it is very important that the question be properly phrased."

"Then how will you phrase it?" said Yehuda Leib.

"I will ask if it is possible for the living to overthrow Death."

There was a long silence now as Bluma and Yehuda Leib pondered this phrasing.

Presently, Yehuda Leib spoke. "Wouldn't it be better," he said, "to be more specific?"

Mammon grinned. "But this is one of Dantalion's snares. The

more specific one's question, the less information one is likely to receive. If I were to ask, *Is it possible for this particular boy, son of his parents, who lives in the place where you dwell, to go to war and overthrow the Angel of Death in order to recover his dead father's soul?* Dantalion might simply say no for any number of reasons. Perhaps it is possible for you to prevail, but not to recover the soul of your father; perhaps there is another town with the same name as yours—any number of details might offer Lord Dantalion shelter for deception."

Gradually, Bluma slowed her feet, allowing Yehuda Leib and the demon pram to outpace her by several steps.

Lord Dantalion.

When she had failed to cut her name away in the second cemetery, Lilith had suggested consulting Lord Dantalion for a solution. That was where she'd heard his name.

When they arrived at his palace, Bluma would have to find a way to ask him how to proceed.

But how could she phrase her question?

Lord Dantalion, is it possible for me to cut away my name?

No—surely he would answer only yes or no.

Lord Dantalion, how should one go about getting rid of one's name?

But *should* seemed like a dangerous word—who was to say if she would agree with what Dantalion thought she *should* do?

Lord Dantalion, if one were to wish . . .

No.

This was difficult.

Bluma reached her fingers into her apron pocket. The spoon was there, cold and sharp as always.

It was almost comforting.

Almost.

Ahead of her, Yehuda Leib had come to a stop.

"There it is," said Mammon, twisting backward over the top of his pram.

"What is it?" said Yehuda Leib.

The three of them were perched at the summit of a low hillock, gazing off through the thickening snow, and at first it was difficult to make out what was before them.

Alone in the middle distance, a tall stone tower was reaching up beyond the limits of the sky, its flat faces as numerous as the stars.

Slowly, Bluma's gut filled with sallow dread; she knew before Mammon spoke.

"That," said Mammon, "is Death's house."

It felt sick to Bluma, wicked; it made her want to crawl out of her skin and disappear entirely.

"Do you think you can take it?" said Mammon.

"I know I can," said Yehuda Leib.

Mammon chuckled.

"But why have you brought us here?" said Yehuda Leib. "I thought you wanted to consult Dantalion."

"I do," said Mammon. "We are on our way. But navigation in the Far Country is not the same as it is in the living lands: things do not remain where they are put. Lord Dantalion resides deep beneath the Dead City; the Dead City lies beyond the Gallows, and the only sure way to find the Gallows is to flee from Death."

Yehuda Leib shook his head. "But I have no desire to flee. I mean to break in."

"Oh," said Mammon, "I know." And with a toothy grin, he turned his beady little eyes on Bluma.

He didn't have to say a word.

Swiftly, Bluma turned and fled.

It wasn't long before Mammon and Yehuda Leib caught up with Bluma.

Bluma heard the rattling of the pram as they drew near, but she couldn't quite bring herself to care. It felt as if there were something huge on top of her chest, something so heavy that she could never hope to lift it off.

Death.

Death was always coming.

She could not catch her breath.

"Bluma?" said Yehuda Leib.

Bluma was shocked by the nearness of his voice. She turned her head to face him, but she could not remember what he had asked.

Her eyes were wide. "What?" she said.

Yehuda Leib nodded and reached out his hand. "Come on."

With a soft tug, Yehuda Leib helped Bluma to her feet, and they began to pace slowly over the snow.

"Are you all right?"

Sudden tears filled Bluma's eyes. "I don't understand," she said. "I don't know how you can go toward that place on purpose. It *hurts*."

Yehuda Leib gave a heavy sigh. "It's just . . . ," he said. "That I don't think I have a choice."

"Of course you do," said Bluma. "Of course. You could get as far away as possible."

"Yes," said Yehuda Leib. "But someone very smart once told me that there's no running fast enough."

Bluma made a sound that had not yet decided whether it would be a chuckle or a sob.

"There are just so many things I still need to know."

"Like what?" said Bluma.

Yehuda Leib's cheek bunched up, his lips tightening. How could he possibly manage to answer this question sufficiently?

Because he wanted to know so much: what his father had liked to eat and drink, say, or which colors had appealed to him, what songs he'd known. He wanted to watch his father build a fire in the family hearth, wanted to see him in a fight. And there were questions, too, questions that he wanted to ask: What had his father's childhood been like? Had he, too, been an unpopular boy? He wanted to know where his father had traveled, what he had seen, which battles he'd fought in; he wanted to know why he hadn't come back home as soon as he possibly could.

Yet all he managed was a shrug. "Everything," he said.

"But, Yehuda Leib," said Bluma. "It's different when the Dark One is coming for *you*. Do you know what that feels like?"

Now Yehuda Leib thought of the dead end in Zubinsk, of the smell of rot and vodka.

"I think so," he said.

"Don't you want to do anything you can to avoid it happening again?"

Yehuda Leib nodded. "That's what I'm doing."

Bluma let out a deep sigh. "Me too."

And all of a sudden, Yehuda Leib remembered the two sides of the cold coin in his pocket: on one, an eye stretched open; on the other, the same eye squeezed shut.

"Well," said Yehuda Leib. "I hope one of us succeeds."

But now a violent shushing split the air.

"*Shhhhhhh!*"

Mammon was sitting up in his pram.

There was a sound stirring nearby—like a million clocks ticking at uneven intervals.

"What is it?" said Bluma, her obscure eyes wide.

Mammon's grin grew broad and toothy. "You've led us well," he said. "That is the song of the Gallows."

Bluma swallowed hard.

"Listen carefully," said Mammon. "You must make no sound whatsoever within the Gallows Grove. You must remain absolutely silent. Do you understand?"

Bluma and Yehuda Leib nodded together.

"Splendid," said Mammon. "Then let's go."

At first the Gallows seemed to be no more than a small copse, each tree bearing one of the hanging dead.

But this was only the beginning.

Before long, the trees and their occupants began to grow thicker, trunks as densely grouped as in a forest, hanged men, women, children, four, five, six to a bough. The nooses here were not of knotted rope, but grew instead like stems from the very stuff of the leafless trees.

There were empty nooses too, hanging and hungry. Yehuda Leib couldn't quite help thinking one of them might rightfully belong to him.

It was while staring up at just one such loop of knobby vine that, with a sick lurch in his stomach, Yehuda Leib realized:

The eyes of the hanged man above him were open.

And they were watching.

Yehuda Leib wanted to back away, wanted to turn and flee, but beside him Bluma caught his attention, her own eyes set and determined.

Yehuda Leib put his head down and pushed the carriage forward.

The hanged were hung so thick that he had to shove his way bodily between them, shifting their bony limbs aside with every move he made. The blowing snow could not make its way in; even the starlight was unable.

Thin fingers with skin like fraying paper twitched and clutched on every side.

He had to turn back. This was going on too long.

But at least he had the cold handle of the pram to hold on to, something outside himself to remind him that he'd had an existence before he entered the Gallows Grove.

Bluma had no such reminder.

And, with a shock, Yehuda Leib realized that they'd become separated. Where had she gone? He could no longer see her or hear her beside him, and he wanted to call out, to ensure that she was still near.

"Bluma?" he whispered.

All around him, the ears of the dead gaped and flexed at the sound.

A soft, sharp shushing came from the pram before him, and quickly, Yehuda Leib recalled Mammon's warning.

He must continue on in silence.

And after an interminable age of pushing through the suspended bodies of the dead, Yehuda Leib saw a glimmer of light ahead.

He was nearing the end.

Soon there was only one hanged man remaining between him and the Dead City: a tattered fellow, more bone than skin, in a long black coat and the bullet-pocked uniform of a solider. A single gold tooth gleamed in his fixed and smiling face.

But something was wrong.

Everything was still.

Bluma was not here.

Where was Bluma?

With a start, Yehuda Leib turned back over his shoulder. The only sign of life in the dense forest of the hanged was the swaying of bodies where he had pushed his way through, and, presently, even this stilled.

Where was she? Where was Bluma?

Ahead of him in the pram, Yehuda Leib heard Mammon whisper a thin warning: "Boy . . . ," he said.

But now Yehuda Leib had begun to panic. Had she turned aside? Had she turned back? Had she been caught in one of the low-hanging nooses?

"Bluma?" he called. "Bluma!"

And his voice echoed out through the night as loudly as the report of a cannon:

Bluma!

Bluma!

Bluma!

Yehuda Leib heard Mammon let out a long, low sigh.

Slowly, each and every one of the hanging corpses turned, revolving in their nooses until all the eyes of the Gallows were staring directly at them.

There was a long and terrible silence.

And then Bluma came crashing out through the corpses, eyes wide in fear and confusion.

Yehuda Leib turned toward the outskirts of the Dead City and began to run, Bluma following close behind. They didn't pause to look back until they were well past the first houses at the edge of the Dead City.

But when they did, Yehuda Leib felt his heart fall.

The final hanged man—the gold-toothed soldier in his bullet-pocked uniform—was nowhere to be seen.

"I *told* you," said Mammon, his voice drawn and angry, "to be silent."

"I know," said Yehuda Leib.

"And of all the things to yell out ..."

"Yes," said Yehuda Leib. "I know."

"I might have to reevaluate our agreement."

Now Yehuda Leib came screeching to a halt in the middle of the snowy street, fixing Mammon with a cutting glare. "Don't," he said, "threaten me."

"How can I possibly enter into partnership with someone who refuses to obey me?" said Mammon.

"Because," said Yehuda Leib, "that's what partnership *is*. And you said in Zubinsk that just bringing us into the Far Country implicates you in whatever we do here, so there's no benefit to be had in breaking off our partnership now. You're just trying to intimidate me."

"I simply cannot believe," said Mammon, "that you would make such a stupid, careless mistake."

"It wasn't a mistake."

At this, both Yehuda Leib and Mammon fell silent.

It was the first thing Bluma had said since emerging from the Gallows.

"It wasn't a mistake," she said again. "I had turned back. I'd lost my way. If I hadn't heard Yehuda Leib calling my name . . ."

Mammon let out a heavy sigh. "You are extraordinarily lucky, girl."

Bluma's shapeless lips were pressed together, white with pressure. "Thank you," she said to Yehuda Leib.

"We have to move," said Mammon. "If word gets out that you've come here . . ."

Yehuda Leib turned the little pram up the street and began to push again.

Only now was he able to look at the corpse of the city all around him.

The hulking shapes of burned-out houses on the outskirts of the Dead City had given quick way to larger buildings—tenements, apartment blocks. Everywhere, doors stood hanging open. Many of the neatly rowed windows above were shattered, their glassy eyes turned into jagged, toothy mouths. Overhead, the slack laundry lines were hung with clothes that had long since gone to abject tatters in the wind, and snow and refuse blew through street and room indiscriminately.

No one was here.

No people, no horses—not even a rat.

No one.

As they moved into the richer and more fashionable portions of the city, their surroundings began to change. Intricate carven masonry adorned the houses, but even it had not been spared its death: the stonework vines and flowers had withered, wilted; soot stained the marble black. Through the broken bay windows, once-fine sitting rooms could be seen to molder, sofas and settees disemboweled of their stuffing, oil paintings worn away to filmy nothingness.

Before long, they found themselves required to weave carefully back and forth in order to navigate the crowds of fallen carriages, hansoms, and carts that littered the street.

Here was an overgrown park, its untended grasses sticking up through the thick layer of snow like stubble through the pale face of a dead man; there was a cavernous market, its unattended stalls piled high with frosty, rotten produce.

The wind was cold, and its long, frigid fingers tore at Yehuda Leib's collar as if desperate to get in.

Soon they came to a wide, frozen river that cut through the Dead City like a scar, and this they crossed along a grand bridge that had tumbled down to the waterline. Ships had lain at anchor when the river froze through, and Bluma couldn't help but think that the masts, fixed at an unnatural cant, looked like fingers reaching up through the ice. They were halfway up the winding switchbacks of the high hill at the center of the city when Bluma looked behind—just to see the masts once more, just to convince herself that they were still inert and wooden—and she nearly jumped out of her skin.

Something had skittered across the road behind them.

"It's all right," said Mammon softly. "It's only a goblin."

"*Only* a goblin?" whispered Bluma.

Mammon smiled cruelly. "I can think of many things you would less prefer to stalk you through the Dead City than a little goblin, girl."

This was not reassuring.

"Perhaps we ought to move a bit faster," said Bluma, her hand straying to the cold metal in her apron pocket—just for the comfort of knowing it was there.

The structure at the top of the hill seemed by far the oldest portion of the Dead City. There were no houses here, no shops or apartments—only ruins of old, tawny stone.

With difficulty, Yehuda Leib managed to rumble the pram up the huge, crumbling stairs that led into the courtyard, eerie and silent beneath its wide blanket of snow.

"Yes," said Mammon, "nearly there." And with a knobbly finger, he pointed at a monumental heap of rubble at the center of the courtyard.

"Inside," he said.

"Are you sure?" said Yehuda Leib, breathing hard. There didn't seem to be much room to maneuver.

"Positive," said Mammon. "In!"

It should've been dark as the grave within the fallen structure, but somehow—and for the first time anywhere in the Dead City—warm, jumping candlelight seemed to illuminate the rocky chamber. But there was no candle here, no lantern, no hearth. All there was within the little sanctum was an empty doorway—battered posts and a lintel—that framed Nothing at All.

Only the rocky wall was visible behind it.

"What is this?" said Yehuda Leib.

"This," said Mammon, "is the way in."

"What are you talking about?" said Yehuda Leib. "There's nothing here!"

He was beginning to fear that this whole misadventure had been a malicious distraction, a wild-goose chase—or, worse, a method of entrapping them with no defenses.

"Tsk, tsk, tsk," said Mammon. "Whatever happened to those keen eyes of yours?"

Yehuda Leib shook his head. "I don't see anything."

"Would you like a hint?" said Mammon.

Yehuda Leib looked as if he might strangle Mammon, but a cooler head prevailed:

"Please," said Bluma.

"Around the back," said Mammon.

With difficulty, Yehuda Leib piloted the pram over the rough, uneven ground to the other side of the doorway.

And all of a sudden, everything became clear.

"*Splendid,*" said Mammon.

From this side, the door could be seen to lead into a wide, warm study hall, in which old dead men bent to the careful scrutiny of thick books by candlelight—candlelight that spilled out into the rocky sanctum through the back of the doorway.

"What is it?" said Bluma.

"This," said Mammon, "is the Yeshiva of Dantalion."

And, having hopped lightly down from his pram, he led the way through the door.

CHAPTER THIRTEEN

Three Questions

Yehuda Leib had never visited a proper yeshiva before, but he had seen the men of Tupik learning in the little study house back home many times.

Immediately he knew that something was wrong.

"Why is it so quiet?" he said.

Bluma stopped to listen. It was true—far and away the loudest sounds were the creaking of the long wooden benches, the turning of pages. There were masses and masses of men here, elders and whitebeards crowded shoulder to shoulder—but none of them ever looked up to pose a question to his neighbor, to verify an interpretation, even to start an argument.

"Look," said Bluma. "They study alone."

"How else could it be?" said Mammon.

"Where we come from," said Bluma, "men study together—in partnerships."

Mammon gave a little chuckle. "Not here."

"Why not?" said Yehuda Leib.

"The only reason a dead man comes to study the Dantalion,"

said Mammon, "is because he is searching for secrets. And one does not master secrets by telling them."

"But how can they be sure," said Bluma, "that they correctly understand what they read?"

"They can't," said Mammon with a smile. "Isn't it splendid?"

It did not seem splendid to Bluma at all.

It seemed very sad and very lonely.

The chamber extended farther than the eye could see in either direction, crowded with readers at long wooden tables. Rising high up into obscurity on every wall were cases and cases crammed with ancient books: parchment and paper and vellum and bark—even clay and stone. Unbound manuscripts, brittle scrolls, jotted scraps filled every inch of empty space. Some books were missing their covers, and some of their spines had broken.

Bluma swallowed hard, trying to imagine how long it would take to lay your hand on a specific book here. A hundred years? Two hundred?

"But how can anyone possibly find the secret they're looking for in all this mess?" said Bluma.

"Oh," said Mammon. "There are no secrets here. In this room, only the supracommentaries are kept—the books about the books about the rumors of what Dantalion has said."

One of the readers nearby was muttering, moving his lips as he read, and Yehuda Leib slowed his pace to overhear.

"'It is written in *Raz Sodekhah*,'" read the old man, "'that Lord Dantalion is none other than the serpent who tempted Adam and Eve in the Garden of Eden, but this is commonly held to be poetic metaphor. The *Daas HaGanuz*, however, brings a rumor that there was a discrepancy in punctuation between the original Ten

Commandments destroyed by Moses at the foot of Mount Sinai and the replacements issued by the Holy One, Blessed Be He. The *Daas HaGanuz* contends that it is this discrepancy, known only by Moses, that is the beginning of the Dantalion....'"

Yehuda Leib turned back to find Mammon grinning ear to ear. "One could study here forever," he said, "and still not come any closer to the secret one seeks."

"But there must be a way forward," said Yehuda Leib.

"Oh," said Mammon, turning them toward a narrow gap between two bookcases. "There is. If one is wise enough to discern the shape of truth beneath the outer layers of rumor and misunderstanding..."

A spindly, steep staircase plunged down into the darkness between the bookcases, one single point of jumping candlelight dancing at its bottom.

"But one may only move forward," said Mammon, clambering downward into the darkness, "if one passes the examination."

The man who sat squinting at his reading beside the candle at the bottom of the stairs was impossibly old. He had fewer teeth remaining than he had eyes, and his beard seemed to be at least half cobwebbing.

"You wish to pass into the second chamber?" he said in a rasping voice.

"Yes," said Yehuda Leib.

"Very well," said the man, sitting up officiously. "Tell me a secret."

Yehuda Leib's heart began to thunder.

Tell me a secret? This seemed like an impossible examination to pass. Was he supposed to tell a specific secret? Or perhaps one that the man had never before heard? What secret could he possibly possess that would be good enough to merit entrance?

But Mammon simply smiled and shouldered past Yehuda Leib.

"No," said the little demon.

No?

"Correct," said the man at the candle, reaching up to draw back a door hidden in the gloom.

"*No?*" said Yehuda Leib. "How can the correct answer be no?"

"Nothing one learns in Dantalion's yeshiva is of any consequence whatsoever," said Mammon. "It is a suit of armor in the shape of an academy. But some benefit can still be gained from studying here—not in information, of course, but in the knowledge of how to discern the truth hidden beneath it. If you were to tell the first door guard a secret as he requested—any secret at all—then you would be divulging it. This would render it no longer secret, which, in turn, would invalidate your answer. Therefore, the only satisfactory response is no."

The second chamber, in which the commentaries were studied, was like the first, only much smaller: the books here might all be held, flipped through, even studied in the normal span of a single human life. The scholars, too, were fewer, ranged about a large circular table at which each man sat backward, facing away from the center of the room, protecting his reading from the others.

Yehuda Leib wanted to linger here and eavesdrop on the muttered reading, but Mammon hurried them along, beneath the circular table and down a spiral staircase to another ancient man who sat reading beside a single candle.

"Ah," said the man. "I see you wish to progress into the third chamber."

"Yes, yes," said Mammon impatiently.

The ancient man began to stroke his long, curly beard, and in the flickering light of the candle, Bluma noticed that it had twined around the armrest of his chair, like climbing ivy.

"I see," he said. "Yes. You have studied long and learned much. But before I admit you to the third chamber ..."

Mammon heaved a sigh, as if he'd had to endure this speech many times before.

"...before I admit you to the third chamber," repeated the ancient door guard, "I must ask you this: In all of your learning and all of your study here, in all the commentaries you've studied, the treatises you've read, what is the number of secrets that you have learned?"

Mammon took a deep chestful of air, as if he intended to blow out the door guard's feeble candle with his answer, but Yehuda Leib stepped forward.

"None," he said. "The number of secrets is none."

"You are wise," said the door guard, and he lifted up a hatch in the floor. "Proceed."

"How did you guess?" said Bluma as they scrambled down the ladder into the dim third chamber.

Yehuda Leib shrugged. "It's the same question as the first," he said. "Only designed to fool scholars instead of students. If it's written in a book, and the book is out on a shelf for anyone to read, it can't be much of a secret, can it?"

"Very good," said Mammon.

The third chamber was as unlike the first as could be—one small square table in the middle of a cramped, earthen room. There were no chairs here, no benches—only a single, battered book sitting open on the table, illuminated in the paltry, flickering candlelight. Before it, a clutch of seven scholars crowded in to read, all at once. As they watched, one of the men leaned forward to turn the page, but his hand was stilled by the tsking of a slower reader.

There was scarcely enough space for Bluma, Yehuda Leib, and Mammon all to occupy the little room at the same time without disturbing the reading scholars, and Mammon turned directly down a long earthen hallway that sloped toward a single flickering candle in the distance.

Yehuda Leib followed, but before long, he found himself looking back.

Where was Bluma?

"I wouldn't do that if I were you."

Mammon had turned to speak to her.

Bluma had drawn near the table, eager to peer around the little group of scholars at the open, battered book.

"That book contains accounts of consultation with Dantalion. It is unbelievably dangerous."

"Why?" said Bluma.

"Because some of it is true."

Slowly, Bluma turned away from the table.

Unlike the two preceding door guards, the man beside the candle at the end of the hallway looked young and hale, with only a smattering of patchy brown beard on his cheeks.

Yehuda Leib, however, was not fooled by his appearance: his eyes were canny and ancient.

"Lord Mammon," said the young man, rising from behind his desk. "The Dantalion gives you welcome."

"Yes," said Mammon. "I've come to seek his counsel in accordance with our treaties."

"Yes, my lord," said the young man behind the desk, laying his reading aside and flipping open a thick book beside him.

But Yehuda Leib was surprised. "Is there no examination here?" he said.

The man behind the desk smiled. "Lord Mammon's treaties provide him access to the Dantalion without the ordeal of examination. For others, though, there is a question."

"What is it?" said Yehuda Leib.

"What it is is not worth your time," said Mammon.

"Why not?"

"Because," said Mammon, "if you answer incorrectly, you won't be allowed to pass through the door, and if you answer correctly, the door will lead you somewhere you don't wish to go."

The young man behind the desk was smiling softly. That didn't seem fair at all.

"Well, what's the question?" said Yehuda Leib.

"Are you sure you wish to hear?" said the young man behind the desk. "Once the question has been put, it must be answered."

"Enough of this nonsense," said Mammon. "I'm here to consult Lord Dantalion. Give me the ledger."

"Very well," said the young man, turning the thick book to face Mammon. "There," he said, pointing to a line in the middle of the page.

With his left hand, Mammon took a spindly ink pen from the desk and scratched away at the paper in the book, crowning his jotting with a large, looping question mark.

"Very good," said the young man, and with a practiced motion, he snapped the heavy book shut.

But scarcely had one hand left its calfskin cover when he reached back again with the other to open it once more. There, tucked neatly into the binding, like a bookmark, was something that hadn't been there before: a cream-colored card. On it, in Mammon's own hand, a long string of letters and numbers had been carefully written.

The ink was still wet.

Carefully, Mammon reached out and took the card, and, as if in answer, an unseen door behind the young man cracked open in the darkness, spilling a column of soft light into the hallway.

"Lord Dantalion will see you now," said the young man.

Mammon took a deep breath and pushed his way through the door. Yehuda Leib leaned forward to try to see around the jamb, but all he managed to perceive before the door swung shut was the sense of a very large room.

The young man let out a little sigh. "Ah," he said, straightening the ink pen on his desk, and he settled into his chair once more.

But he didn't resume his reading. Instead, he looked directly down at Bluma and Yehuda Leib and folded his hands, as if waiting.

Softly, from behind him, Yehuda Leib heard Bluma speak.

"The question," she said. "I wish to hear the question."

A tiny smirk creased the young man's face. "Very well," he said. "But once it has been put, an answer must be given."

"I understand," said Bluma.

With a smile, the young man stood, shut his eyes, and in a singsong tone, as if praying, began to speak.

> *The one true secret that you know—*
> *I brought you to this place.*
> *I am the way that you must go;*
> *I wear your frowning face.*
> *I am the fountain of your fear,*

The secret of the cold;
I'm whispered into every ear,
Yet I am never told.

Yehuda Leib's mind was racing.

The one true secret that you know.

The examinations at the two previous levels had taught him to understand how rare a true secret was: something that only he knew and no other.

I brought you to this place.

Swiftly, as if flying in reverse, Yehuda Leib retraced his path, up through the yeshiva, back out through the Dead City, the Gallows, and the Cemetery, through Zubinsk and the Treasure House and the cold, dark night to that terrible moment in the forest:

The stillness of squirming legs. The reddening of the snow.

I am the way that you must go.

His father, just like him in so many ways—strong, sharp, dangerous.

I wear your frowning face.

What would he look like once his beard came in? Once it began to gray?

I am the fountain of your fear.

His father's grasping hands.

The secret of the cold.

His father's freezing corpse.

I'm whispered into every ear,
Yet I am never told.

All the adults in Tupik must've known who his father was—it must have been whispered into every ear.

Could that be it? Could his father be the answer?

But no—no, his father's identity *had* been told. He'd known it in the end, no true secret.

So what then?

And then he saw it, standing there in the shadows, just behind his father all the time.

The Answer.

Bluma's mind was racing.

The one true secret that you know.

The one true secret . . .

I brought you to this place.

Her hand slipped down into her apron pocket for the comfort of finding what she knew was hidden there.

I am the way that you must go;

I wear your frowning face.

The spoon.

The feeling of turning its handle between her fingers, the pleasant shock in finding herself relieved of the burden of her face.

I am the fountain of your fear,

The secret of the cold.

Even now the spoon's surface was so icy and frost-kissed that it seemed to cling to the warm skin of her fingers.

It seemed incontrovertible.

The spoon. The answer must be the spoon.

But . . .

I'm whispered into every ear,

Yet I am never told.

How could that be? Every ear? How could each of the dead

scholars who made his way down to this desk be expected to have come into contact with the spoon in her pocket?

That couldn't be.

Unless it could.

A dim and terrible knowledge had been growing in her mind for some time now, and she was unsure if she could continue to ignore it.

What was the spoon, after all? Where had it come from?

The One True Secret that you know . . .

Bluma ran the pad of her thumb through the basin of the spoon in her pocket.

She knew the Answer.

The young man took his seat behind the desk.

"What is your response?" he said.

"The answer is—" said Bluma softly.

"I think it's—" said Yehuda Leib.

And "Death," they said at once.

Death.

The young man at the desk showed his teeth in a broad grin. Behind him, the door cracked open.

"Correct," said the young man.

Yehuda Leib took a deep breath. He could see firelight jumping on the other side of the door, irresistibly warm and inviting.

But something was odd. The room into which Mammon had gone had been huge: vast and echoing. But the room on the other side of the door now seemed small—intimate.

Almost cozy.

What was in that place?

He had to know.

Yehuda Leib reached up, grasped the door handle, and prepared to push inward.

"Wait," said Bluma behind him.

With a start, Yehuda Leib wheeled about. He'd almost forgotten that he wasn't alone.

"Don't," she said.

"Why not?" said Yehuda Leib. "I want to meet Lord Dantalion."

"So do I," said Bluma, and with a lunge and a tug, she grabbed Yehuda Leib's arm and pulled the door shut again.

Yehuda Leib was furious. "Hey!" he said, pushing hard against the fixed door, rattling it on its hinges. It wouldn't budge.

"What did you do?" said Yehuda Leib.

Bluma sighed. "Don't you remember what Mammon said? If you answer correctly, the door leads somewhere you don't wish to go."

Yehuda Leib's keen eyes widened.

The young man at the desk grinned. "Your friend is wise," he said.

She was right. "Where does it lead?"

"This door leads to answers—whether they be Lord Dantalion's or your own."

"Our own?" Yehuda Leib was confused.

Until, with a lurch, he realized:

The answer they had just given.

He would've walked through the door to meet his Death.

Yehuda Leib swallowed and looked to the young man, whose grin had not faded.

"Thank you," said Yehuda Leib to Bluma quietly, but she was already moving toward the desk.

"I wish to ask Lord Dantalion a question," she said.

The young man at the desk nodded. "You have earned the privilege."

Bluma seized the spindly pen from the young man's desk, and as soon as the thick book was opened, she scrawled out her question on the indicated line. With the same practiced set of motions, the young man at the desk shut the tome and then opened it again to reveal a cream-colored card between its pages, marked in Bluma's handwriting with a string of letters and numbers. The door behind him cracked open as she removed the card from the book.

"Lord Dantalion will see you now," said the man behind the desk.

With a deep breath, Bluma strode forward and pushed her way inside.

The young man tugged the door shut behind her and took his seat once more.

"And you?" he said to Yehuda Leib. "Do you wish to consult Lord Dantalion?"

"Yes," said Yehuda Leib. "I do."

The book was opened, the pen proffered, before Yehuda Leib had a chance to explain.

"Oh," he said, his cheeks warming with a blush. "I want to ask a question, but . . ."

The young man cocked his head to the side. "Is there a problem?"

"Well," Yehuda Leib said. "I never learned my letters."

"Ah," said the young man, leaning back in his chair. "That is a problem."

"Can you just write the question for me?" said Yehuda Leib.

The young man shook his head. "That would be highly

irregular—I might even say unprecedented. And even if I were to do so, it wouldn't solve the problem."

"Why not?"

"Because," said the young man gravely, "Lord Dantalion is a book."

"A book?"

"Yes." The young man nodded. "A book in many, many volumes. And if you are unable to read the answers he provides . . ."

Yehuda Leib's cheeks were burning. Tears began to fill his eyes. It was the old story, again and again and again: rough, foolish Yehuda Leib, not good enough, not smart enough, making trouble wherever he went. What could he do now? Even leaving aside the question that burned in his chest, both Mammon and Bluma had disappeared through that door. What if he could not rejoin them? What if he was alone down here for good, buried deep beneath the corpse of the Dead City?

He was growing angry.

But all of a sudden, something very strange happened.

The door behind the desk cracked open of its own accord.

"Ah," said the young man, confusion written so clearly on his face that even Yehuda Leib could read it.

The large room into which Bluma and Mammon had gone lurked palpably on the other side of the doorway.

Leaning toward it, the young man behind the desk gave a soft whisper. "Are you sure?"

And, as if in answer, the door inched further open.

The young man turned back to Yehuda Leib.

"Very well," he said. "Lord Dantalion will see you now."

CHAPTER FOURTEEN

Dantalion

When, periodically, each identical page of the thick ledger that sits beside the final door guard of the Dantalion has been filled, having been inscribed with a question by a pilgrim, the volume is retired and replaced with a fresh copy. The completed ledgers are shelved deep in the stacks, and in this way Dantalion himself is fed, grown by the questions people bring to him.

As of this writing, it is still possible to consult these ledgers, and the volume in use when Mammon, Bluma, and Yehuda Leib made their visit is still on the shelf. Mammon's florid writing is there, and his question can easily be read:

Is it possible for the living to overthrow Death?

On the next page, Bluma's tidy, quiet script can be found:

What is my name?

Even the following page, the record for Yehuda Leib's entry into the Dantalion, contains a transcription in neat bureaucratic capitals of the only question he managed to ask while in conference with the Dantalion:

Father? Hey! Hello?

But in order to understand what happened next, one must

flip backward three pages to the page immediately preceding Mammon's.

On this page, a tight, toothy hand has inscribed the question *Is it the boy or the girl?*

Beneath the inquiry, Dantalion's response, in the form of a call number, is recorded:

O 32 J 12 F 166.

This call number would've led the questioner to a book shelved deep in the stacks, the title page of which bears the legend *On the Evolution of Flatware.*

This might seem like an incongruous response at first blush, but once one flips forward to page 166—the page upon which Dantalion indicated the answer was to be found—things become much clearer.

Page 166 is dominated by a large engraving:

An illustration of a fine—though eminently common—teaspoon.

The door swung gently shut behind Mammon, sending an echo into the massive hall like the memory of a drumbeat.

He was alone.

The cream-colored card in his hand read *QB 94 K 7 H 391,* all in his very own handwriting.

He particularly liked the way his *Q*s looped around—he had paid an Italian scribe quite a hefty sum for that *Q,* and it had almost been worth it.

Mammon had consulted Dantalion frequently enough in the past to know the system of organization—Hall QB, row 94, case K, shelf 7, volume H, page 391—but it was still a struggle to reach his answer: from the grand basilica in which he found himself now, he would have to make his way to Hall QB, passing first through Halls A, B, C, D, and E, all the way down to Hall Q, at which point he would turn to Hall Q's offshoots, pass through Hall QA, and finally arrive in Hall QB.

It would be a long and lonely walk—Dantalion had made sure of it.

The halls were huge, round, identical, and imposing. Each was lit by a circular stained-glass skylight far above, bearing the appropriate letter or letters, and the diffuse moonlight that filtered down into the still rows of bookcases was somehow just enough to see by and yet not quite enough for comfort. The bookcases themselves were tall and thin, climbing hundreds and hundreds of feet up toward the vaulted ceilings. Most of their shelves were inaccessible without scaling one of the rickety rolling ladders, but, double-checking his card, Mammon breathed a sigh of relief—only the seventh shelf.

It had always been cold in the stacks of Dantalion, but Mammon wasn't sure it had been quite this cold before. Despite the brisk pace of his step, his sharp teeth were beginning to chatter like a jittery telegraph key.

Before long, he discovered the reason for the frigid temperature: the skylight in Hall O had been partially shattered. Snowflakes wandered down lazily from far above, and all the bookcases on the left side of the main aisle had tilted and fallen.

He would have to make a point of informing Dantalion's attendant. A broken skylight meant an unmonitored point of entry. They couldn't have people coming in to examine the books unauthorized—after all, the catalog of Mammon's Treasure House was somewhere here.

Not that it would be simple for an intruder to find any particular volume without help. The books themselves, in accordance with Dantalion's aesthetic, were scrupulously uniform, neatly organized, and entirely inscrutable to the unguided, each covered in an identical binding of unmarked brown leather.

Mammon's step quickened as he turned into Hall QB—nearly there now—and he made his way swiftly down the numbered rows, pausing at the dim mouth of row 94 to check his card again.

This was it.

He was just setting off in search of the proper bookcase when he froze in place.

Footfalls.

Dashing footfalls.

He could've sworn that somewhere nearby, someone had been running.

But there was no one anywhere to be seen.

This was not entirely unexpected—Dantalion strongly preferred to receive visitors individually, so much so that he had a way of hiding them from one another even when they were in the stacks at the same time.

But few ever achieved the privilege of consulting the Dantalion in the first place. And if Mammon wasn't alone in the stacks, he wanted to know.

Before long, though, the silence had settled again, so solid and heavy that Mammon had trouble even imagining he'd ever heard anything to begin with. Slowly, he turned down row 94.

It didn't take him long to come to case K, and there, counting upward, he found shelf 7.

An orderly rank of little brass letters had been screwed into each shelf, just below the identical volumes. *A, B, C, D* . . . Even these letters were spotless, polished until they shone.

Mammon rolled his eyes. Seemed like showing off.

Once again, Mammon checked his card:

Row 94, case K, shelf 7, volume H.

And there it was, perfectly centered above the little brass *H*: his answer.

Just a few steps up the spindly ladder and he'd have it.

Taking the card lightly in his teeth and the rickety rungs in his hands, he began to climb.

He was surprised to find how excited he was. A part of him had assumed that the boy Yehuda Leib would've simply found a way to get himself killed by now, and that would've suited him just fine. But if the venture he'd proposed was truly feasible . . . well, there might be quite a lot of profit to be had.

It rather made his fingers itch.

Mammon had already begun reaching out to pull volume H from the shelf when he looked up, and he was so startled by what he saw that he nearly let go of the ladder.

Volume H.

He took the card from his teeth and checked again.

Volume H. He had seen it from the floor.

But there on shelf 7 before him, the space designated for volume H was now empty, volume G leaning lightly against volume I.

He had just seen it. Where had it gone?

Mammon peered through to the other side of the shelf, but there was no room for it to have fallen.

What had happened?

Quickly, Mammon clambered back down to the floor. Something strange was going on.

As soon as his feet met the cold marble beneath him, he gave a gasp and a growl.

There it was: volume H, standing at attention, perfectly in place on shelf 7.

With a sigh, he began to climb once more. Perhaps he had been mistaken about the shelf—he could easily have been looking at shelf 6 or shelf 8 from the ladder.

But no: when his eyes flicked up and down to the surrounding shelves, he found them both fully stocked.

And as soon as he looked back again, Mammon gave an involuntary little bark of discontent. He made sure now: it was shelf 7. And volume H was once again missing.

This was nonsense. He'd come a very long way to receive his answer in precise accordance with the terms of their treaty. In his long alliance with Dantalion, he'd never once had to contend with a disappearing book before, and he wasn't about to start accepting it now.

He'd have to have a word with that boy by the door.

Mammon dropped to the floor, went charging down the row, and swung out sharply into the main aisle, but immediately he stopped himself.

There, on the little reading lectern bolted to the end of the row, was an unshelved volume of the Dantalion.

It hadn't been there when he'd first turned down the row—of that he was absolutely sure.

Of course, there was no way for him to be certain that this particular unmarked brown volume was the one to which he'd been directed, but he had a strong suspicion. Taking it in his hand, he retraced his steps back down row 94 to case K.

Sure enough, volume H was still missing from shelf 7.

This must be it.

As was his habit when consulting the Dantalion, Mammon opened the book first to its title page, and there he read:

THE DANTALION
Prophet Margins

"Oh," he said to himself. "Splendid."

Quickly, he riffled through to page 391, where he'd been told his answer would be found.

"Huh," he said.

That was odd. There, in the binding, between pages 390 and 391, was a ragged zigzag of torn paper pennants: clear testament to a page ripped out of the book.

But there was no page missing: 390 led seamlessly into 391.

Something strange was going on.

Mammon looked up from the book with a start.

A sound was echoing through the hall.

Someone had called out:

Hey!

The door swung gently shut behind Bluma, sending an echo into the massive hall like the memory of a drumbeat.

She was alone.

The cream-colored card in her hand read *QB 94 K 7 H 390*, all in her very own handwriting.

It didn't take her long to discern the method of organization. As soon as she'd moved through the entry basilica into the large halls of the stacks, she noticed the letters high above on the skylights.

A. And then, moving into the next hall, *B.*

By the time she reached *F,* she'd noticed the offshoot doorways and determined how to proceed once she came to Hall Q.

She wanted to spend no more time in this place than she

absolutely needed to. The silence and stillness were massive, heavy, weighting her down, as if trying to convince her to join them.

She wanted to find her name, dispose of it, and move on as quickly as possible.

Unconsciously, she found herself striking a compromise between the desire to move quickly and the need not to disturb the heavy silence; she'd begun to step on the balls of her feet to keep her heels from clattering.

The air in the halls was getting colder and colder as she moved forward, and when she first heard the sound, she assumed it was her own teeth chattering.

But it couldn't be: her jaw was clenched tight.

Bluma froze.

Then what was the sound? It was nearby, clattering like a jittery telegraph key.

But there was no one here.

Was there?

Swallowing hard, Bluma began to trot forward, going as quickly as she could without making any undue noise. She didn't even pause to take notice of the dramatic scene in Hall O: the shattered skylight far above, the left-hand rank of bookcases leaning in mid-tumble.

And, more importantly, she didn't even think to skirt the little accumulation of snow that had piled up in the center aisle of that hall.

She didn't think about the footprints she left behind.

By the time she reached Hall Q and turned into its offshoots, Bluma had worked herself into a state. She was sure of it now: someone else was here, following her, chasing her, and she was tired, tired, tired of fleeing—it had been so long, so many steps, so many escapes, from the Dark One and the demons to the Lileen and the soldiers, and she was ready, so ready, to cut her name away, to be unfindable, invisible, and to finally come to rest.

By the time she came into Hall QB, she was running flat out, with no regard at all for how loud her feet fell. She sped down to row 94 and swung inward, passing cases A, B, C, and D, her feet only beginning to slow as she came to I, J, and here was K, and she clambered up the ladder until shelf 7 was level with her eyes, then counted the volumes, A, B, C . . .

There it was.

Volume H.

Bluma breathed deeply and double-checked her card:

QB 94 K 7 H 390.

This was it.

With a sigh, Bluma pulled volume H from the shelf. She made her way back down to the floor and, flipping rapidly, found it:

Page 390.

The type was small and dense, and if Bluma had been willing to linger in the stacks for even a moment, she might've been fascinated to read what was written there.

As it was, though, her eyes were drawn irresistibly, as if magnetized, to one short word near the lower right-hand corner of the page:

BLUMA

There it was.

It was almost too small to mean anything, too minuscule: five little letters practically crushed beneath a massive block of weighty black type.

Bluma's fingers strayed down into her apron pocket and met cold metal there.

But how could she get her name into the spoon?

She had an idea, but she wasn't sure it was allowed. In fact, she was confident it wasn't, but she had come here to remove something from the stacks anyhow.

Glancing left and right, Bluma took hold of the sheet comprising pages 389 and 390, and, careful not to leave her name behind, she tore it from the binding.

There.

She clambered up to shelf 7, replaced the volume above the brass letter *H*, and returned to the floor.

She had it. There, in her hand: the page with her little name on it.

Now all she had to do was dispose of it.

Swiftly, she folded the page, creasing it sharply: halves, quarters, eighths, sixteenths.

It might just fit into the basin of the spoon now.

But something bothered her about this idea. She tried to convince herself that she was concerned about the other words written on the sheet—did she have any right to feed them to the spoon?—but the truth was that a nagging doubt was tickling her brain.

The spoon.

How it both was and wasn't the answer to the door guard's riddle.

What it both was and wasn't.

But every passing moment that she spent in these stacks felt like a risk. Perhaps it was best just to take the sheet along with her and figure it out later.

Yes. That was what she'd do.

With a percussive sigh, she thrust the folded sheet into her apron, careful to keep it in the opposite pocket from the spoon, safely separated—for now.

She had just turned on her heel to track back up row 94 when a terrible uncertainty took hold of her.

Could it really be that easy to steal a page from the Dantalion? She had to check.

She had to be sure.

And so she climbed back up the rickety ladder, took hold of volume H, and drew it down again. She flipped the pages forward, and her heart sank.

Of course not.

There, protruding from the binding, was the ragged remnant of the sheet that she'd torn from the book, but just beside it was the twin of that same page: 390 led to 391, and there, in the lower right-hand corner, was her name:

BLUMA

Bluma's stomach began to squirm. She needed to do something and she needed to do it now.

But what?

Quickly, her feet led her out to the central aisle, and she laid volume H on the little lectern at the end of the row of bookcases.

There it was, staring up at her, square and strong, as if taunting her—her name:

BLUMA

Slowly, she reached into her apron pocket. Cold metal met her fingers.

Fluidly, she drew the spoon out and leaned forward.

It was almost as if the spoon itself were directing the motions of her hand: gingerly, she laid the razor edge of its basin beside the last letter of her name, and, little by little, she scraped the dry ink from the page:

BLUMA

BLUM

BLU

BL

B

There it was, dark and dusty in the small basin of the spoon.

Bluma's name.

With a deep breath, she turned the spoon over itself.

There was a feeling in her throat like a sob, but she swallowed it back.

The basin of the spoon was empty.

Had it worked? Had her name been severed?

How could she know?

Carefully, she replaced the spoon in her right apron pocket, and with a start, she remembered the stolen page.

With trembling fingers, she drew the paper from the left-hand pocket of her apron and unfolded its tidy creases.

There, in the lower right-hand corner, was an empty space:

Her name.

Again, the feeling in her throat loomed up, and again, she swallowed it back down.

She had just folded away the stolen page when she heard it.

A sound was echoing through the hall.

Someone had called out:

Hey!

The door swung gently shut behind Yehuda Leib, sending an echo into the massive hall like the memory of a drumbeat.

He was not alone.

There, at the far end of the basilica, a tall man was leaving through the doorway.

A tall man in a long black coat.

Yehuda Leib's heart jumped, and without meaning to, without even thinking, he spoke his question.

"Father?" he murmured.

But the man was much too far away to hear him—he was already in the next hall—and Yehuda Leib leapt forward to pursue him.

He was making so little progress; just as he would find his way into one hall, the man ahead of him would disappear into the next. Again this occurred, and again and again, hall after hall after hall, Yehuda Leib gaining at most a second or two on the man in the black coat with each door he passed through. He thought, perhaps, about calling out—just to get his attention, to make him slow or wait—but it seemed unwise to disturb the heavy silence in this library.

He would have to catch up.

To Yehuda Leib, the endless halls of Dantalion were not a massive repository of knowledge—they were simply structures, scrupulously regular terrain. Many details leapt to his attention: lecterns, ladders, bookshelves, small brass letters, identical building-block books. The far end of each row of shelves extended all the way to the wall—meaning that the only way to move easily up and down any given hall was through its central aisle. But he also noticed that the double-sided bookcases were open through their shelves— meaning that, in a pinch, one could move between rows by displacing the books.

By the time he reached Hall O, Yehuda Leib's keen eyes had made him very familiar with the orderly layout of Dantalion's halls, and he slowed his feet to make a clearer study of the disarray that met him there.

The letter O had little meaning for Yehuda Leib, and so when he stared up at the broken skylight above, what he saw was the inside of a giant glass eye: the window had been shattered only within the loop of the letter itself, leaving a jagged black pupil to admit the flurries of nighttime snow drifting down from above.

But significant to Yehuda Leib's notice was the fact that there was no broken glass on the floor. This suggested a measure of care—perhaps someone had cleaned up the fallen glass, but this seemed inconsistent with the tipped bookcases, the accumulated snow, and the books spilled out on the floor, their pages waterlogged and even frozen with the cold.

It seemed more likely that the glass had been prevented from falling in the first place. This would've been a difficult thing to accomplish. And why would anyone want to break the window if they were concerned enough to keep the glass from falling? Yehuda Leib could think of only two reasons: that the sound of falling glass might raise an alarm, and that broken glass underfoot could present a dangerous obstacle.

Both of these reasons suggested an intentional incursion.

The tipped bookcases had served as a sort of staircase, then, allowing the invader to climb down quickly and quietly. Some of the books littering the floor were wet but not yet frozen, which suggested to Yehuda Leib a relatively recent arrival, and the accumulation of snow in the central aisle bore the mark of only one set of footprints: small and narrow, heading inward.

This conjured a chilling thought:

Perhaps the invader was still here.

Yehuda Leib swallowed hard. He was out of time. If he didn't want to lose the tall man ahead of him, he needed to be moving.

Ducking through the emptied shelves of the fallen bookcases— he had no intention of leaving unnecessary footprints behind— Yehuda Leib hurried forward into the next hall in just enough time to see the tails of the tall man's coat disappearing through the far door. Yehuda Leib put on an extra burst of speed, but he found himself skidding to a halt as he entered the following hall: the tall man in the black coat was not, as he'd been the last sixteen times, just leaving.

Instead, he was waiting.

The man stood in the center of Hall Q, looking back at Yehuda Leib. It was such a surprise that Yehuda Leib neglected to take notice of his face before the man turned toward the offshoot door— the first turn he'd made since Yehuda Leib had begun to follow him.

Had it been his father after all?

By the time he'd made it into Hall QA, Yehuda Leib had broken into a flat-out run. The tall man ahead of him had too, increasing the gap between them with every stride of his long legs, and if he didn't do something soon, Yehuda Leib would lose him.

"Hey!" he cried, his voice echoing wildly into the stacks.

Hey! came the echo.

He tore into Hall QB, feet clattering hard on the floor, and found himself immediately confused.

He slowed and stopped.

There was no one ahead of him.

The central aisle was completely empty.

What had happened? Where had the man gone?

His footfalls were still echoing loudly as he murmured, "Hello?"

But there was no answer.

Then, turning back the way he had come, he saw them:

Two ranks of Dumah's dead soldiers, piling out of the rows of bookcases nearest the door.

Yehuda Leib sighed. Of course. Why hadn't he seen it before?

Someone was clearing his throat behind him, and Yehuda Leib turned to see the familiar shape of a tall, skeletal man in a long black coat emerging from the stacks just a few rows ahead of him.

It was not Yehuda Leib's father after all. He wore a bullet-pocked uniform, and a single gold tooth gleamed in his head.

Yehuda Leib knew this soldier: the hanged man, the very last he had seen in the Gallows.

Of course, thought Yehuda Leib. *He must've been a lookout.*

How could he have been so foolish?

But there was no time for regrets now.

"Take him," said the gold-toothed sentry, and Yehuda Leib ran.

CHAPTER FIFTEEN

The Retreat

Deep within the halls of the Dantalion, a Nameless Girl crouched, hidden in the shadows, her thin fingers curled tight around the cold spoon in her apron pocket.

There was shouting, cursing, struggle very nearby, but she couldn't see, couldn't understand where it was coming from.

Angry voices. Pounding feet. Volumes began to fall from their shelves, ladders shooting down their tracks seemingly of their own accord, and before she knew it, the bookcases themselves began to tip and fall, bashing into one another like falling dominoes, and she had to go, she was in danger, and again she was running, again fleeing, and she was exhausted and terrified, and tears blurred her obscure eyes as she pelted down the central aisle, her feet sending an echoing clatter ringing out into the wide halls, and she had to get out of here, had to escape, she was tired of the heavy silence that hid all the dangers lurking beside her, and she turned, and all around her the sounds of running were multiplied, and she heard yelling and laughter as she slid into the ruined hall, slipped through the pile of snow, and ran up the tipped bookcases, up and up and up like a staircase, closer to the shattered O, closer and closer, and the echoing cries below her were like a churning whirlpool pulling her downward, and she was so close, could taste the outside air, so close, and the jagged glass of the skylight was beside her, threatening to gash her open, and she had to do it, had to take her chances, and she leapt, and she was up, only the hem of her dress catching and tattering in the teeth of the glass, and suddenly the cold and the silence of the still, snowy night descended all around her.

She was out.

The Nameless Girl took a gulping chestful of burning cold air.

She was out.

But the trap had just been sprung.

Yehuda Leib had been mistaken: the hall had been ruined not by someone trying to find a way in, but by someone trying to control the ways out.

The Nameless Girl was unsure at first—was she seeing a pair of candles in a hidden window? The lights were still and steady as could be—they never flickered.

But they did blink.

A pair of shining green eyes stared at the Nameless Girl through the darkness, and gradually, the shape around them began to materialize: a hulking white cat, a tigress, her thick, knotty muscles coiled tight, prepared to pounce.

The Nameless Girl would've known her anywhere.

Lilith.

The fact of the matter is that if the Nameless Girl had remained calm in this moment, Lilith might not have been confident of who she was—after all, her name had been severed, her face obscured. But Lilith stalked slowly forward, paw over paw, her shining green eyes locked onto the Nameless Girl's hazy face, and the Nameless Girl found herself unable to breathe, thick fear stopping up her breath.

Lilith let out a low growl, and the Nameless Girl's fragrant fear erupted from her in a cloud of misty breath:

"No!"

Already Lilith had recognized the smell of her fear, but when her luminous eyes took in the object that shone cold and keen in the Girl's trembling fingers, outstretched like a weapon to ward her off, she knew:

The spoon.

The Nameless Girl turned and ran.

With a roar, the white tigress Lilith gave chase.

Rough hands. Strong, bruising fingers. Indistinct voices.

Before long, Yehuda Leib's arms were bound behind his back and a sack was pulled over his head.

He was shoved and pushed around corners, up stairs, down corridors. He'd lost all sense of direction. Every moment stretched to five times its normal length as he strained to glean any usable information from the noise, the shuffle all around him.

Soon he was shoved roughly into the snowy outdoors, the cold and the wind rushing in to meet him, and the first words he'd heard spoken since his capture met his ears.

"To the castrum, double time. Noise-and-light discipline. Move!"

Yehuda Leib's arms were taken hold of, and he was forced forward at a quicker pace than his exhausted legs could possibly hope to match. Soon he was being dragged as much as anything, his sliding boots making contact with the ground only once or twice every five steps.

"Lift him," said the voice, and immediately Yehuda Leib became a piece of baggage, jostled and bounced at the swift pace of the re-treating soldiers.

On and on they went through the howling wind, on and on into the darkness, and just when Yehuda Leib thought his brain would be shaken into a thick soup against the walls of his skull, a halt was called.

Stillness—blessed stillness.

"Put him down," said the officer, and with a dizzying impact, Yehuda Leib's feet were slotted into the snow.

A tearing withdrawal: the sack was pulled from his head. Yehuda Leib's eyes began to water—even the pale moonlight, diffused as it was through the falling snow, was nearly blinding.

The sneer of the gold-toothed officer swam up before him.

"Walk, boy," he said.

The walls of the camp were high—ranks of massive stakes as thick as trees, their sides straight and smooth. The tip of each stake was honed to a treacherously keen point, the outer perimeter of the camp jutting forth like the lower jaw of some needle-toothed predator. Guard towers had been erected on either side of the nar-row gateway, and from far above, the guards posted on perpetual watch leered down at him with still eyes. The night was stiff with cold, but no puffing steam issued from their mouths and noses—dead men draw no breath.

Yehuda Leib tried not to stare, but the farther into the camp they marched, the more difficult it became.

The broad road by which they made their entry was flanked on either side by row after row of narrow canvas tents, each bear-ing a layer of accumulated snow to the windward side. There were no campfires here, no braziers or lanterns or even candles to give light or warmth to the cold soldiers, and as a consequence, the men did not gather, did not huddle together and talk—they stewed and paced and chewed their cheeks, polished and double-checked their weapons, in anticipation of orders that could come at any moment, to fight, fight, fight for their lost lives.

Any development, any occurrence that could provide distraction from this thick stew of dread, was seized upon immediately.

And this is why, as Yehuda Leib was paraded down the camp's main road, it seemed as if the entire Army of the Dead made its way out to gawk at him.

One small unit of Dumah's dead soldiers was horror enough to behold—bloodied and bandaged, their eyes dim and empty.

The army at large was exponentially worse: crowds of the Tsar's dead infantry jumbled together with bleeding Prussian jägers and fallen French grenadiers. Among them, several creaking Roman legionnaires, dusty Spartan hoplites, Assyrian lancers, even bare-chested Egyptian charioteers gathered in order to watch Yehuda Leib pass by.

As one, compressed beneath the heavy weight of an impending battle that they were sure must come, they stared.

Not a whisper broke the silence of the camp.

The army was vast, and the road was long, but Yehuda Leib soon saw where they were headed.

At the very center of the camp was a massive tent of rich scarlet.

Inside, a long draped corridor led toward the central peak of the tent. Plinths and pedestals on all sides held up great weapons and trophies of war: Durendal, the sword of Roland; the spear of Lugh; Zulfiqar, the split-bladed scimitar of Ali ibn Abi Talib; even the sling stone that felled the giant Goliath.

"Here," said the gold-toothed officer, pulling back the flap of a small holding cell off the main corridor. "Two inside, two out."

Yehuda Leib was pushed roughly into the small red room, and only looking back did he realize that he had not been taken alone: a second bound figure was slung over the shoulder of a large soldier in the corridor.

The little shape was unmistakable.

Mammon.

A knot rose in Yehuda Leib's throat. He could hardly use Mammon's assistance to bargain if the demon was bound and gagged in the next cell over.

Yehuda Leib was in worse trouble than he'd thought.

"Stay sharp," barked the voice of the gold-toothed officer to his soldiers. "The general is coming."

Yehuda Leib's heart began to pound.

The general is coming.

If the Nameless Girl had not become so accustomed to leaving everything behind and fleeing, she might've been taken then and there.

But navigation is strange in the Far Country—the place you end up is far less dependent upon your direction than upon the way in which you go—and the moment Lilith, who ought to have known better, began to chase her, Bluma was halfway home.

Snow was everywhere. She could hear the swift pads of Lilith's paws gaining behind her, and she ran and she ran and she ran, and soon she was weaving, swerving to avoid crashing into the stones, and there were more and more, thin slabs, grave markers in dense rows and uneven columns, and here the snow was trodden smooth, and there the earth was freshly turned, and before she knew it, she was running past the little iron gate that kept the cemetery out and the town in and her feet were churning the muddy road, and they were carrying her down just the way they always had, every day of her life, down, down, down from the forest and the graves, down toward the light in the window, her front door, and only as she laid her hand on the handle did she realize where she was, and she was tearing back the door, and there, inside, in her father's bakehouse, the men of Tupik were all assembled.

Swaying, muttering.

Prayer.

One by one, they turned their eyes to her. She was sure that someone would shout out her name, greet her, welcome her, but their eyes slid past her.

A girl—just a girl.

The Nameless Girl was breathing hard, panting in the doorway, and the rabbi grimaced, mimed a shiver, beckoned her inside.

Looking back up the hill, she could see a lithe shape prowling, lurking behind the little cemetery gate. Swiftly, she darted inside and slammed the door behind her.

Someone was reciting the Mourner's Kaddish.

"Yisgadal v'yiskadash sh'meh rabo."

May the Great Name be magnified and sanctified.

All the men of Tupik said, "Amen."

Why were they here? Why were they praying in the bakery instead of the synagogue, as they did every other evening?

Slowly, the Nameless Girl picked her way back through the crowd, farther into the bakery, as the voice that spoke the Kaddish rose high over the swaying heads of the assembled men.

Whose voice was it?

"Y'hei sh'meh rabo m'vorakh l'olam u'l'olmei olmaya."

May the Great Name be blessed forever, and forever and ever.

It was only once she'd made her way to the very back of the room that she realized—of course.

It was her father mourning her bubbe.

He was standing in the corner near the cold oven, his arms folded, his head down.

He looked so old.

And slowly, as he prayed aloud, he lifted his eyes to look at her.

The Nameless Girl's heart leapt. There was a moment—just a bare moment—in which her father might've recognized her.

The smile lines at the corners of his eyes gave a little twitch.

But they did not reawaken. The moment passed, and, just as if she were nothing and no one, his eyes slid on.

The Nameless Girl choked back a sob.

What, who had she become? Was she even his daughter anymore?

Turning, the Nameless Girl began to mount the stairs, the final *amen* of the Kaddish rising up behind her. Tucked against the wall, above the linens drawn up neatly, was her bed—but not hers, somehow. Not anymore.

Beyond, in the inner bedroom, she could see her mother sitting on the edge of her own bed in the flickering candlelight, still, staring, deep in thought. She, too, seemed old, the gray in her hair standing boldly forth.

Beside her, Perla Kraindl's mother sat, rubbing gentle circles into her back.

"Your daughter will come back," said Mrs. Kraindl. "You'll see."

But when Bluma's mother spoke, her voice was heavy and flat. "No," she said. "No. I've lost her. I can feel it."

Tears stung the Nameless Girl's cloudy eyes. She wanted to run into the room, to throw herself into her mother's arms.

But, with a lurch, she thought of the blank indifference in her father's eyes.

It would do no good.

Perhaps her mother was right.

Careful not to make enough noise to attract her attention, the Nameless Girl climbed the final flight of stairs to her bubbe's empty bedroom.

Someone had cleaned up. The stones that had fallen from the chimney were stacked neatly in the corner, the dusty mortar swept away. All her bubbe's possessions had been packed up and removed. Only the bare furniture remained, and that, it seemed, grudgingly.

Through the falling snow, the Nameless Girl could see the white tigress pacing back and forth below, weaving impatiently among the stones in the graveyard.

The Nameless Girl let out a heavy sigh, and suddenly, something beside her moved.

She jumped, backing into the corner, arms up, ready to be attacked, and a small gray cat leapt lightly from the rafters down onto the bed frame.

Her bubbe's cat.

It stared at her intently for a long moment.

Slowly, quietly, the Nameless Girl allowed herself to breathe once more.

She knew this cat. She was not in danger.

Was she?

Warily, the Nameless Girl backed away, the cat's small, steady eyes following her as she went.

She had just turned to climb down the narrow stairs when a voice spoke out behind her.

"Wait," said the voice.

In the blinking of an eye, an old gray lady was sitting atop her bubbe's bed frame.

The Nameless Girl had never seen her before—of that she was sure—but still, somehow, she thought she recognized the features of her wrinkled face, the rumpled frown lines on either side of her lips, deep and sure.

Who was this?

"Wait," said the old woman again. "I know you."

"Who . . . who are you?" said the Nameless Girl.

The old woman frowned. "You're the girl who lived here, yes?" she said. "You grew up in this house?"

The Nameless Girl nodded. "But who are *you?*" she said.

"I was your great-grandmother," said the gray lady. "Your alte-bubbe."

In a flash, it all made sense. "Bubbe's mother?" said the Nameless Girl. She could see it clearly now: those were her bubbe's lips—her bubbe's and, once upon a time, her own. "How did you know me?" said the Nameless Girl.

"Oh," said her alte-bubbe. "You never forget the smell of your baby. Or your baby's baby's baby, I suppose."

A wistful look stole into the old woman's eye, and the Nameless Girl was surprised to see that she had shed a tear.

"I'm sorry," she said. "About your daughter."

"Oh," said her alte-bubbe. "Me too. You'd think it wouldn't be quite as bad once you've gone yourself. But it is."

"Well," said the Nameless Girl, uncomfortable in the silence, "it's nice to finally meet you, I suppose. We've lived in the same house all these years—"

But her alte-bubbe cut quickly in. "Not lived. Not me."

"Oh?" said the Nameless Girl.

"Loitered, really," she said.

"What's the difference?" said the Nameless Girl.

"Everything," said her alte-bubbe. "The living can change things—the world around them, even themselves, if they work hard. If you manage to linger after your death, you find quickly that your influence fades."

"But you're still here."

"I am," said the old woman with a heavy sigh. "But I shouldn't be. I died not long before my daughter moved to this place. She had a baby to look after, no money, no husband—no one to take care of her. So I followed her. Just to worry in the shadows. But now she's gone, and I have no one to worry about. Somehow that's what makes me saddest."

"Are you," said the Nameless Girl, gesturing with her chin to the white tigress in the snow, "one of hers?"

At this, the old lady gave a single hooting laugh. "Ha!" she said. "Lilith? Not anymore. She makes a very compelling case when you first come into the Far Country—all about how you were deprived of opportunity in your life, how it makes sense for you to be angry, how you should decide not to move on, stay with her, join her Sisterhood. I bought it for a little while, but it's all a lie. If you pay close enough attention, you'll see: Lilith isn't interested in anything but herself. She's never changed by her Sisters, and little by little, they all become like her. There is no Sisterhood, really—it's all just different phases of Lilith."

The Nameless Girl found herself wishing this didn't make quite so much sense.

"But *you're* the real question," said the Nameless Girl's alte-bubbe. "What's happened to you?"

"Oh . . . ," said the Nameless Girl.

What had happened to her? Death, slowly, incrementally, over the course of many fleeing steps.

How could she even begin?

The Nameless Girl opened her mouth to speak, but her chin crumpled, and her eyes filled with tears.

"Oh dear," said her alte-bubbe. "Come, come." And the Nameless Girl moved quickly across the bleary room to sit next to her alte-bubbe.

"Tell me everything," she said.

And so the Nameless Girl began to talk. She talked about her bubbe—how angry she had been, how quiet and frightening, and how the Dark One had come for her and toppled her, the solid foundation stone upon which the Nameless Girl's life had been built.

She talked about the cold, sharp spoon, about being chased from her bed, about seeing the face that Death keeps hidden beneath her cowl, about how she had to run, had to flee that face, how she would've done anything to escape from Death—about how she *had* done anything.

She talked about cutting her face away so that no one would know her, about cutting her name away so that no one could call her, about how it still hadn't been enough, how at every turn someone found a way to recognize her.

And here her alte-bubbe stopped her.

"Yes," she said. "You ought to be glad."

"*Glad?*" said the Nameless Girl. "I just want to be left alone."

Her alte-bubbe sighed. "There was once a candle that burned in a dark room," she said. "The candle's light was very beautiful, and though she loved to burn brightly, she was terribly afraid of being blown out. The people who lived in the room enjoyed her light and her warmth, drawing close to read beside her or to warm their fingertips, but every time they turned a page or withdrew their hands, her flame would flicker, and she would be afraid that she might go out. In order to avoid this fate, the candle did away first with her warmth, so that the people would not bring their hands near, and then with her light, so that their books would remain far away. This done, the candle's flame became nothing more than a plume of rising smoke. Was she wise?"

The Nameless Girl found that she was becoming angry. "No," she said. "No, the candle wasn't wise. But I am not a candle. I'm a living person. And I can do with my own self what I would like."

"Of course," said her alte-bubbe. "Of course you can. I don't mean to say that you can't. What I mean to say is this: you wish to go unrecognized, uncalled for, unknown, in order to escape the coming of Death."

The Nameless Girl nodded.

Her alte-bubbe gave a wide, frowning shrug. "This you call a life? To wander around forever, cut off from everyone else?"

The Nameless Girl scoffed cruelly. "And what you have is so much better? You creep around in the shadows, follow your daughter from place to place, until she finally dies and you have nothing better to do than sit alone in her empty room?"

"No, it's not better," said her alte-bubbe. "That's precisely my point: it's exactly the same. But I lived many good years before I died."

"And I'll live and live and live without dying!" said the Nameless Girl angrily.

At this, her alte-bubbe chuckled sadly, her eyes taking on a far-away sheen. "This you call a life?" she asked again.

The Nameless Girl was even angrier now, and she rose from the bed now and went to the window.

Below, Lilith sat waiting.

After a long moment, her alte-bubbe spoke. "Do you want to know what it's like?"

"What?" said the Nameless Girl.

"What you're running from," said her alte-bubbe.

The Nameless Girl didn't respond.

"It's nowhere near as bad as you think. You're living your life, going about your business, and you meet someone: a Visitor in Dark Clothes. You have a talk, perhaps, or maybe even not—perhaps your eyes just meet. And the next thing you know, you're in the Far Country. And I'm sure you found it strange, and I'm sure you found it uncomfortable, but you have to understand: it's not for you. It's for people who can no longer change. That's why there's always snow. That's why the sun never rises. You arrive in the Far Country, and you seek out a comfortable, familiar place—a kitchen, a marketplace, a synagogue—and if you manage to avoid the scavengers, the demons like Lilith who try to divert you from what you ought to be doing, eventually you find yourself bored. Listless. Because in your kitchen in the Far Country, nothing's ever finished cooking. In the marketplace in the Far Country, your shopping's never done, and in the synagogue, the service is never through. You become bored. And you decide to move on."

This didn't sound quite so bad.

"And then what?" said the Nameless Girl.

"I don't know," said her alte-bubbe. "I haven't done it yet. But this I can tell you: there's only one building in the Far Country that stays put—a tall stone tower with many sides that reaches up and up beyond the clouds."

The Nameless Girl's stomach lurched. She knew that place. "Death's house," she said softly.

"I can't tell you what happens inside," said her alte-bubbe. "But I can say this: everyone goes in eventually. Everyone. And no one is ever forced."

"But my name," said the Nameless Girl. "My name and my face . . ."

"Yes," said her alte-bubbe. "I fear that you're already two-thirds inside Death's house."

"Is there no way of getting them back?"

Her alte-bubbe shrugged. "Perhaps. But this I know for certain: you're going to have to face Death one way or another, whether to reclaim what you've given away, or to give away your final third. You can hide for a time, I suppose, but . . ."

"There's no running fast enough?" said the Nameless Girl.

"No," said her alte-bubbe. "There's no running fast enough."

"And if I choose to hide, then I do so by giving up who I am."

"Yes."

The Nameless Girl gave a deep sigh.

"Then in order to live . . ."

Her alte-bubbe smiled sadly. "You have to stop trying not to die."

The Nameless Girl turned to the window. She didn't want to think about what she had to do.

"Ah, look," said her alte-bubbe, sidling up next to her. "Lilith's given up waiting."

The Nameless Girl peered down through the snow. It was true: the white tigress was gone.

"Very well," said the Nameless Girl's alte-bubbe. "Shall we go, then? Together?"

"Move aside."

Yehuda Leib's eyes snapped open.

A voice had spoken in the corridor.

With a fluttering snap, the flap of the holding cell was lifted. A scrawny, rat-faced demon in uniform stood outside, flanked by two thick guards.

"Oh, for the love of—pick him up!"

The soldiers who had remained to guard Yehuda Leib stood him shakily on his feet. The rat-faced demon made an ostentatious show of brushing the dust from Yehuda Leib's coat.

"This hardly seems necessary," the rat-faced demon said, and with a sickly sweet smile, he removed the wad of cloth from Yehuda Leib's mouth.

Yehuda Leib worked his jaw, trying to comfort the dry ache within.

"You're not foolish enough to try and run, are you?"

Yehuda Leib shook his head lightly, jostling the tightness in his neck. "No."

"Good," said the rat-faced demon. "Then I think we can dispense with all this nonsense." And, gesturing to the soldiers, he bid them cut Yehuda Leib's arms free. Yehuda Leib rolled his shoulders and wrists, the sensation slowly returning to his numb limbs.

"There," said the rat-faced demon, "that's better," and, beckoning, he said, "Come with me."

Yehuda Leib followed him out into the corridor, soldiers and bodyguards falling in behind them.

"I apologize for all that." Despite his short stature, the rat-faced demon moved at a swift clip, and Yehuda Leib had to trot to keep up. "This is the central castrum of the Army of the Dead. You are here because Lord High General Dumah wishes to speak with you. In just a few moments, I shall present you to the lord high general, and there are a few things you may wish to know before you meet him."

"I'm sorry," said Yehuda Leib. "Who are you?"

"Ah, yes," said the demon. "I apologize. I am Undergeneral Behemoth, chief steward, adjutant, and aide-de-camp to the lord high general." Now the little demon laid a clammy claw on Yehuda Leib's shoulder and leaned in with a dirty-toothed grin. "You will come to know me quite well, I expect."

This seemed like an unpleasant prospect.

"I'm Yehuda Leib," said Yehuda Leib.

"Yes," said Behemoth. "We're familiar with you."

Yehuda Leib had no idea what this meant, but it was hardly comforting.

"There are three things that you may wish to know about the lord high general," said Behemoth. "Firstly, he is called Dumah, which means 'Silence,' and it is not an arbitrary name. His is the jealous silence, the silence that consumes. He will not break it to speak. For this reason, I am often called upon to interpret his meaning for those unused to his methods of communication. This fact notwithstanding, it is very important that, while in the lord high general's presence, you address him directly, and not, as some mistakenly do, me."

Yehuda Leib nodded.

"Secondly," said Behemoth. "It is very important not to resort carelessly to popular slurs in the presence of the lord high general.

As the leader of the Army of the Dead, he is rightly concerned with issues of hierarchy and rank, and he will brook no diminution of his rightful status. Therefore, be sure never to refer to him, as is the vulgar custom, as a *demon*. He is a Messenger of the Eternal, an Angel, no lower than any other, and if you wish to remain in his good graces, you will bear this in mind."

Again, Yehuda Leib nodded. They had begun to approach a thick, rich curtain at the end of the corridor. Light was flickering inside.

"Finally," said Behemoth, "and this may seem simple, but I cannot possibly stress it enough: Lord High General Dumah's anger is quick, sharp, and efficient, and I have never seen him shy away from the furthest extremity of its violence. For this reason, it is extraordinarily important that you do not look Lord High General Dumah in the eye."

Behemoth came to a stop before the curtain and turned to look at Yehuda Leib.

"Do you understand me?"

Yehuda Leib swallowed. "Yes," he said.

"Good," said Behemoth, and he drew back the curtain.

CHAPTER SIXTEEN

The Advance

The chamber of Dumah was still.

A large tabletop model of the Far Country dominated the center of the high, peaked tent, flickering and shifting, rearranging its geography every time Yehuda Leib looked away. He recognized the little ramble of Mammon's Treasure House, the Dead City beyond the thick Gallows Grove. He could even see the castrum where he stood now.

But of them all, only the tall, many-sided tower of the House of Death stood firm, immovable in the center of the map.

Yehuda Leib had just begun to look for the round skylights of Dantalion when he heard the lord high general coming.

Dumah was huge.

He burst in at the far side of the tent, his goblin honor guard following close behind. Dumah's hulking black mount pawed and snorted and bucked beneath him, steaming in the cold, and the honor guard rushed forward to hold it steady as Dumah climbed down.

The general was tall and broad, each of his thick-fingered hands large enough to palm a man's skull. His eyes were sunken black holes deep in his head, and massive muttonchops of moldy blue beard perfectly framed his missing lower jaw. His wide chest was hung thick with medals, each of which, upon closer inspection, turned out to be the relic of a fallen foe—a yellow tooth, a dried toe, a desiccated tongue—carefully set in neat ribbons of stained bandaging.

But all of this scarcely caught Yehuda Leib's notice.

Wrapped tight around Dumah's neck was a scarf: woolen, red, and terribly familiar.

"Lord High General," said Behemoth, bowing obsequiously.

Dumah didn't acknowledge him.

"That scarf," said Yehuda Leib, whispering so that the general would not hear. "Behemoth, where did he get that scarf?"

Now two members of the goblin honor guard reached up behind the lord high general to pull the thick riding coat from his shoulders, and as it came down, one of its buttons caught briefly, snagging the epaulet on the general's left shoulder.

Dumah's fury was blazing and swift: grabbing the offending goblin by the neck, the general slammed him bodily down into the dirt and, with his bare fist, pounded the hapless guard's helmet over and over and over again.

Sounds of screaming, pleading, apologizing filled the tent.

But far, far worse was the silence that fell when they broke off.

Slowly, the general rose and brushed the dust from his knees.

Behemoth cleared his throat loudly and stepped forward.

"Lord High General," he said. "This is the boy, Yehuda Leib."

Now Dumah turned, his interest piqued. Slowly, deliberately, he waved his hand through the air, and Behemoth translated:

"Honor guard!" he said. "Dismissed!"

Quietly, the goblins of Dumah's honor guard dispersed, careful not to turn their backs to the lord high general as they dragged their fallen comrade from the tent.

Dumah stalked across the chamber and lowered himself into a huge wooden chair at the far end. A round table sat beside him, littered with papers, and he shoved several of them aside in order to put his massive feet up.

Knitting his thick fingers together beneath his nose, he fixed his dark eyes again on Yehuda Leib.

Yehuda Leib stood beside Behemoth, unmoving, uncomfortable.

Presently, Dumah lifted one hand to gesture at a low stool next to his chair.

"The lord high general invites you to sit," said Behemoth.

It felt unwise to draw nearer to Dumah. It felt, frankly, unwise even to move in his presence.

But Yehuda Leib was clear-eyed. They, after all, had brought him here. They wanted to speak with him. That was his advantage. And it wouldn't do to shy away from it.

With a light nod, Yehuda Leib strode across the room to where the lord high general was seated but did not, himself, sit.

Again, Dumah gestured to the stool.

"The lord high general bids you sit," said Behemoth.

Yehuda Leib looked at the stool and shook his head, clasping his hands behind his back.

There was a long silence as Dumah regarded Yehuda Leib.

And then, with the raising of an eyebrow, he lifted his feet from the table beside him. Quickly, he sorted through the various documents on the tabletop and found a thick sheaf of papers, which he tossed onto the ground in front of Behemoth.

"Ah," said the little rat-faced demon, bending to retrieve it. "The lord high general wishes to share his intelligence with you."

Yehuda Leib didn't look at Behemoth. "Thank you," he said.

"Two terrestrial nights ago," said Behemoth, "certain omens in the snow and sky indicated to the sorcerers of the Army of the Dead that a significant shift in power had taken place in the Far Country. For this reason, the lord high general consulted with Lord Dantalion, an ancient ally, who gave the following response to our inquiry."

Here Behemoth riffled several pages and began to read.

"'War is coming,'" he said. "'And much will be decided by the weapon that carries itself into the Far Country.'"

Behemoth looked out over the top of the dossier.

"*The weapon that carries itself,*" he repeated, tossing the dossier back onto the table. "This was a compelling piece of information for us to receive. War, after all, is our dominion."

Leaning back in his chair, Dumah cracked the knuckles of his huge hands with a sound like a volley of musket fire.

"The lord high general took this opportunity to commission reports from his various intelligence assets among both the demons and the armies of the living with the goal of determining the identity of *the weapon that carries itself into the Far Country.* There were several possible candidates, including literal weapons, as well as a few recently deceased soldiers and tacticians of note. In the end, though, Lord High General Dumah was far more interested in the notion that you, Yehuda Leib, son of Avimelekh, are the Weapon That Carries Itself."

Now there was a long silence.

Dumah watched Yehuda Leib.

Yehuda Leib was very careful to do absolutely nothing, though his heart seemed to swell in his chest as if his name had finally been pronounced correctly for the very first time.

Soon Dumah inclined his head slightly, and Behemoth continued.

"Yehuda Leib, we wish to offer you a bargain. I am sure that you saw the scale of our army as you came into the castrum this evening. There is more strength here than it is practical to deploy under a single commander, and accordingly, it is our pleasure to offer you the deferred commission of field marshal general of the Army of the Dead, reporting directly to Lord High General Dumah."

Field marshal general? That was as high a rank as anyone could have without being the lord high general himself.

"With respect," said Yehuda Leib, "surely there are soldiers in your army better qualified than me."

"Of course there are," said Behemoth. "But the lord high general is of the opinion that excellence in command relies upon change and adaptation—faculties unavailable to the dead. He wishes his field marshal general to be possessed of both the assets and the liabilities of mortality.

"For this reason, if you accept our commission, we will exploit our contacts and resources in the armies of the living in order to make you more qualified than any other living man of war. You will serve an apprenticeship of some thirty years' length, during which time we will arrange to move you from army to army, commission to commission, so that you may have the opportunity to study with the greatest commanders now living. It will be our pleasure during the term of your apprenticeship to supply your every want as only those in our position are able—with the finest food, clothing, housing, horseflesh, men, and women you could possibly desire.

At the end of this period of apprenticeship, you shall return to this castrum and take command of one-half of the forces of the Army of the Dead, which will be yours to organize and deploy as you see fit, in accordance with the orders of the lord high general.

"You shall have the greatest military career in history. The lord high general has already begun to lay plans for the campaigns the two of you shall execute together, and, having seen only the smallest portion of them, I must say that in accepting this commission, you shall make a legend of yourself."

Slowly, Dumah shifted his hulking mass and raised himself up to stand over Yehuda Leib.

"What do you say?" said Behemoth. "Will you pledge your allegiance to the Army of the Dead?"

Yehuda Leib's heart was racing. This was, of course, an incredibly tempting offer.

But if his time with Mammon had taught him anything, it was that there was nothing so dangerous as a tempting offer.

"Boy," said Behemoth behind him. "The lord high general is not accustomed to waiting."

With a long sigh, Yehuda Leib finally lowered himself slowly onto the low stool before Dumah. "I wonder, Behemoth," he said, "if I might have a word with the lord high general alone."

Behind him, the rat-faced demon gave a scoff, and Yehuda Leib could hear the sneer in his expression as he answered. "Don't be ridiculous. I am the lord high general's most constant servant. Anything you wish to say to him you may say to me."

It was a massive risk, but Yehuda Leib could see no other way forward.

Slowly, just as he had been instructed never to do, he lifted his eyes to look directly into Dumah's.

Dumah stiffened, straightened.

Yehuda Leib did not blink.

And slowly, almost lazily, Dumah waved the back of his hand toward Behemoth.

"But," spluttered the little rat-faced demon. "But, my lord!"

Now Dumah lowered himself back into his creaking chair, careful not to move his eyes from Yehuda Leib's. He lifted his arm and pointed a thick finger at the curtain through which Behemoth and Yehuda Leib had come.

"Are you certain, my lord?" said Behemoth, almost desperately.

Dumah dropped his arm.

Behemoth sniffled, furious, humiliated. "Very, um . . . ," he said. "Very well. I shall go and, uh, check on the other prisoner."

And, with a shushing of curtains, Behemoth was gone.

Dumah leaned back in his chair, raised his eyebrows, and spread his hands wide.

Go on.

"I thank you for bringing me here, Lord High General," said Yehuda Leib. "And I thank you for your generous offer."

Yehuda Leib swallowed. Was he sure about this? If he offended the lord high general, then these might be the last words he ever spoke.

"But I don't think I can accept."

Dumah leaned forward and knotted his thick fingers together beneath his exposed upper teeth. Yehuda Leib's heart clattered in his chest.

"War is coming, yes. But it's not a war that will take place in thirty years. It's a war that has already begun. And as Lord Dantalion has told you, a lot depends upon me. I am the fight, and as soon as I am able, I will carry myself to the enemy."

Lord Dumah raised one open palm as if to say, *Where?*

"There," said Yehuda Leib, and without breaking his eye contact with Dumah, he pointed at the many-sided tower at the center of the model beside him. "To Death."

Dumah leaned back in his chair and began to tug at his muttonchops.

"He's taken something—something of mine. I intend to force my way inside his tower and take it back. If I have to go alone, I will. But I'd feel far more comfortable with your army at my back."

Slowly, Dumah stood and paced his way over to the model on the table. Death's tower rose high into the modeled clouds, its innumerable little faces meeting in a universe of sharp corners.

"At this point you must be asking yourself why you would ever want to tempt a foe as strong as the Angel of Death."

Dumah didn't respond.

"Well, when I overthrow him, he'll need to be replaced."

Dumah's back was to Yehuda Leib now, and he leaned on his map table, one beefy fist on either side of his castrum.

He was thinking. But Yehuda Leib didn't need him thinking. He needed him mad.

"You were an Angel once, weren't you?"

Dumah turned around swiftly, something deep in his dark eyes flashing.

"Come with me, Dumah. Let me win your final promotion. Let me make you the Angel of Death."

Now a long, still silence held the chamber, as absolute as the silence of the grave. Dumah leaned back on his map table, his eyes fixed and thoughtful, his arms folded across his broad chest. Yehuda Leib was tempted to say something more, to prod, to add to his counteroffer, but he held his tongue: there was nothing more to say.

Presently, Dumah stood and flexed his fingers. Slowly, he stalked back to his chair and lowered himself down to sit lightly on its edge. His eyes narrowed as he stared hard at the boy on the little stool in front of him.

Yehuda Leib didn't move a muscle.

Dumah extended his hand.

On a cold, dark night in the middle of winter, an old woman found herself wandering through the forest in search of the small summer strawberries that grow in the shade.

The old woman was unsure how she had gotten to the forest— she couldn't remember leaving home, couldn't remember bundling into her warm clothes. All she knew was that there were berries around here somewhere, and that if she kept looking, she would find them.

These were the best kind of berries, tiny and soft. She remembered them well from her girlhood, when she'd crouched in the bushes, staining her lips and fingertips red: one for her mouth, one for her apron, and so on and on.

She could take them home. She could share them with her son, Zalman, and her granddaughter ...

What was her name?

It seemed to have slipped her mind.

The old woman had just come upon the berries when she heard

the sound, and at first she was sure that she must be imagining things.

But she was not.

The column burst out into the clearing like a ball from a musket: men in ragtag rows, stepping all out of time, their buttons and weapons and uniforms mismatched, and more and more and more men—the old woman had never seen so very many. Now horses came as well, and cackling creatures astride them. Mules, camels, chariots, even a pair of elephants, dead and decomposing, thundered by the old woman in the brambles.

She was not foolish; she kept hidden and did not draw attention to herself. But when one particular boy reached the clearing, she could not help but rise up to get a better look.

She knew that boy. The gray pony beneath him moved dexterously at his urging, as if it were a part of him. In fact, it became quickly clear that the entirety of the column, the entirety of this fearsome army, was simply an extension of his body.

This, of course, was Yehuda Leib.

He had come to retrieve his father.

He had come to overthrow Death.

But something about him had changed.

Around his neck, cinched tight against the cold, was a stained red scarf of wool. He had negotiated its release from Lord High General Dumah as part of their larger arrangement, had listened patiently as its extraordinary qualities had been enumerated by the sniveling Undergeneral Behemoth: it was a very powerful amulet, a protection against harm, stitched painstakingly by a mortal woman for her child, stained with the blood of the child's father, buried with all the dignities of a mortal man. If one of Lord High General Dumah's scouts hadn't recovered it for him in the border cemeteries, it might've fetched a very dear price on the demon market—a noble title, a grand estate, or perhaps even more.

Soon Lord High General Dumah himself came cantering up through the column, riding upon his hulking black stallion, and when Yehuda Leib turned to greet him, the old woman in the bushes saw that the scarf had not been given for nothing.

One of the boy's keen blue eyes was missing, the empty socket covered over with a black patch, and on the lord high general's chest there was a brand-new trophy, a medallion glistening in the starlight:

One keen blue eye.

It had been a dear price to pay. But there are very old laws that govern the drawing up of covenants and agreements, and nothing binds them tighter than the willful giving of blood.

Yehuda Leib had paid gladly.

By and by, the boy and the lord high general moved through the clearing, leading the enormous torrent of the trooping dead behind them, and the old woman was left alone at the berry bush.

But her appetite was gone now. The vine seemed to bear only dried, dead fruits, small black clots that dangled heavily from their stems.

With a sigh, she rose to her feet.

She had become bored.

Now the old lady began to walk again, going in the opposite direction from the army, but moving toward the same destination: a tall, many-faced tower at the very center of everything.

After all—the direction you go matters less than you think.

ᘺ

"They're moving."

Lilith let out a low sigh.

Things were growing more complex by the moment.

"Where are they bound?"

The cat shook her head. "I do not know. But the boy rides before them."

Lilith frowned. "What do you mean, *before them*? An outrider?"

"No," said Lilith's scout. "He rides beside the lord high general."

This was very, very troublesome. The girl was in Tupik, and the spoon was with her. But now Dumah's army was on the move. Lilith couldn't afford to continue waiting here in the forest for the girl's return—the Lileen were exposed, undefended. If Dumah had learned from Yehuda Leib where the girl had gone, they could be vulnerable to ambush at any moment.

But, on the other hand, if Lilith moved too soon, she might tip her hand. Did Dumah even know the Lileen were there, biding their time beneath the trees?

Perhaps the boy had struck a bargain with Dumah on the girl's behalf. Perhaps they were moving to rendezvous with her now.

But what if Dumah didn't even know of the spoon? What if he had different—even better—intelligence?

It was all terribly unclear.

Lilith sniffed, leaning against the tree behind her. "How close are they?"

The cat cocked her head and calculated. "Fifteen, perhaps twenty minutes' march. Do you mean to attack?"

"I don't know," said Lilith. "But I wish I did."

"Sister," said a gray lady, rising from the shadows. "What do you know that we do not?"

"Much," said Lilith through a frown. "And still I do not know enough. But the time for planning may be past. Perhaps the time for action has come."

A pair of shining eyes blinked down from the bough above her head, and another gray cat spoke. "It is a great danger, making war with Dumah. Many of our Sisters may be lost."

"Yes," said Lilith. "But the girl carries a tool of great power."

"Surely," said the cat slung overhead, "there are other weapons."

"No," said Lilith. "Not like this. I desire it. And what is more, I refuse to allow Dumah to have it."

"Then what," said the cat, "shall we do?"

Lilith sighed, unhappy with every option. "Let word be passed among my Sisters: I should like the girl alive if we can have her. But if you must kill her to bring me what she carries, you shall not hesitate."

"Lilith has spoken," said the gray lady.

Lilith had spoken.

"Very well," said the Nameless Girl's alte-bubbe. "Shall we go, then? Together?"

It felt strange, walking through Tupik like this. Everything had changed, and yet all around her, lives plodded forward as if things were the same as they had always been.

Evening prayers. Dinner. Bed.

Just like always.

The Nameless Girl's alte-bubbe led her past the little iron gate into the graveyard on the hillside, but instead of continuing up through the stones and trees, she took a sharp turn. "This way," she said. "I know a shortcut." And, pulling the Nameless Girl behind, she began to circle her daughter's grave:

Once.

Twice.

Three times.

They had separated now, making their tight circles individually around the little hillock.

"Four," murmured the Nameless Girl's alte-bubbe to herself. "Five."

By the sixth circuit, the Nameless Girl's head had begun to swim. Her orbit had been tight, and she'd kept her eyes fixed on the grave. Soon she was downright dizzy, and she stumbled as she completed her seventh circle, stepping sideways to catch herself, treading over the grave.

She stopped, shut her eyes, pressed her fingers to her forehead, and when she blinked her eyes open again, she was somewhere else, the forest dark and snowy, the boughs of its trees reaching out for one another overhead as if eager to blot out what passed below from the eyes of Heaven.

"Where are we?" she said softly.

"Close," said her alte-bubbe. "Look."

There was a wide clearing before them, its snow well trodden and slick, and on the far side of it, the Nameless Girl could see an old woman, hunched, walking, her broken-hipped gait unmistakable.

Bubbe.

Instinctively, the Nameless Girl's body tightened, as if preparing to run to her, but her alte-bubbe laid a heavy hand on her shoulder.

"No," she said. "Don't you see where she's going?"

The Nameless Girl squinted into the gloom. Beyond the trees

on the far side of the clearing, a tall tower of many sides rose high into the sky.

"We mustn't stop her," said her alte-bubbe. "Not if she's decided."

Slowly, they set off to follow from a distance.

By the time they made it to the trees at the far edge of the clearing, the Nameless Girl's bubbe was halfway down the slope, her huddled silhouette growing smaller, smaller, smaller against the mottled stone of the tower. Only now did the Nameless Girl begin to understand how truly huge it was.

She felt uneasy—terribly uneasy.

At first she tried to push this feeling away, thinking that it was only the same churning dread she'd felt at her first sight of Death's house.

But this was not a feeling in her gut. This feeling crept across the back of her neck.

The Nameless Girl pulled up short.

Slowly, she turned back into the clearing.

She didn't see them at first—a thick cloak of darkness hung between the trees—but then they emerged: a woman all in white, neither old nor young, short nor tall, plain nor beautiful, her thick curls hanging loose and free, cheeks rosy with the cold. And behind her, beside her, all around her: a stalking Sisterhood of great gray panthers, their muscles rippling, eyes glowing weirdly in the dim.

"The War Cats," said the Nameless Girl's alte-bubbe, and she gave a deep sigh.

"Hello," said Lilith from across the clearing. "Good of you to stop running."

Neither the Nameless Girl nor her alte-bubbe moved.

"There is no reason for this to be unpleasant," said Lilith. "You have something I desire, a bauble near to my heart. Give it to me, and you shall go on your way without any trouble."

The Nameless Girl was already shaking her head when she heard her alte-bubbe speak.

"You may not have it, Lilith."

Softly, the Nameless Girl put her hand into the pocket of her apron, laying her fingers on the spoon. Lilith tracked the movement carefully with cold eyes.

"Oh no?" she said. "Perhaps you ought to ask the girl."

Now the Nameless Girl's alte-bubbe revolved, closing her into a whispering huddle. "Listen to me carefully," she said. "Whatever you choose to do inside that tower, I am proud of you."

"But *together*," said the Nameless Girl. "You said we go together."

Her alte-bubbe gave a tight little shake of her head. "Sister Lilith has other plans. If you run, I think I can give you enough time."

"But," said the Nameless Girl with a lurch. "But . . ."

"Go," said her alte-bubbe. "And if you see my daughter, tell her I'm sorry."

The Nameless Girl's eyes were crowded with tears as she turned toward the tall, mottled tower at the bottom of the valley.

"Go!"

And, one last time, the Nameless Girl began to run.

Behind her, someone gave a great roar that shook the snow from the treetops.

It had begun.

CHAPTER SEVENTEEN

To War

"No," said Yehuda Leib. "We need to go now."

The Army of the Dead had halted its march just below the ridge that led down into the Tower Valley. Everywhere there was hubbub—tents pitched, cannons cleaned, blades sharpened and polished.

In the privacy of his silence, the lord high general strode through the camp, Behemoth and Yehuda Leib arguing on either side.

"Faster is not necessarily better," said the little rat-faced under-general. "If we take the time to survey the ground . . ."

"Then we give away the advantage of surprise."

Behemoth shook his head. "The tower walls are high and strong. If we don't examine them for weaknesses, then who's to say we'll ever topple them?"

"We don't need to topple them," said Yehuda Leib. "We just need to open them."

"At the very least," said Behemoth, shaking his head, "I must be able to deploy artillery teams up the ridge."

"If you can do it while we're on the march," said Yehuda Leib, "then you're welcome to."

Behemoth rolled his eyes. "What's the rush?"

Yehuda Leib sighed. The Tower of Death could be seen from anywhere in the camp—huge, looming up from the valley, blocking out the stars—and, what was more, Yehuda Leib could feel it: a tightness in his muscles, a cold itching in his hands.

His father was in there.

At just this moment, a sentry came galloping up.

"Lord High General," he said with a bow. "Movement in the trees: Lilith and her War Cats. A girl approaches the tower."

Now Yehuda Leib's heart began to thunder.

"Lilith?" said Behemoth. "What does she want here?"

But Yehuda Leib ignored him, speaking directly to Dumah. "This is it," he said. "We must go now."

Dumah was still, lost in thought. From the broad chest of his deep black uniform, Yehuda Leib saw his own keen eye staring back at him, nestled in a bloom of bloody bandages.

And then, finally, Dumah gave his head a tight nod.

"Very well," said Behemoth, and, with a sigh, he trotted off to issue orders.

It was happening.

Word of the coming charge rippled quickly through the camp. Everywhere the signs of preparation could be seen. Dumah had chosen a massive suit of Japanese armor for this occasion, complete with a fearsome antlered helmet, and his honor guard was busy binding its many plates and panels to him. Behemoth's artillery teams began to harness their heavy guns to teams of rotting horses, and rifles and muskets and pistols were checked and double-checked:

Primed.

Loaded.

On his way to mount his pony, Yehuda Leib saw Behemoth stealing into his little tent, looking sharply over his shoulder as he went. In and of itself, this was unremarkable, but in the warm firelight within the tent, Yehuda Leib caught sight of another face: Mammon, one eye blackened, his arms tied behind his back.

He had almost forgotten about Mammon. As soon as all of this was over, he would have to advocate for his release.

But something tickled Yehuda Leib's mind as he swung up into the saddle:

Why was Mammon being held in Behemoth's tent?

The snowfall had almost entirely broken off by the time they rode, and the contours of the land were clearly visible through the clean white blanket of snow. The visibility was good enough that the entire Army of the Dead managed to mobilize without lanterns, and climbing between the deploying artillery positions to the peak of the ridge, Yehuda Leib felt the army spreading out in the darkness behind him, the chariots and rifles, the horses and soldiers, the spearmen and swordsmen and archers and all, just as if they were his own long arms.

It wasn't fair, what had been taken away.

It wasn't fair.

Beside him, Dumah, a hulking shadow, unsheathed his long sword and gave a nod.

The order was Yehuda Leib's to give.

With a shock, Yehuda Leib felt himself choking up.

He had been so angry—so angry for so long.

Yehuda Leib's vision began to swim; beneath Dumah's massive breastplate, a single tear crept down the front of his uniform.

"I'm coming," said Yehuda Leib softly, and with a yell, he spurred his pony on.

Trumpets blasted. Dumah was beside him, his stallion's hooves sending the icy snow flying up in their wake. Yehuda Leib's lungs were on fire, and he was screaming, his throat aching with the strain, as he charged down the slope, and they came to the long approach, the ground flattening out beneath their mounts, and Yehuda Leib urged his pony forward, faster, and it sprang on with lightning in its legs.

But something was wrong.

Beside him, Dumah was wheeling, turning back to the ridge.

Yehuda Leib and Dumah were at the bottom of the ridge, but the entire Army of the Dead remained above, arrayed for battle.

Only the two of them had advanced on his order.

What was happening?

Yehuda Leib turned his pony's head, trotting quickly to Dumah's side.

"What is it?" he said. "What's going on?"

Dumah's eyes were alive with alarm.

He didn't know.

And all of a sudden, like a bell tolling in silence, they heard it: Sniveling laughter.

With a lurch, Yehuda Leib knew:

Mammon.

There he was, beside Behemoth on the ridge above, a sharp-toothed smile splitting his salt-scarred face.

"Thank you, Behemoth," he said. "I've never owned an army before, and I have to tell you—it's a rather splendid feeling."

"We had a deal!" cried Yehuda Leib, his voice choked with fury.

"A deal?" laughed Mammon. "You were my property, and you attacked me!"

"But," spluttered Yehuda Leib. "But!"

Mammon rolled his eyes. "Oh, spare me."

"You're a liar!" said Yehuda Leib.

"And you're an idiot," said Mammon. "Why should I partner with you? You make unwinnable war on an unbeatable foe, and all so you can steal once more what you took from me in the first place. You must think me such a fool."

"Yes," spat Yehuda Leib. "A dead fool!"

"Best of luck to you," said Mammon. "But as a veteran wagerer, allow me to inform you: the odds are not in your favor."

"You're a snake," said Yehuda Leib. "I don't know why anyone ever deals with you."

"Honestly," said Mammon, "neither do I. And yet there always seems to be someone willing to strike a bargain."

Behemoth shifted nervously beside Mammon.

Yehuda Leib gave a furious yell and lifted his heels to spur his pony back up the slope. All he could see now was Mammon's sick, treacherous little smile, and he wanted nothing more than to bash it and bash it and bash it until it was gone.

But a thick hand reached out and stopped him.

Dumah's dark eyes were sparkling strangely.

He gazed at Yehuda Leib and then turned back to the tower.

The tower.

Perhaps there was something Yehuda Leib wanted more, after all.

Dropping his hand from Yehuda Leib's chest, Dumah hefted his huge sword, gave it a flourish, and fixed his eyes on the army at the top of the ridge.

The message was clear:

Their bargain stood. He would hold off the army while Yehuda Leib made his way in.

"Are you sure?" said Yehuda Leib softly.

Dumah nodded silently, the antlers of his great helm dipping and rising as if in salute.

"Thank you," said Yehuda Leib. "Thank you."

Yehuda Leib wheeled his pony about, and it leapt toward the Tower of Death at the spurring of his heels, the wind tearing past on either side. Behind him, he heard Mammon screech in anger. Behemoth was bellowing orders. The flash and boom of cannon fire cut through the crisp night air, but Yehuda Leib had only one thought now:

The tower.

He had to make it to the tower.

Drums, trumpets, a chorus of screaming voices: Yehuda Leib turned to look over his shoulder and saw that the entire Army of the Dead was charging down the snowy ridge toward Dumah like a massive waterfall intent upon extinguishing a single candle.

There was no time to lose.

But as he turned back toward his goal, his stomach dropped.

His pony was galloping as hard as ever, but the tower had stopped growing larger.

What was happening? Why was he not coming any closer?

And suddenly the words of Mammon came back to him:

Navigation in the Far Country is not the same as it is in the living lands.

Yehuda Leib squeezed his eye shut, fighting to calm his breath.

He must not run from the army behind him; he must run toward the Death before him.

When he opened his eye again, the Tower of Death had begun to grow once more.

But he was not the only one who knew how to make his way through the Far Country. Some of the officers of the Army of the Dead had seen his progress toward the tower and issued intelligence orders to their men, and now dead lancers, cavalrymen, and riflemen began to loom up on either side of him, gaining on the tower just as he was.

Yehuda Leib had one advantage, though: as soon as his pursuers turned their sights on him, their objective shifted, and he surged ahead and out of their grasp.

He must concentrate on the Tower of Death—it was the only way to outrun them.

Now a chorus of roaring split the night, and Yehuda Leib wheeled back in his saddle, looking to the battlefield. A huge phalanx of gray panthers had spilled into the valley, a furious lady in white leading their charge toward the tower—toward him. The War Cats were moving quickly, flying across the snow, and for a moment Yehuda Leib lost control, his heart spinning, slamming against the inside of his chest, and he wanted to run, wanted to flee, and immediately flying paws and beating hooves closed in all around him, cold, dead fingers reaching out to tear him from the saddle.

Again, Yehuda Leib squeezed his eye shut, fighting to calm himself and focus on his goal:

The tower.

The tower.

Only the tower.

Soon enough he'd managed to hone his intention, but the damage had been done: when Yehuda Leib opened his eye once more, the illusion of direction he'd carried with him into the Far Country had been wiped away.

They were everywhere, on every side: the demons and the dead, the War Cats and the cavalrymen, each of them bounding forward toward the rest, scratching and biting, slashing and firing.

They were everywhere.

He was surrounded.

Again, terror began to take hold of Yehuda Leib's heart, but still his pony dodged and pranced, cantering, galloping, leaping forward without impediment.

The two armies were holding one another back.

And as long as he did not lose sight of his goal . . .

With a deep breath, Yehuda Leib fixed his gaze on the huge tower before him, letting the nightmares all around him fade into the darkness.

Death. He was coming for Death.

And no one could be allowed to stop him.

From a distance, the Tower of Death seemed simple, geometric, one flat face of stone pivoting to lead into the next and the next and the next until eternity.

But from feet away, it seemed as if each face were endless.

Yehuda Leib slid from the saddle, and his pony, in a panicked lather, pulled and bucked, fleeing hard back into the battle across the valley.

He was alone, but not for long: on every side, the battle raged. Only the combat of others held his pursuers back.

The tower's stone was mottled, splotchy, and as he drew near, the reason became clear: the tower itself was made of grave markers—slabs and tablets, plaques and plinths—that met edge to edge, rising high up to heaven.

Yehuda Leib cursed quietly to himself. He saw the letters on the gravestones, understood what they were, but he had never learned to read them. Surely one of these graves would proclaim ENTRANCE or I OPEN HERE or something else useful, but if it did, Yehuda Leib had no way of knowing.

Slowly, he began to work his way along the stone wall, tracing the engraved names of the dead with his fingers, looking for something, anything, familiar.

"Yehuda Leib."

Yehuda Leib nearly jumped out of his skin. There, not five grave widths distant, was a girl, staring at him.

"Oh no," she said sadly. "What happened to your eye?"

Yehuda Leib lifted his fingers to his eye patch. "I traded it," he said.

The Nameless, Faceless Girl frowned. "For what?"

Yehuda Leib looked over his shoulder at the battle unfolding all around them.

"Time," he said. "A little more time."

"Well," said the Nameless Girl, "let's make sure we don't waste it, then," and she turned swiftly to the wall of graven names.

But Yehuda Leib was confused. "Do I know you?" he said.

The Nameless Girl didn't turn back. "Oh," she said with a sigh. "I hope so."

Yehuda Leib shook his head in confusion. He could sense her there beside him, even when he wasn't looking—the way she moved, the way she warmed the air . . .

It felt familiar.

Like home.

"Are you . . . ?"

But the Nameless Girl was distracted. "The names," she said. "I think we have to find our way in through the names."

Yehuda Leib nodded. "Yes. But I never learned to read them."

"I can," said the Nameless Girl.

Yehuda Leib pointed. "What does this one say?"

The Nameless Girl squinted at the weather-faded letters in the stone. "'Chaim, son of Herschl and Hindeh.'"

"This one?"

"'Fruma, daughter of Tzipora and Menachem.'"

And, at just this moment, a mournful yowl split the night.

Yehuda Leib and the Nameless Girl turned quickly over their shoulders.

Someone had fallen. Someone important.

Lilith.

Her body was impaled, limp and lifeless, upon a horseman's lance.

She was dead.

"No," breathed the Nameless Girl.

And then, something changed: in the blinking of an eye, one of the great gray War Cats had become a tall, slender woman, and as she strode forward through the ranks of the Lileen, her shift began to fade from gray to pure snowy white.

As one, the Lileen gave a roar of pride and leapt forward against the soldiers again. Lilith, wearing her new self like a well-fitting dress, lunged out to avenge her own death—but not before bending low to whisper to one of her War Cats, a single, slender finger pointing across the valley toward the Nameless Girl at the tower's edge.

The Nameless Girl was transfixed. Yehuda Leib wanted to get her attention, to turn her back to the stone wall, but he couldn't think what name to call out.

Softly, he laid a hand on her shoulder.

The Nameless Girl gave a little gasp of surprise at the warmth of his hand.

"Come on," he said. "I think our extra time is running out."

Swiftly, they worked their way along the tower's face, Yehuda Leib choosing stone after stone, the Nameless Girl reading out name after name. They had just come to a corner and a new face of the tower when the names began to grow familiar:

Yekhiel Tzvi—he'd heard that before.

Nosson Dovid—that one, too.

And then *Avimelekh*.

That name he knew for certain.

Yehuda Leib moved down to the next stone and pointed with certainty.

"That one," he said. "It's that one."

The Nameless Girl leaned in close and read:

"'Yehuda Leib,'" she said. "'Son of Avimelekh and Shulamis.'"

Yehuda Leib nodded.

This was it.

This was his gravestone.

Leaning forward, he let his fingers run over the strange shapes of the letters; lightly, smoothly, the stone swung back, like a door.

And what they saw beyond shocked them.

Outside the tower, the night was cold, crisp, and clear, the snow trickling down from above in small, lazy flakes. But inside, the summer sun shone out bright and warm over a thick carpet of lush green grass, its golden light falling through the open gravestone door onto the thick accumulation of snow outside. Yehuda Leib could feel the warmth bleeding out into the night, and immediately he dropped his knapsack and began to remove his coat.

His red woolen scarf, however, he left in place.

Beside him, the Nameless Girl was motionless.

"Are you coming?" said Yehuda Leib.

The Nameless Girl's eyebrows fell. "It's not my door," she said.

"Well," said Yehuda Leib, opening his knapsack wide to fit his coat inside. "Where's yours?"

But before the Nameless Girl could answer, there was a roar, a yell, and the sound of flying feet and hooves in the snow.

Two lithe panthers were racing across the little emptiness of the valley that stood between the battle and the tower, and horsemen followed in hot pursuit. Quickly, his coat in one hand, his knapsack in the other, Yehuda Leib darted through the open gravestone door.

"Hurry!" he said. "Find your name!"

There was panic in the Nameless Girl's face—the panthers were drawing nearer with every moment.

"I can't!" she said. "I don't have one!"

"What?" said Yehuda Leib.

But there was no time to explain. The gravestone door had begun to swing shut.

The last thing that the Nameless Girl saw before the door closed was Yehuda Leib, gasping, shoving his knapsack forward with all his might, managing, just barely, to slot it into the doorway as the stone swung shut.

And it worked. The door was jammed open—just a hair. Just wide enough for the Nameless Girl to fit her fingernails in.

As it happened, it was not the knapsack itself that kept the door from closing. When the Nameless Girl managed to pry the door back and dart through, one-half of the knapsack fell outside the tower, and the other half, neatly shorn, fell inside. The same could be said for all the items within: one-half of a battered old cup, of a sprouted potato, of an extra cap was inside; one-half, neatly shorn, without.

In fact, the only item in the knapsack that had not been cut cleanly in half by the great force of the closing door was something that had gone long forgotten at the bottom of the bag all the while:

The loaf of challah that the Nameless Girl had given to Yehuda Leib.

And in truth, most of the challah had been shorn as well. Only one very thin, sparkling layer remained uncut, blocking the way open for the Nameless Girl to follow:

The salt in the bread.

And this is how, with cold metal that was not cold metal, with blood-red thread, and with salt, Yehuda Leib and the Nameless Girl came to enter the House of Death.

The Rebbe of Zubinsk lay motionless in his bed, neither awake nor asleep, prayers flying all around him like a thick flock of starlings.

For nearly two hours the first night, the Hasidim prayed, cycling through psalm after psalm. They were all of them terribly moved: worried, impassioned, heartsick.

But it is very hard work to pray with all one's might, and mortal men tire easily. Presently, the group flagged, and one by one they departed for home and bed.

But not all of them.

One of their number, a stranger in black clothing, blacker than the night, blacker than the darkness hidden inside your eyes, remained behind. He had not prayed in many thousands of years, but as soon as his mouth began to shape the words, his eyes drifted shut, and he did not stop.

In the gray light of morning, when the Hasidim returned, they found the dark stranger precisely where they had left him, praying for the Rebbe's recovery with unwavering fervor.

All day he prayed, enveloped by an ever-changing crowd of Hasidim. He did not stop once—not to sit, not to eat, not to rest. By the time the afternoon came around, rumors had begun to circulate: Was he another holy Rebbe from a faraway town? Was he Elijah the Prophet come to advocate for the Rebbe's recovery?

Darkness began to fall once more. A large assembly of Hasidim had grown up around the stranger like twining ivy on the tidy trellis of his psalms, and so fervently did they pray now that it was a short time before someone noticed that the Rebbe was stirring in his bed.

An excited murmur rippled through the crowd, breaking the Hasidim off from their psalms.

Only the voice of the dark stranger chanted on, until, looking up, he saw the open eyes of the Rebbe staring directly at him.

Slowly, the Rebbe raised a gnarled finger to point at the stranger.

"You," said the Rebbe. "You should not be here."

All eyes turned to the stranger, who began to sputter with tearful regret.

"No," said the Rebbe. "You neglect your duty. They have breached your walls. You must go."

Again, the dark stranger fought to object, but before he could manage a word, the Rebbe sat up in bed and bellowed "Go!" with all his might.

The word having passed his lips, the Rebbe collapsed into his pillows.

With a gasp, the crowd of Hasidim rushed forward.

In the mad press, no one noticed that the dark stranger was somehow gone without having taken a single step.

The Rebbe was dead.

CHAPTER EIGHTEEN

The Gilgul

Each of us crosses the threshold of the House of Death eventually, and each of us goes alone.

You stop to let the honey-sweet sunlight warm your skin, and as the fragrance of the grass reaches you, you find that you are desperate to feel it between your toes. You bend to unlace your boots, just as everyone who came before you has done, just as everyone who comes after will do.

The grass is warm, the earth soft and supple beneath your feet.

The only sound you can hear is the light stirring of the breeze.

You are alone now, though there may be hundreds, thousands who come into the estate in the very same moment as you. Even Yehuda Leib and the Nameless Girl, who came in quick succession through the very same door, who stood in precisely the same position at precisely the same time, were entirely alone.

This is the peculiar perspective of Death:

Each of us crosses the threshold of the House of Death, and each of us goes alone.

The Nameless Girl stepped out of her boots and stockings and into the grass. She gave a heavy sigh.

It felt like forever since she'd seen the sun.

Part of her wanted to lean back against the warm rock, to allow the sunlight to flow over her, baking her into the stone.

But the stillness was too sweet, too persuasive. She had come for a reason, and it wouldn't do to rest before she had accomplished it:

She must either reclaim her name and face or else give the rest of herself away.

And until this very moment, she'd thought she knew which she meant to do.

On either side of her, familiar mottled gravestone walls rose up into the sky, their particular names and dates washed away with age. The passage was narrow enough for the Nameless Girl to reach her arms out and touch the stone with both sets of fingertips, and yet, despite the interminable height of the stone walls, the sun always seemed directly overhead: there were no shadows.

This came to seem even more peculiar as she made her way forward to the first forking of the path.

Two branching ways presented themselves, each equally sunny and warm.

Which should she take?

Peering first down the right-hand path and then down the left, she found them practically identical: curves, forks, branches. Lush green grass, thick golden sunlight.

Slowly, the Nameless Girl began to gnaw on her lower lip.

How was she to make the choice?

〰

Yehuda Leib stepped out of his boots and socks and into the grass. He gave a heavy sigh.

It felt like forever since he'd seen the sun.

Part of him wanted nothing more than to lie down and bask in the sweet warmth until the grass grew up over him, drew him down into the soft earth.

But somewhere within, the Angel of Death was holding his father, and Yehuda Leib couldn't rest until he had taken him back.

And so, funneled forward by the high stone walls, he advanced until he came to the first forking of the way.

He gazed for a long while down one path and then the other.

He found them much the same.

How was he to make the choice?

Clenching his jaw, he sighed again and thrust his hands into his pockets.

And what was this in his pocket?

Cold, hard metal.

Yehuda Leib drew it up in his fingers.

An odd coin, heavy, battered, gray. On one face it bore the figure of an open eye, and on the obverse the same eye firmly shut.

He thought back to the moment when, ages ago and no time at all, he had stood across the road from a strange, dark Messenger in Tupik.

He had taken the coin with his own fingers.

If he had only known then what he knew now, would he still have done so? Would he have conducted the stranger into the town? Would he have let him go on in peace?

Almost angrily, he shut his fist around the coin.

And then, in his tight-sealed palm: movement. Drawing his

fingers back, he saw the coin begin to dance, twirling, spinning like a top on its edge.

Now the coin seemed to show the figure of an eye both open and closed at the same time.

And suddenly, with iron certainty, Yehuda Leib knew what he must do.

It had been terrible, giving his eye to Dumah, painful and strange, and he had kept the empty socket hidden away ever since, as much for his comfort as for the comfort of others. When he drew the patch back now, though, the sunlight flooded into his empty eye, filling it with warm, almost fragrant brightness.

Leaning his head back, he dropped the spinning coin into the empty socket, and everything changed.

With his living eye, he saw the branching choices before him, infinite in their variety, opening out further and further, each fork leading to its successor, choice after choice after choice: a maze in which one false turn could steer you wrong.

But with his Death's Eye, he saw in a calmer manner:

It was not a maze, but a labyrinth. One path masqueraded as many. No matter which fork he chose, the destination was the same.

The choice was never false—only the choosing.

The direction matters less than you think.

With a deep breath, Yehuda Leib strode forward.

With a deep breath, the Nameless Girl strode forward.

She was sure she didn't know where she was going, but there was no use in standing still.

Choices had to be made.

Soon the forking paths seemed to come with every second step, choice after choice after choice. The Nameless Girl tried to keep herself moving toward the center of the maze, but the stony ways bent and curved, and, panic growing in her heart, she quickly lost her sense of direction.

She took a turn and found herself on a long, strange path.

Something didn't feel right. Of all the paths in the garden, this one alone seemed to drive straight and unswerving toward the center, and though she thought this ought to feel right and good, she found the walls of the passage narrowing in on her as she went.

Little by little, the stone seemed to squeeze.

Little by little, the light seemed to dim.

Here alone, the walls grew so close together that even the magnanimous sun above could not penetrate their leaning gloom.

Farther and farther the Nameless Girl made her way down the narrowing passage. Soon it was so tight that she could not comfortably fit the span of her shoulders.

Was this right? Behind her she could see the path she had come down widening back out until the sun managed to light its aperture.

Perhaps she ought to turn back.

But no: ahead, through the deepening dim, she could see a brighter light still.

This was the way. The center of the garden lay ahead.

And so, turning sideways, she began to shimmy down the path.

Farther and farther, narrower and narrower.

Now the stone walls were so close to one another that she was afraid her head might not fit. Still she shoved, pushed, but it was no use—all she did was wedge herself in.

Suddenly, the Nameless Girl felt motion on her leg, and she let out a sharp, bright scream that echoed far and wide through the garden of forking paths.

But nothing had taken hold of her.

It was only the spoon.

The spoon, spinning in the pocket of her apron.

With care and difficulty, the Nameless Girl drew it out.

It was somehow very different.

Where before, outside Death's estate, her reflection had dawdled, tarried, arriving late in the face of the spoon, here within, it raced ahead, and by the time the spoon was before her eyes, she found that her furtive reflection had already arrived.

But this was the least surprising thing she saw.

Behind her, in the looking glass of the spoon, she saw not a narrowing passage, not a dim stone path, but a small wooden house, sun-bleached and ancient, nestled in the grass.

The Nameless Girl was astounded.

Turning sharply back over her shoulder, she looked, and sure enough, there it was.

She felt the sun on her face.

The cold, squeezing passageway was gone.

In fact, she could not see any walls of stone anywhere. There was only this: a small wooden house sitting in the grass at the center of the world.

And the door was ajar.

It was with one living eye and one of cold metal that Yehuda Leib pushed his way into the House of Death.

This helped to determine what he saw there, for Death,

mercifully, has a way of looking in the manner most understandable to you.

It was a small hut, simple, nearly bare: a fire in the hearth, an old wooden table, a single worn chair. The floor was made of earth, packed down by years and years of crossing feet. In the corner, an ancient broom had gnarled, warped to fit the pattern of the two grasping hands that had held it day after day.

With his living eye, Yehuda Leib seemed to see the scene lit in the bright light of the sun.

But with his Death's Eye, it looked very, very different: the darkness was thick, so thick it seemed almost substantial.

And with both eyes he saw that every surface—the table, the mantel, the floor, the chair—was covered in flickering candles: beeswax and paraffin, bayberry, tallow, tapers and pillars and votives of all kinds. Some were tall and thin, some short and squat. There were decorated candles with inlays of colored wax, and candles molded into the shapes of animals. Some bore many wicks, some only one. Some sat in small dishes, others in candelabras or candlesticks. A few had even been placed in holes dug into the solid earthen floor. In places, several had melted together in blobs of seeping wax. There were flames that leapt and jumped, huge, nearly as tall as the candles they topped, and flames that flickered and shrank, little more than a glowing ember at the end of a blackened wick.

The supply seemed endless.

As Yehuda Leib took in the assemblage—candle after candle, flame after flame—it became clear to him that there were far more lights in this house than its little area ought to be able to contain.

And yet here they were.

To his living eye, the candle flames seemed strange, redundant:

their light paled in the face of the fire that blazed in the hearth, the sunlight that came streaming through the window.

But with his Death's Eye, he saw another truth: there was nothing here but darkness and light. All he could see was the points of flickering flame. The wax, the candles, the table, the hut—all were choked back, hidden by the thick darkness. Only the bright fire of the hearth gave any illumination to the room.

Slowly, careful not to disturb any of the flames on the floor, Yehuda Leib began to tiptoe forward.

One simple candle on the rough wooden tabletop drew him in—sturdy and straight, neither too wide nor too tall. Its flame burned bright and constant, barely giving a flicker, and though Yehuda Leib could not see it with either eye, the wick that ran down the center of the candle was of blood-red thread.

It felt just like him.

One long stave of wax had dripped down its side, trailing along through the gutter of the table's grain, and if he had cared to follow it, Yehuda Leib would've found that it met up after some ways with the wax trail of another, similar candle not far off: a candle that seemed impossible to describe.

But he was far too taken with his own candle to look anywhere else. He found it fascinating, irresistibly compelling, and he itched to feel its smooth wax against his fingers.

But a voice spoke from the door as he reached out his hand:

"I wouldn't."

With the cold spoon in her hand, the Nameless Girl pushed her way into the House of Death.

This helped to determine what she found there.

It was a small hut, simple, nearly bare: a fire in the hearth, an old wooden table, a single worn chair. The floor was made of earth, packed down by years and years of crossing feet. In the corner, an ancient broom had gnarled, warped to fit the pattern of the two grasping hands that had held it day after day.

Barely, though, had the Nameless Girl come through the door when she shut her eyes and drew a deep breath in through her nose.

What an aroma!

Every surface—table, mantel, chair, and floor—was crowded thick with bowls of chicken soup. Each bowl was different: earthenware, lacquered wood, polished metal, bone china. Even the soup within each bowl was different: some were clear yellow broths dancing with globules of fat; some were carcass soups, cloudy and rich. Some had chunks of meat or vegetables—carrots, potatoes, onions—some had matzo balls, some had noodles. Gouts of steam rose from certain bowls, and some had layers of fat that had separated and solidified on their surfaces.

The Nameless Girl's mouth began to water. She could not say how long it had been since she'd taken anything to eat, but whatever the time, it had been far too long.

Slowly, careful not to disturb any of the bowls on the floor, the Nameless Girl tiptoed her way into the hut.

Hung above the fire in the hearth was a large pot. Inside, she could hear a roiling, bubbling boil, and nearby, just outside the radius of the fire's blazing heat, she could see a stack of upturned empty bowls sitting in wait—though whether they had been emptied or were waiting to be filled, she could not say.

She had just begun to reach out her hand for one of the empty bowls when something caught her notice.

She knew that smell.

And, turning, she found, laid on the seat of Death's chair, a bowl of soup that she might've encountered on any Friday night of her life.

This was it, without question: her bubbe's chicken soup.

There was no use resisting.

The soup in the bowl had cooled, but the Nameless Girl didn't care—she was terribly hungry, her throat parched and dry—and when she dipped the spoon into the soup, the Nameless Girl saw a cloud of black granules dance about the bowl.

At first she thought that this was pepper, but it was not. It was dry ink, powdery black, that had once spelled out a name—though what the name was, no one quite knew.

Desperate for relief, the Nameless Girl lifted the trembling spoon to her lips, black powder dancing in the oily broth, and she thrust it into her mouth.

The soup was wonderfully delicious, as tasty as anything she'd ever had, familiar but surprising, cool but still bright and flavorful, and she swallowed it down hungrily.

As she withdrew the spoon from her mouth, though, the razor edge of its basin nicked the inside of her right cheek, and Bluma yelped.

Bluma.

The soup traveled down Bluma's tight throat into Bluma's cramping stomach.

Tears filled Bluma's eyes.

She had missed her name.

Quickly, Bluma stirred the soup again, the cloudy color of rust seeping from spoon into bowl, and she lifted a second mouthful to her lips. This time the spoon nicked the inside of her left cheek on its way out, but Bluma could hardly be bothered to notice:

Tears were running from Bluma's slate-colored eyes down Bluma's peaked cheekbones. Bluma's lips crumpled as she gazed into the mirrored back of the spoon before her.

Her face.

Bluma's own face.

Her heart had wavered as she'd made her way through the gravestone maze outside—would she reclaim herself or give herself away?—but now she could not possibly imagine giving up her face or name again.

And with a start, she wondered what sorts of mistakes she might've made if she hadn't been trained by her bubbe over a lifetime of Friday nights to know the smell of her soup.

Tilting the bowl, she gave it one final stir with the spoon.

Was it her imagination, or had the soup grown a bit warmer?

Bluma had begun to gather up the last spoonful when her attention wavered.

What was that delicious smell?

Near her bubbe's bowl, another very much like it, but somehow improved—better seasoned, perhaps, with larger chunks of meat, and the bowl itself not simple glazed crockery, but china, decorated with a tasteful geometric pattern.

Now *that* was a soup.

And it was still piping hot.

Careful not to spill the broth, Bluma grasped the bowl at its very brim and pulled it toward the edge of the table, twirling the spoon by its handle lightly between her fingers.

But at that very moment, she heard a voice speak from the door.

"I wouldn't," it said.

Bluma whirled around in surprise, the spoon slipping from her hand to clatter down onto the wooden table.

Yehuda Leib whirled around in surprise. Something had clattered onto the wooden table before him, but his eyes were fixed on the dark figure in the doorway.

Death had come home.

"You," he said.

"Yehuda Leib," said the Angel of Death, "you must be very careful. If you make one false move—if you even breathe incorrectly—it may have disastrous consequences."

"You," said Yehuda Leib again. "Give me back my father."

The Angel of Death shook his head slowly. "I cannot."

"You mean you *will* not," said Yehuda Leib.

"That is also true," said the Angel of Death. "But what I meant to say is that I cannot—it is not within my power."

"You lie!" cried Yehuda Leib, and, looking down upon the wooden table before him, he saw what had clattered there: not a spoon, to Yehuda Leib's eye, but a long, wicked double-edged dagger, and he seized it now, pointing it at the Angel in the doorway.

"Give me back my father!" he said again.

"Be careful," said the Angel. "That blade will sever anything at all it is pressed against, even things that are not visible to your eye."

"I'm counting on it," said Yehuda Leib, and, blade outstretched, he began to make his way through the candles toward his enemy at the door.

"Stop," said the Angel. "You must stop now, before you put out a light that ought to go on burning."

"Then give me what I ask!" cried Yehuda Leib.

"This?" said the Angel, reaching deep into his black coat. "Is this what you desire?"

The small glass bottle held one tiny, fading point of light—barely anything—and if Yehuda Leib hadn't known to look for it, he wouldn't have seen it there at all.

"Yes," said Yehuda Leib through tight-shut jaws.

"This," said the Angel, "is not your father—not in the way that you think. But all the same I will give it to you if, once I have finished speaking, you ask it of me again."

Yehuda Leib could not still his trembling chin long enough to speak clearly, but he dropped the point of the cold blade down to his side.

"Good," said the Angel of Death. "Now consider: What will you do with this light once you hold it? No flame burns here without a wick or candle."

"What," said Yehuda Leib, swallowing hard, "what about the fire in the hearth?"

"Ah," said the Angel with a smile. "Very good. You have noticed the way in which the hearth fire burns, have you?"

In truth Yehuda Leib had not—he had only meant that the fire in the hearth seemed to have been built with logs of wood—but, turning his head now, he saw: the fire burned, bright and hot, but the wood within was not consumed.

"You are quite right," said the Angel. "That is a Light that burns and burns and never goes out. And, Yehuda Leib, if you allow me to keep this"—and here he brandished the small glass bottle—"that is where I intend it to go. It will join the Eternal Light, and some part of it will never go out. But if you should keep it, it would languish, as it has already begun to do, and go out forever."

Yehuda Leib sniffed, tears rolling down his cheeks. "But it was not yours to take."

"No," said the Dark Messenger, shaking his head softly. "But I never come on my own errand."

This all made unbearable sense to Yehuda Leib, and yet he could not stop the fury from blossoming in his chest. "It's not fair!" he said.

"No," said the Angel. "It is not."

"I want him to come back," said Yehuda Leib.

"But he cannot," said the Angel with a sigh. "He must go forward."

Again, the grief bloomed in Yehuda Leib. "But I'm so angry," he said. "And so sad."

"Why?" said the Angel.

"Because you took my father," said Yehuda Leib.

"No," said the Angel. "No. You did not know your father."

And, stepping forward, the Angel reached out his hand.

Stepping forward, the Angel reached out her hand.

"Stay back!" said Bluma. "You cannot have me!"

Now the Angel chuckled.

"No," she said. "It is not your time. And that is why you must not taste of the soup before you."

"This?" said Bluma, staring into the bowl. "But this is mine."

"Yes," said the Angel. "And if you take one bite, you will find it so delicious that you will not stop until the bowl has been entirely drained. That would be a great tragedy."

"A tragedy?" said Bluma. "For me to take control of myself?"

Now the Angel smiled sadly. "Yes."

"Stay back!" said Yehuda Leib, raising the knife in his hand. "You cannot have me!"

Now the Angel chuckled.

"No," he said. "It is not your time. All I require from you is the return of my instrument."

Yehuda Leib's eyes narrowed. "Why? What are you going to do?"

"I am going," said the Angel of Death, "to show you the rest of your father. Would you like to see?"

Slowly, Yehuda Leib nodded.

"Very well, then," said the Angel of Death. "You must give me my blade."

Gingerly, Yehuda Leib took the flat of the cold knife between his thumb and forefinger and held out the hilt to the Angel.

"Good," said the Angel, and, navigating swiftly through the burning candles on the floor, he made his way to Yehuda Leib's side and bent low over the table.

"What are you doing?" said Yehuda Leib.

"Retrieving the balance of your father," said the Angel, and, using the knife's keen edge, he pried a small blot of hardened wax up from the table and handed it to Yehuda Leib.

"There," he said. "You wished me to give you your father, and there he is."

The blob of wax seemed entirely ordinary: pearly white, cool to the touch, its pooled shape strange and accidental.

Yehuda Leib could see the burned end of a spent wick trapped inside the wax, and for a moment he thought about trying to shape it into a tiny new candle, but there was neither enough wax nor enough wick remaining.

The candle was spent.

"Does it not move you?" said the Angel.

Yehuda Leib clenched his jaw. It was only wax.

"I thought not. But all the same it oughtn't go to waste. Come."

Now the Angel led Yehuda Leib across the burning floor to the hearthside, where, above the roaring fire, a great pot full of molten wax was hung.

"Here," said the Angel, and softly, deftly, he used his blade to carve the spent wick out of the hardened wax in Yehuda Leib's hand. Then, laying aside the knife, he drew forth the small glass bottle once more, uncorked it, and coaxed the fading point of light onto the last of the wick between his fingers.

"There we are," said the Angel of Death, and, bending low, he let go of the wick, which floated, smoldering, down into the great unconsuming fire in the hearth.

"Until we meet again," said the Angel of Death to the waning wick.

Yehuda Leib gave a heavy sigh.

"Now you," said the Angel.

"What?" said Yehuda Leib.

"There are two halves to every living soul," said the Angel. "The part that goes wandering about the world, it is my task to retrieve. But the part that stays here with us"—the Angel gestured first to the wax in Yehuda Leib's hand, and then to the ancient pot—"must be returned as well."

Yehuda Leib gazed through the clear wax to the craggy bottom of the pot.

"Now you," said the Angel.

"And what happens to it?" said Yehuda Leib.

"I am not the only Messenger to frequent this place," said the Angel. "Another passes through the door many times each day, bringing fresh-woven wicks to dip into this wax, and when those candles are cool and dry, they are lit from the fire below and released through the window."

Yehuda Leib peered out the window beside the hearth. With his living eye, he saw a bright blue sky filled with summer sun. With his Death's Eye, he saw the wide night sky, filled not with stars but with flickering candles.

"Here," said the Angel of Death. "Now you." And, rising up on his feet, Yehuda Leib dropped the blob of hardened wax into the pot.

"Until we meet again," he said, his voice faltering.

And this might've been the end of things.

But as the wax began to melt, the fire beneath the pot surged, sending a gout of light up beneath the brim of the Angel's wide black hat.

And for the first time, Yehuda Leib saw his face.

"Come," said the Angel to Bluma. "I will show you." And, navigating swiftly through the steaming bowls on the floor, she made her way to the pot above the fire. "If you would hand me your bubbe's bowl?"

With care, Bluma bore the cooled bowl of soup across the room to the Angel by the fire.

"Here," said Bluma.

With practiced reverence, the Angel took the bowl from her hand and emptied its contents into the pot. Then she lifted her spoon in her hand—where had that come from?—and ran its razor edge along the inside of the bowl, scraping every last bit of the soup from the bowl. Finally, she plunged the spoon into the pot and gave it a stiff stir.

"Until we meet again," said the Angel, and she added the now-empty bowl to the stack nearby.

"Goodbye, Bubbe," said Bluma. "Your mother says she's sorry."

Now the Angel withdrew the spoon and laid it down beside her. The Fire flared with warmth.

And it was in this light that Bluma saw again the sight that had sent her fleeing in the first place:

The face of Death.

It was her own, of course—lined and wrinkled, her hair turned to gossamer, but there was no mistaking the slate-gray eyes, the peaked cheekbones.

The face was Bluma's.

"Why?" said Bluma. "Why must you look like that?"

Death frowned, light and tight. "I might ask you the same question. For as much as it frightens each of you to see my face, it grieves me to see each of yours."

Staring into the swirling pot of soup, Bluma realized: Because the Messenger comes for each of us in turn. Because, if by nothing else, we are bound together by her visit.

And in this way, it is a kindness. In this way, the Messenger's terrible face is a reminder that none of us is alone.

"Thank you," said Bluma softly.

But to understand this requires the knowledge that Death's face shifts and changes.

To understand this requires the ability to look past our own deathly visage.

And this is not an ability that all possess.

In the flaring of the fire, Yehuda Leib saw:

The face of Death was his.

With a surge of fear and resentment, he understood. *It is not your time*, the Angel had said, but he ought to have said *yet*.

This Death was his, and as long as it was allowed to survive, Yehuda Leib was in danger.

Heart hot with pain, Yehuda Leib seized the Angel's knife and cut as hard as he could toward Death's throat.

In a flash, the Angel's fingers intercepted, taking hold of the hilt, halting the strike at its very last moment.

"What are you doing?" said the Angel of Death.

"Putting you away," said Yehuda Leib. "Once and for all."

"Why?" said the Angel. "Why would you do such a thing?"

"Because," said Yehuda Leib. "Because you wear my face. Because you are my Death. Because it is to be you or me."

"Yehuda Leib," said the Angel. "You must be careful."

"Yes," said Yehuda Leib sadly. "I know."

"What do you think will become of you if you strike down Death?" said the Angel. "What becomes of the sheep that is separated from the herd? What becomes of the candle left to the wind?"

Yehuda Leib nodded.

"I'll take my chances."

"Thank you," said Bluma softly.

But, turning back, she was shocked to see the Messenger's eyes filling with terror.

Something had happened.

Her fingers, white-knuckled and trembling, were pushing back hard against her spoon, which seemed to hang in midair, its razor edge inching closer, little by little, to her throat.

"Hello?" said Bluma, and again, "Hello?" but the Angel gave no answer. Her eyes were vacant, as if she'd left them behind for other, more pressing work.

What was going on?

It was only with the flare of the fire that she saw it in the back of the looking-glass spoon, and she nearly ignored it, thinking it the blood that had been drawn from the small cuts in her cheeks:

The reflection of a red woolen scarf.

And above it, there, his face.

And she called out his name:

"Yehuda Leib."

"Yehuda Leib."

For a long moment, the boy blinked in confusion.

It was not the Angel's voice that had spoken.

"Yehuda Leib," came the voice again. "What are you doing?"

"I'm going to save myself."

"No, you're not," said the voice. "Take it from me."

Yehuda Leib blinked in confusion. "From who?"

"Look closely," said the voice, and then, softly, "Even here, you're not alone."

Not alone? Yes, he was.

"Look closely," said the voice again.

And, staring hard, he began to see.

By force of habit, he had been favoring his living eye—it saw in ways that made sense to him, were comfortable and familiar.

But if he gave in to the darkness of his Death's Eye, he could just begin to see, in the flickering of the hearth fire: there was another person on the other side of Death.

"Bluma," said Yehuda Leib.

"Take it from me," said Bluma. "You can't hide from the things that make you yourself. No matter how hard you try. Not even from your Death."

"But," said Yehuda Leib. "But he wears my face!"

"Yes," said Bluma, "and she wears mine as well. Look closer."

And, concentrating on the dark eye in his head, Yehuda Leib saw Death's face correctly:

Every face and none, every pair of eyes, every pair of lips, every tooth, every wrinkle, every nose, every hair, each man and woman, child and elder, who had ever lived or would ever live from the beginning of time until its Death.

"She's mine as much as he's yours," said Bluma. "It's not your choice to make."

Yehuda Leib's fingers began to tremble. "Bluma," he said. "Bluma, I'm frightened."

"Good," said Bluma.

Yehuda Leib had spent so much of himself bashing against the cold, razor-sharp fact that he held in his fingers now, and there was nothing he could do, nothing at all, to change it.

Because the darkness shapes the light.

Because the spoon shapes the soup.

Because the dog shapes the herd.

He was so tired.

"Please," said the Angel of Death. "Let me live."

And, with a clatter and a sob, Yehuda Leib let the weapon of the Angel of Death fall to the hard bricks of the hearth below.

CHAPTER NINETEEN

Back

Slowly, tucking its instrument into the folds of its black garment, Death rose from its place by the fire.

"If vengeance belonged to me," said the Angel, its voice flat with suppressed anger, "you may be certain that I would take it now."

Yehuda Leib was still, exhausted, slumped by the hearth, but Bluma rose heavily to her feet.

"Go. You may not remain in this place."

Wearily, Bluma turned toward the thin wooden door.

"That path will not avail you," said the Angel of Death. "For no one may walk in through the door of my house and walk back out it again."

"Then how can we hope to leave?" said Yehuda Leib.

Death was silent as the grave.

"What about the window?" said Bluma.

Death remained impassive.

Carefully, Bluma went and pushed it open.

"But where are we to go?" said Yehuda Leib.

"Can you point us in the right direction?" said Bluma.

"No," said the Angel of Death. "There is none. For you have

seen my face. And therefore every forward step you take from now until we meet again will carry you in one direction only: further toward me."

"Very well," said Bluma. "Then we must not go forward. We must go back."

"But in which direction?" said Yehuda Leib.

"Oh," said Bluma, peering through the open window. "As long as you're moving, the direction matters less than you think. Everyone knows that."

And, stepping up onto the windowsill, she began to back through. "Are you coming?"

From the moment the Angel of Death crossed the river into Tupik until the moment Bluma and Yehuda Leib backed out of Death's house, only the span of seven terrestrial days—the length of the shivah—had passed. The night is long in the Far Country, and ground is quickly covered in the approach to Death.

But progress is much slower moving backward.

For an age, it seemed, they walked blindly back through the grass, the face of Death watching them closely through the window of its little house.

And it was true that the Angel was angry. But it lingered long in watching them retreat for a different reason.

Because until Yehuda Leib had held the Blade That Severs All Things to its throat, the Angel of Death had not understood. And when it heard itself beg for life, as it had heard voice after voice vainly do in language after language, place after place, moment after moment after moment since the very first death had befallen the world, it began to see:

This was the answer.

This was every answer.

And there they were, beaten, bloodied, exhausted: two from Tupik who knew what would have to happen one day and together chose to keep going anyway.

And so the Angel watched through its window in anger, to be sure. But with a sort of fondness, as well.

Because it is a difficult thing to walk backward through the tall grass for the span of a year, even when one is at one's strongest. Time after time, the Angel saw them reach out to brace one another, to catch a fall or bolster flagging strength.

They were two red stitches looped together in the endless scarf of living.

And the Angel would miss them—miss them as friend misses friend, just as the Rebbe had taught.

Until they met again.

Onward and onward.

Backward and back.

Step after step after step after step.

Time ceased to have any meaning. Even the slowly growing distance between themselves and the little house on the horizon meant nothing.

All that existed was the walk: backward, fumbling, blind.

Step after step after step after step.

They mustn't turn, not even for a moment.

Step after step after step after step.

Sun-warmed earth, long, soft grass beneath their bare feet.

Step after step after step after step.

At a certain point, they began to see oddities, artifacts, remnants half buried on either side:

A bullet-riddled breastplate.

A bloodied white shift.

A pair of cracked spectacles.

Onward and outward.

Backward and back.

Soon the debris grew thicker: bleached skeletons, waterlogged books, ruins of stone.

A bearded skull.

A torn prayer shawl.

Onward and outward.

Backward and back.

Day after day.

Week after week.

Step after step after step after step.

The window grew smaller and smaller in their gaze, day after day, week after week, the Dark One watching as they retreated.

And then, all of a sudden, in the teary wake of a blink, the Angel was gone from its tiny window in the distance.

Later, Yehuda Leib would find himself sure that he had known then, but the truth was that there was only the walk—step after step after step after step.

Only the walk.

And only each other: When one stumbled, the other reached out a steadying arm. When one wearied, the other lifted. When one thought they might lose their mind in the endless monotony of backing away, there was the face of the other, just as bored, just as weary, just as determined.

On and on.

Back and back.

Week after week.

Month after month.

Step after step after step after step.

After some time, the grass beneath their feet began to give way to a wide plain covered in sodden black clothing: coats and dresses, hats and head scarves, trousers, stockings, shirts, and shifts, everywhere, as far as the eye could see, dripping with water, twisted, intermingled on the ground.

Before they knew it, there was no grass visible between them and the horizon at all, only the twisted shapes of empty black clothing that squelched and squashed beneath their feet.

On they went.

On and on.

Month after month.

Step after step.

Now the air began to chill, the clothing to freeze, their bare feet to pink and shrink in the cold.

Slowly, the snow began to fall.

On and on, back and back, as the snow accumulated all around.

Soon it became difficult to ignore the shapes on the ground, the dark clothing drawn into relief by the highlights of ice and snow.

The twisted arms seemed to reach out for them, the fingers of gloves to point.

But on they went.

On and on.

And soon there were no shapes at all discernible beneath the snow: only drifts of white that rose and fell, hills and valleys as far as the eye could see.

On and on.

Back and back.

Harder the snow fell, harder and harder, thickening the air with white.

Backward and back, step after step.

The wind was howling.

"Bluma?" called Yehuda Leib.

"Yehuda Leib?" called Bluma.

Somewhere, a bell was ringing.

Arms reached out into the dim white emptiness.

And then, together, as if their heels had caught on the same raised threshold, they fell back.

From the moment they left Death's house until the moment they fell, the span of one terrestrial year—the length of the Kaddish—had passed. The night is long in the Far Country, and ground is quickly covered in the approach to Death.

But progress is much slower on the way back.

With a crunch, Bluma and Yehuda Leib fell side by side onto the snow. Somewhere, a bell had been ringing; its humming decay lingered in the air like the warm scent of last night's fire.

Where they found themselves now, the snowfall had long since stopped, sitting and setting, melting and freezing, until everything in the little glade seemed to be glazed with ice.

Where were they?

They had walked—that much Bluma knew. She could feel it in her legs and her aching, frigid feet, step after step after step after step until they finally fell. Even now, used to months of the pumping

rhythm in her legs, she felt uncomfortable, restless, as if they ought
to go on.

Why had they stopped? What had caused them to fall?

Then, lifting her head from the snow, Bluma looked down at
her bare pink feet and saw what had tripped her up:

There, as if waiting, orderly and neat, her thick woolen stockings lolling out like laughing tongues, were the old boots she had
stepped out of at Death's threshold. Beside them, in a tangled jumble of lace and leather, were Yehuda Leib's.

Gratefully, she sat up, reaching forward.

"Yehuda Leib," she called. She didn't have to look up in order to
know that he was there.

Yehuda Leib raised his head from the ground, and when he
saw the shoes at his feet, he made a grateful little sound: not quite
a grunt, not quite a sigh, but full to bursting with relief.

For a long moment, they sat side by side, slipping their feet into
socks and stockings, passing laces through hooks and eyelets, knot-
ting and double-knotting.

All around them, fat drops of falling water drummed on the icy
surface of the snow.

Bluma stood, working her frigid toes into the warm wool of her
stockings, flexing her feet, stretching her legs.

Yehuda Leib remained sitting in the snow, admiring the sight
of his shod feet.

Somewhere, a bell had been ringing, and before long, Bluma
traced the sound to its source: there, low in the branches of a birch
tree, someone had strung an old bronze handbell, scratched and
battered and green with age.

Softly, Bluma reached up and laid a soft finger to the humming
bell, bringing an end to its lingering tone, and in the newfound

silence of the grove, Yehuda Leib was certain he could hear rushing water.

"Oh," said a voice nearby. "Oh, how good it is to see you."

The voice was familiar—and the face behind it, too—but neither Bluma nor Yehuda Leib had ever heard it speak so clearly before.

"Mottke?" said Bluma.

"Hello," he said, waggling his fingers.

And, all of a sudden, Yehuda Leib understood where they were.

Just behind smiling, slump-shouldered Mottke, he could see the rushing water, the ferry. There was the muddy street that led up into town, and, just beyond it, the first battered houses of Tupik.

"Oh, Bluma," he said, but she had already seen.

"I know," she said, weary, hungry, happy.

"I imagine you would like to cross over," said Mottke.

"Yes," said Bluma, and "Please," said Yehuda Leib.

Mottke's leathery smile deepened. "It would be my particular pleasure."

Yehuda Leib pushed himself up to his aching feet.

"But," said Mottke, "before we depart, there is an uncomfortable necessity to speak of: in order to cross back from the place where you have gone, I must be paid."

"But wait," said Bluma. "Aren't you paid by the community of Tupik?"

Mottke winced apologetically. "I am afraid this is an altogether different sort of crossing."

Immediately, both Yehuda Leib and Bluma began to explore their pockets, looking for anything of value they might have to offer, but Mottke stopped them.

"Your eagerness is dear," he said. "But I have found in my long experience that I am generally better equipped to identify value than those in your position. May I?"

"Of course," said Yehuda Leib.

Mottke's evaluation was quick and thorough, his cracked and callused hands wandering over Yehuda Leib's shoulders, elbows, wrists, reaching behind his head, patting down his front.

It wasn't long before Mottke made his decision.

"Hold still," he said, and, pushing Yehuda Leib's forehead back slightly, he dipped two nimble fingertips into the socket that had once held Yehuda Leib's right eye and withdrew the old coin that spun there.

Cold air flooded into Yehuda Leib's head.

The coin in Mottke's palm juddered, flopped like an unwatered fish.

"Your fare is paid," he said.

Bluma, however, was a more difficult prospect.

Over and over her Mottke went, his face growing more and more drawn with each pass.

"My, my," he said presently. "You carry little that is not a part of you."

Bluma thought that perhaps she might be proud of this fact, except that with every moment, she grew more nervous that she would not be able to return home.

"Is there nothing?" she said.

For a short time, they haggled over the only foreign object she carried on her person—a page torn from the Dantalion that she had neatly creased, put into her apron, and promptly forgotten. Mottke was interested, and he perused it carefully, even reading a section aloud ("'to the breaching of impenetrable walls; to the navigation of impassable ways, yea, even unto the overthrow of Death Itself . . .'"), but he insisted that he could not, as fare for the crossing, accept any stolen good.

It seemed like an impasse.

"Perhaps," said Yehuda Leib, "we can cross together into the village and bring her payment back. Surely we can find something there."

"I can extend no credit," said Mottke.

"Well, then," said Yehuda Leib. "What if I should cross over and return with payment on her behalf?"

Mottke shook his head. "Though I am very glad to see you now, I will be gladder still if I need not see you ever again; it is no simple thing to cross over and return."

Yehuda Leib shook his head in frustration. "But then what is to be done?"

"Without paying the fare, no one may cross," said Mottke. "The rules are very, very old and very, very clear."

"Please," said Bluma. "I wish to pay the fare. I wish to cross over. What can I give?"

Now Mottke shrugged sadly.

A long moment of tight panic passed in the grove, thick drops of meltwater falling all around them.

What could be done?

"I am afraid," said Mottke presently, "that a fare has been paid. I must ferry my passenger across."

"Wait," said Bluma.

"No," said Yehuda Leib.

"Yes, yes," said Mottke. "I know. But without a fare . . ." And he shrugged as if to say, *What am I to do?*

This question hung in the air.

"Here," said Yehuda Leib, frantically unwrapping the scarf from his neck. "Here. This must be valuable. Take it."

"Yehuda Leib," said Bluma. "No."

"Don't be ridiculous," said Yehuda Leib.

Softly, carefully, Mottke reached out and took the scarf from Yehuda Leib's hands.

"Oh," he said. "Oh, this is a very rich price to pay."

Yehuda Leib wanted to describe the qualities of the scarf: how his mother had made it to keep him warm, how it had saved him from capture, how it was stained with his father's blood, how it had returned to him in the most unlikely place and had kept him warm and safe on the journey to Death and back.

But none of this seemed to need speaking. Mottke seemed to know.

"Are you sure?" he said.

Yehuda Leib nodded.

"Very well," said Mottke, and, running his hands slowly down the length of it from one end to the other, he took the red away, leaving behind a scarf of pure, uncolored wool, which he folded neatly and handed back to Yehuda Leib.

And then, turning to Bluma, he spoke.

"Your fare is paid."

"How foolish. How unutterably stupid."

Dumah and Mammon, ancient lords of demonkind, knelt before the Angel of Death.

"In my defense, Most Reverend Regent," said Mammon quietly, "I never believed he would succeed."

"Ah," said the Angel. "Foolish, stupid, *and* cruel."

"And I do hope you'll forgive me, Most Reverend Regent," said Mammon. "But I can't help but notice that Lady Lilith is absent from this meeting."

"Lilith," said the Angel, "has gone into hiding."

"Ah," said Mammon. "I didn't realize that was an option."

The fiery black wings of the Angel of Death flared with fury. "Now as ever, Mammon, your impertinence fails to charm. I do not think you adequately comprehend the dire nature of your situation."

"Yes," said Mammon. "Yes, I was hoping we could speak of that. After all, in the actual event, I *opposed* the boy. At great personal expense, I procured a large army to stop him from reaching you. If anything, I think you ought to consider reimbursing my—"

"You brought him here," said the Angel. "And if Dumah hadn't taken him from you—"

"Yes, yes," said Mammon. "But Dumah *did* take him from me."

"Enough!" said the Angel of Death. "It is my duty to maintain Eternal Order in this realm. I charge you with working to undermine that order, of which charge you are guilty."

"Now, now," said Mammon. "Surely I am entitled to some advocacy, some defense?"

"You are not," said the Angel. "And even if you were, I would know better than to entertain it. You are banished immediately and for all eternity from this country, and none of your properties, titles, or possessions whatsoever may be taken with you."

"Let's—uh—" stammered Mammon, "let's not rush into anything here. What you're suggesting would create a very dangerous power vacuum."

"Your concern is touching," said the Angel of Death coldly. "You keep a steward, do you not? Tall fellow? Fancy trousers?"

"Yes," said Mammon, "but I don't see—"

"All your assets shall devolve upon him. That should keep the status quo."

"I see," said Mammon, swallowing hard. "Yes. I have misjudged the situation terribly. Do forgive me. I shall strive to do better in the future."

"You have no future here," said the Angel.

"Surely," said Mammon, "surely, we can reach some sort of mutually beneficial arrangement."

"Goodbye, Mammon," said the Angel, and with an echoing, ragged scream, the little demon was gone.

Turning to Dumah now, the Angel spoke in a tone far softer than before.

"Brother," he said, and Dumah, bloodied, bashed, and battered, looked up from the floor. "It grieves me to see you here."

Dumah made no reply.

"I would find it a heavy thing indeed to send you away. But if the things I have been told are true . . ."

Dumah was still.

"I am told that you conspired to unseat me, to take my task for your own. Do you deny this?"

Dumah was silent.

"Please," said the Angel. "If it is not so, you must correct me."

But Dumah was silent.

"Very well," said the Angel of Death. "You will stand."

Dumah rose quickly to his feet, and with a sigh, the Angel of Death rendered judgment.

"Dumah, Messenger of Decay, you have strayed from your task. You have erred, and you are unrepentant. The Eternal Order must be upheld. Therefore, as regent in this country, in the Infinite

Names of the One, I strip you of your office and relieve you of your task. You, too, are banished. Go and sojourn among mortal men until such time as you die and begin, yourself, to decay."

Nodding silently, Dumah raised his hand in a final salute.

And then he was gone.

Yankl the schlepper brought news of the Rebbe's death back from Zubinsk the day after it occurred.

Many in Tupik sighed and shook their heads sadly, but Issur Frumkin could not seem to release his grief. He had long relished stories of the Rebbe and his great miracles, long harbored secret ambitions of making his way out through the forest to study at the Rebbe's feet.

But now this could never be. Now he would end up just like his father: a small-town butcher with more learning than he had use for.

This thought was intolerable.

It did not help that Issur's father had always been dismissive and skeptical of the Rebbe's holiness. Now that he had died, Moshe Dovid Frumkin had hardly grown more reverent, and a cluster of sharp little arguments broke out between the butcher and his son in the day following the Rebbe's passing. It was as much for this reason as out of a desire to bid the Rebbe a proper farewell that Issur once again resolved to sneak out into Zubinsk.

That night, he went to bed fully dressed for the road, his open boots and full pack laid at his bedside. As soon as the sun began to peek out over the trees, he would go. He would make his way to the Rebbe's shivah, where he would pay his appropriate respects, and then he would return home again and face his father's wrath.

But that night, lying dressed in bed, he had a dream that changed his plans forever.

In his dream, he was sitting in the Tupik synagogue fervently reading from a prayer book with dry autumn leaves where the pages ought to have been.

Suddenly, a voice spoke to him. It was the Rebbe, seated beside him where a moment ago there had been no one.

Issur had never personally laid eyes on the Rebbe, and so he could not have known, but the image of the old man that appeared in his dream was precisely accurate—every wrinkle and hair in its place.

The Rebbe apologized to Issur that they had never managed to meet—he was sure that he would've been enriched to have Issur as a Hasid.

Issur protested furiously, of course: he would've been the one to benefit, not the Rebbe.

But here the Rebbe cut him off: it was very important—very important—for Issur to understand that while a Hasid might benefit from the teachings of his Rebbe, it was the Rebbe who received the greater enrichment. For a Hasid entrusts a fragment of his soul to the Rebbe for safekeeping and enlightenment, and it is these shards that give the Rebbe his power. Issur, said the Rebbe, had a worthy and beautiful soul, and the Rebbe he would entrust it to would be very lucky indeed.

This comment surprised Issur. He'd never before considered pledging himself to another Rebbe, but the Rebbe of Zubinsk insisted that he must: it was his duty and his destiny.

A parade of imagined sages began to swim through Issur's mind, all curling sidelocks, dark black jackets, long gray beards. How was he to know which Rebbe he ought to follow?

Here the Rebbe of Zubinsk smiled and lowered the cowl of

his prayer shawl. Somehow, all the while, he'd been wearing Moshe Dovid's battered, dirtied shtreimel—the hat that Yehuda Leib had knocked into the muck and ruined.

"The first person, whomever it may be, to mention Everything and Nothing to you," he said, "shall be your Rebbe."

"Everything and Nothing," repeated Issur.

The Rebbe of Zubinsk nodded. "Whomever it may be."

Now there was a sound like wind, and Issur looked down to see that the autumn leaves in his prayer book had all crumbled and blown away.

When he looked up again, the Rebbe was gone.

And with that, Issur woke.

The sun was just beginning to rise.

Swiftly, softly he made his way out of the house, up the cemetery road, and into the forest.

By the time Issur reached Zubinsk, he'd forgotten all about his dream. The crowds there were thick—there had been many Hasidim in town to attend the wedding of the Rebbe's granddaughter Rokhl, and even more had crowded in as news of the Rebbe's passing had spread.

This was why it was so strange to Issur that, when he arrived at the end of the Zubinsk road, there was a girl standing there, dressed for travel, peering down into the forest behind him.

"Hello," she said. "Do you come from Tupik?"

Issur nodded. "Yes."

"What's beyond?"

Issur shrugged. "Nothing. Nothing at all."

The girl shook her head. "That can't be true."

"Well, it is," said Issur. "There's a river and a ferry, but there's no road on the other side. It's just a swampy mess."

The girl gave a frustrated sigh. "That's a shame."

"Why?" said Issur.

"Because," said the girl, "Zubinskers almost never pass that way."

At this, Issur chuckled. "What are you, on the run?"

The girl shrugged. "Maybe a little."

"How can you be a little on the run?"

The girl smiled. "By being mostly somewhere else to begin with."

Issur smiled back. "And what are you running from?"

"Oh, everything," said Rokhl, the Rebbe's granddaughter, "and nothing."

In a flash, the Rebbe's words returned to Issur:

Everything and Nothing.

But how could this be? Every Rebbe Issur had ever heard of had been an old man.

And yet the Rebbe's words were in Issur's ear again:

Whomever it may be.

By the time he came to his senses, she had already turned to go.

"Wait!" cried Issur after the girl who was his Rebbe. "Wait!"

THE DANTALION

Prophet Margins

Hall QB, row 94, case K, shelf 7, volume H, page 390:

... and in those days, there shall come into the Farthest Land,
up unto the very House of Death, a Pair of Eyes That Cut and
a Pair of Lips That Lock, and theirs shall be a terrible peril.

On all sides they shall be assailed by Scavengers: the
Trading Beast, Avaricious, whose weapon is the need of
the Living co-opted; the Silence of the Grave, Bellicose,
whose weapon is the fear of Man misdirected; and the Bitter
Queen, Furious, whose weapon is Woman's righteous anger
misappropriated.

And if they heed the Tempters, then they shall lose
themselves forever, tumbling from their Appointed Path into
the churning scum below the world, where they shall serve
only their captors.

But if their feet carry them through the snares of the
Scavengers unharmed, then, joining together, they may find
themselves equal to any task: to the breaching of impenetrable
walls; to the navigation of impassable ways, yea, even unto the
overthrow of Death Itself.

And theirs will be the choice—the Nameless, Faceless Girl who was called Bluma; the warlike Lion of Judah, Yehuda Leib—whether they shall topple the Great Mottled Tower, or choose to walk the Way Back.

For the Death of Death is the End at the End—no wound may be healed, no injustice remediated when the Great Wheel has ceased its turning.

But if the Eyes That Cut can learn to knit together, the Lips That Lock to live, then, side by side . . .

Here ends page 390.

The rain began to fall on snowy Tupik as Mottke pulled the ferry across the river. Yehuda Leib sat quietly at the edge of the small barge, watching drop after drop after drop after drop slam down into the surface of the water.

How little time it took before they became part of the surface.

Beside him, Bluma drew the folded page of Dantalion from the pocket of her apron and read, but, midway across the river, the letters on the page began to squirm and blur.

By the time she realized what was happening, the rain had washed the page completely blank.

Bluma and Yehuda Leib clambered up and off the moment the ferry barge made contact with the landing, their boots squelching in the mud. Yehuda Leib turned back to thank the ferryman, but he was gone: not on the barge, not on the bank—nowhere. Only when they finally came level with the shack at the height of the rise did they see Mottke there inside, dead drunk and reeking, fast asleep by the stove.

But this was impossible—they should've seen him climbing past them.

Bluma turned back to the opposite bank and scanned the emptiness between the trees for any sign of life.

All was still.

"Thank you," she murmured, and beside her, Yehuda Leib said, "Thank you."

Dusk was descending on Tupik, and between the late hour and the quickly worsening weather, they found themselves climbing the muddy streets alone. By the time they were halfway into town, they'd begun to notice the differences wrought by passing time: a certain run-down cart that had finally broken, a certain outhouse mended and improved. In Tupik's front rooms they saw familiar faces lined just a bit further with worry, familiar heads chased just a bit thicker with gray.

They had passed an entire year backing away from Death, and the year had left its mark.

Now the darkness was falling as insistently as the rain, and, one by one, bright lights began to jump up in the windows of the town.

It didn't take them long to realize what night it was.

In the front window of every house, a Chanukah menorah was set to burn, eight strong, straight candles, raising their warm light up against the darkness outside, and beside each octet a ninth light: the helper candle. Yehuda Leib could not stop himself from thinking of this lone candle—separated, removed—as a sort of herding dog: keeping the others together, keeping the others alight.

From house after house, light shone forth into the street, and as Bluma and Yehuda Leib made their way farther and farther toward their end of town, the anticipation began to grow. How sweet it would be to come back to their own houses, to see the bright lights shining out from their own front windows, to be finally home.

But when they arrived at the house of Yehuda Leib's mother, the window was dark.

Nonetheless, Yehuda Leib pushed eagerly through the front door, tracking wet boot prints across the dusty floorboards, calling for his mother.

But she was not there. Neither were most of her things.

The house had been empty for some time.

They had been gone for a year; Death moves as swiftly as the ticking clock.

Bluma tried to hold back her tears at least until Yehuda Leib showed his own sorrow, and if he hadn't been so dogged, so hopeful, perhaps she would've managed it.

"Here," he said, taking down the rusty old Chanukah menorah from its place at the top of the bookcase. "She wouldn't want us to wait."

With some scrounging, Yehuda Leib managed to find nine mismatched candle ends among the oddments left in the house and fit them into the heavy candelabra. Softly, he chanted the blessings and lit each one in turn.

For a short time, they stood in the empty front room of the dusty gray house, watching the light of the candles blaze and flicker and jump, listening to the pounding of the rainfall on the roof, until: "All right," said Yehuda Leib. "Let's go."

The tremble in Bluma's voice was audible, though she fought to keep it still. "Are you sure?"

Yehuda Leib smiled sadly.

What else was there to wait for?

"Yes," he said.

And, leaving the candles burning in the window behind them, they went back out into the rain.

It was only minutes until they were before Bluma's house, its fragrance of sweet baking bread drifting out like a promise into the muddy street.

Bluma made directly for the front door, but Yehuda Leib continued climbing up the hill.

He had seen something.

In the little cemetery there was a new grave.

Yehuda Leib didn't have to be able to read the stone to know who lay beneath it.

"I'm so sorry," said Bluma, climbing up beside him.

"Yes," he said. "I am too."

And as long as they had watched the candles in her house, now they stood in the rain before the grave of Yehuda Leib's mother.

"I couldn't have stayed, anyway," said Yehuda Leib after a long silence. "Moshe Dovid Frumkin would've made sure of that."

Bluma nodded. "Probably. But it still would've been nice to say hello."

"And goodbye," said Yehuda Leib.

"And goodbye," said Bluma.

"I don't want to go back to Zubinsk," said Yehuda Leib. "But I think I'll have to start there. Perhaps I can hitch a ride as far as Kasrilevke and catch the train."

"And then?"

Yehuda Leib shrugged. "I don't know."

Bluma shook her head tightly. "No," she said. "No, that's no good. I don't care about the direction, but we've got to be moving toward something."

Yehuda Leib's eyebrows rose so far that the patch over his empty eye gave a little jump.

"*We've?*" he said.

"We've," said Bluma, nodding.

"But what about your mother and father?" said Yehuda Leib.

"They've got each other," said Bluma.

"You don't want to live with them?"

Now Bluma wore a light, tight frown. "It's just that there's only so much time until . . . well, Until We Meet Again. I want to see what else is out there. And I've grown used to your footsteps beside me."

This was the first time since learning of the death of his mother that Yehuda Leib allowed himself to cry.

Bluma gave him a little shove, tried to smile and frown at the same time, and somehow succeeded.

"Thank you," said Yehuda Leib.

But Bluma was looking back over her shoulder. "First," she said, "I think I'd like to sit down and get myself dry, though. Maybe eat a few cookies."

Yehuda Leib nodded. "Me too."

"Good," said Bluma, turning down the hill toward the light of the Chanukah candles in her parents' window. "Are you coming?"

ACKNOWLEDGMENTS

I am indebted to Catherine Drayton and Claire Friedman for helping me to lay foundations, and to Erin Clarke and Ruth Knowles for helping me to finish the house. Thanks also to Karen Sherman, Amy Schroeder, Artie Bennett, and Alison Kolani.

My further thanks are due to the members of the Ann Arbor Orthodox Minyan, especially Zvi Gitelman.

This book was largely written in New Haven, Connecticut, where my thanks are due to Mark Oppenheimer and the students of Daily Themes 2019 (eight of them in particular), and to Cyd, Rebekah, Ellie, Klara, Anna, and D. W. Oppenheimer, the members of BEKI (Beth El-Keser Israel), the Westville Shul, and Howard Ratner.

My thanks also to the denizens of many cemeteries, but especially Ann Arbor's Fairview, New Haven's Grove Street, and Þorlákshöfn's churchyard.

Eagle-eyed readers may have noticed loving homages to Indiana Jones and the works of J. R. R. Tolkien in these pages—my thanks to everyone who brought those sterling stories into my life.

In the same spirit, my thanks to Anaïs Mitchell and Rachel Chavkin for *Hadestown*, in which I have found consistent inspiration. Further thanks to Chris Sullivan, whom I have never met, but whose Hermes I still carry with me.

While I'm mentioning inspirations: *The Master and Margarita* by Mikhail Bulgakov. *Hershel and the Hanukkah Goblins* by Eric Kimmel, with illustrations by Trina Schart Hyman. The music of Daniel Kahn & the Painted Bird, the Klezmatics, and Joey Weisenberg and the Hadar Ensemble. Reb Nachman of Breslov. The Maiden of Ludmir.

The house in which I wrote this book belonged to Jack Paulishen and his wife, Michelle. Toward the end of my time living there, Jack died. His legacy needs no contribution from me, but I would be remiss if I didn't pause here to remember him.

That house was also the first home of my wonderful, bright, and beautiful daughter, Lilja Meital, who is napping upstairs as I type this. She opened new doors in my soul when I met her, and every day I am grateful that I get to be her Abba.

Lily, I love you forever.

For the contributions, assistance, and support they gave us in our attempts to grow our family, I offer my insufficient thanks to Melisa Scott, the workers on the labor and delivery floor at the St. Raphael campus of the Yale New Haven Hospital, and to the ljósmæður at Landspítali Íslands.

Finally, my gratitude and love for my wife, Livia, are immeasurable. If she weren't such a private person, I would spill a lot of ink here telling you all about the many ways in which she nurtures me and my work, and perhaps you might begin to understand how I, among all claimants, am truly the luckiest man on earth.

In deference to her preference, however, I will simply close by saying this:

Thank you, Livia.

I love you.

Read on for a sample of
Gavriel Savit's
breathtaking debut novel,

*Anna
and the
Swallow
Man . . .*

What Do You Say?

When Anna Łania woke on the morning of the sixth of November in the year 1939—her seventh—there were several things that she did not know:

Anna did not know that the chief of the Gestapo in occupied Poland had by fiat compelled the rector of the Jagiellonian University to require the attendance of all professors (of whom her father was one) at a lecture and discussion on the direction of the Polish Academy under German sovereignty, to take place at noon on that day.

She did not know that, in the company of his colleagues, her father would be taken from lecture hall number 56, first to a prison in Kraków, where they lived, and subsequently to a number of other internment facilities across Poland, before finally being transported to the Sachsenhausen concentration camp in Germany.

She also did not know that, several months later, a group

of her father's surviving colleagues would be moved to the far more infamous Dachau camp in Upper Bavaria, but that, by the time of that transfer, her father would no longer exist in a state in which he was capable of being moved.

What Anna did know that morning was that her father had to go away for a few hours.

Seven-year-old girls are a hugely varied bunch. Some of them will tell you that they've long since grown up, and you'd have trouble not agreeing with them; others seem to care much more about the hidden childhood secrets chalked on the insides of their heads than they do about telling a grown-up anything at all; and still others (this being the largest group by far) have not yet entirely decided to which camp they belong, and depending on the day, the hour, even the moment, they may show you completely different faces from the ones you thought you might find.

Anna was one of these last girls at age seven, and her father helped to foster the ambivalent condition. He treated her like an adult—with respect, deference, and consideration—but somehow, simultaneously, he managed to protect and preserve in her the feeling that everything she encountered in the world was a brand-new discovery, unique to her own mind.

Anna's father was a professor of linguistics at the Jagiellonian University in Kraków, and living with him meant that every day of the week was in a different language. By the time Anna had reached the age of seven, her German, Russian, French, and English were all good, and she had a fair amount of Yiddish and Ukrainian and a little Armenian and Carpathian Romany as well.

Her father never spoke to her in Polish. The Polish, he said, would take care of itself.

One does not learn as many languages as Anna's father had without a fair bit of love for talking. Most of her memories of her father were of him speaking—laughing and joking, arguing and sighing—with one of the many friends and conversation partners he cultivated around the city. In fact, for much of her life with him, Anna had thought that each of the languages her father spoke had been tailored, like a bespoke suit of clothes, to the individual person with whom he conversed. French was not French; it was Monsieur Bouchard. Yiddish was not Yiddish; it was Reb Shmulik. Every word and phrase of Armenian that Anna had ever heard reminded her of the face of the little old *tatik* who always greeted her and her father with small cups of strong, bitter coffee.

Every word of Armenian smelled like coffee.

If Anna's young life had been a house, the men and women with whom her father spent his free time in discourse would've been its pillars. They kept the sky up and the earth down, and they smiled and spoke to her as if she were one of their own children. It was never only Professor Łania coming to visit them; it was Professor Łania and Anna. Or, as they might have it, Professor Łania and Anja, or Khannaleh, or Anke, or Anushka, or Anouk. She had as many names as there were languages, as there were people in the world.

Of course, if each language is for only one person, then eventually a girl begins to wonder, *What is my father's language? What is mine?*

But the answer was quite simple—they were speakers of other people's languages. Everyone else seemed tied down to only one, at best to two or three, but Anna's father seemed to be entirely unbound by the borders that held everyone else in the wide and varied landscape of Kraków. He was not confined to any one way of speaking. He could be anything he wanted. Except, perhaps, himself.

And if this was true of Anna's father, well, then it must have been true for Anna, too. Instead of passing on to his daughter one particular language that would define her, Anna's father gave her the wide spectrum of tongues that he knew, and said, "Choose amongst them. Make something new for yourself."

In none of her memories of him was Anna's father not saying something. He lived, in her memory, like a vibrant statue, molded in the shape of his accustomed listening posture: right knee bent over the left, elbow propped against the knee, his chin in his palm. He adopted this attitude frequently, but even when so silently bound in attention, Anna's father couldn't help but communicate, and his lips and eyebrows would wriggle and squirm in reaction to the things people said to him. Other people would have to ask him what these idiosyncratic tics and twitches meant, but Anna was fluent in that language, too, and she never had to ask.

She and her father spent so very much time talking together. They talked in every language in every corner of their apartment, and all throughout the streets of the city. Of all people, she was certain that he liked talking to her best.

The first time Anna realized that a language was a compromise shared amongst people—that two people who spoke the same language were not necessarily the same—this was the only time she could remember asking her father a question that he could not manage to answer.

They had been making their way home from some outing or other, and it had been growing dark. Anna didn't recognize the part of the city where they were walking. Her father was holding on to her hand very tightly, and his long-legged strides forced her to trot to keep up. His pace quickened, faster and faster as the sun dipped beneath the rooftops and then the hills beyond, and by the time it happened, they were practically running.

She heard them before she saw anything. There was a man's voice laughing, loud and jolly, so genuinely amused that Anna began smiling as well, excited to see whatever it was that was making the laughter. But when they arrived at the street from which the sound was coming, her smiling stopped.

There were three soldiers.

The laughing soldier was the smallest. She didn't remember the two others very clearly, except that they seemed impossibly large to her.

"Jump!" said the smallest soldier. "Jump! Jump!"

The grizzled old man in front of them did his best to follow this direction, hopping up and down pointlessly in place, but there was very clearly something wrong with his leg—a bad break, perhaps. It was plain to see that he was in terrible discomfort. At great expense of effort, he kept his voice silent each time his shoes hit the cobblestones, despite the pain that twisted his expression.

This seemed to delight the small soldier even more.

Perhaps the most difficult part of this memory was the pure and unreserved delight of that laughter. In Anna's mind, the soldier was speaking—and, for that matter, laughing—in Herr Doktor Fuchsmann's language.

Herr Doktor Fuchsmann was a fat, nearly bald man who always wore a waistcoat. He had spectacles and a cane, which he used to help him shuffle around his small pharmacy all day long. Herr Doktor Fuchsmann was a man who giggled, and whose face was almost always turning red. In the short time that Anna had known him, he had snuck her more cookies than she had ever even seen in any other setting.

And the small soldier was speaking Herr Doktor Fuchsmann.

Anna was confused. She could understand neither the soldier in the context of the doctor, nor the doctor in the context of the soldier. So she did what any child would do in such a situation.

She asked her father.

If Anna's father had not been the man that he was, and if Anna had not been hearing and speaking and thinking, in part, in German for as many of her seven years as had the potential for speech in them—in short, if her accent had not been so compellingly native—this story might've ended before it began.

"Papa," said Anna. "Why are they laughing at that man?"

Anna's father didn't answer. The soldier turned his head.

"Because, *Liebling*," he said. "That is not a man. That is a *Jude*."

Anna remembered that word exactly, because it changed

everything for her. She thought she knew what language was, how it worked, how people pulled in different words out of the air into which they had spoken in order to shape their outlines around them.

But this was much more complicated.

Reb Shmulik didn't say *Jude*. Reb Shmulik said *yid*.

And this soldier, no matter what language he was speaking, was as different from Herr Doktor Fuchsmann as he wanted everyone to know that he was from Reb Shmulik the Jew.

In 1939 a group of people called Germans came into a land called Poland and took control of the city Kraków, where Anna lived. Shortly thereafter these Germans instituted an operation entitled Sonderaktion Krakau, which was aimed at the intellectuals and academics of the city, of whom Anna's father was one.

The day appointed for the execution of Sonderaktion Krakau was November the sixth, 1939—Anna's seventh year—and all Anna knew that morning was that her father had to go away for a few hours.

He left her in the care of Herr Doktor Fuchsmann shortly after eleven o'clock, and then he did not come back again.

It was not uncommon for Anna's father to leave her with his friends when he had some pressing business to attend to. He trusted her enough to leave her alone in the apartment for brief periods, but on occasion, of course, he needed to be gone for longer. She was still very young, and from time to time someone was needed to look after her.

Anna's father had done his best to insulate her from what had been going on in the city, but a war is a war, and it is impossible to protect a child from the world forever. There were uniforms in the street, and people yelling, and dogs, and fear, and sometimes there were gunshots, and if a man loves to speak, eventually his daughter will hear the word "war" spoken, furtively, aloud. "War" is a heavy word in every language.

Anna remembered vaguely that there had been a time before this heavy word had descended on every side of her like the weighted edges of a net, but more than the figure or face of any particular person—more even than the brief impression she had managed to form of her mother—what principally characterized her memory of that time was the vibrant outdoor life of an exuberant city: chatting strolls in public parks and gardens; glasses of beer, or cups of coffee or tea, at tables on the sidewalk; mothers and lovers and friends calling names out across reverberant stone streets, hoping to catch and turn a beloved head before it disappeared around a corner. Those had seemed like days of perpetual warmth and sun to Anna, but war, she learned, was very much like weather—if it was on its way, it was best not to be caught outdoors.

In his final months Anna's father spent quite a bit of time inside with her, talking and, when the inevitable need for silence arose, reading. He meant very well, but most of the books he had in the house were still far beyond Anna's level, and so she spent much of her time with one particular book, a thick volume of children's stories drawn from every source. Whether they were from Aesop or the Bible, or Norse myth or Egyptian, they were all illustrated in the same comforting nineteenth-century hand, with pen and ink, reproduced there on thick, heavy paper.

Anna missed that book as soon as she was separated from it. Even before she missed her father.

For the first two or three hours after noon on the sixth of November, Herr Doktor Fuchsmann acted just as he always had toward Anna, teasing and laughing over his spectacles while the shop was empty, and immediately ignoring her as soon as the bell on the door rang a new customer inside. There were many fewer cookies now than there had been in past days, but Anna understood—Herr Doktor Fuchsmann had explained the dearth with reference to the war. This was a common practice, one with which Anna had already become quite familiar—whenever someone remarked something out of the ordinary lately, it seemed to be explained by pointing out the war.

Anna still was not certain what precisely was meant by this word "war," but it seemed, at least in part, to be an assault on her cookie supply, and of this she simply could not approve.

The shop was much busier that day than Anna had ever seen it before, and the people who came in after Herr Doktor Fuchsmann's relief seemed mostly to be young Germans in subtly differing uniforms. Even some of the older men in suits came in speaking a bright, clipped-sounding German that, though clearly the same language as the Herr Doktor's, seemed to Anna to lean forward with tight muscles, where his sat back, relaxed. It was all terribly interesting, but Herr Doktor

Fuchsmann became nervous when she paid too obvious attention to anything his customers had to say, and so she did her best to look as if she weren't listening.

He tried to mask his growing anxiety as the day drew on, but when the time came to close down his shop and Anna's father had still not returned to collect her, Herr Doktor Fuchsmann began to worry very openly.

Anna was not yet terribly worried, though. Her father had been gone for longer before, and he had always returned.

But now there were gunshots in the streets from time to time, and dogs barking constantly. Herr Doktor Fuchsmann flatly refused to take Anna home with him, and this was the first seed of worry in her. He had always been so sweet to her before, and it was confusing that he should suddenly turn unkind.

Anna slept that night beneath the counter of Herr Doktor Fuchsmann's shop, cold without a blanket, afraid to be seen or to make too much noise as the streets filled up with German in the growing night.

She had trouble falling asleep. Her worry kept her mind just active enough to prevent her from nodding off, but not quite so active that she could stop herself from growing bored. It was in this never-ending threshold of a moment that she missed her book of tales.

There was a story near its back, a story at which the cracked binding had grown accustomed to falling open, of a spindly wraith called the Alder King. Anna loved to stare at his picture until her fright reached a nearly unbearable height and then to shut it away. The fright disappeared reliably with the Alder King, trapped there between the pages of his book, and she longed to shut up her gnawing worry with him now.

In the morning Herr Doktor Fuchsmann brought Anna a little food. It comforted her, but by lunchtime it became clear that he meant not to keep her around. He was very apologetic, telling Anna that he would send her father straight along if he came back to the shop for her, but that he just couldn't have her in his shop anymore.

Everything he said made sense. Who was she to argue?

Herr Doktor Fuchsmann locked the door behind him when they left to walk Anna to her apartment. There it quickly became apparent to her that her father had locked his own door when they had left for Herr Doktor Fuchsmann's the day before. Herr Doktor Fuchsmann never learned this, though—as soon as they were within sight of the apartment building, he excused himself and hurried back to his shop.

Anna sat in front of the door to her apartment for a very long time. There was still a part of her that was sure that her father was on his way back to her, and she tried as best she could to prune her worry and encourage this certainty to grow in its place. Surely, he would be back soon.

But he did not come.

Whenever she felt her surety fading, Anna tried the apartment doorknob. Over and over she tried it, each time becoming slowly, thoroughly convinced that, in fact, her father had not locked her out, but that she had simply not turned the knob hard enough.

As much as she wanted it to be true, though, the door never budged. In days of peace, sometimes such fancies can prove true. Never, though, in times of war.

It felt like an eternity to Anna, sitting there, and in a sense it was. To a child, an empty hour is a lifetime. Anna sat there for at least two or three, and if it hadn't been for old Mrs. Niemczyk across the hall, she might've sat there waiting for her father until the war stopped her.

Mrs. Niemczyk frequently complained to Professor Łania (and others) that he and his girl spoke too loudly too late at night, but Anna's father had been convinced that she simply didn't like their bringing Gypsies and Armenians and Jews into the building. Mrs. Niemczyk spoke only Polish, and only very little of it at any one time. In all her life she had never spoken one word directly to Anna, though the old lady had frequently spoken of her to her father in her presence, usually to tell him how he was failing to bring his daughter up properly. Needless to say, she was never a particularly happy sight to Anna, and Anna was a girl who was rather well disposed to meeting people.

Shortly after Anna began her wait in front of the apartment door, Mrs. Niemczyk left her apartment briefly to run an errand. Her eyes lingered on Anna as she passed down the hall, and upon her return they didn't move from Anna once until she shut the door of her apartment behind her.

Anna wasn't sure what she thought Mrs. Niemczyk would do, but the old lady began cracking her door open every so often to check and see if the little girl was still sitting in the hall, and every time Anna saw her, what little of Mrs. Niemczyk's face she could see behind the door looked somehow better and better pleased.

If it hadn't been for old Mrs. Niemczyk, Anna might very well have stayed to wait for her father.

If it hadn't been for old Mrs. Niemczyk, Anna might very well never have met the Swallow Man.